BIG NICK ENERGY

KRISTEN BAILEY

Storm
PUBLISHING

Ebook ISBN: 978-1-83700-177-4
Paperback ISBN: 978-1-83700-179-8

Cover design: Emma Rogers
Cover images: Shutterstock

Published by Storm Publishing.
For further information, visit:
www.stormpublishing.co

ALSO BY KRISTEN BAILEY

Sex Ed

Five Gold Rings

Textbook Romance

We Three Kings

Hot to Go

Glow Job

Souper Mum

Second Helpings

Has Anyone Seen My Sex Life?

Can I Give My Husband Back?

Did My Love Life Shrink in the Wash?

How Much Wine Will Fix My Broken Heart?

Am I Allergic to Men?

Great Sexpectations

ONE

BATH, DECEMBER 2018

'And the final round is all about books set at Christmas!' cries our host behind the bar wearing reindeer antlers, a red and green holly-print festive suit and a bow tie. 'First question! The opening chapters of *Little Women* are set at Christmas, but what are the names of all the sisters in the March family?'

Where does one buy an outfit like that? When else would you wear it? Christmas Day itself? I wouldn't be able to digest my sprouts looking at that. His tone and stance tell me he's the most excited person in this place, which figures. Everyone else in here is at different stages of drunk, and here for the social. I'm not really sure how driven they are by the grand prize of twenty-five pounds, a box of luxury crackers and a meat hamper.

'Oh, my wife loves this one. The one with Darcy. Lizzie, Jane... right?'

I sit at my corner table near the misted-up window, eavesdropping on the team on the table beside me, named 'The Myrrh the Merrier' – three older men, all with pints and Christmas jumpers, one of them armed with reading glasses and a pen.

'Mary?' one says cluelessly.

'Amy, Jo, Beth and Meg,' I mutter, my hand covering my mouth.

One of them turns to look at me. 'Bev?'

'Beth,' I say and laugh, hoping the quiz host can't see me. Is this breaking quiz rules? Will I get thrown out?

He winks back at me, giving a thumbs up. 'You want to join us? We could do with the help...' he whispers. 'We'll give you a cut? Our chipolatas?'

'Dave...' one of the others intervenes. 'She's a young girl, mate...'

He realises his gaffe and blushes instantly. 'Off the meat hamper obviously. Christ, I'm not a perv. I'm sorry...'

I smile broadly. 'You're lucky it's Christmas. It's fine. I knew what you meant. You can have that answer for free, in the spirit of giving,' I say, putting a hand to my chest. I'm in a Nirvana t-shirt, trainers and jeans. I'm not exactly dressed for festive fun. 'I'm actually waiting for someone.'

'A date?' Dave asks.

'A boyfriend.' They all smile and seem quite happy for me.

'Question two! In *The Christmas Carol*, what is the name of Scrooge's fiancée?' The whole table look at me. I stare at the gaudy gold bells hanging off a garland next to us. All their thumbs go up again.

I'd kill in this quiz. But it's not why I'm here. I look at my watch. He's half an hour late. I look at my phone, no messages so I take a prolonged sip of red wine to fill the space. I'm sure we did say our pub for 7.30pm. It is our pub because this is exactly where we met, over by the bar, festooned with the same foil decorations and plastic Santa signs. That was a year ago, a night when this popular university haunt was filled to the brim with students all overflowing with the merriment of the season. A sea of Christmas jumpers with a heavy scent of meaty crisps and mulled wine. I can remember them playing Band Aid and a group of students standing on stools all took on different personas to sing along. Bono was especially mullered. It was rammed, and the man next to me was so close that I could smell the Paco Rabanne wafting off him.

'Seeing as we're standing so close to each other, I should tell you that I'm thick,' he said. I smile as I remember it. At the time, I frowned, puzzled; wondering why he was divulging this information to me.

'Hi.'

'What's your name?' he asked me. I paused, then turned to look at him; he was reasonably handsome with sandy blond hair, cool slate-coloured eyes. I liked the bobbles on his jumper which showed me it was well-worn and loved.

'Kay,' I replied.

'No, I asked you what your name is?'

'I'm Kay.'

At this point, I decided he was definitely thick. Or drunk.

'Oh, I thought you were telling me you're OK. Kay, like the letter?' he said.

'But not. I don't work for MI6,' I explained.

For some reason, he found that hilarious.

'Is... short...?' he said.

I tried to make out his words through the racket of Mariah Carey now warbling over the sound system. Was he being rude? I stood on my toes because I was keeping it casual in jeans and trainers. 'I'm five foot six.'

He leaned into me and I flinched a little. 'I asked if your name was short for anything,' he said.

Oh. 'Katherine – but everyone calls me Kay.'

'I'm five foot ten in case you were interested.'

'Interested in you or your height?'

He grinned. 'You are very funny.'

I hate to say that was all it took but that was, pretty much, all it took. I remember someone at the other end of the bar ordering six complex cocktails so it felt less awkward to relent and engage, to let my defences down. I mean, it helped that he wasn't horrible to look at; he had the sort of face that creased into a different shape when he smiled, which he did often. I like a face where I can read the laughter so clearly. He asked me if I was a fan of Christmas and then he offered to buy me a drink. It was a sincere gesture, not lecherous, bordering on gentlemanly, and in the student population of Bath I'd rarely seen that. It was in the spirit of his name, he said.

'You haven't told me your name...' I told him.

'I believe I have. I'm Nick.'

I thought back to his opening line. '*Oh*, I thought you told me you were thick.'

That now-familiar smile spread across his face. 'Would you like to find out?'

I cocked my head to one side. 'Are you talking about your penis?'

He roared in reply. 'God, no. I meant do you want to know if I'm stupid or not.'

And with that there was a certain look, a real definite possibility that this had legs. 'So you're Saint Nick, are you?'

'Yes, I am.' I felt an instant warmth as he said that. I liked the festive vibe but also that he felt good, safe.

'Then I will have a rum and Coke, Saint Nick. Would it be cheeky of me to ask for nuts too?' I said.

'You can have nuts too. It's Christmas after all and I always deliver.'

'Always?'

'Always.' There was a certainty in his look, the way his eyes came to life, fixed on mine.

The memory makes me smile as I unwrap my scarf from my neck and ruffle out my auburn curls. That initial chemistry, the buzz of it is still imprinted into my mind and fired up all over again, just from glancing over to the bar where we met.

'Can you believe it's still raining? It feels as though it's been raining for months,' a voice says from behind me, and I recognise it instantly. Nick. He puts an arm on my shoulder and kisses the back of my head before I turn to greet him. He hasn't changed since we first met; still the same shaggy blond hair, woolly jumper and jeans, the usual pint of stout in his hand. 'Sorry. Lectures overran and then the landlord paid us a visit,' he says, hanging his coat on the back of his chair.

'It's fine. I've been enjoying the quiz.' I see Dave and his mates have clocked Nick and they raise their pints at me. I hope they got the question about Dr Seuss right. 'Did you get your essay in on time?' I ask, leaning over to put a hand in his.

'Yeah. By the skin of my teeth,' he replies, taking a long gulp of his drink.

I can see the stress etched in Nick's face. It's been a long term and he's had a lot of coursework, while I've been in endless tutorials on Virginia Woolf during the day, and working shifts in the uni bar in the evenings. Christmas will be a welcome break, a time to be a couple again, see family and drink our woes away. Our time at university has evolved in this last year – we used to come here for wild nights in large groups of people from halls, evenings that would lead us into nightclubs and down empty streets at three in the morning, getting told off for setting off car alarms and urinating in people's gardens (not me). But now, this pub feels more like our local, a place of special significance in our relationship.

'I was thinking back to when we first met here,' I say affectionately. 'When I couldn't hear you tell me your name because of the noise.'

He half smiles. I thought that was a particularly funny moment of note, but maybe not. God, he is stressed. He takes his hand out of mine. 'God, I don't think I can do this.'

'The pub?' I enquire. Maybe it's the noise. 'We could go back to mine, it's cool.'

He rubs his hands down his thighs and exhales slowly. Behind him, the man in the Christmas suit starts to rove around the pub with his microphone for a music round. Finish the Christmas lyrics. I can see why that might induce stress.

'Is this about Christmas? I know you're upset I can't make it to yours, but I really want to spend it with my nana. A bit of space at Christmas wouldn't be awful.'

He shakes his head, a little too seriously for my liking. There's the stressor.

'A bit of space?' he asks me.

'In Christmas week? It'll go quick,' I say.

He looks at me for a moment too long. 'What if that space was...extended?'

'The whole Christmas break? Three weeks?' I guess. 'Did you cave? Are you going skiing with Olly and Si?' I ask him.

Nick takes another lengthy sip of his drink and looks me in the eye. 'Or what about longer?'

It's then that I realise what's happening. A year means that you can read words in people's eyes, the way their face isn't creased with laughter anymore. There's a whole host of emotions in his face instead, a whole different shade of blue that speaks guilt, fear, sadness.

'Nick, are you breaking up with me?'

But as I manage to utter that sentence, a microphone is thrust in my face. The words are loud, echoing through that space, the music muted in my honour. The whole pub freezes and turns to look at us, sitting opposite each other at this dark wooden pub table.

'Not quite,' the host says, forcing a laugh, realising he has a duty to save this. 'Would you like another go?'

I look at him. 'Tis the season to be jolly,' I say blankly.

The man's jollity has turned into silent caution. 'You are correct and this means you can go to the bar and get a free drink.' He slides a sort of token in front of me and waits. In fact, the whole bar still looks at us, waiting. *Sod the quiz, we have drama in the corner of the pub and that is worth the cost of our quiz entry fee tonight.* Nick, who looked uncomfortable before, now looks as though he's in the stand of a public court.

'You can do better!' a drunken voice sounds from across the pub, and a small table of women cheer.

Don't react, Kay. Don't. But I feel so empty, so confused. Something surges up in me, and I pull the microphone, still in the quiz host's hands, towards me. 'Why?' I ask Nick. No one in this pub cares about that meat hamper anymore.

'You must have felt it too?' he mumbles quietly, choosing not to broadcast the moment.

'Felt what?' I question, the microphone whining with feedback. I feel a whole pub lean forward to try and eavesdrop.

'Like we've grown apart.'

'What did he say?' someone at the back of the pub asks.

'They've grown apart,' the host says, leaning into the microphone. Nick looks mortified but I will admit, the tables glancing over in anger and judgement are helping here. Because since that day I met Nick here, I've laid down roots and let our branches intertwine. I let him into my life, we've felt the sun on our leaves, we've experienced the rain and the cold, but all the while it was together, always growing together. To put it bluntly, he was inside me last night, so I don't really understand this at all.

'Seriously, can we go somewhere else to do this?' Nick says, leaning over. Dave and his friends next to us are sitting with their arms folded, piercing him with their stares.

'No,' I say into the microphone, my fingers clenched tightly around my wine glass.

That table of ladies cheers again. 'He's a cliché, babe!'

I can't think straight right now, I'm just trying to keep it together. I've been completely ambushed, in the very place where our relationship started, and I can't figure out if he's being cruel or whether he wanted to give this moment some full-circle significance. But if he's going to ambush me with bullshit reasons about why our year-long relationship is over then he can be waylaid too.

He inhales deeply, looking me in the eye. The host points the microphone at him. Nick looks at it distastefully. 'We've been together for a year and it's been amazing,' he tells the pub. 'But I feel this... you and I... has come to a sort of organic end.' A lady a few tables down scrunches her face up and shakes her head at him. He needs to stop it with the plant metaphors. But maybe that's my influence rubbing off on him. 'In a few months, I'm going over to

New York to do my MBA. She wants to travel. I think now's the time to work on ourselves.'

'CLICHÉ!' someone shouts. 'You just want to get out of buying her a Christmas gift, you cheap git!'

I look down at the table, my bottom lip wobbling, and I take a large gulp of my wine to steady myself. I guess however he did this it was always going to hurt, it was always going to feel as if my heart was bleeding emotions that were seeping into every part of me.

'Ask him if there's someone else?' a woman shouts.

He puts his hands in the air and stands up. 'There is no one else, I promise. I'm so sorry, Kay.'

He shakes his head and covers his face with his hands; if he starts crying, I will throw something at him. I suspect most of the pub will. I feel dumbstruck, nauseated. The Christmas decorations in this place sparkle and wink at me. I wish they wouldn't do that.

I grab the microphone again. 'Did I do something wrong?' I hate myself for asking that question, but I'm simply trying to figure this all out.

'No. And it's not you—'

I put a hand up. 'Don't finish that sentence.'

'It's—'

'Piss off.'

The pub cheers collectively, as if someone has scored a match-winning goal.

My swearing silences him. I don't know what else to say. In my bag under the table is a notebook with a list of all the gifts I've bought for his family. I went to a farmer's market and bought a bottle of sloe gin for his sister. His mum wanted cheese knives. I usually cut my cheese with a normal knife but whatever floats your boat, Marjorie. I got him a blue/slate-coloured jumper that matches his eyes. I have a feeling he's bought me nothing apart from this bad, bad news.

'I really still want to be friends though,' he says.

I look back at him blankly. This feels rehearsed now; perhaps he's putting on a performance so the patrons don't turn on him.

'Please stop,' I beg him. I move around in my wooden chair, the cushion worn and uncomfortable underneath me.

'Do we have to do this here? In front of all these people? It doesn't have to be like this.'

'So this is now *my* fault?'

The pub quietens.

'Please. If you no longer want this then I will accept that, I will graciously move on.' I bite my bottom lip to stop myself from crying. 'But don't ambush me in a public place and then ask me to be your friend.'

The crowd cheers again.

'Kay...'

'Because I love you, Nick,' I say assertively, loudly. No microphone needed. The pub goes deathly silent. We met in this very bar, we spent the evening together, I abandoned all my friends that night and we went back to his house share and had scrappy, fun sex in his single bed. And he called me back, and we spent a year together. I was in love, a feeling I've never been so certain of in my whole life.

I look up at him. For God's sake, Nick. React. Let me know this hurts you too.

But he doesn't. He grabs my hand and holds it to his mouth and kisses it. Every motion seems to be happening underwater. He then takes another sip of his drink, pulls his coat from the back of his chair and leaves. I can't even look at him. I hear booing. I think someone just threw a bag of honey-roasted nuts at him. How fitting, how very full circle.

'Are you alright, love?' someone whispers, pushing an open packet of crisps in my direction. I look down at the crinkle-cut McCoys and then around the pub to see everyone glancing over, speaking in hushed whispers. I am mortified. Do I go to the toilets? I've seen the toilets here, I don't think I want to cry there. A single tear rolls down my cheek, I wipe it away swiftly. 'Well, that was fucking embarrassing,' I mumble.

'For *him*,' Dave says. 'Go get this girl a brandy or something,' he says to the quiz host, still hovering. 'Put it on my tab.' He wanders off as Dave pulls his stool next to me. 'Would it be weird of me to give you a hug? I've got a daughter your age.' I nod and he wraps his big burly arms around me. 'I'm sorry, love.'

'Don't be.' I cling on to Dave tightly. Up close he smells of lemons and thyme, which is surprisingly comforting.

'You know, maybe he needs to go off and do his thing and then perhaps when he comes back, you could give it another go?' I smile faintly at him trying to find a positive in all of this. 'What's that thing they say? My wife has it on a fridge magnet. "If you love someone let them go, if they come back…"'

'Who's the cliché now, Dave?' one of his mates says. They all laugh. I still can't find the emotion. I feel so completely sucker punched by what has happened. I stare into space at Nick's empty glass, his empty chair, an empty space at a bar where I once stood with him, not understanding anything he was saying. 'Make space?' The quiz host returns, carrying a tray of drinks. We all look up at him curiously.

'Mate, I said one brandy,' says Dave.

'Yeah, every table in here said the same,' he says, placing a bottle of red in front of me and various other drinks. I look up, expecting to feel mortified, ashamed, but people are nodding, raising their glasses.

'You deserve better, babe!' a woman shouts.

'Nick rhymes with prick…'

'AND THICK!' someone adds. And that's what it takes for the tears to finally roll down my cheeks: the protective kindness of strangers, the shock, and the memory of meeting a boy in this pub for the very first time. A boy I thought I loved. A boy who's just dumped me. Three weeks before Christmas.

TWO

LONDON, DECEMBER 2021

'What the hell, Nana? This is bloody huge. What are we going to do with it!' I'm outside my Nana's small maisonette in a mews in the corner of west London staring at the Christmas tree in front of me. I'm about five foot six and this thing is twice my height, so basically, my nana has bought herself a tree over ten feet tall. It's illuminated by the glow of the streetlights as a winter mist descends on the day. 'Please don't tell me you dragged this back from the market on your own?' I ask as she stands there giggling.

'Of course not, you daft cow,' she says.

'Did you steal it?' I ask her. This is the sort of tree they erect outside shopping centres and drape in lights to please the shoppers and create a vibe.

She doubles over laughing, in her brightly checked wool coat and fluffy lilac hat. On her feet are the New Balance I bought her, because I told her she's getting old and I can't have her shuffling around in glorified slippers, not on these cobbles. 'Do you have a saw?' she asks.

'Yeah, I carry a saw around in my backpack most days.' I live in a house share in Brixton. We barely have enough forks to get us through the day, let alone working tools. I look up at the tree again, amazed at the sheer ridiculousness of it. 'Have you asked your neighbours?'

'Not yet. I called you first to have a look because, you've got to admit, it is funny. Plus, your phone is better than mine, so you can take pictures and we can put them on the Facebook.'

She stands next to it, working out how to pose. To get the right perspective and both of us in frame, I'd have to either lie on the floor or stand at the end of the road.

'Pull it down and we'll get a picture of me sat on the top as the fairy,' she jokes.

'You'd get pine needles up your minnie,' I say, and she almost keels over laughing. 'Pose next to it like a normal person.'

I'm unsure what pose Nana's going for but she's got a leg cocked up, embracing the tree like a koala, but with a face as if she's presenting a gameshow prize. This picture is one hundred per cent going on our Christmas cards next year.

'It's your fault,' she says, walking around the thing and admiring it.

'My fault you've got a giant tree outside your tiny house?' I joke.

'You introduced me to that Facebook Marketplace.' I did do that last year. Nana got into Facebook as a way of keeping up with me and my travels after I left university. She would like pictures and leave comments, usually reminding me to keep spare money in my bra. Her world changed completely when I taught her about emojis.

'Yeah, so you could get useful bits and bobs – jars and side tables,' I say.

'There was this fella giving away trees. With only a week to go until Christmas, he said they'd all go to waste otherwise,' she says. I take a moment to consider her reasoning. People normally pick up furniture on there, old clothes, baby items. I scrunch my face up, throwing my head back to look at the size of this thing.

'And you didn't think to check the measurements?' I say. 'You always check the measurements.'

'You know me, I don't care for inches,' she cackles.

I smile in return to see her so happy. 'Some chancer giving away Christmas trees? You didn't give him any money, did you? Your bank details?' I say, wondering if my lovely trusting nana has been scammed.

'Nah, he said it was his business. Lovely looking boy. Strapping's the word. Good old-fashioned hunk. I asked him if he was single and said I had a lovely granddaughter. You'd look good together.'

I shake my head in silent resignation. Nana got a free giant Christmas tree, perved over the delivery boy, and then tried to set him up with me. Lovely. 'But the strapping hunk dumped the tree here and didn't think that maybe your little maisonette wouldn't have the ceiling height for this? You don't know how wide it is. How are you going to see your telly through the branches?'

'He did say something but I told him I'd sort it out. I've got help,' she says, unperturbed. 'That would be you, by the way.'

'Did the hunk have a name?' I ask her.

'You're not going to call him up and tell him to take it back, are you?' she asks, her eyes round and sad.

'I want to check he's kosher.'

'He is. He had a van and everything. He let me hug him.'

'Bet you enjoyed that,' I say, cheekily.

She wriggles her shoulders at me, sticking out her tongue. 'It's big but isn't it lovely?' she says, trying to change the subject and peering up at her tree proudly. I look up. There is something to be said for a tree of this stature and magnificence; it turns this cobbled walkway into Trafalgar Square. How would you put lights on it though? I'd have to climb out the bathroom window and hang off the gables. It smells nice too. Earthy and fresh, like Christmas. I run my hand along a branch of waxy pine needles as Nana puts a number in front of me. 'He said he worked on a farm.'

'In London? That's a great big scam if ever I saw it, the only time you see Christmas trees around here are in front of supermarkets and petrol forecourts.' I dial the numbers on my phone and put it to my ear as it rings once before being answered.

'Hello?' The man's tone is deep and gruff.

'Hi, yeah... are you the man who just sold my grandmother a tree from Facebook Marketplace?' There's a silence on the end of the phone. 'Hello?'

'I sell a lot of Christmas trees. You'll have to be more specific.' I don't care if this man is strapping or not, his surly tone makes me immediately dislike him.

'Little old lady near Shepherd's Bush. She said she hugged you?'

'Oh yeah... Doris. I didn't sell that one. It was donated.'

'I know that, but you saw the size of her, the house... You didn't think that maybe she'd need assistance? That maybe that tree wasn't for her?' I ask him.

'She said she'd be OK. Said she had someone who would help. Are you having a go at me? It was free. That was an £200 tree.'

'And she's grateful for the gesture but—'

'Look, it's my busiest time of year. No offence, but that tree was given in goodwill,' he returns defensively.

'I know but she's old. I wanted to make sure that you're... kosher,' I say.

There's a pause. 'In case I was a scamming thief looking to case your gran's house and mug her?'

'No but...' I realise this man on the other end of the phone is not taking kindly to this phone call. 'If it was *your* grandmother, you'd check.'

There's a silence again. 'Bloody wazzock...'

'Excuse me?' I say angrily though slightly amused by the insult.

'Not you. I'm driving.'

'You shouldn't be talking to me then if you're on a phone,' I reply, sounding more prim than usual.

'So now I'm a reckless driver as well as a scammer. Anything else?'

'Well, I was just—'

'Yeah, Merry Christmas to you too.' And then the line goes dead. I don't care what the man looks like, that was just plain rudeness, free tree or not. My brow furrowed, I look up to see Nana still looking up at her tree in wonderment, as if it's the best thing she's ever owned. It's the sort of look you want to bottle because it's pure happiness.

'Your Christmas-tree hunk was a little rude,' I say.

'He was lovely in person,' she reminds me. I'm not sure why I'm having to tell my nana that looks don't maketh the man.

'You didn't ask him if he had a saw when he was here?' I ask her.

'Yeah, I should have asked him, eh? Hello young man, show us your tool...' she says in lusty tones.

I shake my head at her. 'Won't your neighbours get aggy?'

'They won't care! Him next door left a fridge outside his front door for a month,' she says. I look at her, grinning away. Only you, Nana. She's the sort who'd get a free Christmas tree on Facebook, who'd buy fifty packs of loo roll if it was on offer. When my first book came out this year, she bought ten copies and asked me to sign them all. She always carries one around in her handbag and tells everyone she meets about me.

'And what happens when this thing moults? Your hoover won't be able to cope,' I say.

'But it'll be like waking up in a forest every day,' she says, her eyes pleading, still hopeful there's a chance we can get this thing through the front door. 'I can be like Snow White.'

'You got enough baubles?' I ask.

'I'll go down the park and look for pinecones and berries. And Poundland will sort me out.'

I smile as I think of Nana down the park with a plastic bag, collecting pinecones. She'll be a little woodland creature with a project. She'll take pictures of that tree for me and send them all on WhatsApp because I've shown her how that works too.

'Your ceiling is eight feet max. This is never going to work. Could we chop it into firewood?' I ask.

She opens her mouth at me as though I've said something sacrilegious. 'We can't do that! It's a Christmas tree.'

'Why not? I don't think there's a superstition related to burning Christmas trees. We could take it down the allotments, compost it?'

She looks at me in horror that I would even be considering this. 'Kay, every time a Christmas tree doesn't reach its full potential, an elf dies,' she says, making that myth up completely on the spot.

'Do they now? Define full potential,' I ask her.

'They've got to wear all their decorations, be lit up and see people through the season. It's their destiny.'

'Or an elf dies?' I say, eyebrow raised.

'Yeah. They disappear into thin air in a cloud of glitter; it's a terrible thing.'

I try not to laugh. 'Has the cold got to you, Nana? Have you been at the Bailey's again?' I say, biting my lip. I love the joy she's getting from this, how it's minus two out here – her breath is fogging the air and she's jogging from side to side to keep warm – but she still wants to stay out here, with her tree. I take off my gloves and slide them onto her hands. I sigh and give Nana a hug, and she wraps both arms around me tightly.

'You sent a pic to Mum and Dad yet?' I ask.

'I have. They told me I was mad and then they sent me a pic back of them lording it up in Australia. Sunshine and bare feet at Christmas, that don't make any sense to me,' she says, looking disgusted.

It's one thing we agree on at least. Christmas should be cold, wintry, with snow, scarves and mulled drinks. Despite my mum's insistence we go and visit them now they've emigrated, we both said it wouldn't feel right at this time of year.

'Don't you have a tree already?' I ask her.

'It's that fake one; it's rubbish compared to this.'

'Ah, but if you dump that one, won't an elf die? What about all that destiny gubbins?'

'Only counts for real trees,' she says, winking. The wink always gets me. It's something she's done since I was little to get me to join in with her secret plans. Let's have sweets when no one's looking; let's have secret chips on the way back from school; let's sing along to Barry Manilow whilst we do the dishes. It's been a long day and I was hoping to snuggle in bed with a Christmas film when I get home, but I guess I'm now a lumberjack. 'There's that fella at the end of your street, the plumber? I can knock on his door and check if he has a saw,' I say.

She beams at me. 'You're so smart. That happens when you go to university, you know,' she says proudly.

I laugh again. 'Then maybe we can try and get some of this tree inside. Keep those elves alive.'

'You've got a good heart, Kay Redman,' she says, beaming. She does a little jig on the spot, excited to see my cynicism and practicality fade away. I've now been suckered in to helping her big Christmas tree dreams come true.

'You, Doris Redman, are as mad as a Christmas hatter.'

'It's why you love me.'

She may be right.

THREE
LONDON, DECEMBER 2023

'We trust you, love. We've hardly seen her in three years, so only you would know what's best for her?' my dad says, and I close my eyes to hold back the tears. I try hard not to let my emotion travel down the phone, but I'm sorely disappointed that my parents have chosen to stay away at this moment rather than help with the situation or give advice. They're just going to throw money at it and hope it means something.

I watch Nana now as she sits in the day room of this nursing home, looking out of the window at the garden. Her maisonette was very much in the heart of the city, around the corner from bustling markets, the Tube station, shops and life. But maybe that was the problem: as her memory faded and doctors gave us their diagnoses of how she would fade further and struggle more with everyday life, somewhere built up and busy was the worst place she could be. After numerous calls from the police telling me they'd found her again, lost and unable to tell them who she was, it was time to step in, make sure she was safe and had care round the clock. 'Dad, I'll call you later, yeah? Have a look online, see what you and Mum think?'

'Will do. You're a gem for this, thank you.' *I love you, Dad*, I want to say but I don't reply. I hang up and walk over to Nana, running her fingers along the tinsel hanging from the window frame. 'They've got a garden, Nana. Isn't that lovely?'

'So I can do my sunbathing in the summer. Get my bikini on,' she says with a wink.

'Bag yourself a boyfriend,' I say.

'Oh, behave,' she says, nudging me.

'They've got tulips, look,' I say, pointing.

She gives me a look like she's embarrassed for me. 'Those are snowdrops, darling... and supposedly I'm the one losing my mind.'

I laugh as she threads a hand into mine. We've walked around a few of these places already, always hand-in hand. Nana with all her questions, usually asking about the availability of hot water and whether I can still smuggle her in teacakes. This one hasn't been awful. This day room is well-lit, decorated in pastels and light wood; Christmas decorations are up and there's a mixture of chairs, sofas and tables, shelves well-stocked with board games. Beyond the hallway, I can see a group of ladies playing mahjong, a TV room showing an old Christmas film, and another place where a group of people have easels up, painting.

'Do you think they do life drawing?' she asks me. I laugh. 'I prefer this place to the other one. That one smelt of Cup-a-Soup and bleach. This one's got nice curtains.'

I've been poring over brochures and websites for weeks now, looking at contracts, prices and medical provision. Nana's simply been scouting out the soft furnishings. This one would give her a lovely private room overlooking trees and the river, the menu looks varied, and most importantly, Tuesday night is bingo.

'I liked the room. We could really make it your own, bring your own things in. We could hang some pictures.'

'Would my Netflix work here? Could I watch my shows? I'm still on that one with the firefighters. Got two more series of that.'

'Yes, and I'd give you my password to Prime too. They've got great stuff on that.'

She nods. I glance at her, seeing all the anxiety and fear in her eyes, and it breaks my heart. She's not resistant to this but I think she knows it means life is moving in a certain direction, away from independence, towards a time when her mind will leave her completely and she won't remember all the things that make her life what it is.

'Can you visit whenever you want?' she asks me.

I hold her hand tightly. 'I will be on call whenever you need me, but I'll make it here once a week at least.' I feel a lump lodge in my throat. I still don't know if that's too much or not enough. I'd come every day if I could, but the last few months have shown me that I couldn't juggle work and being Nana's carer, and that fills me with incredible guilt.

'Don't do that, lovely,' Nana says.

I shake my head. 'I just... I wish I could do more.'

'I don't want you here all the time, you daft thing,' she says. 'Popping in at one in the morning to say hello? I'd tell you to sling your hook.' I pull a face, knowing she's trying to make me feel better about it all. 'I will be fine. When did they say I could move in?'

'New Year? Gives us Christmas together,' I say. 'We could do something special.'

'Get a bigger turkey?'

'We could go away?' I suggest. Maybe we could escape to a dreamy Christmas market in Germany, toast this next adventure with spiced cookies and mulled wine.

She shakes her head. 'Nah, let's spend it in my house. Maybe we'll have a day in London. Go to a gallery or something, get an afternoon tea somewhere posh.' I nod, trying not to tear up. 'Hey, do you remember that Christmas when I got that stupid big tree off Facebook and you had to saw it up in the street?' she says.

The episode comes to mind again. I'm curious at how her brain and memory work. 'That buggered my hands, do you remember the blisters, the splinters?' I say, giggling.

'And didn't something jump out of that tree?' she asks.

'A mouse. Leapt out at me from the branches.'

'Then you screamed, told me you were going to get rabies, waving that saw around like a loony and then the neighbours...'

'Called the police.' We both stand there, broad grins on our faces.

'And when the police came, you sweet-talked them into helping us,' I remind her. It was peak Nana on form. She was a little old lady who'd been scammed by the internet and she didn't want to be a nuisance.

'You went on a date with one of them!' she says, pleased as punch to be remembering her matchmaking skills. That night, Nana really had been on form.

'Lewis, his name was Lewis.'

'Hold up,' she says, a little worried. 'Did I go to your wedding and not remember it?'

I shake my head at her cheeky smile. 'No. We only lasted a couple of months.' He was good at trimming Christmas trees but had debatable sexual fetishes involving feet, which wasn't great when his smelt like cheese. I don't tell Nana that much.

'I'm sorry that didn't work out,' she says, taking my hand.

'I'm not,' I joke. Since university and a move to London, my love life has followed quite the trajectory and Nana has witnessed a lot of it; the highs, the lows, the laughs, the tears.

'You will get married one day though, won't you?' she asks me.

'Maybe. If the right man comes along.'

'I'd just like to come to your wedding. That's on my bucket list, you know?' she says, and my heart prickles to hear her use that term, to look forward to the future. 'I'd wear the biggest hat. Something with fruit.'

'So you'd have something to snack on all day,' I joke. She sticks her tongue out at me, and I see that adorable, wonderful woman I know so well. 'We could have a dance to "Copacabana". I'd be Lola, you'd be Rico. We'd act the whole thing out.'

She takes my hands and starts humming a bit of Manilow to herself. I dance with her on the spot and spin her round. I think whatever the future holds, I have to make this happen now, don't I?

We both separate, dancing on our own, a strange version of disco-salsa.

A cough in the background, however, gets our attention. It's the lady showing us round, formal and well-presented in a suit and gold name badge. *Please don't think we're strange and tell us there's no room at the inn now.*

'I'm so sorry...' I start to say.

'I take it the dancing is a good thing?' she says.

Nana nods. 'Am I allowed to dance here?'

'We actively encourage it as a means of keeping fit. We have classes.'

Nana looks at me and smiles sweetly. 'Then me and my granddaughter will see you in the New Year.' She grabs my arm and squeezes it tightly, pulling me in as close as she can.

FOUR

LONDON, DECEMBER 2025

'Are you sure those deadlines aren't too tight? Two books by the first week of January?' my agent, Davinia asks, as she sips on her Christmas cocktail, the glass frosted with salt and sugar.

Davinia always brings me to places way out of my comfort zone. I'd be happy sharing plans over a Nando's, but she always tells me to come to these flash-fusion London eateries – the kind with lots of different glasses to drink from, seasonal specials and menu items with tiny printed numbers that could either be the calorie count or the price. But then that is Davinia. She has the sort of publishing flair I thought would infuse into my bones once I became an author, that laissez-faire cool where she can sit there and nibble casually at her edamame, in her black designer co-ord and her dark sculpted bob, while telling me about trends in children's literature. I, meanwhile, am the anti-chic. I'm clashing leopard print with bright tights and Doc Martens and I've put a whole dumpling in my mouth that was far, far too hot. I may need surgery on my tongue after this.

'As long as it fits in with the illustrator's schedule then I'm fine,' I say. I mean, it won't be. I'll be very relaxed until just after Christmas and likely spend that last week of the year in a mild panic, in my pyjamas, my flat filled with paper, words, regret and leftover trifle.

'Then...' she says casually, downing the rest of her drink, 'I love you. I say that a lot, I know, but you're by far my easiest client. You write your lovely bear books, you deliver, people buy them, you don't go all pass-agg in your emails,' she says, blowing me a kiss. 'Plus you always send me cookies.'

'Don't the others send cookies?'

'Lordy, no. There's one... I won't give names but he sent me a basket of kombucha. What the hell am I going to do with that?' I want to say drink it but instead I smile as a waiter comes over with the bill and she doesn't look at the total, which makes me think she's definitely not solely living off her cut of my royalties. Ever since I signed with Davinia five years ago, my series of bear books have been out in the world, and sales are steady if not setting the world alight. There was a point when it all first happened where I imagined merch and a BBC kids' series that would pay for my retirement. Yes, I thought I might be in my chaise longue phase of authordom by now. But no. I do still take pics of my books when I see them in shops. I move them to the promo tables when no one's looking. I get fan mail but also I write at the kitchen table, and I have another job to keep the lights on.

'I'll keep working on the rights deals. I have strong hopes for France and Sweden but once we have a series of ten then that will help.'

'Then I will work towards ten,' I say.

'You are a dream,' she says, studying my face. 'And what about you, my lovely girl? Tell me what else you have going on in your life?' This is why I hold on to Davinia dearly. Not that agents were rushing to sign me but there's a maternal streak in her questions about me and my life which shows that she cares. It's why I gravitated towards her.

'Everything's OK, Davinia.'

She pouts at my response, pushing at the bridge of her brightly rimmed glasses. 'And you're spending Christmas with your grand-mother? How is she?'

'She's doing fine... good days, bad days, but it's to be expected.'

I've always confided in Davinia about Nana's circumstances, as when I first signed with her, Nana sent her a thank-you card and gift along with photos of me as a child. They still exchange Christmas cards. Davinia cocks her head to one side to hear news of her, aware that what's happening to her fading mind still hurts my heart.

'Remember to reach out to me if you need help there. You know I have a soft spot for Doris.'

'I will.'

'And what else? Give me more.'

I'm not sure what she expects me to say. I could lie and say my days are full and exciting and read like a young social media influencer. I love London, I do occasionally go out, but I also enjoy sitting at home and scrolling through my phone. Do I tell her I've just found out about Korean skincare? I've joined a gym, they've got Lady Gaga spin classes. I don't think that's what she wants to hear. My pause intrigues her. 'You see, I took another of my young twentysomething authors out to lunch the other day. She ordered five cocktails and sat there and told me about a ridiculous weekend she spent in Bratislava and then whipped out her new tattoo. But you're just... OK.'

I shrug. 'I really am OK. You see, I write, I work... at the library. I'm organising a charity book drive,' I say excitedly.

'That's lovely,' she intervenes. 'Admirable stuff.' That's definitely not what she wants to hear. That's the polar opposite to a mad weekend in Bratislava.

'And I go on exceptionally bad dates. I do have a life,' I argue.

'How bad?' she asks me. 'I've been married for too long, I crave hearing your young-people stories.'

'Nothing exceptional. No sparks, a little dull. A little tiring, truth be told. There are a lot of weirdos out there. I had a man tell me about an ingrown hair on his back. When they pulled it out, it had coiled and measured six centimetres. He showed me a picture that he'd kept on his phone.'

Davinia sits there laughing, adjusting the patterned scarf around her neck. 'Please tell me you didn't sleep with that man.'

I shake my head. The fact is I did because I hoped there'd be something; I craved spark, I thought it might ignite in the bedroom and, I'll be frank, I'd spent a lot of money on waxing that I didn't want to waste. Let's just say the sex was like a box of damp matches.

'And there's no one else?'

Again, I shake my head. I do have the occasional play on Tinder, there have been one-month flings that haven't really stood the test of time, but sometimes I wonder if it's better to not chase it, to let it come to me. The chasing is tiring, confusing and, in a city like London, bloody expensive.

Davinia sits back in her chair and studies my expression, but mostly my hair. People do this; it's auburn and wild and sometimes I don't have the strength or energy to control it. 'Oh, my beautiful Kay. I want you to have some fun. You're in your twenties in London. You're on the precipice of greatness and the rest of your life. I don't want to hear that you're just OK.'

'Define fun then. I have no real urge to get a tattoo,' I say.

'Let go. I know it's been stressful with your grandmother but you're so very young. I see a girl in there who needs to let go, experience real joy, get into the bones of this city.'

'Bones?' I say.

'In both senses of the word,' she cackles. 'God, if I was your age again, I would spend a lot more time embracing my freedom and sleeping with handsome strangers. Don't get me wrong; I love being married, but I'm likely going to go home now, talk to my husband about turkeys, and then we'll fall asleep together, me listening to a podcast and his orchestral flatulence.'

I laugh, but there is a smidgeon of truth there. After university I did go travelling and loved the wild freedom of it. But maybe, in recent years, I have been preoccupied by my commitment to Nana, writing and trying to build a career. Maybe I've got the balance all wrong.

'Well, when you find where all the handsome strangers hang out then please let me know.'

'I will keep my eyes open. I will send you co-ordinates when I find them.' She smiles. 'When I see you next, I want to hear about a lusty encounter, filled to the brim with knowing looks and moments of intense longing.'

'Alright, Mills and Boon. Remember, I write books about bears, for kids.'

Davinia chuckles and looks at her watch. 'Right, as much as I love you, I need to go and scour the shops and find something for my mother-in-law.'

'Does she like kombucha?'

She laughs as we both move out of our seats, putting on our coats and heading towards the door. 'See... beautiful and funny.' I blush at the compliment as we walk out into the biting cold, which forces me to hide my face in my scarf. 'Maybe the season will provide. Santa will send you the perfect gift. I can feel it, Kay,' she says, looking up to the blue sky above bustling Covent Garden.

I look up too, wondering if a handsome stranger will just fall out of the sky. 'That would be far easier, you know, if the perfect man came down my chimney this Christmas.'

'If you're into that then let him, my dear,' she replies.

'Davinia!' I shriek, linking arms with her, our laughter misting the air.

'Have an exceptional Christmas, lovely girl. Remember: fun...' She goes in for the customary double kiss.

'And bones.'

'Indeed,' she says as she walks down the street away from me. 'Have a walk around. It's the best city to be in at this time of year. Saint Nick will deliver, trust me.'

I pause for a moment, thinking about when I last heard those words, and look up at the sky again, waiting, wondering.

'Pardon me,' a voice sounds, as someone barges past my shoulder.

I turn instantly. 'Santa?' It's a man dressed in an admirably high-quality red velour suit with what appears to be his own white fuzzy beard, though the Nike rucksack and the Asics ruin the illusion somewhat. 'I'm so sorry, I should have looked where I was going.'

'No harm done. I won't report you to my elves,' he says, wagging a finger. We both laugh. I think it's because we know from the flush in our cheeks that we've both indulged in a bit of festive daytime drinking. But there's also a childish sense of glee in meeting Santa, whatever your age. He salutes me with his gloved hand and tucks his thumbs under his rucksack straps. 'Merry Christmas, young lady.'

'You too, Santa.' I watch him as he skips away, thinking about what Davinia said. Maybe I need to follow the magic and see where it takes me. I just hope Saint Nick doesn't think I'm interested and stalking him. He's cute, but he's three times my age.

FIVE

'I'm going to countdown from ten,' the street performer says to the crowd, 'and then when I get to one, I'm going to jump through this hoop, over these people, spin five times in the air and then land, right there. I call this move the Nutcracker because if it doesn't go well...'

I should be petrified as I'm one of 'these people'. One of the four this man picked, because I'm the sort who has one of those happy, gullible faces and always stands in the wrong place. Either way, instead of exuding fear, and because Davinia and I had cock-tails and wine, I howl loudly at this joke to the bemusement of the tourists next to me who really have no idea what's going on. They look at me as though I've lost my mind. *He's going to parkour over our asses.* I'm not sure if it's too late to Google Translate that so they know what's coming.

Have some fun, that's what Davinia said. Follow the magic. You're in London. It's December and you're in glorious, light-filled Covent Garden. It's where Christmas goes to be a little bit extra, where every sense is assaulted by the festive season. In the metal frame of the iconic market building, every inch of space between the little cafés and boutique shops is filled with fairy lights, dazzling giant bells and winding red velvet ribbons. Inside the piazza, I hear the echo of brass instruments playing Christmas carols and the place is awash with people in bobble hats and big coats carrying large shopping bags. The place glows, as if it's been waiting all year to unleash its Christmas onto people. It's a good a place as any to infuse myself with that Christmas spirit, to feel some cinematic version of the season deep within my soul. I mean, a man dressed as an elf in Nike Air Max might flatten me in the next thirty seconds but at least I got to smell the chestnuts roasting around the corner. I got to die inside Christmas.

'Right, let's all get clapping…' the street performer continues.

I clap along. The tourist beside me (Jurgen from Austria) stares me down, as if he thinks we should try and keep as still as possible to survive this. He may have a point.

'Ladies and gentlemen, welcome to London. My name's Jack and if you like what you see, remember don't run away, do think about giving me a little something. I want to upgrade and get my mum something from John Lewis for Christmas. And 5-4-3-2…'

Jack does a strange lunging move. The crowd still clap but their voices are deathly silent. He runs along the cobbles at great pace and leaps into the air – a Christmas ninja. I close my eyes. The crowd roar above the buzz of the market building, and the shoppers follow him as he spins through the air and lands perfectly where he said he would. Everyone explodes with noise, I whoop loudly with my arms in the air and hug Jurgen. I hope he doesn't think I'm stealing his phone. Jack takes a bow. Little children run up to him. It really is a marvellous thing. I go into my handbag and find my wallet, walking over to him so I can add to his festive bucket adorned with tinsel. A woman drops in ten pence and I scowl at her. Were you not entertained?

'God bless you, kind lady,' he says as I drop in a fiver. 'Thank you so much for taking part.' He pulls out a candy cane and puts it in my hand.

'You are very welcome. Thank you, that was awesome.'

'I am available for birthdays, parties, bar mitzvahs, weddings… Or later, if you fancy a Christmas drink,' he says, winking.

I pause, biting my lip. Hold up. Is that what Davinia meant? 'That's very kind but...' I think this might be an act. He's also in very stretchy pants and I can see the outline of his yule log. I part with a few extra coins. 'I have a... date...'

Jack holds his hands up to his mock broken heart and I grin. 'Well then I hope you both have a very merry Christmas...'

'You too,' I say, turning around to walk away.

'Ladies, ladies... we're looking very festive. Where are we all meeting later?' I hear him say behind me. I look over my shoulder. A bullet dodged maybe, but can you imagine Nana's face? He could somersault through her nursing home, juggle some satsumas – she'd love him. It'd be a meet-cute for the ages. We met on the streets at Christmas. He jumped over my head. He'd be all banter, boundless energy, that wouldn't necessarily be awful... No, Kay, keep the stretchy pants at the forefront of your mind. It pains me that when I think about my dating life, I really am scouting out all the available options. Why don't I go and chat up the statue man who's spray-painted himself silver?

Davinia is right. Having taken the day off work, I may as well take advantage of all this festivity, so I keep strolling to see what other magic I can find in Covent Garden. I could check out more of the big decorations, grab a festive drink, sit on the stone steps and watch tourists order massive jacket potatoes, thinking that's what we Brits are famous for. But inspiration suddenly strikes; with a bit more shopping to do, this is the ideal place to scope out special and unique gifts in the antique markets. I make my way through the piazza, past misted windows filled with patisseries and jewellery boutiques. Nothing will make Nana happier than a bit of used china that looks as though it has a story. It would add a homely, stately touch to her very normal room. I stop though. Nothing will make *me* happier than a Ben's cookie. No queue? White chocolate and cranberry? Fresh out of the oven? Yes. Very much, yes.

The antiques market at Covent Garden is opposite the main, glitzier piazza building and consists of a line of stalls and tables, roughly organised, badly lit but all selling curious wares of old china, vinyl, clothes and always one man with a big box of spoons. It's one of those lovely places where you can spend hours sifting, admiring, thinking about all the stories behind these well-loved objects.

I saunter through, wrapping my black wool coat around me against the cold, glad I opted for thick tights and boots. I reach in my bag and put a dark green beanie over my curls, getting carried along by the shuffle of people.

Vinyl. Yes, please. I flick through dusty album sleeves, some wrapped in plastic to let me know they're rare and more expensive. Something novelty for Dad that I can send over to Australia for a laugh. I see it: *The Golden Voice of Demis Roussos*, with Demis on the cover exposing his manly chest rug in a kaftan like a Greek god. It's as if the Christmas gods are here, blessing me with their gifts. 'Will you take a tenner?' I ask the man at the stall.

He looks up at me, smirking. 'Of course.' He then breaks into a tuneful version of 'Forever and Ever'. He has a wonderful tremolo. I hand over my money, putting the vinyl under my arm and keep walking along. It's the man with the box of spoons! The slightly controversial man with his war memorabilia, a table stacked high with books, not in any discernible order, which makes my little librarian heart sad, but I go over to have a moment, to flick through sepia-coloured pages and run my fingers over creased spines. My favourite thing to do is read dedications, or see if any have been signed and then given away. *For Barry. You'll never read this but you'll still put it on your bookshelf and tell everyone I wrote it and that's why I love you.* I grin broadly.

I continue walking behind a couple, hand-in-hand. They pass a vintage clothes stall and he puts a hat on her head. She smiles and poses. That's the magic, isn't it? Someone who doesn't mind having a camera roll full of pictures of you in a tartan beret. The neighbouring stall does a good line in dreamcatchers and blankets with giant wolves on them. The next is a table of jewellery. This is the table with the stories. Lost rings, stolen necklaces, artefacts of relationships laid out for people to inherit. I'm drawn to a pair of beautiful jade earrings, but then look at the price tag and move on.

'Please... you're most welcome,' a stallholder says as I approach her array of wooden tables, stacked with antique china, cups, saucers and teapots galore. Bingo. I look up at the stall name. *Clementine's*. I smile for no other reason than it's a Christmassy name and I ate five of them this morning because at this time of year, vitamins. I stop and look over the shelves and brown cardboard tags attached to everything, prices written in lovely calligraphy. 'Anything you collect or looking out for?' she asks, as I admire her gorgeous orange scarf and matching fingerless gloves.

'I'm just browsing. Is that Spode?' I ask, spotting an immaculate blue and white china teapot nestled in amongst the tin cups. Nana would lose her shit over that. It'd be all purpose to her – Earl Grey in the afternoons and gin as the sun went down.

'Girl knows her china then.'

'I got an education from my nana. She believes an afternoon tea should be done right. You've got some lovely pieces,' I say and she beams proudly. I like her ruddy cheeks, the way she's wearing two coats to keep the cold out. 'How much for the teapot?'

'This has got a bit of a chip on the lid so fifty quid alright? Brand new these fetch over one hundred.'

This is when I should haggle but the smile on her face makes me think that would be a little too cheeky. 'Then you have yourself a deal.'

Another gift done, I'm dead good at this. She reaches for the teapot but another person on the stall suddenly intervenes. I look up. 'Clemmie, the man down there said he'd take the cups and saucers and the teapot for £150.' I feel my shoulders go down. I've been gazumped over a teapot? Surely I've got a better stake in this piece as the actual owner has sold it to me. It's Christmas. It's for Nana. The warm Christmas spirit is evaporating off me, something inside telling me I need to put my game face on instead. *Bring it, teapot thief.* I look down across the tables, noticing the stall extends around the corner. I walk across to negotiate with this mystery punter, my nemesis. But as I do, I stand there and see him staring back at me, confused.

Hold up. How do I know you? Are you in my spin class? Are you a neighbour?

No. *You?* I haven't seen him in... since the night in that pub when...

He smiles and it changes the shape of his face, his slate-blue eyes. He waves. It really is him.

Nick. Nick Coles.

'It's fine. The lady can have the teapot if she wants,' he says, still smiling, a hand casually placed in his coat pocket.

I am speechless. He's standing there, a Dickensian Christmas shopping apparition. How did he appear out of nowhere? Plus, this isn't fair. It's glowed-up Nick Coles – older and wiser, in a really well-tailored navy suit, a dark wool coat, a striped-burgundy scarf wrapped around his neck, his sandy-blond hair well-styled. I remember those eyes.

Clementine is looking at me worriedly, as if she can see that the joviality I had running through me before has gone. Perhaps she's not sure what that means with so many breakables in the area.

'I have other teapots if you want to see those? I've got a lovely Royal Albert – I'll throw in a milk jug with it,' she says, as she and her colleague try and de-escalate the situation. I don't think there's a lot to de-escalate. I'm not angry per se. I think I'm in quiet shock. This is a man I've not seen for eight years. Last time I saw him was when he dumped me. In the pub.

I shake my head. 'It's fine. Let him have it. I'm not going to fight over china,' I say jokingly. I wave to him and he strides over to my side of the stall. As he gets closer, a strange feeling of fizziness comes over me. I can't tell if it's nerves or excitement.

'I thought it was you. It's the hair. Completely unmissable.'

He looks into my eyes, the fairy lights from the stall illuminating the angles of his face. I smile because as much as a face changes over time, there's still something there to recognise. Eight years, Nick Coles. I'm not sure he gets to open with a line about my hair, though I am happy I used the good conditioner this morning.

'Nick fucking Coles.' As I say it, I feel the grin spread across my face.

Opposite us, Clementine and the other woman who works on the stall hold a teapot each, watching. I wish they'd pick up a teacup and saucer and have a sip to break this tension. I don't know how to follow this up. Is it good to see him? I get the same feeling as when my neighbour's cat comes into my garden and stares at me through my kitchen window. It's very unnerving. Why is he here?

'Can't believe it's you,' he says, studying my face, his gaze falling to the outline of my face, my lips. *Yeah, don't do that.*

'It is me,' I say, unable to hide a touch of dryness in my tone.

'You look great.'

I sigh. Unfortunately, he does too. Nick was one of those exes where our break-up was unexpected, and it was deeply painful because my heart was young and naïve. In university, my expectations of love were curated around books and TV and so when I met him, I thought I'd met a forever person. This was what love looked like, it was cutesy, fun, and involved brunch. When it finished I therefore, mourned him dramatically. I cried. I ate a whole tiramisu in my pyjamas. I think about that sad idealistic girl now and cringe. Why did we break up? Is it terrible I can't remember?

'You look... healthy,' I say.

He chuckles. That wasn't a joke. He works out now, and I can see the better fit and quality of his attire. He smells nice and that is a terrible thing to pick up on so quickly.

'I forgot how funny you are... Always knew how to make me laugh,' he says to the ladies at the stall, both of them enjoying the sort-of reunion, a bit of Christmas magic unravelling here.

'"Knew." He speaks in the past tense as I haven't seen him in nearly ten years,' I tell them.

'Is there a story there?' Clementine asks me, hopeful that it's a good one. Maybe we were separated by war, a desert island, warring families. Maybe this is a love story for the ages.

'We used to date,' Nick says, affection in his voice.

'Before he dumped me in a pub just before Christmas.' Not that type of love story, Clementine.

Those words instantly transform the hopeful glances of these two ladies into grimaces. They both look at him expectantly, waiting for his explanation. I find this all very good fun.

'We were young. Hand on heart, I made a terrible mistake,' he says, though I know that's directed at me. I try not to react, instead watching the ladies as they warm to his words. 'I mean, look at her, right?'

I'm not sure what to say. Young love is like that, I guess. Relationships can be brief, passionate, but usually fizzle out on a whim. We had some good times. He was excellent at buying me flowers and cuddly toys. However, he did dump me, that much I remember, and then he disappeared. Time and distance meant he quickly got erased from my mind and I moved on. I still can't shake that secret thrill at seeing him again though.

Clementine smiles at me. 'I'd be more inclined for you to have the teapot if he was an absolute wanker,' she says. I smirk as Nick pouts in her direction. There's solidarity there if ever I needed it. 'I can sell him sweet FA if it would be a good way to get back at him.'

'Or maybe I can buy you the teapot?' Nick adds. I try not to let my emotion show. Clementine's colleague on the stall keeps looking Nick up and down. He's giving off a kindly aura, and I remember that generosity, the way that he would buy drinks for a whole group of people he didn't know. Clementine looks at me for cues. 'Is it for your nana?' he asks. Nick met Nana on a number of occasions whilst we were going out. I'm pleasantly surprised that he remembers her.

'Yes.'

'Then you really should have it. Please let me buy it for you.'

He keeps trying to prolong the glance between us. I force myself to be civil. This should be a nice moment but it feels as though he's trying to buy my affections here. 'I can buy my own teapot for Nana. Thank you though,' I say.

'Well, maybe I can get you something else?' he suggests.

I look around the stall, trying to find something really bloody expensive which I could then re-sell to buy myself a new bicycle.

'Let him get you something,' Clementine's colleague says, still trying to save the situation.

'Maybe some nuts?' he jokes.

'We don't sell nuts,' Clementine says, looking confused.

But the line does make me smile. It's a nice thing, to know how much an ex remembers, how much they think about you. I did move on from Nick. I graduated, travelled, I had relationships with other people and grew, all on my own. But I sometimes wondered about him, about us. Don't we all? On a cold night, unable to sleep, I'd sometimes scroll through my hall of fame, stalking people, seeing where they ended up. He was part of that roll call of people. To be honest, he was my first big love. So seeing him so suddenly is a jolt to the senses, thinking about halcyon moments lying with him in sunny fields, wrapped around each other, draped off each other in clubs, in bed, having sex. Eight years ago, Kay. That was a very long time ago. That was back when I had a fringe. I'm glad I grew that out.

'I'm good. Thank you again though,' I say to him, a little tickled that I hold power here. He can't seem to be able to look away from me.

Clementine's colleague looks up at me. 'Seriously?' She looks between the two of us. 'Where did you two meet?'

'We went to university in Bath,' I say.

'And almost ten years later, you're both here in front of Clemmie's stall, meeting over a teapot? That's got to mean something, right?' she continues. 'It's Christmas, lovely. Maybe it's worth a second pop,' she says, looking Nick up and down. '*I* would...'

Nick looks down at that moment, trying to hide his embarrassment. Well, he does wear that suit well. He side-eyes me. I have no idea what this is. He could be married by now, with kids. I could very well be in the same situation. This is a chance meeting between two people who once knew each other. Intimately.

'You have to admit, it could be fate,' Nick says with a grin. 'It is quite the thing to bump into you again.'

I look down, trying to keep my smile to myself. I have no idea what to say. I watch as he hands over a bunch of notes to Clementine, much more than what the teapot and all his haul is worth.

She looks down at the money and over at me. 'What do you think?' she asks me.

She appears to be still debating the morality and emotion of the situation. I nod. I'll take free Spode if it's on the table. I'm not stupid. And if it leaves you quids in, Clementine, then you take this man's money. She and her colleague start to wrap everything up in sheets of newspaper.

'Thank you,' I say, finally catching Nick's eye.

'Will you tell your nana I bought it?'

'No,' I say.

He laughs in return and there's a strange feeling of electricity in remembering that sound. 'I really can't believe it's you,' he says again, a strange look of wonder in his eyes. I can't believe it either. 'Do you live in London?'

'West London, Shepherd's Bush.' I'm not sure why I divulge that information so quickly. 'You? I thought you lived in New York.'

His eyebrows shoot up. Damn. That does mean I have looked him up since. 'I did but I live in Fulham now. I work for the Wiseman Brothers in town.'

'That explains the fancy suit.'

He keeps grinning because that infers I've been looking at said suit.

'Fulham's not far from Shepherd's Bush.'

I nod, wondering where this conversation is leading. I could walk away here. We've ascertained that I still look good, we live near each other and we dated a long time ago. Is it worth flirting with history? But then, like a flash of lightning, I think about the moment he dumped me. It wasn't me, it was him. We needed space. Maybe we could be friends? And a bitter feeling like bile rises up in me.

'Well, maybe we can—'

'No,' I reply, shaking my head, laughing. I wait as Clementine hands me my teapot and winks at me. She gets it. 'Thank you so much. Your stall is amazing. Have a lovely Christmas.' Nick looks a bit confused, collects his own assorted plates and cups and follows me briskly.

'Umm, what do you mean, no? You didn't know what I was going to ask,' he says jokingly as I try and traverse this maze of a building.

'Oh, I do,' I say, still walking as quickly as I can amongst the crowds. 'Look at all this fate in action. Maybe we can meet up for a drink, reminisce, catch up...' I jest.

'I don't see what would be so bad about that.'

I stop for a moment by a stone pillar as Nick looks at me, a brooding look to his face, trying to lure me in. I don't deny there's a flutter there, as light as a butterfly's wing, a curiosity. But then flashbacks of our break-up come into view. It's why I'm toying with him a little.

He continues to glance at me, warmly. 'How have you not changed in nearly ten years? What's your secret?'

Korean skincare. The problem is he's not changed either. We are just both grown up versions of ourselves. It's a strange thing to see him close up, looking this good, this polished, because every other memory I have of him is fuzzy, with him in straight-leg jeans and bobbly woollen jumpers. 'I drink a lot of water. I don't date wankers who dump me in pubs anymore.'

'Ouch. I possibly deserved that though,' he sighs, realising that perhaps I have more sense than to bounce back into a flirtation that didn't end well the first time. He takes a long deep breath. 'Kay Redman.'

'Saint Nick,' I say, a little too softly, but suddenly thinking of what Davinia told me outside that restaurant, about the universe delivering. Well, the universe thinks it's pretty funny, giving me something secondhand.

He smiles. 'Highly appropriate that we should have bumped into each other at Christmas then.'

'Perhaps.'

'Look, I think we should get a drink. Are you free now? Maybe a hot chocolate? With no hope or agenda or anything; it would be nice to chat, to catch up.'

This should be the moment where I say no. I have a teapot and a glorious Demis Roussos vinyl in my shopping bag. I can circle back and get some earrings and old poetry books from that stall I walked past earlier. That would be a power move. To leave him and what we had in the past. That said, in the last hour, my agent told me to go out there and have some fun, she felt so strongly that the universe would deliver. Nick used to deliver. Quite well, if I remember.

'One hot chocolate,' I say.

He smiles again. One drink.

SEVEN

I shouldn't be here. I mean, I should be here because this is a nice cosy café with its scents of gingerbread and its jingly Christmas folk music, and I have a cinnamon bun in front of me that's bloody delicious, but I shouldn't be keeping the company in front of me. Nick Coles. With his cool blue-grey eyes like a cat, his strong jawline and intriguing smile. I really thought he belonged in the deepest recesses of my history. Why did I agree to this? Is it because he bought me a teapot? But despite my best efforts to ignore it there is something that sits here between us, a strange energy. We can't stop looking at each other and grinning.

'Good buns?' he asks me.

Oh dear, don't try and do that. Don't throw around these puns that could be vaguely sexual, because innuendo was the foundation of how we got together the first time round, and that's both rude and unfair.

'They're very good, thank you,' I say, nodding.

I stir the cocoa into the whipped cream on top of my hot chocolate and put a spoonful into my mouth. He smiles to himself. 'You still do that?'

I will assume he's referring to the cream thing. I also do it with the foam on my cappuccino. I've done it for years. This is

better as there are sprinkles on the cream. He remembers that?
'Yes.'

'Funny the little things you remember,' he says. I don't know what to make of this. Why are we here? To debrief what happened nearly a decade ago? But I can't deny there's something mildly sexy about this. To be here with someone from the past that I once cared so deeply about. There is mystery here, and my thoughts are full of what-ifs and memories. Is there a chance to rekindle something? No, Kay, he dumped you. Have some self-respect. Look how well you thrived without him. Look at what he missed out on. Revel in that power. That said, I am under no illusion that he seems different now, with his sharp haircut and the suit that fits well at the shoulders and cuffs. I'm glad I had my agent lunch so I also look half presentable. We grew apart, that's for sure, but in opposite directions. In that way, I just always assumed he was a placeholder relationship, a lesson, shaping the way I looked at myself, the world, love. But now we're here. And strangely, I remember Dave in the pub telling me a corny line about setting someone free. That's what happened. And now he's back.

'So how was New York?' I ask him.

He leans forward, resting his elbows on the table. He's taken off his suit jacket so he's sitting there in his shirt and tie. *Don't look at the curve of his shoulders.* 'Intense. A good place to call home for a while. I did a lot of growing up there.'

'I bet the bagels were good,' I say. I don't know why.

He grins. 'They were pretty amazing.' I take a bite of my cinnamon bun so there's something in my mouth which will prevent me from saying anything else really stupid. 'What are you up to? Are you still writing?' he asks.

I look at him as he says this, my mouth full, surprised. I didn't write when we were at university, so this is something he's researched or discovered through the internet. 'I am.'

'I bought that book about the bears. I gave it to my niece,' he says. 'It was cute.'

'That's kind, thank you.' So he's been keeping tabs too.

'And are you still working with the library service?' he asks.

He really has been looking, eh? Was he watching from a distance? Comparing our journeys? Was today even a coincidence at all? Because if not, that's weird. I pull my drink closer.

'I am.'

'Then you're still Kay with all the words, all her books. That's a good thing,' he says, looking genuinely pleased for me as he tilts his head to the side. I find myself looking at the line of his neck, wondering what's underneath that shirt. I shake my head to scold myself.

'Well, it's not as if I was going to leave university with an English literature degree and suddenly become an accountant,' I say.

'You'd be surprised. I bet many of your year copped out and became teachers, lawyers... you always wanted to write books. I'm glad you're doing that.'

The kindness and support in his words make me melt a little in my seat. 'And you became a finance person...' I say.

He chuckles under his breath. I hope he knows that it'll take a lot more to impress me. 'Yes, a finance person. That's what it says on my name badge.' *Please don't try to be funny.* I watch as he takes a sip from his latte and a bite out of a gingerbread snowman. He leans back in his chair, beaming at me. There is eye contact briefly and I have no choice but to return the gesture. I've forgotten how a smile transforms him, how it makes his eyes crinkle, how it is instantly magnetic and charming.

'So how did you know about my books?' I ask him curiously.

'I checked in. It was good to see you doing so well. Don't tell me you didn't do the same,' he says, smirking.

'Of course I didn't. That was a very long time ago. I moved on and pretty much forgot about you. Actually, when I saw you in that market, I almost called you Rick.' He laughs, loudly. *You bastard.* 'I saw you with someone else in your pictures?' I ask, not knowing if that's perhaps a step too far because, yes, I did look once. Maybe twice.

He stops for a moment, that smile hiding away from me. 'We were together but not anymore. Her name was Neve.' The way he almost spits out her name makes me think it didn't end well. I won't dig. He sighs but then returns to the conversation. 'For a few months there was a musician fella, you went to his gigs.'

'Doug. He played the drums.' He had questionable political beliefs and I once saw him kick a cat. 'We weren't together long. Stalker.'

'Takes one to know one,' he says.

We gaze at each other over our mugs, sitting there in silence for a moment, sipping at our drinks, the windows of this place misting up. 'We were super young when we went out, eh?' he says, breaking that silence. 'I'll always be sorry about the way I ended it all.'

'In the pub, during the quiz,' I say, remembering the pretty savage way that pub turned on him.

He grimaces to remember it. 'I mean, it was particularly spectacular though. Someone threw a packet of nuts at me. I got a bloody lip. Every time I went in there after, people would heckle me.'

I try not to laugh. 'There were positives. I won a meat hamper that night.' It's true. After he left, I was persuaded to get quite drunk and finish my night helping three middle-aged men win a pub quiz. They gave me the hamper as recompense for my very public shaming. The chipolatas were outstanding.

'I can't excuse my behaviour. I was a dick back then.'

I take a sip of my hot chocolate because I don't know how to react. He's right, but I wasn't expecting him to own his behaviour with such clarity and magnanimity.

'Then I am grateful for the apology. We *were* young,' I say.

'And whatever happened, I had a lot of affection for you. We had a good year.' I sit incredibly still as he says that. I guess it's easy to say in hindsight, but he's right; there are good memories, and they are the ones I return to when I think of him. 'And I regret never telling you that much, just walking out that day.'

I feel a surge of emotion. This is the sort of closure we all need at the end of a relationship, but I'm unprepared for it, today or at any time. 'You missed out.' He missed out on someone who would have been his biggest champion, a hilarious sidekick. I also make the best cookies.

'Yeah,' he says wistfully, taking a deep breath. He looks totally at ease in my company. 'Seeing you now, I totally get that.'

It feels wildly lifting to hear him say that. 'I appreciate the sentiment and the gesture.'

'That's very formal,' he replies jokingly.

'It's because we're grown up now. I'm trying to be mature. You're in a suit.'

His smile broadens. 'I am.'

'Do you have plans for Christmas?' I ask.

'And that's a very mature line of conversation.'

'Well, that's me now. I'm not that same girl who used to live off pasta and sauce and water down my juice.'

He grins again. 'I didn't think that for a second. I'm spending it with my family.'

'And how are Marjorie and Lester?' I ask. His eyebrows lift again, as if he's impressed that I have remembered their names. He forgets that's what I do. I remember the names of all my primary-school teachers, the names of mums of friends I used to have tea with. It's my pub trick. 'Has your mum made her Christmas pudding yet?' It was a family recipe with a mountain of dried fruit soaked in a whole bottle of rum. I was invited to a strange ritual at their house where I was asked to stir it.

'She has. They are well, thank you.' He leans over the table. 'And your parents? Your nana?'

'All good. I won't tell Nana you bought that teapot for me,' I say. 'She wasn't a fan at the end.'

He laughs heartily, gaining the attention of a table next to us.

I sit back in my chair, running my hands through my hair. 'Christ, Nick. What are we doing here?' I look over at him in his chair, sitting back so I can see how well that shirt really fits him.

Both of us still in a state of complete bemusement that we've popped up in each other's lives again, at this precise moment. 'Are you dating anyone?'

He pauses for a moment. 'No. You?'

'No.'

'So maybe that lady at the stall with the plates had a point,' he says.

'That you're a wanker?'

Again he laughs, and for a moment I feel that emotion too. The idea that it is slightly ridiculous to have bumped into each other after all this time. I've had a decent eight years without him. OK, I didn't fall in love with anyone, but I thought my time with Nick was done. He was a stepping stone to a greater purpose when it came to my love life. He wasn't the one. Could we have a second chance at this? Did we grow apart just to grow up?

'God, you look great...' he says again, slowly.

'You look OK too,' I say, pulling a face to take away the intensity of his stare.

'You said I looked healthy before,' he jokes.

'That's a positive adjective.'

'You could use another adjective,' he suggests.

'You look well.'

'And wellness is everything.'

'There are industries dedicated to wellness.'

'I am aware.'

He leans forward across the table and I feel his leg against mine and I don't move away. There's a feeling emerging that I don't mind it there. That I like it. I watch him staring at me. I almost encourage it. Because despite any bad feeling I may have had towards this man, to be here now, opposite him, listening to his compliments, hearing him say he's missed out, feels strangely powerful and I want more of it. Do I reject him now, go nonchalant, or do I lean into this?

But then I also remember a feeling I once thought was love. A deep feeling of liking, wanting him. You and I had sex. We were intimate. And maybe another feeling joins the mixer now. I think it's lust and, well, that trumps it all sometimes. I lean in. This could be a really big mistake, couldn't it? Or maybe the lady with the plates did have a point.

I rest my hand over my mouth. 'You look very well,' I say, staring him in the eye.

'You want to get out of here?' he asks me.

Have some fun. Bones. Hell, why not?

EIGHT

'Hold up there, sparky,' my friend Lucy says. 'What have I told you about that? When you eat from a bad buffet, do you go back? You don't.' I would possibly take her more seriously if she wasn't dressed as a snowman, but I stand in the library letting her lecture me before the toddlers arrive.

'Was it good though?' Helen asks, propping her glasses up on the bridge of her nose.

'Don't encourage her,' Lucy says, sticking a finger in the air.

'Maybe the kitchen had a bad day,' I say.

'That's giving them excuses. There are so many decent buffets out there. I can't believe you went back for seconds,' she says, clearly unimpressed.

'I went back a few times, to be fair,' I admit. At the risk of sounding greedy, it wasn't simply many times on the one night. It's a hook-up that's had legs. We've met up twice since for drinks and food that, yes, has led to more sex, but I'm not angry about it. I think I may be mildly surprised and energised by the experience. 'And all those times have been pretty...'

'Moreish?' Helen says, grinning.

I can see Lucy still has her reservations; she narrows her eyes at me. 'I went to a buffet once and got sick off a chocolate fountain.'

'Is that an analogy for something else?' I ask quizzically, but she cackles in return, shaking her head at me as she readjusts her top hat and belly, making her way into the kids' section of the library. Today is one of many events in our library in Hampton Grove, trying to ensure our kids get into the season. I wear a knitted elf dress with colourful tights and a matching hat and we've called in Lucy to dress up and dazzle us all with her drama and dance skills. She's an old friend from university who still lives locally and does all of this for kebabs and bottles of wine.

'How many colouring pages do we need?' Olga asks. 'I'm keeping an eye on these. Last time, the kids were feral and they didn't colour properly. I am rationing the crayons. No scissors.'

Olga, Helen and I run this library in a large Georgian building that sits on a grassy hill outside this leafy suburb of London. I've been offered jobs in the more modern libraries around here but they all look like leisure centres. Despite all our attempts at modernisation, the nooks and crannies of the building still remain, and you get to walk into this place with its history, wooden window frames, original fireplaces and high ceilings, and find a book or a story that suits. Helen and I have spent an age decorating it, putting tinsel, garlands and fairy lights on every tabletop, so much so that Olga occasionally wears sunglasses indoors, but it's what makes this place magical. We wear Christmas hats, we theme the displays and have sweets for the kids. Olga is less enthused. She works here to improve her English so all the books are at her disposal. Libraries are for reading and quiet. Not little unpredictable children who don't use the colouring pages properly.

'I can supervise the little ones,' I say to Olga.

She looks at me, nodding. 'That is a good trade then. But I also want news about this boy you had seconds with.' Despite her severe tones which match her severe cropped haircut, there is a warmth to Olga in how she paints her nails different colours and loves a homemade knitted hat. 'I am happy you have found your way back to this buffet.'

Helen laughs again, tapping away on her computer but leaning over to listen in. She wants in on the gossip. Both of them are married so they always love news of my single shenanigans. I watch as Lucy starts to welcome a few little ones into the children's section. 'I bumped into someone I used to date at university. We may have...'

'Done the ol' fandango?' Helen says. I love Helen's Christmas jumpers, her thick London accent and the way she always has her blonde hair up in a perfect ballerina bun. She's the sort who always keeps us in tea, biscuits and gossip. It's because of her that I know that the people who run the bakery in town are also swingers on Sundays.

'Yes,' I say, scrunching my face awkwardly. It was also very good sex. I think back to the memory of that day we left the café. I assumed we might go to a hotel, or worse find a quiet alley, but instead a black car showed up and a driver called Francesco drove us to Fulham, to a flat that Nick calls home. Was it fancier than my maisonette? It had a lobby. I walked through it thinking my boots were noisy, amazed at how I could see my reflection in the floor. And then we took a lift up to a flat that overlooked the river. There was a balcony, a kitchen island, bifold doors, all those signs that we were older now, and grown up. Well, Nick was. I don't have bifold doors. I have a window that opens out onto the back of a Chinese restaurant called *Wok This Way*.

'No Christmas tree?' I remember saying as I walked in. There were no photos up, no soft furnishings, and more importantly – because that's what I look out for – no books.

'I'm getting round to it.'

But then he walked over to me and we were inches away from each other. 'You do look fucking good,' he whispered, and I felt full of bravado, completely attracted to him so I moved towards him and we kissed. A moment so intoxicating, so filled with desire for him, where he propped me up on that posh kitchen island with its fancy sink and solo fruit bowl and I wrapped my legs around him.

'We had sex on an island,' I tell them.

Olga furrows her brow. 'Like in the middle of the Thames?'

'No, a kitchen island,' I say, trying not to laugh.

'Kinky,' Helen says, winking. 'Did you use anything on the island?'

'Such as?'

'A... pasta server?' Helen continues, giggling. A few parents walking past look at her strangely. Christ, Helen. I don't know what she and her husband get up to and I don't want to know. We made love on the island and there was something so familiar and right about it, but also a feeling of disbelief that this all came from wanting to buy the same teapot.

'You scrunch your face like this when we ask about the sex.' Olga demonstrates said face. 'Why?'

The children's section has filled up now and Lucy puts on music, dancing around and asking the children to follow her. 'Because... Lucy may have a point. I've moved on since university. If it didn't work out then, why would it now?' I ponder.

'Why did you break up?' Helen asks.

'We were young. Last year of university, we were going in different directions.'

'So the road is forks, and now it comes back to one,' Olga says. Naturally, with her strong Eastern European accent we think she's talking about someone fucking a road. The best part of my job is working out the conundrum of her English.

'The road forked, yes.'

She takes out a notebook she keeps in her dungaree pockets and makes a note.

'Then maybe it's come back together for a reason. What does he do?' Helen asks.

'He's in finance.'

'Marry him,' Olga says immediately.

I put my hands in the air. 'Really?'

'Security, pension, nice holidays, you can do big shop in Waitrose,' Olga says.

'How rich? Does he have money to fix the roof?' Helen asks.

I look at both of them judgementally. 'Are you telling me to sell myself to a man so we can fix the library roof?'

'You're doing it for the community, for the kids, for all the books,' she says, winking. 'It's not a silly thing to consider now you're a bit older. The women in Austen's books were always looking for gentlemen of a certain stature and fortune so they could be married off.'

'And only one time in a hundred did they end up with a Darcy,' I reply, shaking my head. 'We'll see. We're meeting for drinks tomorrow. I'll ask him to write a cheque then.'

'Or shag him first then ask him for the money. Work for that dollar,' Helen says, still sitting at her desk as a library patron approaches. 'Hello, sir. What can I do for you?'

He looks at the three of us curiously. 'I have books to donate to your Christmas drive,' he says, a small box in his hands.

I walk over. 'That's very kind of you, sir. I'll take them.'

'I saw your flyer in the supermarket, how's that all going?' he asks me. There is kindness behind this man's eyes. I hope he's told his wife he's put a lot of her Nicholas Sparks in this box. 'It's a marvellous thing you're doing.'

Helen and Olga stand there beaming behind me as I chat. It was a thought really that came to me in November, trying to collect as many books as I could to give away to the community. Some I would donate to schools, others to nursing homes and other community centres. We'd wrap them up and put on events and readings. It was a small idea that's snowballed into something larger, and I'm grateful that people have bought into it.

'Thank you. That's very kind.'

'Also, while I'm here, I'm looking for a book for my wife. It's called *The Pisces*.'

The erotic fiction novel about the woman who has sex with a merman?

'I believe Helen can help you look for that,' I say, grinning.

'IT'S SNOWING EVERYONE!' I turn to the noise in the corner of the children's section. It's not snowing, not even close, but the clamour has increased to a roar and I realise that I've left snowman Lucy on her own to fend for herself. She can't see down past her snowman belly, I hope she's not trampled on a toddler. I scurry over and find that she's got them all joining in the chorus of *Frosty the Snowman*, with actions, and the kids all look up at her, fascinated. I didn't realise the song came with actions. She's got her own sleigh bells. But then she gets to a line about melting and does a dramatic dying scene like the witch in Oz. Did she just throw ice cubes everywhere? A toddler cries. Christ, Luce – get up. She jumps back up and sees me smiling in the corner.

'Everyone, this is my special elf friend, Kay. Can we all wave at her?' A little toddler marvels at my green and purple dress and she's instantly my favourite person here. Yes, I am an elf but I am not dancing; this is what I'm buying Lucy a kebab for. 'Now kids, tell her, don't date Nick. She can do so much better.'

'Don't date Nick!' an excitable five-year-old shouts out. Some parents look supremely confused.

Lucy laughs, rubbing her snowman belly. 'Right, kiddios. I believe there's colouring and craft, and then I am going to read a story!' she says, her eyes widening. The children are mesmerised. She is very good at making this little corner of the library come to life. I grin as they start running to the little tables we've set up, everyone wondering why there are only two crayons on each table. Olga wasn't joking.

Lucy wades over to me in her costume. 'I will take an extra-large doner with chips if you please. Did you see me melting? Wasn't I convincing?'

'Pick up your ice in case the children try to eat it,' I say. It may be too late though. It's already melted, leaving small puddles everywhere on the carpet. That had better be ice. I hope all the babies walking around have nappies on.

'Oh, also the little tosser in the Chelsea shirt asked me why I'm not a man. Snowmen should be men apparently.' I look around in case anyone heard that. 'So I told him someone nicked my snowballs.' I watch the one-year-olds stumbling around with crayons in their fists; all that glitter being sprinkled will make Olga's head spin. She'll have to get the hoover out. 'A heads-up in case someone complains.'

'Thanks for telling all the little ones about Nick,' I say, linking an arm through hers.

'This is why I'm here. I always tell my sisters, old meat is bad meat,' she says, seemingly unaware that little ears are still listening.

'Which is a meaningful phrase in many situations, especially in the run-up to Christmas.' My face is taut from trying not to giggle.

'Exactly. Especially when it comes to pork, bad pork can make you very ill... OOOH, GLITTER! Look how fancy you've made that! I think you're going to get one of Frosty's special stars for that!' Lucy walks away, winking at me.

I do love how she yo-yos between festive cheer and sheer indecency, but most of all I love how she does all of this for free. We got a quote in from a RADA man who wanted four hundred pounds and a dressing room.

Bad meat. It was good meat, to be fair, though it feels a little inappropriate to be thinking those thoughts while surrounded by little ones. I'm single. He's single. Maybe enough time has passed to not get too het up about why it ended, maybe we're older and wiser now. We had certainly matured in the bedroom. There was a whole ton of spark, we were both more confident, more relaxed, we both had acquired more moves and there were tender moments of lying there, laughing, reminiscing about the naïve youngsters we used to be. I can't lie: strewn across his king-sized bed, glancing into his walk-in wardrobe, there was also something slightly attractive about a man who had his shit together, who could offer security, a future. Last month, I had a brief dalliance with a man who thought he could map out his future on cryptocurrency and ads on Instagram.

Lucy circles the room and I look at the time. Kids this age don't have the longest attention span, so time for a few more songs and a reading and we might be done. I signal to her to take her seat.

'OK, my little snowboys and snowgirls, let's all sit together in my magic circle and get reading.' That carrot for a nose really adds something; she's even wearing silver Converse. I'll have to buy her a drink to go with that kebab. She picks up the book and a big smile spreads across her face. Oh dear, what on earth did Olga pick? '*What Is In Santa's Sack?*' I widen my eyes but look at all the parents who hide their sniggers too. 'Who knows, eh? Is it furry? Is it big? Will it fit down my chimney? Let's find out shall we, children?'

NINE

I'm waiting outside the Natural History Museum in London, looking through the thick iron railings, wondering if I have got this completely wrong. Nick told me to meet him here. I assumed we were going ice skating because the seasonal rink appears to be open; the bright white of the ice, the fairy lights, the Christmas tree and the tinkle of music filters through. That would be an excellent, festive, first official date. Both of us wrapped up warm, holding hands, gliding around under the shadow of one of London's finest buildings. But no, he said that we're having drinks. I was told to wear something nice. Men don't know what those words mean, do they? It runs the gamut from black trousers and a top to black tie, so I went with a dark-green jumpsuit. With my hair, I'm always aware I look a little like Poison Ivy but hey, at least it's seasonal. Did I get this wrong? Was it a bar or hotel opposite the Natural History Museum? I look up at the building towering over me. I've always loved it, the way it brings back memories of school trips, how back then the grandeur and majesty of it would take my breath away. I search for my phone in my clutch.

I'm outside.

So am I.

Is he though?

'Boo.' I jump in fright then laugh to see Nick behind me. I put a hand to my chest to calm myself. He takes my hand tenderly and steps back, looking me up and down. 'Gorgeous,' he says, a hand reaching for my face, and he pulls me in for a kiss under the streetlights. His cheek is soft against mine, I feel the warmth of his breath and the gentle touch of his lips. I relax immediately as he puts an arm around me, both at the contact and knowing I read the dress code right. We part and I check him out, realising he's in a tux with a black tie, his haircut is fresh and he has one hand in his pocket, posing as if he's on the red carpet. It's very swish and debonair. I'm suitably impressed.

'I hope you've not hired this out on my account,' I say. I really hope he hasn't because all we've done so far is indulge in a few dates that have led to some pretty energetic sex. We've traded a few cheeky texts, but whatever this may be is still in its infancy, baby steps before we decide if it's a good idea.

'God, no,' he says, as we walk through the gates and proceed up the path to the stone stairs at the front. He puts an arm around me to shield me from the cold. 'There's an event I had to attend here, and I had a plus one. I thought it might be nice.'

'A wedding?' I say, worried that I haven't brought a gift.

'No, just a small work drinks thing. Is that OK?'

I smile. I think so. It feels big for a date but I guess I'm also flattered that he thought me a suitable partner to introduce to his colleagues. We walk through the doors where others are queueing to go in, the ladies in a selection of cocktail dresses and what I hope aren't real fur coats. He puts his hand into mine and squeezes it tightly. It's a reassuring feeling and I squeeze back. However, when the crowd clears and we walk through reception, I stand there for a moment to take it all in. Holy balls. This is not a work drinks thing. I had that with Helen and Olga back in the first week of December. We went to a bar that had tapas and wore novelty earrings, and Helen wowed us all with her conversational Spanish that she's been learning on Duolingo. This is an event. In the main hall of the museum as you walk in, a blue whale skeleton sits there regally, and all around the room are tables festooned with candles in jars. Lights and verdant greenery hang from the large stone archways that frame the galleries. A large tree at least twenty feet high sits near the back stairs, glowing with warm light and velveteen decorations. Amongst the well-dressed are waiters in bow ties and gold antlers carrying silver trays of champagne and assorted hors d'oeuvres, while a swing band plays a selection of classic Christmas songs on a stage to the side. I laugh under my breath as I stare at it all, wide-eyed.

'Your coat, madam,' a waiter says, handing me a small cloakroom ticket.

'Yes. That is my coat and... thank you,' I say as he takes it away. It's an H&M overcoat, my name is written on one of the tags as I'm a touch possessive like that about my coats but no one needs to know that. I let out a breath, very glad I didn't go for the black trousers and fancy-top option tonight.

'You OK?' Nick asks, looking over at me.

'A small work drinks thing...' I say, repeating his words and raising an eyebrow.

He smirks. 'Are you impressed?'

'I will be if they have those little Yorkshire puddings with the beef.'

I walk past an ice sculpture of Santa. I think that may be a vodka luge. This is not how I usually do this place. I usually come here for an afternoon and learn random facts about fossils, catching the light through the large circular stained-glass window that now sits dark and lifeless above us. I'd be sitting on the stone steps and people-watching with a café flapjack.

'You got fancy in your old age,' I say to Nick as he walks alongside me. He smiles broadly, effortlessly stopping a waiter and taking two glasses of champagne, handing me one. I will take it this isn't a seven-pound bottle of Prosecco from Aldi. I take a prolonged sip. Of course it isn't.

'That went down well,' I say, a little too loudly.

He smirks. That is our conversational currency at the moment, these small moments of banter that hark back to that moment when we first met. I shake my head at him, my eyes continuously drawn to this boy I used to date, who's blossomed into quite the man.

'I guess I thought I could do that later. Bringing it up now seems a little premature,' he whispers into my ear. His hand goes lower down my back, resting above the curve of my hips. 'We could find a little dark corner.'

I now regret wearing the jumpsuit. 'Somewhere near some old bones.'

He laughs loudly and I'll admit that even though I don't think it was even in the vicinity of my best jokes, it's a kick to amuse him. 'Is that what we're calling me now?'

'An old bone? Well, if the shoe fits.' He slaps me playfully on the backside and I jump, sticking my tongue out at him. 'I will hold you to that, Saint Nick.'

'Oh, there will be nothing saintly about it.'

He stands dangerously close to me, his arm wrapped around me, and I look at his face – so familiar and so strange at the same time. *Who are you?* There is a deep attraction there. I think it was always there when we were younger, but he seems different to the person he was eight years ago. Back then he was young, a little selfish. I survived our break-up because that's what young hearts do, but have things changed enough for us to give this another go? Does this also feel right because it feels a little wrong?

'Colesy! How goes it?' a man suddenly says, approaching us. Nick lets go of me, takes the man's hand and shakes it vigorously. 'Tough day on the markets, do you know how the FTSE panned out?'

I smile, clutching on to my glass to hear the poshness of the accent and because the topic of conversation goes well beyond my sphere of knowledge. The man is similarly in a tuxedo, accompanied by a lady partner with sleek blonde hair and a stunning black backless dress.

'Mad day but I'm not talking shop now, Phil. It's time to drink. This is Kay. Kay, this is Phil and his wife, Meribelle.' I wonder if she's named after the ski resort or the Nintendo game anime character? I'm going to think neither. I put out my hand and shake theirs to introduce myself.

'This jumpsuit is gorgeous, is it vintage?' Meribelle asks. If that's how we're describing ASOS then let's go with it.

I nod. 'You're very kind. Your dress is also beautiful.'

'Oh, this old thing, last season's Gucci,' she says. I feel a lump in my throat as she says this because I picked up my clutch on a food shop at Tesco last year. This isn't my crowd, not one little bit, but I try to keep up appearances. 'Are you in finance too?' she asks.

'Oh no, Kay's in publishing,' Nick intervenes. I frown before quickly correcting my expression and giving a polite smile. It's not a lie per se but I stop for a moment to get that story aligned in my head. I guess we haven't really traded in much chitchat since we reconnected. He knows I collaborate with an illustrator and write the occasional kids' book. Does he know I spend the majority of my time in a community library though? I'm a beast with the Dewey decimal system. Can I unleash that knowledge now? It pains me that maybe this won't be of any worth to them. There is another reason why he may have lied though, and I'm unsure how I feel about that.

'Wow,' Phil says. 'Any of the big five?' he asks.

To hell with it, I've had a drink and it's a fancy night. 'Penguin.'

'Do you know Roger Miley? He's one of their editorial execs? We climbed Everest with him two years ago.'

'Oh yes, Roger. How's his knee?' I say. I have no bloody idea who Roger is but, truth be told, if I'm being asked to participate in this game then I want to have fun with it. Please don't tell me Roger doesn't have knees.

'His knee?' Meribelle asks. 'He's always been one of the fittest people I know.'

Shit. 'Oh yes, I believe he hurt it playing in a pickleball tournament. I think he strained his patella.'

'I'll have to send fruit,' she says. Well, at least Roger will have got something out of this.

I want to move this on but I smile at Nick who seems to be in a light panic that I've brought pickleball into the conversation. Do I bullshit about Everest now? I've seen pictures of it but that might be harder to fake and I've only had one drink.

'Kay mainly works in acquisitions and commissioning at Penguin,' Nick tells them. I turn my head swiftly to look at him. I do? OK, I can drag this out. Do I have to talk about Roger again?

'Yeah, mainly liaising with agents and new talent.'

'Anyone to look out for? Who's the next big thing?' Meribelle asks. 'I'll have to tell my book club.'

'Well,' I say, nodding and thinking what gets loaned out the most in our local library, 'fantasy with erotic leanings is always going to sell big. I think the romcom is going to start making a strong comeback.'

Phil snorts immediately. 'Fodder fiction then for lovelorn idiots.'

I stop in my tracks. 'You say that but it accounts for a large proportion of the market. Nothing wrong with people wanting fiction that's hopeful, bright, that soothes the soul.'

'Well, you would say that if you're getting all the profits,' Phil says, guffawing in reply. I reckon Nick can read in my eyes that I instantly dislike this man. Can I hit him? Nick may remember that I hit someone in a pub once when we were together because he told me Jackie Collins was crap. I bet Phil reads fictional war books, speaks in tactical talk and has slightly masochistic tendencies that come out in the bedroom. Still, I keep smiling along with this charade. 'Colesy, brandies later and we can talk about that merger offer,' he says to Nick, doing a strange click of the fingers and pointing action at him.

'It was lovely to meet you,' Meribelle says, putting an arm to mine. She'll feel this jumpsuit is synthetic won't she?

They walk away and Nick turns to me sheepishly. 'I am sorry.'

I fake a laugh. 'Publishing?'

He sees the confusion in my face. 'I panicked and I didn't want them to judge you. They're a bit high and mighty with all their Everest and Gucci talk.'

I feel a swell of disappointment that he would feel the need to keep up with the Joneses, but maybe I need to accept his excuse that he was trying to be protective. I take a sip from my drink and look out into the room again. Behind him the swing band break into song and people congregate on the dancefloor, including one man in a white tux jacket. 'He looks like Marty McFly's dad,' I say.

'Who?' Nick asks, looking at me. And for a moment, I remember something that didn't quite click with us. He never had a huge amount of pop culture knowledge. I am very much a film quotes and song lyrics kinda girl and that never translated with him. He used to look at me as if I was speaking in tongues. When I visited his family, they were very highbrow, happiest with a BBC4 documentary on the origins of space or Greek philosophy on the TV. There is time and space for both, I feel. I think it's good pub quiz knowledge to amass as many random facts as possible.

'*Back to the Future*,' I say.

'The one with the car.'

I nod, smirking. He senses me mocking him. Well, he's told complete strangers a lie that shows that he doesn't think my profession is good enough for public consumption. I think that makes us even.

'Can you tell the next people that I'm a screenwriter and that I summer with Scorsese in Sicily?' I say. 'It's a bit more glamorous than pickleball with Roger.'

He laughs again as someone walks past with a platter of tiny Yorkshire puddings, each topped with a perfectly cooked piece of rare steak and horseradish. 'You were saying,' Nick says.

'He delivers again.'

'Always,' he says, whispering into my ear.

TEN

It's been a while since I went on a date and I'm not sure how they are supposed to pan out, but I think it's common to spend time with said date.

It all started very well. Nick and I walked around and took lovely selfies with the lights and skeletons. I followed a waiter around until I'd had my fill of Yorkshire puddings and beef, a few crispy prawns and smoked salmon blinis and, well, the champagne did go down well because I've had three glasses and am now cradling a very beautifully spiced winter negroni. It was the mingling that was the killer. Pretending I knew Roger was fun but every other meeting and conversation has been less so. There were a lot of balding men talking about finance, the size of fish they'd once caught and their holiday homes. I played along to start with but there's only so many marlin and mountain lodges in Switzerland you can hear about before realising a lot of people in this room are absolute asshats.

> Where are you? I'm stood next to a very big rock.

I look down at my phone, at a message I sent an hour ago. It's not particularly sexy, which is why he's likely not replied, but it hasn't even been read. I'm not sure what to do now. All I did was go to the toilet and I took a bit longer because I am wearing a jumpsuit but when I went back to the spot where we were standing, he was no longer there. Or maybe I went back to the wrong group of greying old men. Since then, I've walked around on my own trying to track Nick down, trying to work out if I've been dumped by someone who possibly hasn't changed much at all. If so, then that sucks. What if he's so knee deep in financiers, he hasn't noticed I'm not by his side? What if he left with someone else? What if he's hurt? Oh God, he could be passed out in the gents. Or mugged. Maybe I should check before I think the worst, of the situation and of him. I head over to the darkened corridor and hover by the door to the gents. Do I shout in? Maybe I should try and look for him as the door swings open and closed.

'Ummm, are you OK?' a man asks me as I stand there, slightly bent over, peering inside. I look up. He's got particularly curly hair and is wearing a red velvet tuxedo jacket and Vans on his feet. I feel an immediate affinity to him.

'I was looking for someone. I've kind of lost my date,' I say.

'I can check for you. What's his name?'

'Nick.'

He swings the door open and heads inside and I hear his voice shout out. 'Is there a Nick in here? Nick? Nick? Your date is waiting outside.' I'm impressed that he's doing such a thorough job of this. I wait a couple of minutes before he reappears. 'I'll take it that he didn't make an appearance?'

I shake my head. 'Thank you for checking.'

'I checked the stalls, no feet. Unless he's hiding, which would be weird,' he says. He notices the concern in my face. 'Have you called him?'

I twist my phone in my hand. 'Yeah.'

He grimaces as he tries to figure out what that means. 'Then what an absolute fucker if you ask me. Are you OK?' I hold up my negroni. I don't know who you are, curly haired stranger, but I have alcohol so I'm fine. I'll just leave here and spend the rest of my evening kicking myself for being so stupid and investing my time in that man again. I'll also take a few more canapés for the ride.

'I'm Jasper.'

'Kay.'

'You're not in finance are you?' he asks, scanning down to my heels.

'No, is it obvious?'

'No, it's a bloody relief, that's all. Come...'

He starts to walk, beckoning me to follow as he turns down another corridor by the gents to a group of people propped up by a display of ammonites. They've set themselves up with bottles of champagne and a platter of assorted canapés, sitting on assorted tables that have been dumped there.

'Troops, this is Kay. Some financier wanker has abandoned her so she is now in our party.' I turn to him, glad to have been adopted so immediately. 'We are IT... Frank, Leo and Leo's wife, Maggie.' They all put their hands up in turn as Maggie pats a table space next to hers. 'We don't bite. Come, join our little shindig!' She is warmly drunk in her sparkly blue dress which I recognise instantly as last season's H&M.

'Say that again? Someone left you at the party?' Frank asks me.

'Yeah,' I admit, slightly ashamed.

'It's cool. Nick, you say?' Jasper says. 'You're with the right people. I can shut down his computer Monday, upload a virus or something, pour a can of Coke in his hard drive.'

'We have our ways and means,' Leo says, winking at me.

'So is this a long-term boyfriend? First date?' Maggie asks me.

'He's just someone I used to date and bumped into and I thought I'd give it a second go. But it's been a strange evening... I guess I'm a different breed to the people swanning around that room.'

'So, normal then?' Maggie says, and they all cheer, raising their glasses. And then downing their glasses. I agree, this is normal. The drinking but also the joy. From walking around out there, the joy really seemed to be missing from this so-called party.

'Oooh! LUGE!' Jasper suddenly shouts out, holding his empty glass aloft.

'Jasper, no,' Maggie says.

'Maggie, yes.' He steps aside and I see it glistening in the shadows.

'Shouldn't that be out...' I point out into the main party, recognising it from before.

Jasper is doubled over laughing. 'Oh, it got sidelined because...' He goes into the shadows to wheel out the trolley it's resting on and I look at it curiously, flinching slightly as luges remind me of university nights filled with dentist chairs and continuous shots. The difference is that this one is shaped as Father Christmas.

Jasper still can't stop chortling. 'So I don't quite know who designed this but look...' He grabs a bottle of Grey Goose underneath the trolley and pours it into the back of Father Christmas, the stream of vodka then emerging from his mouth.

'That's...' I mutter.

'Because that's what we all want to see – Father Christmas vomming out vodka,' Jasper chuckles.

I cock my head curiously to watch while Maggie angles herself under the stream to catch a bit in her mouth, Leo filming her as she swallows her shot then stands up, both arms in the air in celebration.

Leo peers at his phone in hysterics. 'This video looks like you're into some very festive kink, wifey.'

'When I saw it out there, they had shot glasses,' I say. 'Or I guess you could snog him to get your vodka? It might look less dubious,' I suggest.

'The lady has spoken!' Jasper says, raucously. 'Come on, Kay with the good hair, that's one way to get over one Nick, snog another.'

And I giggle at the thought but they all start to clap and cheer me on and maybe it's the negroni or the ice-cold feeling of date failure in my veins but I jump down off that table. Why the hell not? I reach into my clutch and grab my phone. 'Maggie, right? If I'm doing this, I want a video too.'

'Of course...' she says obligingly.

I go up to the trolley with the luge. Santa is conveniently at eye level with me and I beam at him. Alright, Nick? I can't stop giggling. Merry Christmas. Maggie puts her thumb up and I go in to catch the falling vodka emerging from Santa's lips. Crikey, that's cold. I hear Jasper in hysterics as I put my hand to Santa's arse, for video purposes of course. I close my eyes for the authenticity.

'Excuse me, I was wondering if you'd seen a lady... she's wearing a green jumpsuit...'

My eyes ping open as I hear the voice at the end of the corridor and I try to back away from the ice sculpture but feel a tug on my bottom lip that makes me flinch. What the actual? I side eye Leo who runs over to Nick, realising who it might be. Maggie stops filming but looks up at Jasper who doesn't know whether to laugh or run away.

'I'm stuck,' I say in muffled tones. I put my hands on Santa's chest trying to extricate myself from the ice as Jasper covers his face.

'Oh shit, we're so going to get fired for this,' Frank says, trying to help me.

I look further down the corridor past the melee of waiters and bottle fridges to see Nick engaging in conversation with Leo. He hasn't seen me yet, thank God.

Jasper follows my gaze. 'Shit, is that the date?' he asks. 'He's fit. I know him, new guy on the fifth floor.'

'Yeah... but... I...' I say, gesturing at my immediate situation. I was snogging and now am stuck to an ice sculpture. Could I lose a lip? I am half-laughing, half-mortified.

'Jasper,' Maggie says, clicking her fingers to get his attention. 'Let's wheel her around the corner. You good to walk with me, help me push it?' she asks. I'm not sure I have much of a choice, but we wheel ourselves as slowly and carefully as possible into the shadows of a little alcove out of sight.

'I think we did see her. She was looking for you but then went home when she couldn't find you. Sorry, mate...' We all go silent, listening to Leo cover for me. Given he doesn't really know me, he's doing an excellent job. 'She was pretty upset.'

'Crap. I just got caught up with one of the senior execs and then...' I listen to Nick carefully from the shadows. 'She didn't deserve that.'

'No, I guess not. Maybe a text might help? Or a big gesture to get back in her good books, eh?'

'Perhaps. Thanks. Leo, isn't it? Head of IT?'

'Yeah. Nick, right? From the fifth floor?'

'Yeah. I should get back and show my face.'

I stand there for a moment, listening, pondering. At least he acknowledged that this evening may not have been great for me. At least it wasn't a complete abandonment. I hear his footsteps pad away. I'm still trying to remove my lip from this ice when Frank reappears with a small glass full of water. 'It's room temperature. Physics dictates that it should... work...' He tips a little onto my lip and, as if by magic, my lip flips back to my mouth, slightly cold and swollen but attached to my face. I had had visions of the fire brigade being called that weren't great.

'Oh my... you are a genius,' I say to Frank as he looks at me with relief that this wasn't a complete disaster.

'Are you alright?' Maggie asks me, putting an arm to my back.

'I'm mortified but crisis averted, eh? Did you get a video?' I ask her.

'And many photos,' she giggles.

'Then it was all worth it,' I say, taking my phone back. I laugh at one of the photos and the fact I'm really going for it. I send it to Lucy and then put it back in my clutch.

Leo returns to us and I nod to thank him for his stellar work. 'Are you going to find him?' he asks me. 'I think he knows he's effed up.'

I shrug my shoulders, thinking of my options, knowing that Nick has returned to the party and all those bores. 'Oh, I think I've had enough excitement for one evening. I reckon I'm going to call it a night. Thank you all though. That was quite a moment.'

Maggie comes to give me a hug and Jasper puts his arm out to offer me the half-drunk bottle of vodka. 'Bye, Kay with the nice hair.'

'Bye, Jasper with the Vans,' I say, blowing him a kiss.

'SEE! They do go with this suit!' he says to the group, and they all wave, wishing me a merry Christmas. I turn back to look at them, grinning widely, glad that they were there to save my evening, happy to see the friendship and joy they obviously share as a work family.

I walk back into the bustle of the main hall, looking out across the large crowd and see Nick deep in conversation with a group of silver-haired men. It doesn't look as though I'm missed or would add anything to their chat. I think I'm going to go. There was something in me that thought this wasn't the best idea, and maybe tonight proves as much. We are from very different worlds. I go out into the foyer of the building, handing my cloakroom ticket to a waiter, loitering as he goes to fetch my coat.

'Are you the management then? It's been awful service all night, I hope you do investigate that. Our company has spent a lot of money on tonight.' The lady's complaints seem to carry louder given the high ceilings and tiled floors of this place, so I have no choice but to eavesdrop. I turn slightly to see her frosty blonde hair, long and sleek, a face that looks vaguely familiar. She turns to look at me for a moment and then storms off. I suppose she didn't get one of the wagyu sliders.

'Your coat, madam...' a waiter says.

'Thank you.' Do I check my name tag inside too? Of course I do. As I put my coat on, I walk over to the person who was on the receiving end of that woman's harsh complaints. 'Hi...'

'Evening, madam.'

'I wanted to say I had a lovely night. The service was exceptional, well done,' I say warmly, hoping they haven't noticed the half-drunk bottle of Grey Goose under my coat.

Her shoulders drop, she stands a little bit straighter for the feedback. 'That is very kind, madam. Thank you. Have a lovely Christmas.'

'You too.'

I turn to leave, exiting through the large wooden doors, not even looking back. I'd assumed the chill outside would be unbearable but the alcohol in my system tells me otherwise. Am I a tad disappointed? Maybe. But it's still reasonably early and I know there's a matcha café in South Kensington, so my evening might be saved. My phone suddenly pings. And a message pops up from Nick. Perhaps there was no signal inside.

> Where are you? Have you left? I'm so sorry. Can I find you? Make it up to you?

I stand there for a moment looking at the message. I could go back. Do I dare go back? But then my phone starts to ring. I smile and answer it.

'WHAT THE ACTUAL?' Lucy shrieks, and I hold the phone back from my ear. 'Are you still there? Can I come?'

'I'm actually leaving. Where are you? Do you want to grab something to eat?' I ask her.

'Urgh, I can't. I've got another hour left on this gig. Come to me? I'll ping you the location. We can do something after?'

'Will it be fun?'

I hear sleigh bells in the background. 'Have we not met before? Of course it will.'

ELEVEN

The one thing about London is that it is very green. Unlike most cities, it is punctuated by beautiful parks, large spectacular trees and a winding river that's like its spine. I love walking through it at Christmas, taking in all the lights wrapped around every building, the inkiness of the sky, the puddles on the ground reflecting all that light and making everything glow amber, watching people wrapped up, scurrying across streets to get inside to the warmth of the buildings. And then getting to the outskirts of the city on the Tube, to see more green spaces, more trees, the quiet night of the streets. It is lovely but I am starting to get a little worried that Lucy gave me the wrong location here. I've grabbed an Uber from the station and we're driving into darkness. This is when I find out she's leading me to a warehouse rave on an industrial estate. We drive down this winding road where the trees are a little taller, the shadows a little darker.

'Are we sure it's down here?' I ask Egon, my Uber driver.

'It's what the map is saying, my love. I can turn around to the main town if you want,' he says, a worried look in his eyes that I'm assuming the worst of him and where he may be taking me. *Don't worry, Egon. I've got my keys out ready to attack you if this is the case.*

'Well, maybe a bit further.'

However, the location then seems to jump out at us from the darkness. A carved wooden sign is lit by fairy lights to mark the entrance, and long lines of wooden fenceposts show rows and rows of Christmas trees, all illuminated, standing there proudly. I read the sign: *The North Christmas Tree Farm.*

Egon rolls the car to a stop at the top of the driveway and looks up at the lights, his mouth agape. 'This is like the movies. I thought they only had these sorts of places in America,' he says, amazed. 'I bought my Christmas tree from the back of a pub.'

I nod, equally amazed but also slightly worried why we're here. Lucy moonlights as a lumberjack? I can't imagine her on a farm. I don't think we're in the right place. Unless Lucy thought this was a joke. I sit in the car and look out the slightly misted window, cars drive in and out of the entrance with trees squeezed into boots and strapped precariously to roof racks. Then, out of nowhere, I see an elf running towards the car. Lucy? I open the car door and step out.

'You found it!' Poor Lucy. I made her dress up as a snowman and now she has gone full elf, from stripey tights to clog-style shoes with bells. The bright-green dungaree dress is a little brief but she makes up for it with drawn-on freckles and a cute Robin Hood hat. She wraps her arms around me. 'Come and see my Christmas wood!' she says, waving her arms in the air.

'Lady, I don't have the straps or the space to carry a Christmas tree,' Egon shouts from the driver's seat. He looks infinitely bemused by Lucy, as if he's stumbled on an alternate Christmas reality.

'It's OK, Egon. It was a one-way trip,' I say. 'Thank you, five stars all day long!' I must be tipsy.

He smiles. 'Then I will leave you. Merry Christmas, ladies!' His car pulls away as I stand there looking at the farm and at Lucy, who threads an arm through mine and leads me up to a series of log cabins in front of all the trees, their frames covered in baubles and ribbons. It doesn't seem real, it feels as if we're in another country.

Around the cabins, a fake snow machine pumps out white foam everywhere to give the impression that it's snowing.

'Explain?' I ask Lucy.

'It's a Christmas gig. People come here to buy their trees. I'm an elf to make it more sparkly and fun. I give out candy canes, pose for photos, entertain bored children. It pays well and I'll get a free turkey from the farm shop. Mum is holding out for this turkey.'

I love how nothing phases her, how she juggles these numerous jobs that border on the ridiculous, but pay the bills. She was in a bike accident a few years ago, one which could have very well ended her life, but she seems to have come out of it more determined, a bit more Lucy, which I never thought possible.

'This place is...' I start to say, looking around at the festive décor.

Lucy leans in. 'You didn't hear it from me but it's overpriced. People come for the experience, similar to picking pumpkins from a field rather than going to the supermarket. It's something to do, all that making memories shite,' she says. 'Oh my goodness, that's the fanciest hot chocolate that I ever did see!'

A family of four come out of the shop, all in matching Fair Isle. Mum carries a paper bag of cookies and decorations whilst the little ones cradle paper cups of hot chocolate with candy canes.

I look at Lucy who has gone from Christmas cynic to magical elf in a matter of seconds. Give this girl an Oscar. I stand back for a moment as she stoops down. 'It was so lovely to see you, come back soon!' she says, and from nowhere she gets a handful of glitter and sprinkles it in the air. I don't know whether to laugh or be impressed as she poses for a photo and then waves them off as they go to their car, a Christmas tree tied to the roof rack. 'Except don't come back soon because why would you? To buy another tree? Piss off home. It's late and I want to get bladdered. Wave with me, Kay!' They all get in the car and drive away, and I'm not sure why but I wave too, much to the family's confusion.

'But seriously...' I say, turning around and walking back

towards the log cabin, 'This place is pretty magical. Look at the snow! All of the lights!' I'm mesmerised by the charm of it all. 'It's so earthy and green.' I may spin at this point.

'Crikey, how much have you had to drink?' she giggles.

I reach down into a deep pocket in my coat and pull out the half-drunk bottle of Grey Goose. It's actually now more like two-thirds drunk as I had some sips on the Tube like a festive lush. Lucy smiles at the bottle, leading me through one of the smaller cabins where another elf sits with a card machine, classical Christmas music being piped in behind him. This elf seems to be a worker elf because he wears a North Face puffer coat and heavy-duty gloves.

'Nate. Please tell me they were the last ones? Any others sneaking around?'

'My sister told you that when we're on the floor, you must call me by my elf name,' he says dryly.

Lucy chuckles. 'I am so sorry, Twinkle.'

He nods and I'm immediately taken with his humour. 'Last ones, Sparkle. She was an influencer, she wanted to take a lot of videos and then bartered with my brother for a discount. He was not impressed.'

'Is he ever? This is Kay. I'm giving her a tour and then I'm headed out.'

'Is she buying?' Nate asks.

'No,' I say hesitantly, but he looks immediately relieved, turning off the music and shutting up his cabin.

'If my brother comes looking then I'm in the shop, defrosting my baubles,' he says.

We both laugh, watching him march away as Lucy ushers me into the farm. There is really something lovely about it, how we're on the outskirts of the city so the sky is a bit clearer, and the stars shine that bit brighter. By this cabin, some trees have already been cut down and wrapped with beautiful tags that say *take me home now* in calligraphy font.

'They're a bit forward, but OK then,' I say, reading all the tags.

I turn to see Lucy laugh and take a sneaky sip of the vodka before she passes it back to me so I can have a swig. I was warmly drunk in the museum before but now I'm verging on that sort of drunk where I think I could run home in heels but also devour a whole plate of chips with garlic mayonnaise, damn the consequences. Beyond the cabin is a field, beautifully lit up with lanterns and light-filled trellises. The Christmas trees stand in rows in an almost military fashion; their shadows look as if they're wearing billowing skirts, waiting to dance. I bite my lip as I take it all in, amazed at how lovely it is.

'So if I wanted a tree, I have to saw my own down?' I ask Lucy.

We walk to the edge of the field and take a seat on a large hay bale.

Lucy says, 'No, it's family run and there's a brother or cousin who runs out and does that. They let people hold the saw for photos but when they used to allow people to fell the trees themselves, they got hurt. There's a story that a granny got crushed and they had to pick pine needles out of her chin.'

I shouldn't laugh but I do because I'm drunk. I stretch my arms to the sky and get up from my hay bale, having a sway to the Christmas music in the background. Lucy looks on, smiling. 'You look happy but I want to ask why your evening ended so early.' She has another shot of vodka.

I puff out my cheeks. 'I got my lip stuck to an ice sculpture.'

'OK, so you had to leave?'

'No, I probably would have got thrown out for snogging the ice sculpture and not using the shot glasses like a sensible human being. But it was a very high-end, snooty party. Lots of bellends. I felt out of place.'

'Look at you keeping the insults seasonal,' she says.

I curtsey at the compliment.

'Where was it?'

'Natural History Museum.'

'Fancy. And Nick?'

I pause for a moment and look out into the night sky, watching the flashing lights of a plane overhead and a crescent of silver moon hanging there. 'He kind of abandoned me. It was a work social and he disappeared for an hour. I don't think he meant to, but it was a bit... tedious, and for a work party you would have thought there'd be...'

'A conga line at least,' Lucy jokes. I think of Meribelle and her Gucci doing the conga, the Macarena, getting on down to the cha-cha slide. 'Sounds like a duff party. I'm sorry. Told you so though,' she says, sticking her tongue out at me.

'Told me what?' I enquire.

'Don't go back for seconds. I know I only met him once or twice, but I never could see you with a serious finance sort,' she says.

'Lucy, we went out for a year,' I remind her.

'Yeah, but that's a university relationship. It exists in a bubble of cheap rent and even cheaper alcohol. Do you want to know what I remember about him?' she says. I shake my head. 'We had food and he ordered you some breaded brie shit. He didn't even ask what you might want. He just ordered for you.'

'He did?' I say, trying to rewind back to the memory.

'Red flag for me but I don't really like men telling me what to do. If someone ordered a burger for me and I didn't want a burger then I'd throw it back at him.'

'Which I feel would make for a very successful date,' I say.

'Well, this all confirms what I thought, finance people usually live in the echelons of their own self-importance.'

Thinking back to how he lied about my real job, this is perhaps true, but there is also no denying that we bumped into each other for a reason. And if you think about all the people you could bump into on any day, in any city, it feels as though there was a reason to drift back into each other's lives, a sort of magic and coincidence you can't quite explain. I keep going back to our year of dating too and all the good parts of being together. We went on a city break to Dublin, he supported me through the time when my aunt passed away, and we had a lot of fun together. A fun that we've relived in recent days, a spark we've re-ignited. I think back to his body angled over mine, a synergy, realising how well we still fit together. Sexually, he's delicious and he's giving off this strong *Suits* energy that's suave, mature, alluring. I realise I'm thinking all of this but still swaying.

'You should be single with me, get an ugly cat and we can go out every weekend. Order what we want, when we want,' Lucy says.

'Why does the cat have to be ugly?' I ask.

'Because they're always the most unloved ones. All the love you have in that beautiful heart of yours, channel it elsewhere.'

I smile and blow her a kiss, extracting the compliment from her words. I do another strange swaying but spinning dance move and turn towards the fences by the field, my head tilting slightly as something gets my attention. 'What's that?'

Bizarrely, they look like a set of aluminium speakers, wrapped in white material, but I can't see any wiring. They sit on red-framed stands rested against the fence.

'They're the netting machines,' Lucy says. 'For the trees – so people can take them home all slim and compact. You thought me and the trees may be the star attraction here but really people stand there for ages and watch the netting machines.'

I suddenly realise what she's talking about. 'Ohhh! The net thingies for the trees. I love those!' Lucy looks at me, laughing, as if she's not sure if I'm drunk or genuinely excited about this apparatus. It would be the latter. I get excited about these in the same way I do about the machine in the supermarket that slices your bread for you. They are both genius feats of engineering. 'Can we put something through it so I can see it in action? My clutch?' I hold up my bag.

'Nah, that's too small.' She looks over at the trees and then over her shoulder. 'They've got the big trees out. You'd have to help me,' she says, pushing one of the funnel-shaped machines away from the fence. And that is the beauty of a friend like Lucy. She's only had a few shots of alcohol but there is something about her that will always exude fun and can-do. This is how she will make her friend happy this evening. She goes over to the fence and picks a massive tree. 'It needs to go in trunk end first,' she says, dragging it through. 'You go fluffy branch end and push the bastard in.'

This must look odd to any outsider but I am very excited, falling over myself as I try to get hold of the treetop. 'You ready?' she says. 'I grab the wood, you yank.'

'Oi, oi...' I say, and we both explode into fits of giggles.

'Three, two, one and...' I don't know what happens next. But Lucy yanks incredibly hard and, because I'm still laughing, I seem to hold on to a branch of the tree a little too firmly because I lose my footing and slip. Into the funnel. My face lands in a sea of pine needles and I scream as she continues to yank.

'LUCY!' I say, half-shrieking, half-giggling. I can't see her as I seem to be halfway through this funnel, my arm still attached to this tree and I can hear Lucy's jingly shoes and the sound of her in absolute hysterics.

'Oh my God, you were supposed to let go. I can't...' she says, bending over to have another laugh.

'It's... help... pricks... all over my face...' Naturally, a comment of that nature doesn't help and I can hear her stumbling around in laughter and then fumbling for her phone. Is she taking photos? 'You'll have to pull me out.'

'I can't, it'll bugger the netting. I'll have to pull you through...' She's still giggling. Meanwhile, I strangely understand how it feels to be a baby mid-delivery and stuck in your mum's birth canal. 'Can you breathe?'

'Well, I'm not underwater.' I start laughing at this point. This evening seems to be a comedy of errors, from the ice sculpture to this. All I can hear are her jingly shoes trying to get in the right position and the sound of her exerting herself.

'HEAVE!' I scream, and she stops to have yet another laugh. And just like that, I find myself on the other end of the funnel, still holding on to this blessed tree but wrapped snugly in layers of white netting. The force with which she pulls me through means I land on the ground with a thud. 'Fucking OOWW...'

Of course, my pain comes secondary to Lucy's amusement and, even though my vision is obscured by layers of webbed netting, I can still hear her howling. And then, strangely, the sound of my own voice saying HEAVE. The cow filmed it, didn't she? I do hope she has scissors to get me out of here.

'JESUS CHRIST!' The voice comes out of nowhere, echoing around the place. It is Christmas but I suspect the man himself has not made an early appearance. It's a man's voice and he doesn't sound particularly happy or amused. 'Lucy, please tell me that's not a customer.'

'Chill your beans, bossman. It's my friend. It was an accident,' Lucy explains, not particularly bothered that the person standing over us is her boss. Oh dear, is this going to get her fired? I am still laughing but also feel darts of worry for my friend. Is he a nice boss? Will he get the joke?

'That's what they always say. Have you been drinking?' I hear him say. Oh my God.

'It's Christmas,' Lucy explains.

'It's machinery. Your friend could have died,' he says, clearly not pleased.

'It's not a wood chipper,' Lucy retorts.

'I am very sorry, it was all my idea,' I pipe up. It might be a little bit funny that this person netted up like a mackerel is starting to talk. I hope he's laughing and will start to get the joke.

'Are you OK, miss?'

'I landed a bit awkwardly but I'm OK. I really am sorry.'

I hear the sound of the machine creaking and his heavy foot-steps circling around me. 'Lucy, in that drawer there's a cutter. Pass it here.' I start to hear the sound of snipping. 'Miss, I am conscious that I don't want to cut your clothing or your skin so do tell me if I'm too close.'

There is something about his voice now that he's stopped telling Lucy off that is soothing, a low register with a touch of earth to it. He rests his hands on me to gain purchase and turns me and my tree friend around. His figure comes into view a little more and I feel my body go taut. I'm not sure if it's the firmness of his grip or the fact that a blade is so close to me. And then I suddenly see light, a hand comes in to push the branches of this tree away from my face. I look up. *You're shitting me.*

Santa?

TWELVE

There's no other way of saying this. I am sitting in Santa's office. It's a nice office – wood is an overriding theme, from the panelling to the desk to a couple of ornately carved chairs. Santa also knows how to do Christmas. He has two trees in each corner of the room, tastefully decorated in red and white, and, in keeping with the woodland Scandi theme of the place, a fire in a black cast-iron log burner crackles away giving the place warmth. There are lots of family photos on the walls, a bookshelf of art and travel books, and there's a well-worn red patterned rug in the centre of the room. I sit there with my mug of coffee, sipping quietly, leaning over to see a computer switched on. There's a film paused on the screen that I believe is *Home Alone*. Santa watches the best at Christmas. There is also a bowl of sweets to the side of his desk. I look around and take one. Lord have absolute mercy, it would seem that Santa likes crispy M&Ms. I take another one. The door opens and Santa appears again holding a bright-green medical box. I hold the sweets in my mouth.

'Is the coffee alright?' he asks. 'Help yourself to biscuits if you want.' He points to a plate on the desk. I take one tentatively. Naturally, the biscuit is ginger with a perfect snap. It crumbles as I bite into it, meaning I have to pick crumbs out of my hair. Santa looks at me curiously.

'Did you make these?' I ask, trying to break the tension.

'I don't bake. I leave that to the elves,' he says, a little too seriously. I find that comment funny in my head so I laugh. I may also snort which must be attractive. He doesn't laugh. *You're supposed to be Santa. Where's your jolly?* I watch as he sifts through the medical box. The problem here is that this man is not Santa. This dude is young. He has the red fur outfit and the big black boots but the red coat is not done up. It's hanging there so I can see he has a white fitted t-shirt on underneath. Santa's not been at the cookies. The beard is his own but dark brown, and he has green eyes. No hat, slightly-longer-than-short brown hair, and tousled. This is most definitely not Santa and not someone I'd picture being Lucy's boss.

'Then my compliments to the elves,' I say, trying to snap myself out of staring at this very attractive man.

'You know, this might be better if you perch yourself on my desk,' he says. I choke a little on my coffee. 'Saves my knees.'

I nod quietly and put my coffee down, going over to the desk and sitting there, waiting. He grabs a chair and comes over, looking at my knee and taking it in his hand. *You've got big hands. Don't look at his hands.* When I went through the Christmas tree netting machine, it would seem I tore fabric off my jumpsuit and have a nasty graze. When Santa saw it, he invited me in to administer first aid and a warm drink for the trouble. It sounded gentlemanly but it turns out there's also an incident form to fill out for health and safety so I can say I got in that machine voluntarily and wasn't pushed.

'Where's Lucy?' I ask, trying to engage in chitchat to mask my embarrassment.

'Tidying up, getting changed. She'll be through in a minute,' he says.

'You're not going to fire her for this?' I ask.

He chuckles under his breath. 'No. Funnily enough, you're not the first person to jump through that machine and you won't be the last. Bloody TikTok generation has a lot to answer for.' He opens some packets of gauze and medical wipes. 'And Lucy Callaghan is many things but she is also one of my best employees. The kids love her, she gets us good reviews, even if she does flirt with a lot of the dads who come through the door.' That sounds like my friend. I breathe a sigh of relief I've not cost her her job. I watch as he traces his fingers through the tears in my jumpsuit and grabs the underside of my calf. That's a firm hold and I breathe in to feel his fingers wrapped around me. 'I am sorry about your onesie.'

'It's a jumpsuit.'

'Same thing.' Not really but I try and hold back my laughter. He rips at a small patch of material to get to my knee and winces to see the blood. 'Does it hurt?' he asks. I hope it might appear to him that I'm brave and can withstand pain, but the truth is the alcohol in my system is helping to numb everything.

'It stings a bit,' I say.

'Well, it's going to sting a bit more, sorry...' he says, and he dabs at the blood and dirt with an antiseptic wipe. I wince a little and he looks into my eyes. I stop wincing. *Yeah, don't do that.* Why can't I breathe? He blows on it gently. Oh dear. I don't think that's how you do first aid. I don't remember doing that on the course I took in the leisure centre. He dabs at the graze with cotton gauze. 'It's not too deep.' He really needs to stop saying that sort of thing.

'Yes, I think amputation won't be necessary,' I say, coughing to get the words out. Am I blushing? I feel I'm blushing and that's not a good colour with my hair.

'It's a shame. We have good saws here.'

'I bet you do. Are they tenon or hack?'

He sits back as if he doesn't know whether to laugh or be confused at my terrible version of flirting, talking about his tools.

'Those are tools for indoor carpentry. We tend to use a bow saw, a chainsaw for the bigger trees. You know your saws then?' he asks.

'I know what I remember from technology at school. I made a money box once. It had a hole... at the top.'

'For the money?'

'Yeah.' I have a feeling this is why I have not managed to pin down a man yet. Look how amazingly charming I am with my wood talk. The charisma is off the scale. I should now tell him how I made a doorbell in Year Nine and burnt my finger with a soldering iron.

'I once helped my nana saw a Christmas tree.' He nods again. I mean, that's the whole story in its entirety. I remember a few splinters and the mouse that jumped out at me. He reaches into the box and starts to unwrap a few plasters. I notice they're covered in an elf pattern. 'Your medical supplies are Christmas themed?'

'That's my sister's doing,' he says. 'You'd be surprised the number of kids who fall over in this place. She also makes us wear the outfits so the whole farm is more of an experience. Gets the punters in.'

'Which is why you are Santa,' I say. 'Do you normally wear a hat?'

'I do. I draw the line at a beard though. Gets in the way.'

'Of?'

He gives me a confused look. 'The sawing of the trees.'

'Of course.' I wasn't thinking of anything else, I really wasn't. I want to tell him this is likely why the punters come in, because he looks like the sort of Santa who has trousers with Velcro sides ready to let people sit on his knee and tell him what they want. I won't say it, but he is distractingly good-looking.

'How's your ho-ing?' I ask. Yes, because that is a better thought to air aloud.

'My gardening hoeing is exceptional. The other ho-ho-ho-ing needs work. It lacks gravitas.'

'It really needs to come from the diaphragm, doesn't it? Ho-ho-ho.' I went very deep there. Again, he doesn't even smile but gives me a look as if I've hit my head harder than he thought, and he may need to run through some concussion protocol.

He takes all the rubbish and supplies and puts them in a bin next to the desk. 'Did you want me to check if you have any other cuts or bumps?' he asks plainly. What is he hinting at? To do that would surely mean me stripping here so he could examine me more closely.

I hold my arms up to look at my own elbows. 'All clear. Only my ego damaged.'

'I don't have anything in my box to fix that.' He talked about his box. *Don't laugh.* His eyes seem to gaze at the outline of my curls at this point. 'You seem to have a whole tree stuck in your curls though. That's a lot of pine needles. I can get a brush out of the stables? Give you a—'

'Groom?' I smile, looking down. I think he just compared my hair to a horse. I take back everything I said about the saws. This is primo flirting if ever I saw it.

'That's not what I meant.'

'I'll shake myself out later,' I say, wondering about the nest I've acquired up there and how I'll shake it out. Like a dog? Or Taylor Swift?

He stands there for a moment, holding back a grin, both of us not really knowing what to say. *Santa, from that t-shirt, I can see you have pecs.* My eyes go up the line of his jaw, over to his eyes. It feels a little indecent to be perving over Santa. 'Could I get you to sign this form?' he asks, breaking the moment.

'Oh, the incident form. Sure.' I look down at it, signing my name away. 'Did you want my telephone number?' He looks up at me and hesitates for a moment. 'For the form, there's a gap here.'

He forces an awkward smile. 'If you want. You can also tick the box so we don't bombard you with emails about trees and stuff.'

I summon up a smile hoping it might lighten the mood, but nothing. 'I am very sorry I got caught up in your machine. I hope I haven't broken it. Thank you for looking after me.'

He looks at me and shrugs his shoulders. 'I'm glad you're not broken, Lucy's friend.'

'My name is Kay,' I say, giving him back his clipboard and pointing to my name.

'As in Peter?'

'Yes, except I'm a woman.'

'And not a comedian.' I think he's implying I'm not funny. I'm not sure if that's a bit rude. It's true that today I was not at my peak, I was injured and traumatised. 'Well, thank you again, Lucy's boss.'

'I also have a name...' he says. 'I'm Nick.'

'You're joking, right?' I say immediately.

He looks supremely confused. 'You have a problem with my name?'

'No,' I say, backtracking and hoping I've not said that too quickly or offensively.

'Nick North. Nice to meet you, Kay.'

THIRTEEN

'So basically, I've entered the season of Nicks,' I say to Lucy as she leans her elbows on the restaurant table grinning at me.

'It's just one of those names, isn't it? Like Tom or Sam. You don't register when there's more than one,' Lucy says, unbothered that I'm being plagued by men of the same name during this festive season. There must be a festive message in all of this.

'Miss Kay, long time no see,' Jin, the waiter, says in welcoming tones.

'You say that, Jin, but I was in here last week,' I joke, and he laughs, the Santa hat on his head slipping down over his brows. 'This is my friend, Lucy.'

He looks at me confused. 'Miss Kay, did you fall in a bush?'

I obviously didn't shake my hair out hard enough or should have taken up Nick's offer of a horse brush, plus I am a little sore, battered and torn. A brief visit to the bathroom beforehand showed that I also have a large purple bruise appearing on my thigh the size of a steak.

'Kind of but I have lived to tell the tale.' My use of idioms is throwing him.

'Then I am happy you are alive. You ready to order?' he asks.

'A Tsingtao for the lady, jasmine tea for me, some dumplings and two of the stewed beef noodles, extra chilli oil on mine.'

'Perfect.' He nods and takes his leave. I do love this place. It's round the corner from my flat, open all sorts of hours to account for the hospital staff in the vicinity, and is authentically Chinese. From the very basic décor, the chopsticks piled in a container in the middle of the table, the white paper tablecloths – the sole nod to Christmas being a lot of tinsel – and a Santa figurine at the bar next to one of those nodding gold cat statues. Given tonight's events, I've also realised I haven't really eaten much except canapés, a ginger biscuit and two stolen crispy M&Ms, so sustenance was needed and this felt the perfect place to get that.

'You let me order for you there,' I say to Lucy as she sits back in her chair next to this fully misted window, colourful fairy lights wrapped around the restaurant sign.

She sticks her tongue out at me. 'It's different when there's real genuine love there. So Nick, my boss Nick? That could work,' she says nodding, sparked by the idea.

'Or not. Give a girl a second to recover from the last Nick. He is incredibly good-looking though, no?' I ask, curious why she hasn't noticed this before.

'Maybe. He's kind of grumpy though. He has occasionally called me flighty which I take great offence to,' she says.

'I think I get the grumpy. He didn't really get my jokes,' I say.

'Figures. And you're one of the funniest people I know. He can be super surly. Serious. I couldn't imagine sleeping with him. He'd be completely humourless. One queef and he'd not laugh. And you need to laugh when that happens. His beard is also maybe too straight.'

'That's a thing?' I ask.

'That's someone who's anal, who can't let go. The sort who won't dance at parties and pairs his socks.' I nod, wondering how pairing socks became a bad thing. 'So are we thinking rebound? I could hook you up possibly?'

'Lucy, no. He's lovely to look at but I don't do grumpy,' I say, memories of my sub-standard date disaster before coming into view. Perhaps the festive message here is to give Nicks a wide berth for now.

She pouts. 'Well, at least let me fill you in on him. I find him intriguing, but for me, there's a few red flags,' she says, as drinks and a bowl of warm nuts arrive at the table. Lucy sits up and takes a few in her hand, the white paper tablecloth rustling under her as she arranges herself. 'Lives at home, very family orientated. Nate the elf is his youngest brother and there's another called Noah who's got a zillion kids and a sister called Nell who calls the shots. In fact, all the women in that family do. Mum is Italian and they listen to their mum. They do everything together to the point where I thought I was working for a cult because they do those group-photo shoots where they're all wearing white.'

I nod and take it all in. Head to toe in white, that man would look like fit Jesus. Still festive.

'I've never seen him wear trainers,' she continues.

'OK.'

'That means he isn't cool. I've never seen him date or mention a girlfriend. It's all about work. That could make him gay or asexual but the likelihood is that there's a story there, an ex who broke him which implies crushing emotional damage.'

'And what is he? Does he do anything else except Christmas trees? That's a very seasonal career?' I ask, pouring out a small cup of Chinese tea.

'Oh, they have this beautiful farm shop and café that does well all year round. The fresh pasta is off the chain; I think it's won foodie awards. And then they have this nursery, fruit picking in the summer, they grow flowers... it's all very fucking wholesome,' Lucy says sneeringly. Lucy, since I've known her, has never really bought into the idea of wholesome. She prefers a life of adventure and experiences, so I can see how someone like Nick doesn't really appeal. 'And Nick makes furniture or something. I don't know. I'm only ever there in December.'

'To get your free turkey...'

'Exactly.' She studies my face as Jin brings a plate of extremely crispy-looking dumplings to the table. I tap my chopstick to the underside of one and a happy feeling runs up my spine. 'How you met is a meet-cute for the ages though. He cut me out of a Christmas tree netting funnel. He was dressed as Santa. We could play the video at your wedding reception,' she says, laughing.

I hit her with my napkin, telling her to help herself to a dumpling before they get cold. 'They make them fresh, they've got chives and prawn in them.'

She reaches over, looking me in the eye. 'I can make that happen you know, if you want to go there?'

'I don't,' I say.

'Or if you're into Nicks this season, my mate, Eve, has a dad called Nick. You could make it a thing.'

'Is he fit?'

'He's in his sixties. Cracking paunch.'

I choke on a bit of ginger as she draws a heart in the misted window of the restaurant and writes the name Nick in it. I spy it there curiously. She then draws a cock and balls because that's what Lucy does.

As my jumpsuit is ripped and my thigh is starting to throb with pain, I call it a night after noodles, leaving Lucy to call herself an Uber to take her to a party in Peckham. It's been an eventful evening that I think calls for a bath and a cup of herbal tea to cleanse my system of alcohol. I also have Christmas Lindt that was meant for someone else that I can jump into. I don't know what it means when the prospect of getting cosy under a duvet with chocolate and pyjamas is exciting. I may break open the fluffy socks, a hot-water bottle and a film. *Home Alone*. If it's good enough for Santa…

I've been living in Nana's maisonette since she left, and I've grown to love this little terrace off the main road, cobbled and made up of different-coloured doors. The maisonettes inside are small but have enough character to make up for it, and at Christmas, we all put in the effort to ensure the exterior lights are all hanging from pillar to lamppost to make this little corner of London all the more magical. As I walk up to my red front door though, I see something outside, a round shadow. I walk up to it curiously and notice it's a large bouquet of roses, sitting there with a note addressed to me. I go and pick it up, opening the envelope.

I'm sorry x.

I sigh deeply, my breath clouding the cold air. There are at least thirty red roses here.

'I really am sorry,' a voice says from the shadows.

'MUUAGRH!' I scream, and Nick emerges from the darkness. Museum Nick. 'We are in London. You don't do that, I could have...'

Nick stands there laughing. 'Made a very funny guttural noise?'

'Attacked you with my front door key? Like a ninja,' I say. I stand there for a moment as my panic dies down. 'What are you doing here, Nick?' I ask, a slightly pained expression on my face to see him, his bow tie loose around his collar.

'I wanted to apologise in person for tonight,' he says, walking towards me. 'After you went to the bathroom, I got caught up with the senior execs. I had to go and help a colleague who was crazy drunk and got very ill. I had to call a driver, get him home which is why I went MIA.'

I listen to his explanations quietly. It's a reasonable excuse, I guess, and I start to feel guilt that, in his perceived abandonment, I walked away thinking the worst of him.

'I'm sorry I left. I had waited and walked around for an hour. You didn't reply to my texts,' I say, and he scrunches up his face, letting me know he feels bad about the situation. 'It was also not really my scene. There's only so many shares and investments a girl can handle, you know.'

He laughs again, heartily. *You see, this Nick understands your comedic value.* 'I know. Finance people are not very good at partying. It did get better as the night went on.'

'Did people actually dance?'

'Oh, we moved on to liquid assets and venture capitalism.'

I giggle under my breath. 'Thrilling.'

'It was the wrong sort of place to have a date and I am very sorry I left you,' he says.

'I seriously thought you'd dumped me in the most spectacular fashion,' I jest.

'But why would I do that?' He steps closer to me. 'When I've just found you again.' I feel a breath catch in my chest to hear those words, the romance of it in the low lights in the street. He shrugs his shoulders. 'I like you, Kay. It feels easy to be with you, even after all this time. Do you feel that too?'

I nod quietly. 'It feels like...' I want to say 'home' without it sounding corny, but there's a strange comfort I get from being around him. He reminds me of a time when life was more fun, less complicated, and it's warming to feel that at a time when my idea of home is so confused. 'It feels nice.'

'Only nice?' he whispers, tilting his head, taking my hand in his.

I grin but his expression suddenly changes when I walk more into the light and he sees that my jumpsuit is ripped. *Don't look at my hair.* I didn't realise my curls had this much capacity to hold so many pine needles. 'Shit. Did you fall?'

I pause for a moment, wondering how to explain this. No, I went to the outskirts of Greater London and visited a Christmas tree farm, I then fell through a netting machine and got rescued by a hot Santa, also called Nick. 'I may have tripped outside the museum and fallen into a Christmas tree,' I say. 'Those negronis were potent.' His face immediately shifts to concern and care, and I pout. 'I'm fine. I got fixed up. I found food. Seriously, how long have you been waiting out here?'

He shrugs his shoulders and puts his hands in mine. Long

enough to potentially develop frostbite. I look up at him. This is very confusing. I left that museum tonight thinking this was done. We are from different worlds. We had our moment. It's done. But he's here, with a large bouquet of roses, wanting to apologise, still looking pretty damn sexy in that tux. I'm also not the sort of person to turn away someone in this cold. 'Better pick up those flowers and come in then, eh?' I say.

'Are you sure?' he says.

I lean over and kiss him on his cold cheek, my body folding into his, still loving how familiar and magnetic that feels. 'I'll put the kettle on. Do you want a hot-water bottle?' I ask him.

'Sexy.'

'I thought so.'

FOURTEEN

'I bet he stole those flowers out of the museum,' Helen says as she organises books off a wheeled trolley. 'Where on earth are you getting thirty red roses in the middle of the night?'

'It is London,' Olga says. 'I reckon there is someone you could call if you paid them enough money. That is nice, so many flowers. That is the sign of a gentleman.'

There was something very sweet about it all, the flowers, the gesture of turning up unannounced, the contrition in his tone. However, once he came into my maisonette, he was less gentlemanly with the way we had sex on the stairs. Turns out it is easy to get out of a jumpsuit when it's already ripped to shreds from a Christmas tree netting funnel.

'So what does this mean?' Helen asks. 'Are you dating?'

I don't know the answer to that one. He stayed the night, he ordered in breakfast for us, he stayed long enough for it not to feel like a dirty one-night stand. There was a moment in bed where it felt like we'd rewinded to 2017, our bodies entangled in my double bed as the winter sun streamed through the windows.

'I have no idea, but we're meeting tomorrow night again for what he describes as a proper date,' I say.

Olga claps her hands. 'And soon we will have money to fix the roof. You put out a few more times, yes?'

Helen looks me in the eye, as if searching for my thoughts on the whole matter. I would let on if I knew myself. It's Nick from university. There is a real comfort to be with him; he knows me already so I can totally be myself with him. In fact, the years have done us both well, we're our own people, we've grown up and know what we want from a relationship – it's none of this young love where we're trying so damn hard to please all the time. And both of us are floored by the magic of it all, carried by a feeling that the universe has asked us to give this another go. That feels like something beyond our control, a power greater than us. So with the chemistry still there, there's excitement at being thrown back together and seeing where this goes. The road forked for a reason – so we could grow – and now we have come back together with a wealth of maturity and experience under our belts. This could be a great love. The key word there is *could*.

'Maybe you should see how it all goes? Don't jump into anything if you don't feel ready?' Helen says, offering a more considered opinion. 'Christmas will do that to you. Some fairy lights and a whiff of cinnamon and most girls will just drop their knickers.'

A person appears at the counter looking a little perturbed. 'Excuse me, do you have a specific biography section?'

'We do,' Helen says. 'Over by the sofas, near travel, bottom shelf.'

'Is that what gets you going then, Helen? A bit of Christmas?'

'Well, John and I probably have more sex at Christmas but solely because it's a means of staying warm so we don't have to put the heating on.'

I laugh, a little too loudly given it's a library, but she returns me a look, one which reads care and worry that as much as we joke, she wants me to find something authentic. She offers me another chocolate from the tin behind the counter. Such is the way with libraries at the moment that everyone comes in with sweets and gifts to say thank you for looking after them all year, for giving them our recommendations and pointing at the right shelves, and I guess for also being guardians of somewhere safe and reassuring.

'Oh dear, rugrats approaching,' Olga says, and we turn to see a crowd of toddlers race through the door. We often see the same faces at the moment as Lucy appears to be a big selling point – the kids are starting to come dressed up in onesies and Disney costumes. I'll admit, it brings a bit of life to this old building and turns this library into the community centre it deserves to be.

A woman comes up to the counter with a huge pile of baby books. 'For your drive?' she says.

'That is so kind, thank you.' I slip the bag underneath the counter and then look to the clock, realising an important element of our story-time session is missing. Lucy is many things but she's usually punctual, so she has time to get changed and get into character. She only has ten minutes to get through the door. I go to my bag and get out my phone.

> Lovely, I am sorry. I've got a fever and feel crappy
> so won't be able to make today. Sending someone
> else to take my place 😉

Why is she winking at me? Will I know this person? She works in the theatre so I assume any replacement can do the whole character thing and come in costume. I only hope they'll let me pay them in kebabs. I mean, this isn't a complete disaster. If no one turns up then I can read. I am wearing Christmas themed clothing, I can attempt reasonable accents. Or we can wheel out a television and show them *Frozen*. Helen can sing.

'Holy mother-of-pearl,' I suddenly hear a voice mutter. I look over at Helen whose face is a deep blush. Has someone been graffitiing in Lee Child again? But I follow her gaze to the front door, to the person standing in the foyer, reading signs. *Hold up. I know you.* He opens the door and looks around the place. It's Nick. Christmas-tree Nick. Dressed as Santa. He sees me and waves, walking over as Olga and Helen look at me, wide-eyed. I don't know why but I straighten out my Christmas-themed pinafore dress and check the corners of my mouth for remnants of chocolate pralines.

'Kay, isn't it? Hi,' he says, standing at the counter. A woman looking to borrow a book goes in her bag and retrieves her glasses to get a better look.

'Nick.'

'YOU'RE NICK!' Olga shrieks, and I look over to her mortified expression. The problem is they only know about the other Nick. It's early, I've not had time to fill them in about the events of that night and this Nick presently stood in front of us. This Nick looks at me curiously, assuming that he's become the subject of Christmas office gossip.

'This is another Nick,' I whisper, before turning to him. 'He works with Lucy. I assume you're the person she sent to help us out,' I say, turning to him and trying not to smile. I know Lucy and I am calling bullshit on her fever story. She still thinks old Nick dumped me in a museum. She doesn't know he came back and had his reasons for leaving me at that party. So this is Lucy in her infinite wisdom trying to set me up with a new Nick. She's probably somewhere outside, hiding in a bush, rubbing her hands together that her plan is coming together. I look at Nick's outfit; he has a hat, his robe is tied up with a black belt and he's wearing black leather gloves that in my mind look a tad kinky. That is so wrong. This is Santa.

'If I am a suitable replacement. She rang in ill at work and explained the situation. I thought it would also be an opportunity to return this.' I look down at his hands to see a black cashmere scarf, my name written in the label, one that I obviously left at the farm that evening. 'Does your mum still label your things then?'

Helen and Olga can barely talk because they're trying to work out why studmuffin Santa has my scarf and why he isn't the other Nick.

'I lose things,' I say. 'Lucy didn't say you did this sort of thing. I thought you were a farmer.'

'I'm not a farmer,' he says a little grumpily. *Yes, you're good looking but we still need to work on that snappiness.* 'But I have nieces, nephews. I've read many a bedtime story.' Olga lets out a little noise at this point, like air squeaking out of a balloon. 'Lucy said this was important. She was crying on the phone. She didn't want to let the children down.'

Give that girl her awards already. The children would have coped. 'This is really out of your way.'

'Not really. I had to deliver some trees in town. It fit in with my schedule.'

I swear Olga and Helen are holding hands, watching this entire interaction.

'I also can't pay you. I normally pay Lucy in kebabs.'

'Then I'll do it for free,' he shrugs. 'Glad to see you got all the greenery out of your hair,' he says, his eyes tracing my curls again. I realise I'm also wearing very fetching antlers on the top of my head.

Helen swings her head around, as if she's wondering if this man found me in a tree, or whether I did something with him in a bush? She seems comically angry that I failed to mention any of this, and instead wasted time telling her boring stories of roses and people I once went out with at university.

'How do you deal with being around all those trees? I swear I had pine needles everywhere when I got home.'

'Everywhere?' he says, with his head tilted curiously. Well, in enough places for the other Nick to ask me how exactly I fell into that Christmas tree. 'Hazard of the job.' I suddenly get what Lucy means when she says there's a serious streak there. That should have been a joke.

'I smelt lovely though,' I continue.

'That'll be the pine.'

I nod, smiling. I know. A little girl in a reindeer onesie runs through the doors and immediately sees Nick standing there at the counter, her eyes following his tall six-foot figure up to the ceiling. She stares at him open mouthed for a moment. 'Who are you?'

He bends down. 'I'm Santa.' I notice Helen angling her head to take a better look at his arse as he does so.

'You don't look like Santa. Why's your beard brown?' she asks, reaching out to him without hesitation.

'I had it dyed.'

'The Santa at the shopping centre is old and fat. You're not fat.'

'I went on a diet,' he says.

'Was it SlimFast?' she says sweetly. 'My mummy went on that to get ready for Lanzarote.'

'Lila, I told you not to run ahead...' her mum says following her in, a rucksack on her back and a small Tupperware of carrots in her hand, her hair scraped back into a messy bun. She trots in and sees Santa and then looks to me. 'Who on earth...?'

'Mummy, it's Santa,' Lila says.

'Hello, Lila's mummy. I know you...' Nick says, and Lila's mummy gives him a look which says if that were true, she would have remembered. I'm also interested to see where this is going. He turns back to Lila. 'Did you know your mummy keeps me informed to see if you should be on my good list? She tells me you like *Lilo & Stitch* and carrots which is good if you're a reindeer... they help you see in the dark.' Lila giggles sweetly. 'You ready for story time, little missy?'

'Yeah,' she says. Nick puts his hand out for her to fist bump but before she can, he opens his palm to reveal a little chocolate coin.

'Thank you, Santa!' she says, before running off. Lila's mum looks at him curiously before following her daughter to the children's section.

Helen, Olga and I stand there staring at him.

'How did you know she liked *Lilo & Stitch*?' I ask.

'She had a Stitch rucksack,' he says, as if it wasn't plainly obvious to the rest of us. 'I assume I'm headed through there then. What am I reading today?'

'We're starting with *Mog's Christmas*,' I say.

'Classic. OK then. You coming?' he asks.

'I think I already did,' Helen mumbles under her breath, and I giggle.

'Yeah,' I say, flipping the countertop up and turning to Helen and Olga before I accompany Santa to the waiting kids. Those two need to stop grinning like absolute buffoons. I scoop up a pile of carefully selected children's Christmas tales. Christmas Tree Farm Nick is here. This is a very strange example of worlds colliding. I don't think many would agree to do this, so why is he here? What has Lucy told him? Why does he smell so nice? That's not pine.

'Thank you for doing this, it's very kind of you,' I say.

'I thought it might be an interesting diversion from carting trees around all day,' he says, looking around the library. 'All your trees in here are fake.' There's a hint of disapproval in his voice.

'It's a money thing. Fake means we can cart them out every Christmas and not have to spend precious council budgets.'

'I can hook you up. Free of charge, in the interests of community spirit,' he says.

I smile. 'That would be amazing. We could mention it on our social media, give out flyers for the farm on the desk if you want?'

He nods. He turns a corner into the kids' section, and compared to the usual bedlam that accompanies Lucy's arrival, the crowd go quiet. A mum at the back dribbles a bit of cappuccino out of her mouth.

'What the...' another mum mumbles.

'HI, SANTA!' Lila screams.

'Hello, Lila! So... my very good friend, Lucy, sent me today to read you stories? Who wants to hear a story?'

Yet another mum puts her hand in the air. I look at how he has complete command of that room and all of the people in it.

'Ho-ho-ho,' he bellows, and all the kids laugh. I stare at him strangely. You were right, Nick. The ho-ho-ho-ing needs some serious work.

FIFTEEN

This is going to get confusing, isn't it? Two Nicks. Should I number them? Or perhaps I should call them by their surnames: Coles and North. That sounds like they should sell organic fruit and veg boxes and deliver them to your door. Nick A and Nick B? Old Nick or New Nick? This is a very seasonal dilemma, in any case.

Either way, I'm currently walking through the nearby street market with Santa Nick, on an enforced lunch break that Helen demanded I take even though I have a cheese sandwich in the work fridge.

'The man has come all this way, Kay,' she said. 'The least you can do is feed him.'

'I could give him half of my sandwich,' I told her. But by that point, she had my lip gloss out of my handbag and was applying it for me.

I do love this street market around the corner from the library, bustling with noise and life. In a sea of half-empty high streets and identikit shops, I enjoy walking past fruit stalls where men in fingerless gloves and bobbled woolly hats are trying to sell me boxes of mangoes and hocks of ham. As Christmas approaches, the stalls are decorated with tinsel and lights, the bakery stall sells boxes of freshly made mince pies and that man with the roast chestnuts sits on the corner, waiting. I swear he's following me around. Santa Nick walks next to me in jeans, a checked shirt, brown boots, a navy reefer coat and a grey woollen hat. The ladies who sell the artisan cheese boxes and chutneys elbow-nudge each other as he walks past, but he remains completely oblivious.

'I'm glad you brought a change of clothes,' I say, looking over at him as the winter sun catches the angles of his face.

'Thank you for letting me change in the staff room, I'm not sure I could have done this dressed as Santa,' he says.

It wasn't me who let him change. That was all Olga who was excited about him being half naked in the library. 'You'd have fit right in, there's another Santa over there,' I say, nodding towards one with a charity bucket outside a pub whose glasses are his own and whose beard looks highly flammable. He may also be drunk but it's Christmas so I don't judge. Nick looks unimpressed by my attempts to be slightly comical and glances over at me, forcing a smile. 'You were excellent by the way, a very good Santa. I am so grateful.'

He nods sheepishly. 'I have a big family. I'm used to kids.'

'Do you have kids of your own?' I ask.

'No. I have a cat.'

'You fathered a cat? You're a miracle of science then...'

'Well, no, I rescued her.'

He didn't get the joke. I choke with a sense of embarrassment. 'What's her name?'

'Kay.' My eyes move from side to side. I have the same name as his cat? 'It was a joke. Her name is Bonnie.'

I don't laugh. 'Does she have a brother named Clyde?' I ask.

'That's the dog's name,' he says. OK, the jokes are getting through. Maybe? This feels slightly less painful. I wrap my checked woollen overcoat over me and try and hide my smile in the scarf wrapped around my neck. 'So how do you know Lucy then?' he asks.

'University. Same drama society. Have you met her sisters?' I ask.

'I think Beth and Emma have dropped by the farm?' he says. 'So you're also an actress?'

'Oh God no. I was a backstage, scriptwriter sort. I did English Lit at university and now I...'

'Work at the library...' he says. Is that a dig at where my degree took me?

'I also... that third book you read today. The one about the bears...'

'*A Beary Merry Christmas*. Yeah, I didn't get the rhyme scheme on that title...'

'I wrote that.'

I see his mouth round in shock. 'Oh, that's not to say the rest of the book wasn't excellent. You wrote that?'

I nod. I did. 'Yeah, that Christmas rhyming was to capitalise on the season, but I work with an illustrator and we've written a series of books about those bears.'

'So you're famous?'

'Naturally, paps are waiting around the corner,' I joke.

He looks at me almost quizzically. 'Well, I think that's pretty cool. Do you write under your own name? Kay Redman, right?'

I pause for a moment to hear him say my whole name, the way the growl of his voice almost whispers it. 'I write under a pseudonym. K. M. Barrett. The idea was that if I ever wanted to diversify into erotica then it wouldn't sully my reputation.'

'Is that what you were thinking?' he asks. 'You'd write erotica?'

My cheeks glow a little at the thought. 'No, it was hypothetical. I'll stick with families of bears in bow ties for now.'

He smiles. I bite my lip because you can sense it's not a natural stance for him, to let go, to be free with his emotions, and I think back to what Lucy said about him being anal. Given we've just spoken about erotica, this, of course, makes me giggle to myself. I hide my mouth in my scarf again. He looks over at me curiously. 'Well, let me at least support you. I'll buy copies for my nieces and nephews.'

'Thank you,' I say, surprised by the gesture. 'Did you say your friend's van was up here?'

'Yeah, I think so,' he says. It turns out I don't have to buy Nick a kebab, as he knows one of the food vans up here in this market and suggested we pay it a visit. 'He does stints on the farm, we got him in for autumn events. I provide him with his pork.' Don't laugh. He's talking about produce. He works on a farm. Don't be juvenile. Plus, I don't think he gets me. Whatever this is, if I compare it to the other Nick, the chemistry and the banter is really not flowing as well as it should. 'And this is it.'

We stop at a small food van with a couple of tables out front decorated with bottles of condiments and a fair bit of festive greenery. I look up at the name of the van. 'Getting Piggy Wit' It'. I burst out laughing. 'That is amazing.'

There's that half smile again. As soon as the owner clocks Nick, he waves his hands in the air, a huge grin on his face. 'Nicholas North, my old mucker. How are you, mate?' The owner wears a t-shirt with his company logo on, a bandana and apron, and leans over the counter to shake Nick's hand.

'I was in the neighbourhood. Hank, this is Kay, she works at the local library. Kay, this is Hank,' he says.

He swiftly raises his eyebrows to Nick who returns a stern look. I do think back to when the other Nick introduced me the other night, how the introduction wasn't as quick or authentic. 'The library? The old building near the park? Love that place. How's the book drive going? I keep seeing flyers for it everywhere. I'll drop by some stuff one day.'

'It's going OK. And yeah, thank you – you're welcome any time,' I say.

'Excellent... so I'll assume you're here for some scran?' he says.

'Yeah, I'll have a hog roast special, chilli relish on mine and extra crackling? Kay?'

I stop for a moment mainly because I'm mesmerised by the smell of the roast pork, sage and cranberry, and the fact he has a bucket of crackling just sitting there.

'Umm, I guess the same. Do you have apple sauce?' I ask.

'Does the Pope like Jesus? Of course, lovely. Make it myself.'

Am I drooling? I think I am. How did he know I absolutely adore a hog roast? Did Lucy tell him? It's the sort of thing you don't see a lot – the vans and stalls make an appearance around autumn and wintertime, and even then, the quality varies. I once went to an evening wedding reception that was putting on a hog roast, though I didn't care much for the cousin who invited me. I watch as Hank masterfully slices through rolls and starts layering them with meat and trimmings.

'So how's the family? I think Nell has asked us to do a couple of weekends, yeah?' Hank asks.

'Yep. Look forward to having you there. Family are all good. Busy with Christmas. Did you get your tree?'

'Of course. Absolute beauty. It's what my boy's good at. Pork and wood,' he says, chuckling at his own joke. That was funny, but Nick looks down, blushing and shaking his head. As he does, Hank turns to me, pointing at Nick and putting a thumbs up, mouthing the words *top bloke*. I nod.

He finishes creating our rolls and then wraps them in paper, handing them over. I go into my handbag to get my wallet. 'How much do we owe you?'

'Nothing,' Hank says. 'Put your money away.'

'But I owe Nick here.'

'Then you'll have to think of another way to repay him.'

'Hank,' Nick warns him.

'Mate, you are the reason I can keep this van open and have a livelihood. Begone with both of you, tell your mates, do that social media stuff. I'll see you at the farm and you at your lovely library,' he says.

Nick whispers his thank yous as we walk away. I don't wait. I take that loaded bap in my hands, all warm and fragrant. I inhale it deeply and then take a bite, my teeth snapping at crispy crackling, the apple sauce tart and slightly warm against the tender meat and soft bread of the bap. I don't care for anyone called Nick now. I'm going to run off and marry this sandwich. I sigh and close my eyes.

'You OK?' Nick asks me, interrupting this love affair.

'I'm in love…' I say, my mouth full.

'With Hank? He's engaged I'm afraid,' he says, biting into his roll effortlessly. How does anyone look good eating like that? I eat messy. I know there is stuffing on my upper lip.

'This is astounding. This is one of the best things I've ever put in my mouth.'

He stops chewing for a bit. I know what I said and I don't care for any alternative meanings there because that is the goddamn truth. If I know this man is here then sod my cheese sandwiches, I am coming here every day until the library shuts down for Christmas.

'Shall we keep walking?' he asks.

I nod, my mouth full of food. We walk away from the market, down an alleyway that leads to the river and find a bench along the path; above us strings of lights hang between the lampposts. Steam rises from our food and I hold mine to my chest almost protectively, in case a city pigeon or small dog comes for me.

'Enjoying that, are we?' he asks. I am also aware that I must be making noises to express my satisfaction. Those noises must be slightly suspicious.

'Hmmm. I'm sorry,' I say suddenly. 'He asked for some social media love. Was I supposed to take a picture of it first?'

He shakes his head. 'It's fine. I think you can follow and like or whatever you do on social media. I'm not one for taking pictures of my food, in any case. It seems to be a curse of our generation.'

I nod. I am a picture taker on occasion but only so I can retain the memory of something particularly pretty. I once ate a blood orange and custard pastry from one of these bakery stalls that is in my favourites folder. We both sit there, quietly eating as I pick crumbs off my coat and scarf.

'Hank mentioned a book drive before? What is that?' he enquires.

'Oh, it's a crazy idea I had back in autumn. I'm collecting books and wrapping them, handing them out at old-age homes, schools, hospitals. I've got visits planned too.'

I go into my bag to get a flyer out and show him. He glances over it.

'You made this flyer?' he asks. I'm not sure he should sound so surprised.

'I'm very good on Canva,' I reply.

'I like the fonts,' he says. Is it terrible that this is the sort of compliment that arouses me? *Thank you. I'm a fan of something sans serif with cursive leanings.* 'And all those dates? Before Christmas? That's a lot to take on.'

'Oh, that's me. Classic over-achiever. Good ideas...'

'Good heart...' he mumbles. As he speaks, he almost recoils as if he may have said too much. I sit there for a moment, reading the genuine emotion in his tone, side-eyeing him as he takes a big bite out of his sandwich.

'Thank you. I hope it comes together and I can make it work.' It is a labour of love and the intent is there, but I may have underestimated how much work it would actually take. I put out flyers and posters thinking handfuls of books would come in but what's happened is that people have seen it as an excuse for a good purge before Christmas.

'Is there any way I can help?'

'Well, now that you mention it, I could do with a Santa...' I say, half joking.

'Really?' he says, and I can't decide whether he was serious about the offer of help. 'I guess I could, links into my name at the end of the day.'

'Saint Nick...' I whisper, feeling a little disloyal as I say it.

'That's me. Well, you know where to find me if you need me.' We both bite into our rolls at the same time. I'm not sure what was agreed there. I hope he didn't feel obliged to offer help. But then it felt like he almost backed away. I try to work out if he's panicking that perhaps he's overstepped, or he's coming across as a bit indifferent. 'Or we could contribute in other ways. We give away trees and hampers sometimes from the farm, we could work together. Like a collab, as my sister would say.'

I laugh at the way he says the word 'collab' with a snarl on his face. 'You're making my innocent, well-meaning book drive sound very boujie.'

He shrugs. 'It's an idea. If you want it. If it appeals.'

The problem is, Nick, physically you do appeal. But there is another Nick in the picture and maybe I should bring him up, but I'm still so unsure about what this is – this collab, this set-up by Lucy, this bench picnic.

I take another bite into my hog roast roll, the snap of the crackling hitting once again. 'Fuck me...'

'Excuse me?' he says, slightly shocked.

'Oh, the crackling. It's very good, isn't it?' I say, half blushing. 'Crackling is an art form and your friend has mastered it. The number of times you get a bit of crackling and it's...'

'Limp?' he suggests.

'I was going to say chewy and inedible but if you want to go there,' I smile. Is this warming up? It could be because I've got his friend's pork in my hands and am extraordinarily sated, but a feeling of confusion overwhelms me. He leans over and picks what is possibly a small piece of onion out of my hair. The contact, the closeness, makes me sit still for a moment, looking over at him, staring at the outline of his lips. 'You should have brought your horse brush out with you?' I joke.

'Perhaps. You've also got sauce...' he gestures. Oh dear, he's going to get close, isn't he? Wipe a finger at the corner of my mouth so I look up and into his eyes intently, caving from the contact. I instinctively stick out my tongue to try and stop this from happening. But instead, he offers me up a napkin. 'Yeah, it's kind of all over. A full beard of sauce. I don't know how to fix that. I'll leave it with you. Do you have any wet wipes?'

I look back at him blankly. No, I don't.

SIXTEEN

I will hazard a guess that the majority of people who live in England will ice skate with the theme of *Bolero* in their heads. I wasn't born when Torvill and Dean made history in Sarajevo or when they made their comeback in Lillehammer, but they remain cultural icons. Nana loves the figure skating and it was a love that was passed down – I have the fondest memories of afternoons spent in front of her telly in her flat, watching people glide across the ice, throwing each other about, landing as if they hadn't just been spun around six times by their ankles. We cheered in her living room with the sea-green shagpile and gave rounds of applause to everyone. Once Nana picked a flower out of a vase and threw it to the floor.

Naturally, a passion for the sport doesn't translate to ability. I can manage to stand on the ice and push myself across it in a measured fashion. Don't ask me to spin. I can just about change direction and that involves putting my hands in a set position to keep my balance.

'Seriously, the ones who go in the wrong direction should be fined,' Nick says, as he goes to put a hand into mine. That's not the greatest idea as it might put me off-balance, but I like the way he holds me close, pulling my arm into his body.

As for second dates, Old Nick (his official name) has done well here. He remembered my strange fascination with ice skating and booked us a slot at Somerset House, by the river, one of the most perfect places to spend Christmas in London with its towering golden Christmas trees, the ice rink framed by the old stone buildings of the house, a perfect starry night sky above us. Nana would adore this. She wouldn't skate. She'd sit by the side wrapped in a blanket and take it all in, heckle me, shout bravo for any flourishes of decent skating. I need to take a thousand photos of this for her, throwing poses, and buy her something from the gift shop for when I next see her. I'm not sure why recalling her in this very moment feels so warming if bittersweet.

'All OK?' Nick asks, his hand still firmly in mine.

I snap back to the rink, smile and nod. It's bizarre to see Nick finally out of formal dress. He's in jeans, a blue woollen jumper with a white shirt underneath and a Canada Goose coat. 'So do we go round and round?' he asks.

'Yeah, for the full hour, unless you had a routine you wanted to dance out?' I ask.

'I could try and lift you,' he says. 'You might have to take your coat off though.'

I pull up to a railing to steady myself. 'People tend to go in circles, stand around, chat, fall down, get up.'

'Right,' he says. 'Have you ever stacked it before?'

'Plenty. Once you get past the shock and the embarrassment, it can be funny. Physical comedy is always a winner.'

We wait for a moment, watching everyone else whizz past us. There are a number of families enjoying an evening out, kids with penguin aids, their faces full of joy at gliding across the ice, wrapped in matching hats and mittens. It's also very much a date-night kind of destination – there are lots of couples in different stages of dating – the hand holders, the newbies, the ones who may have been at odds about being here tonight, one of them skating around furiously and the other standing with their arms crossed by the skate exchange.

'I feel I should have opted for the knee pads?' he mentions.

'And look like that...?' I say, my eyes guiding him to a man near us who is a tentative skater, padded up to the hilt, with a helmet and elbow pads – his date looking at him curiously, wondering how she's going to survive the next fifty minutes.

'You're fine as you are,' I say, kissing him softly on his cold cheek. He looks at me and kisses me on the lips, softly. If we're rating romantic moments that I've experienced in my lifetime, this is up there – the stars, the tree, the lights all seem to glow as he kisses me on the ice. I am not immune to romance and it's hard not to be affected by the magic of it all, so I close my eyes to take it in for a second.

'You OK there, miss?'

'Uh-huh,' I say, looking up at him and basking in the full beam of that warm, crinkle-eyed smile. In this moment, it feels as though he's come into my life and swept me off my feet. The big Christmas party in the tux, the roses, the uninhibited and familiar sex, and now this – it's all romance as it should be, someone getting everything right. And I think of other dates where people have failed to achieve this, rookie mistakes like the guy who gave me supermarket flowers with the price tag still attached. Not just a price tag either – a yellow sticker to let me know he'd got them out of the bargain bin. And that bloke who thought a meal deal was a nice dinner out. Nick has climbed to the top of some imaginary dating ladder beating them all. I feel spoilt and incredibly cared for, impressed by the thought he's putting into everything.

Nick reaches up to my black wool hat and pulls it down a little over my curls. 'We went ice skating in Bath that time, remember? I think that's where you taught me to skate.'

I laugh at that memory, intrigued that he would want to recreate it. 'You had that woolly hat with the ear flaps,' I remember.

'God,' he remembers with horror. 'I was a sartorial disaster then, please try and forget a lot of that.'

'Do you still have your leather bomber jacket?' I ask.

'Well, fashions come and go. This time in ten years when we're still skating in circles, we'll joke about this again.' My pause must tell him that what he's just said comes as a minor surprise to me. We're keeping this incredibly casual. Maybe he's talking about the ice skating feeling monotonous and never-ending. 'That wouldn't be such a bad thing, would it?'

'Ten years' time?'

He shrugs. 'I doubt we'd be alone though, right? Most likely we'd be ushering kids around the ice.' He draws my attention to a family zipping around, the dad picking a boy up and making him explode in hysterics as he floats around, kicking his legs. Words like those should fill me with joy. This is a man who's projected this date into the future. He wants to have kids? With me? I'm assuming that, rather than us escorting random children around this ice rink. 'I've said too much, right?'

I shake my head. 'You've caught me by surprise, that's all. Let's just take this slowly, Mr Coles. Maybe live in the moment.' He smirks. I think because when we dated before, the roles were very much reversed. I was young and in love and thought about our life beyond university, and he was possibly the reverse. I won't lie. I signed my name with his surname for practice. I imagined our kids. I even named them: Mabel and Benjamin. They would have really loved ice skating. 'I'm just... it's been nice to be back in touch. It's felt...reassuring.'

I wonder if I've said the wrong thing. I'm not sure if that's what great love is built on. Reassuring is a word you'd use to describe a nurse or a mortgage advisor. But I mean it in a good way; this does feel familiar. We've done all the legwork to get to know each other. It feels, for want of a better word, easy. 'It's been an unexpected week. I don't hate it,' I say jokily, leaning into him as I skate.

'The opposite of which means you love it?'.

'No comment.'

'None needed. Here, reach into my pocket,' he says.

'I think that goes against the code of conduct,' I say, smiling, but I reach in and pull out sweets in a striped paper bag. I untwist the paper and peer in.

'Red strawberry laces, your favourite,' he says.

'You remembered?'

'I remember things too,' he says, shrugging his shoulders, and I put one in my mouth to mask my shock. He used to show up at my student flat with bags of these and we'd race to see who could eat one the quickest, the strings hanging down from our mouths and us both in hysterics. I offer him one and he untangles a strand. 'We probably both need the sugar too if we're going to be going round in circles for an hour,' he says, using his tongue to sweep the string into his mouth.

He pushes himself off the railing and skates off, waving at me, beckoning me over. This feels right, this is how being with someone should be, but I can't help but feel guilty that in the back of my mind, the other Nick sits there almost looking on. *Why have you popped into my head at this precise moment?* I don't think that Nick would ice skate. I can't imagine him going round in circles having fun. Would he stand at the side, refusing to participate? I didn't hug him after that day in the library. I was almost scared to touch him, so I shook his hand, which makes us official social acquaintances. I find him very attractive, but I find Henry Cavill attractive and I happily admire him from afar. I have no idea what he thinks of me but I saw that look of horror he gave me as I was eating that hog roast roll and had sauce all over my face like a feasting Christmas zombie. We've made a half-arsed agreement to possibly work together with this book drive, and that's it.

'Come on!' Nick shouts at me from over the way, waving his arms around trying to keep his balance. I skate over, guiding him to safety, tripping slightly, my arms flailing to regain my balance.

'See what I mean, physical comedy,' I joke. 'So what do you want to do after this?'

'The hand in my pocket obviously triggered something then,' he says, as we set off across the ice together, following the crowd of people.

'No, I mean food?'

'There's a Jägermeister tent. I think they do raclette if that's your bag? If not, there's a French bistro across the way. *Le Manger.* It's a patisserie by day but does a mean steak-frites at night too. I've been there loads with…'

He doesn't finish his sentence, I assume because he's been there with someone who isn't me. I should be glad that he doesn't bring that person up but I am curious, and a look returns to his face that I've seen before. It's wistful, sad even, and I want to take that look away or at least find out who could have evoked that emotion. I know he's not been single for the eight years since we broke up at university but the topic of conversation hasn't really come up about that space in between.

'I can do steak-frites,' I say, to continue avoiding that conversation. 'I might have to have an early night though; I've got to be in the library early in the morning, quite a lot to get through.'

'I'm sure the kids will survive without story time for one morning – call in sick,' he says casually.

I look over at him and pause for a second before answering. 'It's another event. It's a book drive that I've set up – people are donating their old books and I'm re-gifting them in the community.'

'You're giving out old books for Christmas?' he says, pulling a face. 'Do you want me to ask my company? Maybe we can sponsor it so you can give out new books?' he says. 'We do it all the time for school fairs and stuff.'

I keep skating, trying to get out of the way of a particularly uncoordinated individual but I can't help feeling a little hurt.

'There is something about re-gifting that's nice though, right? Repurposing a book so it can find a new owner?' I suggest.

'They're not dogs, they're just books,' he scoffs. 'Leave it with me, I'll make some calls. Don't create work for yourself.'

I don't reply because I'm not sure what to say. I have a lot of love and pride for the book drive and it hasn't felt like work. It feels like something good in a season of consumerism.

'Or maybe you could help? Come down, join me on visits? You

might be surprised,' I say, trying to get him involved, to let him see what I actually do.

'I'm not sure I can fit it in around work but you crack on,' he says. It's a weird, casual rebuttal of my invitation but it sits there uncomfortably, similar to indigestion. Do I say something? I really should be able to voice that hurt but I can't. Luckily we're both ice skating so it's easy to avoid eye contact. It's simpler to keep moving.

'You should write more, you know?'

'I am. I've got some deadlines for the New Year.'

'You should make more time for it. Don't waste your talent,' he remarks.

'I'm contracted to write the rest of the series of bear books, it's going OK,' I say. What is he hinting at? That he thinks my ambitions aren't lofty enough or that my library work is a waste of time? I think what he's saying is well meaning but it unsettles me; I try so hard to be an author, but sometimes I do find it hard to validate my writing or define my success.

'Maybe I can see if Phil and Meribelle can talk to their contact at Penguin.'

'Maybe. I mean, I have an agent who does that for me.'

He squeezes my hand. 'Well, make sure she's looking out for you financially. That she's getting the best deals for you. You deserve the world.'

And it's a compliment. But it almost isn't. I don't want to ruin this perfect moment, the romance of this date, with a conversation about me, my career and what I do and try to do with my life. It feels better to push that down. We can talk about that another time. And out of nowhere, I can suddenly hear the soundtrack of *Bolero* in my head, drowning out his words, and the festive music being piped in from above. It makes me think of Nana and I wonder what she'd make of this conversation if I told her. I used to report back on dates – have her squealing with laughter when things had gone horribly wrong. I remember telling her about when this Nick dumped me in the pub. She told me to post him prawns in a padded envelope. She'd love the ice skating but there would be parts of tonight she'd be less keen about. And for one clear moment I hear her voice clear as a bell in my head, saying, 'You've got a good heart, Kay Redman.' I think about another Nick who echoed those words. I push the thought aside. Not now. I just look up, at the stars trying to peek through the clouds, swaying my arms from side to side as we keep skating, continuing to go round and round in circles.

SEVENTEEN

I love the library, I do, but there are moments when I don't and that's right now. I'm here on my own at night and, because of my overactive imagination, I worry that the ghost of a Georgian noblewoman who was tragically strangled to death by her cheating husband is going to appear and start haunting me, asking me to avenge her death. That's the problem with having a library in an old building that creaks and has corners that seem to suck the light out of the room.

I keep wrapping the books on the table next to me, looking at the pile that seems to be growing, not shrinking. I was right. This idea of the book drive was great in theory and spirit but I have overwhelmed myself with the task. I over-advertised and people have flooded me with their old books. And not just good books, we get bags of random free books people got with their Happy Meals, colouring books that have already been coloured in, Shakespeare that's been annotated. It's sorting the wheat from the chaff, wrapping each book and then preparing for these events I've planned. I did not think this through, at all. I rest my head on the table, trying to work out how I've let this snowball, but then hear a squeaking sound in the depths of the library. Maybe we have mice. Not friendly Cinderella mice, urban mice who will come and eat my face. I grab a pair of scissors from next to me on the desk. I should have asked Olga to stay. I should really learn self-defence. To protect me from urban mice and Georgian ghosts. A knock on the door raps loudly, piercing the silence, and I scream, holding the scissors aloft.

I pop my head through to the foyer and see someone standing there, holding something large and pointy. I squint a little, another sign I think I might need glasses, but then realise who it is. *You? New Nick?* I don't recall us arranging a meeting and this is the second time he's done this, pop up when I least expect it and when I haven't had time to plan an outfit. Today I'm in a jumpsuit with Converse, what Olga calls my 'fun mechanic' outfit. My curls are bundled on my head, my lips and skin dry and tired from a day of work and the central heating in this place. He knocks again. I put down the scissors and quickly get lip balm from my handbag before scurrying over to unlock the door. He waves at me through the glass panels.

'Hi?' I say as I open the door, the cold prickling my face.

'You look surprised,' he says, his tone deadpan, his face scrunched that I'm not happier to see him.

Why must you always be so good-looking? Have a day off or something. 'I am. Did we arrange to meet?'

'No but I rang and told your colleague Helen that I would be here to deliver the trees,' he says, his arms rested against the tree next to him. 'She said it'd be alright. There'd be someone here to receive them.'

I smile faintly. Helen and Olga were especially quick to take their leave tonight and I see a plan in motion here, one that will mean I will not be bringing in nice cakes for them tomorrow.

'I must have missed that message. Come in,' I say, opening the door fully and allowing him to enter. He seems dressed for work today. He's wearing a fleece with the company logo, heavy-duty yellow work gloves, dark-blue jeans and brown work boots, that same grey woolly hat on his head. It's not just one tree, he seems to have three that he hauls in with ease and they're not tiny. They're at least seven-footers, majestic in relation to the dinky five-foot plastic ones we have.

'I brought stands too that you can borrow. I figured you're a library, you'd be good at getting them back to me,' he says.

'Will there be fines if not?' I joke.

'No. I trust you,' he says. I stop for a moment, accepting the compliment. I lead him through to the main part of the library so we have space to open up these trees. As soon as he gets through, he looks around. 'Where are your workmates?' he asks.

'Only me,' I say a little shyly, hoping he's not figured out Helen's ruse.

He looks me up and down. 'You'll have to help me erect them then.' I bite my lip; he said the word 'erect', but nothing. He's totally straight-faced, looking at me and waiting for an answer. I nod. 'Where do you want me to put this one?'

I lead him over to a space nearest the desk. I watch him as he lines up the stand and then takes a cutter to the nets around the tree.

'Any random women wrapped up in there?' I joke.

'Hope not,' he replies. 'Right, I'll get the trunk in and then you do the screwing.' I look at him, begging him to at least smile so I don't appear puerile and inappropriate if I react, but nope. 'Get on the floor so you can line it up.' I do as I'm told as he lifts the tree and places it inside the holder without straining or discomfort. I, however, seem to be in that familiar place of being attacked by pine needles again. 'Is the trunk central?'

'Uh huh,' I say, my hands going to the wingnuts on the stand and tightening them as hard as I can. I'm glad he can't see my face but this is taking effort.

'Screw a bit harder.'

Well at least I can giggle to myself under the foliage. He then does a strange thing, shaking it to see if it's secure enough, and pine needles flood me again. My hair won't survive this. I crawl out and stand up, looking up at the tree. 'Woah, that's a big boy.' The problem is I'm not delving into innuendo here, that is an impressive, majestic tree. It's the way the branches curl up at the bottom, as if it's doing a little curtsey.

'It's a silver fir. Put a little water in the tray to keep her healthy,' he says, looking on proudly. 'That way you won't lose too many needles.'

'That's good advice, thank you.'

He smiles and then comes over to me, using his massive gloves to reach out and brush my face. He's unfeasibly close. 'You're covered again.'

'Seems to be a theme with me,' I say, grinning awkwardly. 'Any other Christmas tree tips for me?'

'Put the lights on from the bottom.'

'Noted.'

He looks at the tiny fake tree next to the desk which looks a little sad in comparison. 'What's with those ornaments?' he asks me.

'Oh, we get the kids to make them. I did a workshop and they wrote the name of a book they want for Christmas on there and then went a bit crazy with the glitter,' I explain. He doesn't say a word, but I have that same feeling Old Nick gave me when he seemed to be judging my library activities. *I am a grown woman who should really be doing more with her life than arts and crafts.* Nick goes over and reads a few. 'Thank you for the tree. Shall we get the others up?' I ask.

He nods but is also looking around the library, intrigued. 'That's a lot of books...' he says, nodding to the table I was working at, piled with books, rolls of brown paper, tape and Christmas ribbon.

'You have no idea.'

'Oh, is that for your book drive thing?'

I nod. 'This is just a small fraction of the books.' I walk him over to a storage cupboard and turn on the light. At the last count, we were at a little over four hundred and more come in every day. 'I'm wrapping them with little tags and stuff...' I say, hoping my panic at the task in hand doesn't show. As my name is attached to the drive, I want things to be done well, I want the books to be presented nicely.

His eyes scan the room and then back to me. 'You're going to wrap all of these books yourself?'

'I'm an over-achiever.' Who doesn't mind the occasional paper cut. Helen takes a box home every night to help but I don't let Olga near them as she really can't wrap for shit.

'Well, I mean it, I can help,' he says, his tone warm and authentic. He reaches into his pocket and pulls out the flyer I gave him last time we met. 'I also looked at my calendar and I can be free when you need me.'

I think about our last meeting and the way he had offered help. I guess the problem is when you do voluntary endeavours, people can be quick to offer their assistance but those promises are often reneged on quickly. The man has staying power. Don't overthink that. 'Well then, that is very kind of you.'

'You're welcome, Kay.'

And he looks at me intently and smiles. That is a good smile and those eyes are very, very green. I feel a breath catch in my chest, everything around him stopping for a while. It's so intense, I have to remember to exhale.

'Can I get you a cup of tea for your efforts? One of our customers baked us a Christmas cake? It's a bit boozy but edible?' I say, trying to find words and clarity.

'Yeah. Then we can get those other trees up. I can help here as well?' he says, pointing at the books and wrapping paper.

'You don't have anywhere to be?'

He shakes his head.

'How's your wrapping?'

'Learnt everything I know from Dr Dre.'

'You made a joke,' I say, surprised.

He looks at me curiously, seeming slightly insulted that I've pointed that out. He takes off his hat and puts a hand through his hair. Don't stare, Kay. 'Better cut me a slice of cake then. We've got our work cut out, eh?'

Did the Xmas Tree Man arrive? Enjoy! Hope he gets his wood out! X

I look at the message on the phone and turn it over immediately so Nick can't see. I am appalled, Helen. I really am. It's coming up to eight o'clock now and Nick has been here in the library for nearly two hours, helping me position trees, envelop them with lights and laughing at how one little boy wrote on a bauble that he wanted *Fifty Shades of Grey* to give his mum. And I think I've found something super attractive about this man that trumps everything else. He can wrap. The way he glides scissors around the paper, how he doesn't wing it with paper size but measures out the books first, the way he folds his corners and doesn't get frustrated by the tape dispenser. It's a thing of beauty to watch. And he can tie ribbon like people on Instagram do, looping it around his fingers expertly. I can't be lustful and stare at him. I went ice skating two days ago with Old Nick and it was romantic, he talked about our kids and we went for dinner afterwards and had sex. I think we're going out and in terms of my own morals and to give that a chance, I can't be perving on New Nick and imagining things about his hands.

'So tell me about your farm again? What does your mum do?' I ask, trying to focus on civility.

'So my mum really helped my dad turn the farm into an all-year-round business. The café is our biggest earner and then we have a small nursery, holdings for fruit-picking in the summer,' he says. Sitting down with him has also been a way to find out more about his history, his family, and as Lucy explained, it's super wholesome and organic.

'Lucy mentioned to me that you also build furniture?' I ask, hoping he doesn't mind that we've been chitchatting about him.

'Yeah. I have a small carpentry business on the side.'

'Like Jesus?' I say, slightly embarrassed that I don't know any other carpenters to compare him to. I know that's a shit joke from the look he gives me.

'What do you make?'

'I'm into chairs at the moment.'

'Edge of the seat stuff,' I say. The look on his face tells me he didn't get that joke at all. 'Sorry.'

'And you write?' he asks, trying to change the subject from my awful sense of humour.

'When I'm not here, yes.'

'These bears you write about, are they based on anyone?' he asks.

I give him a look. I think he's being funny. 'Well, yes, because I know a lot of bears who wear bow ties and hats,' I say. 'I don't know... I had a stupid idea once that wouldn't it be funny if you had a family of bears – brown, polar, panda – and they all lived together and had bear adventures.'

This he smiles at. 'I loved the Christmas one I read the other day. How they had to pull Santa's sleigh because the reindeer got food poisoning.'

'All my writing is very much steeped in reality,' I say, trying to sound like an earnest author. 'But in all honesty, I love writing fiction, a story that creates joy and helps a kid believe in magic and storytelling. And it turns out talking bears are quite the thing.'

He doesn't reply but pulls at a length of tape and nods to himself. Is he another non-believer? In me or my brand of Christmas spirit, I'm not sure, but it makes me go quiet too.

He picks up a book and holds it up: *Poetry for Lovers*, flicking through the pages and starts reading aloud.

> 'I do not resemble your other lovers, my lady
> Should another give you a cloud
> I give you rain
> Should he give you a lantern, I

> will give you the moon
> Should he give you a branch
> I will give you the trees
> And if another gives you a ship
> I shall give you the journey.'

He looks at me as he finishes, slowly closing the book. Do not react. It's a good- looking man reading you love poetry in a sort of husky growl that makes me want to weep. It's nothing.

'Corny?'

'Yes,' I say, trying to joke.

He starts to wrap it.

'Meanwhile, more corn here,' I say, picking up the next book on the pile, a rather hefty cookbook, slightly dusty and untouched. 'Look at this whopper!' I say a little too enthusiastically. I see him smile out of the corner of my eye. This is what I do, I cover up awkward moments with my weird sense of comedy. I flick through the pages of the book. One thing I've found out is that people donate books without checking them first. I've found travelcards, receipts and, well, a library book that should have come back to us in 1994. Worse are the books with inscriptions, the thoughtfulness given away to someone else. That always hurts. I hold the book to the side shaking it out, when a letter floats out.

N,

My wonder, my joy, my love. You are my heart and I do not want to spend another day without you next to me. I think about us all the time in some future drenched in light and happiness. Love you, always.

K x

I pause as I read it and the emotion makes my eyes glaze over to see the coincidence of the initials, this wonderful testament to someone's love in my hands, separated from its owner. I flick through the remaining pages of the book and find several other letters in there, as if they've been put in this heavy tome to flatten them out or keep them safe. Deep down though, I know that maybe I shouldn't have them.

'Is someone not a fan of the River Cottage then?' Nick asks, noticing my hesitation.

'It's just... this...' I pass him the letter and he reads it. 'There are more, dozens of them from N to K and back again,' I say, holding one of them gently to my chest. I can't put an age on them but sometimes the paper is thick, and other times they're on paper ripped out of what appears to be a school notebook. I scan them, they do go mildly erotic at times but what comes across most strongly is the depth of feeling. You get the idea this was a love story for the ages.

Nick reads through some of the letters and I see a glimmer of a smile. '*Love you, always. Even when you steal my duvet and leave cold cups of tea everywhere.*' He looks up at me earnestly. 'Is there any way to trace the writers?' he asks.

'I could try, but these books came in from a lot of different places,' I say, wondering whether it's possible.

'Got to be worth a shot though, eh?' he says. And again, he gives me a look. He seems to want to say more, ask more. If not then why is he here, wrapping books for people he doesn't know, weeks before Christmas? And for a moment, Old Nick comes into view, the way he laughed all of this off. I've never seen him wrap a present in his life. What if he's shit at wrapping?

'Nick... I...'

'Shit,' he suddenly says, looking at his phone. 'How is it eight already?' There's confusion in his eyes. 'I have to get back to the farm. We're on a late opening.' He reaches for his hat and rises from his chair. 'I'm sorry to rush like this,' he says, collecting up the plastic netting on the floor. 'I wish I could have helped you hoover or something.'

You also hoover? I need to stop this. 'I'm sorry, I should have ordered in dinner or something to thank you.'

'No thanks needed. I came because...'

Say it. Then I'll know. I'll know for sure.

'I... you know...' he says mumbling. He looks at me intensely. 'Charity.'

My face drops. Oh.

EIGHTEEN

'Maybe I could give you a quick makeover so you could see the effects of our radiant glow foundation. It's really good for filling in those fine lines,' the woman says, scanning my face.

I'm not sure if this is really the best way of making a sale but I look into the magnifying mirror on Elena's counter and stare deeply into my pores and the lines of my face. I don't usually care too much about them – Nana always says a face with marks is one that has lived – but I think Elena is trying to tell me it's one that's not cared for enough, so I should now buy her products so I can cover it all up.

'If you buy the foundation today, you get a free lipliner and we can put you into our draw for a £500 beauty hamper.'

'I was looking for a fun eyeshadow,' I say.

She looks at me blankly. Fun? Eyeshadow is a serious endeavour. 'Have you thought about concealer?'

Tell her no. Tell her you're happy with your face as it is. But I can't. 'Merry Christmas,' I say, before scurrying away. Is it bad that I'm a Londoner and I've never been to Harrods before? I think sometimes it can be too intimidating to walk through those hallowed doors, to be deluded enough to think you might be able to afford anything. As I look upon a whole shelf of snail moisturisers at £100 a pot my assumptions are proved right. This whole beauty section is a mirrored, brightly lit arrangement of counters, leather stools and women with slicked-back hair and strong lips who look like dental hygienists. This is not Superdrug where I can try stuff out on the back of my hand and go, hey, it's five pounds and not tested on animals, let's give it a go.

As it's Harrods, the Christmas music is also strong and orchestral. No Bublé here, and the decorations around this place hang precariously off the ceilings. There are giant glowing reindeer and baubles as big as the moon, the lights glow, and the greenery is real and fragrant. As much as this is way beyond my wallet and usual shopping experience, this place does feel magical. As soon as I walked in, the marble floors, the way the ceilings extend up along striking white pillars, the art deco features, the complete grandeur of it, it's movie shopping. Something to watch from afar and admire as opposed to partaking in.

'Rose Chérie?' a woman says, approaching me.

'Oh, I'm sorry. I don't speak French,' I say politely, wondering if maybe I'm so chic today that I look French. I'll take that. It's a vintage checked wool coat, I get a lot of compliments about it.

'Oh no,' the woman says, reverting back to a disappointingly snooty London accent. 'It's a perfume. It's Guerlain.'

'Yeah. I'll have a...' I thought she might spritz me but instead she hands me a small white strip of paper and the only place I've seen those are in the doctor's office when they test for urine infections. She watches and I think she wants me to smell it. 'That's lovely. I can smell the rose and the... chérie?'

She smiles at me, knowing that I don't belong, but then her attention seems to be taken with a figure next to me who approaches closely and slips a hand inside my coat and around my waist. 'I'm so sorry I'm late. Have you been waiting long?' He leans in to give me a kiss on the cheek.

'Madam was sampling our new fragrance at Guerlain,' the lady with the white strips says, simpering.

Old Nick goes to smell it. 'Wow. That's insanely good. Did you want it?'

Do I? I think we should look at the bottom of the bottle for the price first. But they both stand there and look at me. 'I'm undecided for now. I may do a bit more sampling over in...' I look around. 'Dior. Thank you though.'

The woman knows I'm lying but she smiles passive-aggressively and lets us walk on. Despite a few minor reservations about Old Nick, there is something very comforting about him at the moment. The way he has no qualms about draping an arm around me or looking for a hand. After ice skating, we spent the night together and had a morning of buying coffees and then kissing each other goodbye at the train station and going our separate ways, off to work. And the way I asked him if he had his keys, and the way he straightened out my scarf felt normal, as if we're in a relationship even though the terms of what this is haven't yet been discussed.

'So is this your regular shopping spot then?' I joke. 'Are we here to do a big shop in the food hall downstairs?'

'Not quite but we can go there later. Peruse...'

I nod. All I was told was to meet him here, in Harrods for three o'clock on the dot, so I do wonder why now. There are restaurants and cafés here. Perhaps we're having a fancy afternoon tea. Or are we doing champagne and oysters? That is super classy. I really should have worn heels instead of boots for that.

'I like that coat on you. Suits you,' I say to Nick, scanning his outfit. He's wearing a tan wool-style trench today over jeans, boots and a black polo neck.

'Oh, it was a gift,' he says, frowning slightly. 'I never know if it suits me.'

'You wear it well,' I say.

He leads me over by the hand to the lifts that again scream luxury with their brass-plated buttons and lit-up store directory. We go inside the lift and he finds my hand again, next to a few other shoppers and excited children. Lower Ground. I guess the food hall it is, to find posh truffles and caviar. He smiles to himself and I do wonder what he's thinking about because he seems happy, and whilst I feel comfortable in his company, things linger in my mind. Little conversations about my writing and career and, maybe more importantly, New Nick. New Nick who can wrap books and gives me Christmas trees for free but who I think, the last time I saw him, may have referred to me as charity. He feels sorry for me? Yeah, that's definitely not how I want to feel in any sort of relationship with anyone.

'Lower Ground Floor,' a polite voice says as we arrive at our destination, and Nick leads the way, letting me exit the lift first.

'Come...' he says but I examine the signs on the wall and we head away from the food hall. 'You're still super Christmassy right?' he asks.

'Yes?' I say, confused if he thinks that's a bad thing.

'Then we are exactly where we need to be,' he says, gripping my hand tightly.

He leads me through to another hallway and there are labelled arches, decorated brightly in red ribbons and nutcracker-soldier statues greeting us. Christmas. They have a whole Christmas department. I walk through and it is the sort of magical place I always wanted to go to as a child. Stuffed Harrods bears piled high, toy locomotives whizz through model villages decorated with snowy mountains, and walls of ornate decorations in every feasible colour, stacked like gloriously bejewelled pieces of fruit. Nick notices my mouth is agape and laughs. Are we here so I can get emotional and stare at everything? Nick cocks his head, telling me to keep walking until we get to a wooden sign, sitting in swathes of white, glowing material made to look like ice. *Santa's Grotto*. I look at Nick curiously to see the small queue of children there, and an elf with a clipboard at a lectern ticks off everyone's name.

'Maybe we have to book?' I say. 'Plus, I'm twenty-seven,' I remind him, conscious of the small kids in Christmas jumpers and super-cute velveteen dresses surrounding us.

'I have a booking – Nick Coles,' he says, ignoring me and turning to the elf.

'Of course, Mr Coles. Please go through.'

I turn to him, unable to speak. We're going to look very strange with all these children. Isn't there an age limit for these sorts of things? Will I have to sit on Santa's knee? I keep walking through a labyrinth of lights and decorations. Along the way, there are displays of animatronic penguins, singing and dancing, one of whom pops his head out of a little igloo to say hello. I feel an overwhelmed joy at the cuteness of it all, the dedication to creating something so special that a kid will believe in everything Christmas is about. I look up, noticing Nick taking a photo on his phone and turn to smile.

'I can't believe you. You booked this?' I ask.

'You love Christmas. This is one of the most festive places I know. Mum used to bring me here as a kid. I thought I would share in the joy.' We stroll past kids completely enamoured, elves following them around, playing games with them and asking them questions.

'Madam, sir...,' an enthusiastic elf says, approaching us. 'Do you want to step up to the naughty or nice machine? We can find out what list you're on if you're interested to know?'

I push Nick forward. 'Oh, I'm very interested,' I say playfully. Nick stands on a giant golden scale and a huge arrow on the ball bounces up and down, landing on NAUGHTY. Some children gasp in disbelief but I bite my lip.

'I demand a recount,' Nick argues and he comes over to hug me, kissing me gently on the cheek. 'As long as you don't mind naughty?'

I shake my head. We walk on until we get to a large wooden door and Nick introduces himself to yet another elf, who nods. As the door opens, I think about all the Santas I've ever met, charity ones in the street, school-fair ones, even ones who work in Christmas trees. This one just beats them all, hands down, no contest. He is actually so authentic, so real I let out a little gasp. He sits in a library, surrounded by books, garlands and a little log fire with a magnificent Christmas tree next to it, golden and dazzling. He doesn't wear a hat, but that beard is genuine and luxurious, he's got apple cheeks and a ruddy complexion. He's portly and has the sort of syrupy voice and smile that makes you want to share all your life secrets immediately.

'Ho-ho-ho! Miss Redman and Mr Coles – how are we today?' The voice is like warm melted chocolate. 'Do come in.' We're ushered in to sit on a red and gold sofa. I'm curious as to how he knows my name but also why he's not questioned the lack of children in the room. 'Look how lovely and grown up you look. When was the last time I saw both of you?'

I giggle, covering my mouth. The last time I visited Santa in this manner was in a garden centre and he smelt of pilchards. 'It's been a while, Santa. You look very well.'

'I need to lay off the cookies,' he says, patting his belly. 'But thank you, dear girl.'

'Would you like to hear something funny? You share a name with Mr Coles.'

'Your name is Santa?' he jokes.

'No, I'm a fellow Nick.'

Santa reaches out a hand. 'Then the privilege is mine, Nicholas.' I grin, wondering if it's bad form to get out my phone and take a selfie. 'So, I will assume you have written your lists? What do you want for Christmas?'

I pause. I really do not know. Is it strange to want to ask Santa for UGG slippers and a reading pillow? I feel this is Harrods Santa and he may be able to get more for me. World Peace and a holiday to Hawaii? I shrug my shoulders. 'I haven't really thought about it, Santa. I would like... everyone I love to be happy.'

Nick laughs. Santa stops for a moment, his smile flattening before nodding and looking me in the eyes. 'That is a wonderful thing, Miss Redman.'

'Well, if she's asking for that, can I grab a Ferrari if your elves can make them?'

Santa switches his gaze to Nick, cocking his head to one side. 'My elves can make anything.' He seems to write these requests in a large manuscript he has in front of him. 'It was lovely to see you both. I hope you have a wonderful Christmas!' The tone and volume of his voice are perfection. *I want to stay in here for longer, to chat to you all afternoon but I know I can't be selfish, it's Christmas after all. The children need you.* 'Before you go...' He reaches into a sack by his Christmas throne and takes out a Harrods teddy bear with a Santa hat and hands it to Nick. I am instantly jealous and hope he has one in there for me. Instead, he reaches down and takes out a little square box. 'And I believe this is for you.'

A strong emotion runs through my body at this moment. Panic. It grounds me to the spot like a massive spear. No. No, no, no. We've literally reconnected in the past fortnight. This is ridiculous. He isn't going to...? And in front of Santa? I take the box and unfurl the red satin ribbon, opening it cautiously to reveal a pair of earrings. Just earrings. I don't know why but my chest deflates, and I can suddenly breathe.

'Well, what's your answer?' Santa asks excitedly, looking over at Nick, almost urging him to get down on one knee.

We both turn to look at him, me shaking my head slowly. It's only then Nick gets it, looking strangely aghast. 'Oh no, the little box. They're earrings. I didn't think that through, did I? I'm so sorry. I just... I thought it was cute with Santa and... we've...'

'Two weeks,' I explain to Santa.

'TWO WEEKS!' Santa exclaims. 'Shit... sorry... I swore. Santa shouldn't swear,' he says, his old wrinkled face going very pink. 'I shouldn't have assumed...'

Nick looks at me, searching for my reaction. 'I... you love Christmas.'

That I do, I think to myself, still trying to sift through my emotions here.

'And he obviously likes you very much to go to all this trouble,'

Santa interjects. 'Those are lovely earrings as well. What can I say? Us Nicks have impeccable taste,' he says, winking.

'I went with peridot because they're your birthstone,' Nick says.

'They are my birthstone,' I say, leaning over to hug Nick to thank him. He remembers these little things about me, and I can't help but fall for that, to know that behind this big gesture, there's also kindness there, someone who is invested in me. 'Thank you. I love them, all of this. I love...'

But I don't finish my sentence. That's way too soon. Instead, I wrap my arms around him and embrace him tightly. There is something here, isn't there? A spark that was lit almost a decade ago, a familiarity there that means I can rest in his arms and feel safe. Maybe I need to give this a chance. I look up at Santa gazing at both of us, smiling. What do I want for Christmas? Maybe it starts with this.

NINETEEN

I believe that in my obituary they will write: Kay Redman, author, decent human being, over-achiever. Died on a trunk road near Brentford, next to her really shit red Renault 5 filled to the brim with books, dressed as a reindeer. Please little car, please start. I turn the key again and the engine emits a dying splutter, and a light shines on the dashboard. The book drive starts today; I'm supposed to give out the first of my books but ironically, I can't drive anywhere. I admit defeat and put on my hazard warning lights, exit the car and head to a grassy bank behind a barrier to protect myself, watching as my breakdown seems to be creating traffic and people are starting to scowl and beep their horns. I look down at my phone and fill in the details of the breakdown on my app. *We are experiencing a higher number of callouts than usual. Someone will aim to be with you in ninety minutes.* Great. I don't know what to do. Do I go on YouTube, open the bonnet and try and fix the fault myself? Do I try and get the books out of the car? But then, because life has a cruel sense of humour, it starts to rain. That horrible cold winter rain that makes the air feel sharper, more bitter. The books should stay in the dry. I, meanwhile, put my hood up, the antlers of my onesie pinging up, taking shelter under a nearby tree because my umbrella isn't in the boot of my car. It's at work in the staff room. Shit.

'Move your car, you twat!' someone shouts at me.

I stare back blankly. 'I would if I knew how!' The man beeps his horn at me and I wave a fist at him like an angry old man.

What to do? I look down at my phone again. These are the moments when I miss having a family the most – ride or die people you could call and they wouldn't question a thing, they'd show up. Mum and Dad are enjoying their retirement in Australia and I don't deny them their fun, but at times it feels lonely not having them near. In her prime, Nana would have shown up with a taxi and helped me deliver these books. She'd have loved getting involved and swearing back at angry drivers. I scroll through my phone list and hover over Old Nick's name. *Are you that person now?* It'd certainly be a test of our young relationship. But he'll be at work. I don't want to drag him out of important finance things. I see another name and smile, dialling it immediately.

'What's up, Kay Kay?' the voice sounds.

'Please say you might be free, Lucy?' I ask, realising my bottom jaw might be chattering.

'You sound cold. Are you OK? I'm at work, at the farm,' she says.

'Nah, it's... Did I ever tell you about my book drive I was doing? I seem to be stuck. My car's broken down in the middle of a main road. Are you mid-shift though? I need...' I need help but I also need a friend.

'Jump in a taxi, babes? Have you called recovery?'

'I can't leave my car. Recovery says they'll be over an hour.'

She pauses for a moment. 'Oh, love... look, leave it with me. I'll sort it. Can you drop me a pin with your location?' And I smile broadly because it's the response you want, the sort that drops everything, without question.

'Thank you, I love you.'

'You soppy cow. Help is on the way, dear.' I hear the jingle of bells in the background as she hangs up and I stand there by the roadside, just in time for someone to drive through a growing puddle and splash me. Seriously. Thanks.

There's something about waiting that always gives me space with my thoughts, and as a consequence, I tend to think about life in too much detail. Maybe my car breaking down is a sign that this book drive is a terrible idea. I need to give up the ghost. This is time I could be spending with Nana. It's time I could be writing. It's time I could be spending with Nick. This is the universe telling me not to distract myself with other things. Maybe people don't want these books at all. People don't read anymore. They want iPhones and gift cards. How silly to think any of this could make a difference. The rain hasn't stopped. It falls in diagonals so the parts of my onesie where my coat doesn't cover my legs are soaked through. Any make-up I was wearing has probably slicked off my face, from the rain but also my tears. This is not a winning moment.

I've been here for about twenty minutes when a truck suddenly pulls up behind my car. I can't take another person shouting at me so I try and hide behind the tree, watching as the two men in ponchos and work boots go over to my car and look through the windows. One of them opens the driver door and checks inside. Shit. Are they trying to steal it? *Hold up. I know you.*

'Nick?' I say, peering out from behind the trunk of the tree.

He looks up at me, squinting through the rain before climbing over the railing and heading over to me. 'What are you doing behind that tree?'

'Waiting for...' Damn you, Lucy. I realise what she's done here. 'I always thought you shouldn't wait in your car when you break down.'

'But you're... wet through. It's raining.'

No shit, Sherlock. I don't think my mood needs him to state the bleeding obvious right now.

'Why are you in a jumpsuit?'

'It's a onesie. Why do you keep confusing these things?'

I don't know why his inability to identify all-in-one clothing upsets me so much but he looks at me brusquely, and I frown despite how relieved I am to see him.

Another person emerges next to him, side-eyeing Nick curiously. 'I'm Noah,' he says, waving. There's a softer shape to his face but he has the same eyes. He scans my bedraggled chic curiously.

'He's my brother,' Nick clarifies. 'We were doing a delivery and Lucy rang to tell us you were in trouble so...'

He came to the rescue. Of course he did. 'Do you guys know anything about cars?'

Noah turns to me. 'I know that one's a bit dead. Maybe we push it into that lay-by ten yards up there and then at least it's out of the way?'

Nick doesn't look at me for permission. He heads over to the barrier, steps over it and almost has command of the traffic, the way cars slow down and part for him like Moses. He then goes into the car to release the handbrake, steering and pushing as Noah pushes it from the back. I should help but I stand there quietly to watch this manly show of help, embarrassed if immensely grateful.

They return to the grassy bank next to me. 'Thank you,' I say sheepishly. 'I... I guess I should wait for the AA if you wanted to be on your way?'

'Lucy said you were on your way to your book drive?' Nick asks. The water drips off the hood of his poncho. Inside his face is perfectly dry, as if he hasn't even broken a sweat.

'Yeah, the car is packed with books.'

'Then load them up in the truck and I'll take you there,' Nick says, as though it's a very uncomplicated solution to this matter.

'But... my car...'

'Noah will stay with the car. Where do we have to drop the books?' Nick asks me.

'Isleworth.'

'Literally down the road.'

'But...'

'Kay, it's pissing it down. You need my help. I told you to get in touch if you needed my help. I am giving you my help.'

Noah gives him a sharp glance at this point because there's a sense of rebuke in his tone. I guess the rain doesn't help but I look at him and exhale, exasperated by the events of the day and probably even more by this man telling me off. 'Then I guess... thank you?'

We all move back to my car and take a plastic crate each, making two journeys to their truck to load the books in, trying to shield the books as best we can. As they are loaded up, I turn to Noah. 'Seriously, you don't mind waiting?'

'Half an hour away from grumpy bollocks here won't hurt,' he says. 'It's all good, Kay.'

He smiles as he says my name and studies my face. I'm not entirely sure why but I hand him my car keys.

'Thank you.'

'When you're both done having a social,' Nick shouts from the truck, flashing his lights. I run to the side of the truck and jump in, realising I'm going to leave great puddles of rainwater all over the seat and the floor of the vehicle. I am appreciative of the help, but I can see where Nick gets his grumpy reputation from. There is an efficiency there laced with a healthy dose of impatience. He pulls the truck away carefully and we wave at Noah as we drive past.

'Will he be OK?' I ask Nick.

'He's a grown man with 4G. He'll be fine. There's a towel in that bag if you need it,' he says. 'You're kinda...' *Please don't say wet again.* 'Soaked.'

'Kinda?' I should tell him the rain has seeped into my knickers but I'll keep that to myself. 'Is this your towel?'

'It's my gym towel.'

'Is it used?'

'No,' he says, apparently confused at why he would be offering me a sweaty towel. 'I was going to the gym later.' He goes to the gym. Probably why he can push cars so easily. I take off my coat and bury my face in the towel, drying my hair as much as I can, which collects water like a sponge. The car is silent, bar the squeak of the window wipers. Where's his Christmas music? 'That is a lot of books in the back there, Kay. Were you seriously going to deliver those yourself?' he asks, as I try and rearrange my curls.

'It was going to be a quick drop off at the women and children's refuge. I can carry plastic crates very well on my own,' I say.

'Dressed like that?'

I pull at my onesie self-consciously. It was fun, fluffy and cute an hour ago but I guess Rudolph probably never had to wait by a flyover in the rain. 'That was kinda rude,' I tell him.

He seems taken aback at my retort. 'I'm only saying that because you're all matted and soggy. You should plan better. Your car's a bit of a crate too.' Well, now I'm deeply offended. That car's done me well over the years; it's survived university and numerous trips to beaches and suchlike. It's almost a part of my family. 'We have vans at the farm. Let me help,' he says.

'But... I don't want to impose...'

'I'd say if you were imposing.' I have a feeling that he would.

'I saw you at the library, juggling all those books, wrapping them up. You've got an event at an old people's home on Friday, yeah? I'll drive you. I'll do the Santa thing. Don't do this alone.'

I still don't care for his tone but there's something there, a simple add-on at the end of that sentence that is affecting and humbling. Maybe since Nana went into the home I have been doing too much on my own. I write alone, I live alone and I haven't known how to do things any other way.

'I don't get you,' I tell him sullenly. He looks at me, confused. 'You're offering help but you're also making digs at how I go about things.'

'I'm not. All I'm saying is if you're going out dressed like a sad wet bear then plan better. Pack an umbrella.'

'I'm a reindeer,' I say, pulling up my hood so he can see my antlers.

He says nothing but gives me a look that tells me he finds my need for fancy dress ridiculous. I even wore UGG slippers for authenticity. Some would applaud the commitment.

'Well, even reindeers don't do Christmas on their own. Santa needs a whole flock to pull his sleigh.'

'A herd,' I reply. 'Reindeer herd. It's a flock of sheep.'

'Or seagulls.'

'Mine-mine...' I caw.

'*Finding Nemo.*' He got the reference. But he doesn't laugh despite my rather brilliant impression of a sea bird. I look over at him, hands firmly on the steering wheel, clenching it tightly. *Why are you so tense, so humourless? Because this is an inconvenience and I seem ungrateful?* Maybe I need to break the surliness and just accept his offers of help.

'What are your trucks like? Are they roomy?' I ask him.

'We've got white vans with decent load dimensions,' he says seriously.

'Will it have this?' I ask him, pointing to a Santa on the dashboard that wriggles his hips every time the truck stops.

'That's not mine, it's Noah's. He thinks it's funny,' he says.

'It is, no?'

'No.'

I look over at him. *I am thankful you're here, I really am but it's supposed to be the happiest time of the year.* I grab his towel and unzip my onesie a little to expose my neck, drying as much rain as I can down to my cleavage. However, as I do, the truck brakes suddenly and I feel the pull of the seatbelt against my shoulder.

'Bloody wazzock!' Nick shouts out angrily. The combination of his volume and the sudden jolt of the brakes makes the hairs on my arm stand on end but there's something about that word too. I laugh. It's something you don't hear these days. But when did I last hear it? On a phone. A man. A man who delivered a Christmas tree to my nana. A really big Christmas tree. Oh my. *You?*

TWENTY

'Oh my God, did you fall in a river or something?' Nick asks as I walk through the door of his apartment. He stands opposite me, giving casual and relaxed vibes in grey joggers and a hoodie, bare feet on the floor. I have no idea how I look but it's not relaxed. It's sodden and damp, a cold in my bones and veins. After the other Nick helped me transport my books, we returned to my car and he and Noah waited with me until the AA man (Larry) eventually arrived and told me my car was dead as a doornail which I told him was a very timely Dickensian reference that no one else got. Anyway, the car and I were towed to a garage and then I called an Uber and came here because Nick invited me round for dinner. I think the Uber driver might charge me for flooding his car but I'm so done with today. I need somewhere warm, somewhere I can collapse. Somewhere with a towel.

'I've had a day. My car is dead, I was stranded and...' I moan.

'Why didn't you call? I could have helped?' he says, sounding concerned as he ushers me inside and takes my handbag which seems to have absorbed all the rain.

'You were at work. I had to wait for the AA. Just... nightmare.'

'I could have sent help. A car maybe? I can't leave a reindeer stranded at Christmas.'

See? He could identify the onesie. He has not batted an eyelid that I look like a big matted soggy mess. He comes over and straightens my antlers. 'Did you get your books delivered?' he asks, disappearing into a room off the kitchen to get a laundry basket. I nod, not divulging how. It was the other Nick who flew in to save the day but I'll admit since realising he was the very abrupt man I spoke to years ago about the ridiculous Christmas tree he gifted my nana, that there's a strange feeling there I can't shake. He was rude, so rude, and even though he's now offered to help me with the book drive, I can't get over the extremes of his personality. 'Here, put all your wet things in here and I'll throw what I can in the dryer.'

Because here is someone who has just showered me with kindness since we've been re-acquainted. I know him much better. I exhale deeply to be in the warm, marvelling at his domestic efficiency and his desire to help. I immediately feel the warmth of his underfloor heating on the soles of my feet as I remove my socks. 'Shall I just strip here?' I ask him.

'Well, I won't complain... let me get you a robe...'

He disappears again as I try and undress, peeling my onesie off me. He returns with a dark-grey fluffy robe and wraps it around me, kissing me on the forehead. 'I must look a state,' I say, looking down at my knickers that have gone completely transparent.

'You're freezing. Come with me...'

He reaches down and takes my hand, leading me to his bathroom where he starts to run a bath, pouring in bubble bath. I sit on the edge, watching him. As he glances over, I can see him smiling there and I feel incredibly warmed by the fact he doesn't care what I look like. I can show up at his doorstep and he's brought me in and taken care of me. It harks back to a time at university where we'd revel in joint hangovers and crawl to lectures looking our absolute worst. His bathroom has a window overlooking the Thames and I watch as the rain calms and the river twinkles from streetlamps and boats passing through.

'I was going to order in food tonight but you get first dibs. What do you fancy? Something warm? Soup? There's a good ramen place nearby?'

I tense my body, noticing that my fingers are all pruny and wrinkled. 'Perfect. Can I get something with egg and pork belly?'

'You can.' He comes over to me and embraces me tightly and I sigh to feel his body heat but also the fact he wants to look after me this evening.

'I'm sorry. Once I regain feeling in my joints, I might be up for something a bit more sexual.'

He laughs. 'Is that why you think I invited you over?'

'Well, no but...'

'I'm sure if I was in the same situation you'd do the same for me.'

'I would,' I say, my cheek resting against his chest.

He unwraps the robe from my shoulders and kisses one before looking me in the eye, reaching around to unhook my bra and then bending down to remove my knickers. I close my eyes, grinning as he does it because the intimacy of it sends a shiver down my spine. 'Get in, warm up. I'm going to order us food.' He lends me a hand as I step over the side of the bath, and the water, the bubbles, the heat of it, is an instant relief, leading me to make an extraordinary sigh of joy. Nick chuckles to hear it. 'Good?'

'Magnificent. Is that lavender?'

'It is. Good nose. I do enjoy a calming, relaxing scent after a long day at work,' he jokes.

He leans over to give me another kiss on the forehead, not before lighting a candle on a shelf nearby. 'Dumplings too, you like dumplings, yeah?'

I nod, my eyes closed in contentment as I continue to thaw out in the water, and I see his eyes glance down to see my nipples poking out through the bubbles. I catch his eye as he grins cheekily. Was this a ploy to see my naked body? I really don't care. He escapes into another room to get his phone and I suddenly hear music coming out from somewhere. Ibiza chillout sounds. The lights dim. God, this is lovely. Can you rate baths? Because this is definitely in my top ten. I glance at the toiletries on the side, looking at the shampoos and scrubs that Nick uses, smelling them and looking around at how immaculate it is. I have issues with my grout but not here, it's sparkling clean. He returns minutes later and I watch as he hands me a glass of wine. I lied. This is now the perfect bath.

'Get this down you,' he says.

I nod, sitting up as his eyes travel down again to watch the bubbles sliding off my skin. 'You're an angel. Your bath is singing to me, by the way.'

'It's a good bath like that,' he jokes. He drags a stool over to sit nearby and keep me company, his fingers gliding over apps as he orders food. I take a sip of my wine and watch his body leaning against the wall, the curve of his shoulders. Maybe I should have called him before, maybe I shouldn't have had any doubts that he would have showed up for me. 'All done. How are we feeling?'

'Warmer.'

'That is good. You soak in there for as long as you want. How's the car?'

'Most likely dead. It's my old Renault 5,' I say.

'Shite, the Ronald McRocket? That thing is still driving?'

He's remembered my car had a nickname and the many trips up and down the M4 we once shared in it. 'It doesn't have a second gear but it's been a good run-around for many years.'

'May he rest in peace.'

'Amen.'

'Did you need another one?' he asks, sipping at his own glass of wine, reaching over to top up mine.

'A car? Well, I didn't drive a lot anyway living in London, maybe I need to start relying on public transport.'

'We'll get you a new one, no bother.'

I take a sip of wine as he says this. *We?* We'd go car shopping or pick one off the internet? Or he'd buy me a brand-new car? That is too much. He's already bought me those earrings. I'm happy enough that he's run me a bath. I'm a simple girl, really.

'Or we can wait. Give me a chance to mourn the old car first,' I say. 'Actually, you probably don't but do you have anything I could tie my hair with? I'm starting to turn into a feral mermaid, the curls go a bit mental with the damp.' I shake my hair around. I just need it out of my face so I can enjoy this wine a bit more. 'Anything, I'll take a rubber band if you've got it.'

He smiles but goes to a drawer under his sink and pulls out a scrunchie. 'Will this do you?'

He hands it over. It's black and silk. I shouldn't think anything of it but I do. 'Is this yours? For when you're doing your skincare and stuff?' I ask, pulling it over my hands and grabbing my hair into a bun.

'Yeah, I do love a face mask,' he jokes but he realises there are questions forthcoming. 'Well, we all have relics from relationships past, eh? Things we inherit.'

'Indeed. For me it's usually hoodies.'

'You women are awful when it comes to hoodies, you really are.'

I sit there, sipping on my wine, waiting for the story of the scrunchie. 'Scrunchies have amazing other uses, you know? I tend to use them on rolls of wrapping paper to keep them tidy. I sometimes tie off bags of crisps with them.'

'That is ingenious,' he says, and I see a sadness return to his eyes, one I've certainly seen before.

'How much did she hurt you?' I ask him.

'Unfathomable amounts,' he says. I can almost feel his hurt, the way it makes him visibly gulp and rub his hands together.

'I'm sorry. You could also burn the scrunchie.'

That makes him laugh, and it's a relief to see the sadness dissipate from his face. 'Maybe not while it's still attached to your head though,' he says.

'Ideally not.' I don't push because he's being lovely and I don't want to bring up anything that might cause conflict and emotion in him. 'I feel I've been greedy too. Did you want to come in the bath? There is room. Now my hair is tied back.'

'Food comes in twenty-five minutes.'

'More than enough time then,' I say.

I watch as he takes off his hoodie and t-shirt in one fell swoop and then pulls off his trousers and underwear. I am impressed at the speed of action but I tilt my head to the side to admire his naked body, the line of his back down to his arse. He steps over the enamel and entwines his legs around mine, sitting opposite me. He smiles, putting a hand to my much warmer knee, our bodies submerged and entangled below the water line. A hand grazing the inside of my thigh. 'Top up?' he says, reaching for the bottle of wine. I nod, sitting up, meeting him halfway so he can kiss me tenderly on the lips.

'Thank you. For this,' I say.

'Never thank me. I don't think you'll ever understand how much you circled back into my life at just the right time, Kay.' There's maybe some hidden meaning there, but I know that at this point, being here with him feels good, right. 'But I've got an eye on that hoodie. Don't you even think about stealing it,' he says, laughing. I laugh back.

TWENTY-ONE

'Kay, look at the antlers, they are lovely,' Janey, the lady sitting at the reception desk, says.

'They jingle and everything,' I add, shaking my head from side to side.

She laughs. 'Then that is perfect.' She pushes the sign-in book in front of me, looking at my festive dress and red Doc Martens with glittery laces. Don't tell me I don't know how to make an effort. As this is one of the first events in my book drive, I wanted to pull out all the stops.

'People are very much looking forward to this book event, you know?' she tells me. 'Some of our residents get a little lost at this time of year.' It's probably the reason why I made this home my first port of call because I saw it with my own eyes last year when visiting Nana. It wasn't people who'd been abandoned per se but ones who missed out on the magic that led up to Christmas, because it should be a season, not simply a few days.

'I'm glad,' I say, trying to balance the boxes of books near the counter. I gaze up and around at this place. I love the effort they put in to make it look as colourful and homely as they can at Christmas, the fact that every colour is represented in their decorations, the fact none of it really matches. Behind the reception are bits of string holding cards up, tinsel around every door and window frame, and coloured lights flashing hypnotic patterns.

'Is it just you?' she asks.

'Oh, no. I've brought Santa,' I say.

She peers around me until she sees the door of the home open again and, in costume and holding two boxes of books expertly under his arms, in walks Santa himself. Janey stares up at me and then back to him. *Yes, I know. He looks more like an underwear model but work with me here.*

'Janey, this is Nick.'

She giggles. 'Well, I knew that already.'

'A pleasure, Janey,' he replies, and she adjusts herself in her seat.

'Where am I going with these?' he says, turning to me.

'Right down that corridor to the day room. It's signed, you can't miss it. I'll join you in a second,' I say.

He smiles back at me. Since Nick rescued me from that lay-by with his brother, I've leant into him offering me help with this book drive but with renewed reservations, now that I remember he's that idiot I spoke to on the phone when Nana had that massive Christmas tree delivered. I haven't said this to him, but it's certainly diluted any attraction I have for him. Anyway, today he picked me up from the library, dressed as Santa, and we drove over in his Christmas-tree van and I'm finding out many things about his driving habits. He changes the radio station when Christmas music comes on, he carries a healthy supply of gum and his truck is very clean. It's nothing like my beat-up old Renault 5, now to be scrapped because of a fatal oil leak. I think you can also tell a lot of things about a man from the way he drives and what I've learned from him is that he's not a speeder but doesn't take lightly to bad wazzocky drivers. He's sensible but will also wave at a child on a zebra crossing. I watch as Janey leans over the counter and follows his figure down the corridor. 'You do know where we are, right? Half our lot have pacemakers and are on all sorts of cocktails of drugs. They'll see him and pass out.'

'Or maybe he's exactly what they need to see to cheer them up,' I joke.

'Are you and him courting then?' she asks.

'No.'

'What's wrong with him?' she asks. 'He looks like the sort who'd get about.'

You know what, Janey? He very well could be, but I don't really know a lot about this bloke. I know parts of his family history, he's a bit serious, he's good at wrapping gifts and knows a lot about Christmas trees. We hang out together now, it would seem.

'You'd have to ask him yourself. He's just...' I'm not even sure I can call him a friend. At present, he feels like a seasonal acquaintance. '...Santa. I'll just pop up and fetch Nana. I'll come back for these books in a moment.'

She smiles broadly as I make my way to Nana's room on the second floor, treading through these familiar hallways of beige carpets and floral prints on the walls. This place will never really fill me with a sense of comfort, but it's bright, the staff have become familiar, and like the social bunny she is, Nana's always participating in bridge or karaoke night. As I approach her room, the door is ajar and I see her sitting up in her chair, watching *Loose Women*. As soon as she sees me through the door, she jumps up and shuffles over in her slippers to greet me.

'Oh, my Kitty Kay. Look at you, all Christmassy! How are you, lovely?' There is something about her arms wrapped around me that will always feel right. 'Have you grown or am I shrinking?'

'It's Christmas. With the amount of chocolate I'm eating, it's likely that I'm growing,' I joke.

She hits me playfully. 'Less of that, you're lovely looking. So Christmassy. I love it. Let me look at your face.'

She does this more and more now each time I visit, taking prolonged looks at my face, as if she's hoping it'll help her failing memory. 'Katherine Michelle Redman. Twenty-first of July,' she says.

'You are right,' I say, and she kisses me on the forehead. I go into my bag and get out some things for her that I always buy. She likes a gossip magazine, hand cream and those gummy foam sweets shaped as teeth and lips. Sometimes she gives them out to her mates who don't have teeth so they can sit around the day room and laugh. She goes around her room, straightening out things, her silvery-brown hair still tightly curled on her head, her glasses on a string around her neck, nestled in a lavender cardigan. 'These scones are from Helen,' I say, putting a Tupperware on her bedside table.

'Helen. Your mum was called Helen?' she says.

'Mum's called Diane, Nana. Your daughter-in-law, Diane? Helen is someone I work with,' I remind her. Her eyes look into mine, searching but completely lost, and I try and smile to reassure her. 'It's alright. You know Diane. She married your son, Fred.' She nods but I've lost her. And this is the bit that always hurts. It's a sign that she's not with me, I can see the frustration in her eyes and it floors me that I can't do anything to help her, I can't rebuild those memories as much as I can't fix this, any of it. 'Who are the flowers from?' I ask, nodding towards a vase by the window, trying to change the subject.

'Oh, that's Jim, one floor up. I think he's a bit sweet on me but he's a bit dim. When we play Scrabble, he's a four-letter-word man, maximum.' I marvel at what she does know, what she does remember. As long as she remembers me. 'You also need to explain that thing over there,' she says, pointing to a basket in the corner of the room. 'That arrived in reception last week, they all thought they got this place confused with Buckingham Palace.'

I look down at the Harrods hamper in the corner. After our little visit last week, Old Nick arranged to send this here as a gift for Nana. After his big gesture of the earrings, we walked around Harrods and Nick spent the hour buying things. Not that I asked for any of it but we went to the food hall and he filled a basket full of cookies and tins of tea and truffles, telling me it was all for family and friends, asking me for advice. Advice? I drink three types of tea: normal tea, Earl Grey when I feel posh and fruit tea that sits in the back of my cupboard. And then he said he'd send something to my nana. Harrods didn't do those teeth sweets apparently. Funny that.

'Who's Nick?' she asks, asking me to sit down on the edge of her bed. 'Kay and Nick, imagine my surprise to see a young man's name there on the gift card.'

I have been here in the weeks since I reconnected with Nick but I've not said a word, mainly because when we did break up the first-time round, Nana declared him a mortal enemy for life. 'Nana, do you remember when I was at university and I dated that boy...'

'Nick,' she says, his name dripping out of her mouth with disdain.

'Yeah, we bumped into each other again and we might be going out. Kind of.'

Nana stares into space. 'Was he the one with the earring like a pirate?'

'No.'

'Shorts in winter?'

'No.'

'*This white wine tastes like lighter fluid,*' she says.

I laugh. 'Yeah, that's the one.' I hadn't remembered that. Nick had come round for Sunday lunch at Nana's and had been snooty about the wine. Nana left the table and went to find a bottle of lighter fluid so Nick could make the comparison for himself.

'Explains Harrods then. He used to buy me flowers though. Is he still posh? Snooty?' she asks.

'I think he's mellowed a little. He's very generous, kind. We went ice skating. You'd have loved it. What's in the hamper?' I ask, not mentioning that we share baths now too.

'Oh, all sorts. That lovely lad, Milosh, who works in the kitchens here, I gave him some bits – the gourmet chutneys and nuts. And Ivy upstairs, I gave her the loose tea so she can do her readings.' I smirk to know everyone's futures in the building will be a lot posher. Nana takes my hand. 'I won't comment but is he nice to you? Are you happy, lovely?'

'I'm happy because I'm here with you.'

'That's a shit answer.'

'Nana!' I retort in shock.

'We're always happy when we're together,' she says, resting her head on my shoulder. I curl my body into hers. Am I happy? Who knows? At this moment, I want to snuggle up on her bed, read out trashy magazine articles together and then watch a bit of a TV show while she makes fun of everyone's clothes. That will always be my definition of happy. But Old Nick is showing me that he cares, and I feel looked after, and that is a good thing. A knock on the door suddenly gets our attention and we both glance up.

'Hi. Yeah, the woman at reception told me you'd be here. They're ready in the day room,' Nick says. 'They all thought I was a stripper. They all wanted to come and sit on my knee. I thought I'd best come and find you.'

I laugh as Nana leans into me. 'Kay, I'm not going completely doolally, right. That's Santa at the door, yeah?'

I nod. I don't think I have the energy to tell her how he fits into the story though. Four-foot-eleven Nana stands and looks up at six-foot Santa. 'You're a big fella, eh?'

I smirk and look down to the floor. 'Santa, this is my nana. Nana, this is Santa.'

Nick looks at me. 'Your grandmother.'

I nod. I wasn't entirely clear with him why we were coming to this particular nursing home, but he knows now.

'I know you,' Nana says. 'I'm sure I know you.' I see her searching through her memories, a pained expression on her face. I exhale because I don't want to confuse her any further.

I put an arm around her immediately. 'Nana, remember you got a Christmas tree delivered once to your house. That big one? This was the fella who delivered it.'

Nana seems relieved that her mind isn't playing tricks on her but Nick looks confused that I haven't mentioned this connection before now.

'Oh, that was a lovely tree. How are you, young man?' she says, her eyes sparkling.

'I'm very well...'

'How have you forgotten my name? I'm supposed to be the one with dementia. I'm Doris.' As soon as Nick hears that she has dementia, he looks over at me, studying my face. 'I guess I only remember the naughty ones. You're far too good.'

'Then you don't know me very well at all,' Nana says, cackling. 'How come you two know each other then? Did I miss something?'

'I went to his farm one day and got stuck choosing a tree and Nick helped me.'

Nick smirks to hear the word 'stuck'. But Nana looks at me for a moment. Yes, you heard that right. This is another Nick. She shifts her gaze between the both of us trying to work us out, a cheekier glint in her eye than I would like to see.

'Can I walk you over to the day room, Doris? It would be my pleasure,' Nick says, offering her an arm.

'A polite Santa too,' she says, her eyes widening at me. 'Can I offer you something to eat before we head over? I've got truffles from Harrods.'

Nick takes one look at the box and pulls a face. 'Oh, that's far too fancy for me. Save those for your important visitors. I see you've got those teeth sweets though. I'll take one of them.'

Nana leans over to her bedside table and opens a packet. 'Here you go.'

'Thank you kindly,' Nick says. He puts the teeth sweet in his mouth, then grins. 'Do you like my new veneers?'

I stay quiet and watch both of them laughing together. Nana does the same thing with her sweet.

'Did you get those in Turkey? They're beautiful,' Nick says. Still chuckling, Nana turns back to me. She just winked at me, didn't she?

TWENTY-TWO

'And that was the end of that story, as the sun set amber on the horizon and the sky shone as blue as it ever did,' Nick says, as he finishes the chapter of the book he's been reading out in this super-festive day room. I like the fact that Nick sits in a high wingback chair so it vaguely looks like a throne. He reads very well. There's good diction there, a wonderful tone to his voice. In another life, he could make a good living out of doing radio ads. 'He looked into my eyes, searching for a counterpoint to his own soul, to see if the sun could rise with me, for a lifetime.'

There's a small crowd of about thirty residents sitting here listening, and I swear we all sigh at the same time to hear him, his tone making us all swoon, even the men. I cock my head to one side at how he grins at that last line. *Who even are you?* He closes the book and then rubs his hand over the cover, almost as if he's thanking it. An old lady in the front row in a pink cardigan sits up, as though the magic of his words may have cured all of her ills. That said, the man next to her in his tartan slippers is asleep, but there was something about that reading that was a little bit magical. Nick glances over at me and smiles. Yeah, that's not allowed when you're dressed as Santa. This is plain wrong for him to transform himself into someone so alluring and attractive. I don't know what to do with the intensity of his look so I just put my thumbs up at him.

'Now take off your clothes!' someone shouts, and I sincerely hope it isn't my grandmother.

However, I am grateful that this means Nick isn't looking at me anymore. Instead, he puts his hands in the air to calm down the furore and blushes deeply. I don't get this new New Nick. It turns out that when he's around anyone aged sixty or above he transforms, and all his jolly spills out, he shares jokes, laughs and well, one of these ladies has him up and dancing, pressing herself up against him. He gives her a little twirl and everyone claps again. OK, calm down, Fred Astaire. I guess I should feel something – this is mildly endearing – but the fact is, *I* did this. I came into this room and set up all the books, I laid out mince pies and teacups and now I'm sitting here working the tea urn, watching as he gets all the limelight in his Santa suit and kindly flair. He is usually the most serious man I've ever met and now he's dipping a lady in slipper shoes. I take one of my mince pies, peel back the foil liner and take a confused crumbly bite.

'Where on earth did you find him?' Janey asks me, sipping on a mug of tea, not able to avert her gaze. He's done dancing now. We watch as he sits down at the day-room piano and starts playing. Of course. Now he's Elton John. Next he's going to show us he can do magic tricks and paint us a picture. A few start singing along, their arms linked as he conducts them in this makeshift singalong.

'At a Christmas-tree farm,' I mumble, noticing quite randomly that he has very good posture, the way his legs are slightly parted, the way the material of that costume clings to his thighs.

'You're funny,' she says.

Oh, she thought I was joking. 'No, seriously, he sells Christmas trees.'

We both look on as the man I thought was asleep suddenly sits up and impresses us with his vibrato.

'That might be why he was offering to replace our plastic trees.'

'Yeah, he likes a real piece of wood.'

'Don't we all, hun,' Janey says, sniggering. 'Well, this is the biggest crowd we've had in here for a while. Thank you again, it's lovely for them all to do something a bit different and get a gift too.'

I see a man across the way unwrap a beautiful leather-bound edition of *Moby Dick* and a warm expression creeps across his face as he perches his glasses on the bridge of his nose to fold open the first page. That's all I'm here for, that moment when someone opens a gift and there's a look of complete surprise, wonder and contentment that it's exactly what they need in that moment.

'You are very welcome,' I reply. 'While I have you here, can I ask about Nana? How's she been?'

Janey comes over to sit by me, turning her chair towards mine. It's one of the advantages of being here that they always keep me in the loop, that the care feels very personalised, full of kindness. 'She is a joy, full of laughs.' She pauses. 'She's had some bad days recently where her frustration peeks through, but we're keeping a check on that to gauge how it may be affecting her overall mood.'

I nod and smile, watching Nana over Janey's shoulder, tinsel wrapped around her head as she joins in a very animated version of 'Jingle Bells'. I didn't realise she could kick her leg that high but it tells me that she is surviving here, she's having fun, that despite my guilt and my worry, she is OK and there are people constantly looking out for her.

'Can I also just check, the last payments have been coming from Mr Redman but with top-up from yourself, is that right?' she asks. I nod, taking a deep breath. When we put Nana here, we knew that it would come at a cost but we've been bumbling through trying to make it work. I'll need to sell a few million more bear books, possibly rent out one of her bedrooms, to make this all work, but we will continue to keep her here. 'Then that's totally fine – I will adjust the receipts to match.'

'Oh... and I have a book for you too,' I say to Janey, digging through a box under the table. I hand over the package. 'One day I saw that you were reading Rebecca Yarros and these books are similar if you're into vampire kings – just beware, it's all a little kinky.'

She opens the book and grins, leaning over to give me a little hug. 'The kinkier the better, gets me through the night shifts,' she winks. 'Could I get a signed picture of Santa too? That would also help.'

'What would help?' a voice says from behind us.

My eyes widen to hear Nick standing there, wondering who's taken over at the piano because it still seems to be playing. Janey smirks quietly to herself. 'Alcohol. We should have done mulled wine. Helps them all sleep better too,' she says, shrugging her shoulders at me.

'I don't think many of them need the alcohol,' Nick comments, nodding at an old man with a walker who may be twerking.

'Yeah, he shouldn't do that. He's just had a new hip put in,' Janey says, scurrying over to intervene.

I can hear Nick laughing as she does. I can't bring myself to look at him because I have absolutely zero poker face. Him connecting with my nana and dancing around this place being nice to the elderly is a little confusing for me.

'I'll take a cup of tea if you're serving?' he says.

I turn around, trying to act surprised and deeply nonchalant that he's there, up close, some perfect embodiment of Santa. *Why does he smell so nice? Like freshly sawn wood and vanilla cookies.* 'I can do that...' I say, putting a teacup to the black nozzle of the urn. 'How do you take it?' As I say that, I think how it could sound vaguely sexual.

'Black, one sugar.'

'Black? You have your tea black?'

'Yes. I'm lactose intolerant.'

'Then how do you drink all the milk the kids leave out for you?' I ask, trying to focus on cups and saucers and also checking my reflection in the big shiny silver urn.

'I sometimes pour it down the sink,' he says.

'Santa, that's so bad.' For some reason my intonation changes when I say that. I'm standing by a tea urn, this is not the time to be remotely sexual and I don't think that way about him anyway. It's not allowed. I hand him his cup of tea and look into his eyes. 'There are also mince pies. I baked them myself.'

'You did?'

'No. I bought them in I'm afraid.'

'You should have said, we have great mince pies at the farm. Next time.'

Next time. I've agreed to all of this, haven't I? We're likely spending all this time together and we haven't really defined the parameters of our acquaintance yet. 'That would be lovely,' I say.

'You never mentioned that thing about your nana's Christmas tree. That we've spoken before on the phone?' he says, curious.

I smile to myself. 'You know what, I only worked it out myself a few days ago. When I was in your truck. Do you remember it?'

'Unfortunately no. Was I rude?' I nod that he's at least self-aware. 'I'm not a phone person,' he says. 'I'm sorry. I think I do remember your nana though. Cobbled mews address?'

'That's her. She's not someone you forget, my nana.'

I glance over at her fondly and I see his gaze following mine. 'Your grandmother has some stories about you,' he says, cradling his teacup in the palm of his hand.

'Is it the one where I saved all those cats from a storm drain?' I ask.

'You did that?'

'No.' I was just trying to sound brave and hilarious.

'She told me about how you once got your head stuck in the railings outside the chip shop and they managed to free you with a giant tub of frying oil.'

I now refuse to believe my grandmother has dementia. She's lying to us all. 'Her memory isn't what it used to be. She must be thinking of someone else,' I say.

He pauses for a moment, taking a sip of his tea. 'You should have said she was here,' he says.

I look up at him, struck by the concern and empathy in his

tone. I don't know what to say. Because to tell him about Nana would divulge something sad, which means this is more than just being casual acquaintances. It's the kind of thing you share with friends, people who mean something to you so they can lend you support, advice. And there are times when I don't want to talk about her, I don't want to face the truth that her being here means she is moving further away from me.

'I meant, so I could prepare, put on more aftershave. I could have brought her a gift,' he suggests, reading my pause.

'That makes it sound as if you want to chat up my nana and that's slightly inappropriate.'

He laughs and it softens that stony exterior I'm so used to, that deep throaty sound that he rarely engages in. He pauses to take another sip of tea. I see how he still avoids my mince pies though. 'By the way, you know those letters you found the other day in the library? I hope you don't mind but I did some digging, went on some community sites and put the feelers out to see if anyone recognised them.' Behind him people are still dancing and singing as he says this, one of them being my nana. She looks over intently at our interaction and smiles broadly. 'Because I read through all those letters and it's quite the story.'

'You read the letters? There were about fifty of them, you read them all?' I ask, surprised.

'I did.' I can still see Nana watching. Is she pulling smoochy faces? 'I'm enjoying the mystery of piecing together their love.' I turn to him as he says this, exhaling slowly. 'And if they've lost pieces of their story then I think it's nice for them to have them back, to have reminders of that love.' He holds my gaze as he says that, before turning back to glance at my nana and then back at me, his expression full of compassion. He read all those letters. He knows.

I cough to cover up my emotion. 'Any joy?'

'Not really. I'll let you know if anyone gets in touch. It would be nice for that story to have a happy ending.'

'We all love a happy ending,' I say, trying hard not to smirk. He doesn't even flinch.

'K and N,' he mutters.

'That's quite a coincidence, eh?' I say, trying to downplay it all. It's then he looks me straight in the eye, a gaze so steady and soft I feel the rest of the room slow down, quieten around me. 'Karen and... Neil,' I say, suddenly trying to break up the tension. 'Or Kevin and Nigel. We have made assumptions. Maybe they're both men.'

'K is definitely a woman,' he says. 'N describes parts of her intimately that tells me she's a woman.'

'Oh.' I fidget in my seat, trying to not catch his eye.

'Or who knows? He could be a Nick,' he says. 'Maybe there's a second Nick out there.' And I'm suddenly snapped into the room. That's the problem. There already is.

TWENTY-THREE

'I feel like I'm in a cage and people are watching me eat,' I say to Old Nick as I peer out of this igloo on to the water, passers-by looking over curiously from the docks.

'They're just focused on me, don't worry,' he says, smiling and giving a regal wave to the people looking on.

I giggle and he reaches under the table to hold my hand, kissing my shoulder and cuddling me in close. This is the problem with this Nick, it's how he pulls me in with big romantic gestures like these. *Let's go for dinner*, he said. *Something on the water*. So we walked down to Canary Wharf and I thought we were going to get tacos but suddenly we were on a floating igloo, decorated in fairy lights, a cute ceramic fondue pot at the centre of the table. It's romance, and let's be frank, it's super cheesy.

'I don't really know what's driving this?' I ask him, looking around at the plastic roof. Even though there's a soundtrack of jingly Christmas music playing, it's hard to not also hear the lashing of the water off the sides of this fancy dinghy we're on.

'I think they're remote controlled so we won't float out to sea,' he reassures me.

'That would be a great story though. Remember that time we ended up in the North Sea in that blow-up boat.'

'We had to make the fondue last for days...' he says. I laugh. Possibly a little too loudly as we're in an enclosed space, but deep down, I know I do this out of guilt too. Here's Nick who is not just taking me out to dinner and a movie. He's thinking about our dates, he's really spoiling me, looking after me, treating me to all that this glorious city can offer. It's luxury I've never experienced and all of it is completely enthralling, such a special gift in a way. However, two days ago, I also spent an afternoon with Santa Nick and I can't help but think he slowly revealed himself to me in ways that he hadn't done before. Not like that. I still have only ever seen him clothed, but there was the way he instantly connected with my nana, his ability to charm his way around that room was endearing, his empathy completely floored me. But I have to turn away. It's the right thing to do. Because he's a man who I do book stuff with, we don't even hug or shake hands, and right in front of me is a man in a floating boat investing time and energy into me, into us. I have to give this Nick a chance.

I tuck my hair behind my ear. 'I'm wearing the earrings by the way,' I say, showing them off and he beams, putting a hand to my cheek. Maybe this too is the difference between the Nicks. The natural way with which he comes in to touch me, the intimacy we've shared since we met where there's been no hesitation. We know each other, we search each other out physically when we're together. I know this man. In a world of relationship labels, all I know is that being here with him feels right.

'God, your hand is frozen...' I say as I put my hand over it.

'I didn't plan. Stupid me to think they'd have a log fire on a rubber boat,' he jokes.

I slide in closer to him and place my blanket over him. 'They also gave us hot-water bottles,' I say, handing him one.

'And nothing screams sexy like a hot-water bottle down the pants,' he jokes, his bottom jaw chattering. 'Remember that date I took you on and I got hypothermia.'

'You grew icicles off your hair, all Leo in *Titanic*.'

'Didn't the boat sink in that one?' he says, winding his arms through mine.

'Yeah, the difference is if we sink I reckon I can breaststroke it to a ladder over there. I reckon I could also save the fondue.'

'And not me...?' he says.

'Women and fondue first.'

His laughter is everything but I like the way it makes him feel more connected to me as he scooches in close, trying to extract all my bodily warmth. It's possibly not the candlelit glowing romantic moment he envisaged but there is something special about being able to look up to the stars and enjoy being in each other's company.

'You mentioned you saw your nana,' he says, as we continue to look skyward. 'Did she enjoy the hamper?'

I won't tell him she gifted the posh tea to the nursing-home medium. 'She did.' I sit there for a second wondering what else to say. She's poorly, Nick. Her mind meanders and can't find the memories and my biggest fear is that she'll forget the love I feel for her, that her light will diminish so quickly and so catastrophically that it may consume me. But I don't want to share it at this time, I'm not sure why. 'It was very kind of you and generous.'

'Well, we all deserve treats this time of year. I'm glad.'

His eyes return to the earrings, getting out his phone. 'I knew they'd suit you. Come, we should get a selfie, maybe?'

'OK?' I say, half reluctantly but also a little surprised that he would want to do something to record the occasion so publicly. This is what couples do, I guess. I get into the frame and pose, watching as he adds it to his Instagram story. '*Date night x*' reads the caption. I smile.

'Also, I think we should talk about the earrings too,' he says, nudging me, jokingly. Instinctively, we both know what he's talking about. After the very grand gesture of Santa gifting me that little box, and assuming he was assisting a proposal, neither of us talked about it. We continued to shop, we had the most incredible sushi, we went back to his flat, we had sex. We've even shared a bath together and it wasn't discussed. We didn't talk about that little moment at all. 'I didn't bring it up last time because... well, we were trying to thaw you out but just to check, were you expecting a—'

'No,' I say, cutting him off instantly. 'Dude, it's literally been weeks. I wasn't even expecting the whole Santa thing. I was not expecting a...' We laugh as neither of us can even say the word. It was a twist of fate that brought us back together and our time together has been unexpected, but it's far too early to project into the future yet. 'I mean, when we spoke at the ice rink, you did talk about our kids, so I was a little unsure,' I joke.

He chuckles softly. 'I'll take that. But... if we were to talk about this, what it is, where we're going?'

I look into his eyes. I think they're reading hopeful and it pains me to say anything he might not want to hear on open water.

'Headed towards the Thames?' I joke. He reaches down below the blanket and grabs my hand. 'Fun, I think we're having fun.'

'Fun,' he says deliberately.

'Did you want honesty?' I ask.

'Always,' he says, arranging the blanket over both of us.

'Maybe I am being cautious because I don't know what this is. A chance to go down memory lane or is it a second chance at being you and me again?' He nods, a look telling me he doesn't quite know either. 'The sex is good?'

He bursts out laughing. 'It is pretty good.'

'Pretty...?' I ask.

'No, you're pretty. You always were.'

'I'll take that compliment, kind sir,' I say, beaming. 'So maybe I am holding back from defining us or taking us too far into the future because I don't want to get hurt like the first time,' I say. I hope he reads the sincerity in that because there is truth there, there is uncertainty because of how it finished the first time. I mean, there is also another Nick but I won't bring that up now.

'I appreciate the honesty,' Nick says dolefully. 'And I am sorry that I ever hurt you, I really am. Like I say, I was young.'

'We were young,' I remind him. 'You were kind of a first love.'

He looks a bit surprised at the revelation. 'So I'm one of your all-time great loves then?' he asks, smiling.

'You are... something.'

'Something.' He says that word slowly, tenderly, still in that flirtatious manner that I've become accustomed to. And there is something there, I feel it now. That energy between us that's heady and addictive and he leans over to kiss me tenderly. Did we resolve or define anything? Not really, but this is fun. With the blanket covering us though, Nick has other ideas of what that fun could look like. A hand that was on my thigh moves around the curve of my legs, fighting with the layers of my coat until he gets to the waistband of my trousers. He stops kissing me to hold my gaze.

'You forget this boat is see-through...' I whisper as his fingertips brush my stomach.

'The blanket isn't though,' he says, softly into my ear. 'Plus my hands are very cold.'

'That's what the hot-water bottle is for...' I say, kissing him swiftly on the lips again.

'Go on, it's Christmas...' he says, his lips searching out my neck. I look around. There are other boats bobbing about, the odd person on the wharf and docks. 'I mean, this is fun. Giving you an orgasm right here, right now, could be very, very fun,' he whispers.

I bite my lip and don't stop him as his fingers reach over and under my waistband, sliding down under my knickers. The feeling is insanely electric as he looks me in the eye, my breath quickening to feel the softness of the contact, our faces barely touching. He was always good at this, even at university I was thankful someone had trained him up for me. No notes. 'Do you like that?'

'Uh-huh,' I say, trying to summon up the words.

'Tell me what you want,' he whispers.

My mind wanders, smiling – whilst we're still on the boat? People can see us, can't they? But what he's doing feels incredibly good and I crave him, a stirring delicious feeling soars through me. I want... But as I dare to say it, the boat jolts to a stop and a curtain is unzipped. Have we floated back to shore? To the docks? Shit. Does this thing have CCTV? I look around, and a man stands there in a woolly hat and fleece and looks at us both cosied up underneath that blanket.

'Howdy folks... and welcome back to dry land. How was your ride?' He knows, doesn't he? It must be written all over the blush in my cheeks. Nick moves his fingers and I let out a little squeal.

'Sooo festive and it's lovely to be out on the water...' I say, gesturing out towards the wharf in case he didn't know there was water out there.

'You're lucky. Rained yesterday, proper wet one.'

Nick chokes on his own laughter and the man looks at him strangely. 'Well, we'll leave you docked here to finish your fondue. Let us know if you want any more wine,' he says before walking away.

'You need to finish your fondue?' Nick whispers.

'Is that what the kids are calling it these days?' I reply, before both of us descend into giggles, leaning back into our seats, his eyes full of joy and his face creasing with laughter, changing into a shape that I definitely, most certainly remember.

TWENTY-FOUR

'So France is a yes which is amazing because the French are a difficult market. They want to change the titles about so we're playing with rhymes but... You know what? No. I don't want to talk about book shite, tell me about this Nick boy.'

I love how Davinia has pretended to call me and talk about my career as a children's author when really all she has done is see a glimmer of a picture on an Instagram story and has rung to investigate.

'It was a date.' Where he fingered me next to a fondue, but I might leave that bit out for purposes of decency and to spin this into more of the romantic story that she's expecting. I feel a little hot under the collar to remember it though, the urgency of the moment, the way we left that boat and kissed so passionately in the foyer of his building, in the lift, outside his front door, and translated that energy so perfectly into the sex that both of us were seeking.

'I need more than that...' she says.

'He's someone I dated at university and we've since reconnected and we're having fun. That's what you told me to do, yes?'

'I did,' she says, and I hear her satisfied smile on the other end of the phone. 'I do like it when my clients listen to me. I'm full of excellent advice. Am I thinking it's too soon to buy a hat?'

'Yes. God.' Because Davinia, you don't know the half of this story. It's somewhere between a fling and a dalliance with the past. All at once, I can get wrapped up in it and it makes me giggly and curious to see where it could go, what it could be, but then I'm taking this phone call standing outside the house of a man I've also been spending a lot of time with. And get this, Davinia – they're both called Nick. Is there a children's book in this? *That's Not My Nick*? It could be one of those pull and reveal books – which one will she choose? 'But thank you for that reminder that I needed to put myself out there. Turns out the universe did have plans.'

I hear her clapping on the end of the line and it's amusing to sense her excitement. 'It's fucking Christmas is what it is. All that love glows in the air this time of year. I'm so happy. But yes, France is a go, and deadlines? Are we still on for those first weeks in January?'

In fact my social life has suddenly ramped up so that might be a no, but how do I tell her? 'Of course.'

'And I want updates. Not blurry photos on Instagram that mean I have to call you up to find out what's happening. Please. Promise?'

'Promise.'

'Bye, lovely girl.'

She hangs up and I stand underneath a tree, pulling my winter coat around me. Does Facebook still let you update your relationship status? Because my God, it is so complicated. I do like Old Nick, very much, but New Nick pops up in my thoughts every so often. I guess my worry, therefore, is whether there's an honest thread running through any of this and it all makes me a little nervous.

I'm here today to map out the rest of the book-drive schedule with Nick now that I don't have a car and he's going to be taxiing me around in his van. We could have done this on the phone, I feel, but he insisted I come round. I think back to what Lucy said. He lives at home so I may meet family, I may have to interact with other people. Is it also strange that I'm preoccupied with what he may be wearing? What does New Nick wear at home when he's relaxing? Pyjamas? If it's a onesie, I will laugh. I head down the garden path to this house, a three-floored terrace in a leafy suburb of St Margarets, terracotta tiles on the porch and, naturally, two potted Christmas trees flanking the door, lit up and sparkling. I ring the doorbell before stepping back. Maybe I should insist we do this by text to avoid any embarrassment. Or perhaps I can... The door opens and I look at an empty space in front of me before looking down.

'Hi!' The little girl in front of me has a big bush of curly brown hair and is wearing Christmas-tree pyjamas.

'Hi! I'm... is this where Nick lives?' I ask her.

'UNCLE NICK!' she squeals, still not taking her gaze away from me. 'UNCLE NIIIIIICCCCCKKK!'

There's a banging of doors as a familiar figure appears in the hallway. I smile because this is not what I imagined Nick to be wearing at home. He's in a black t-shirt with jeans, but he also has a superhero cape on and a pair of cat ears on his head. He quickly removes the ears when he sees me and puts a hand through his hair. He looks at his watch. 'Monkeys, I didn't see the time. You're here.'

'I am,' I say, still hovering on the porch, smirking at the way he said monkeys to hide his swearing.

'Are you moving in?' he asks plainly, looking at the wheeled suitcase behind me.

'I also wanted to drop off some books. I've been busy wrapping these ones at home. I took the bus.'

'Oh. Yeah, I forgot you didn't have your car. You should have got an Uber,' he says, as if I'm a little stupid.

'I like the bus.'

'I like the bus too,' the little girl says, and I am glad to have a public transport ally.

'Can I leave them here?'

'I guess,' he replies.

The little girl looks at the interaction between us curiously. He takes the suitcase from me and our hands graze for a second. I can also see he has a fetching glitter candy cane tattoo on his lower forearm. I smile but don't quite know what to say next. This is weird, isn't it? I notice that the little girl winds her way around her uncle's legs expecting a formal introduction. Maybe she'll help me make this less awkward. I bend down and put out a hand for her to shake. She giggles at the formality. 'I'm Kay, by the way... it's lovely to meet you.'

'I'm Sofia.'

'Like Sofia the First?'

She curtseys to confirm as much. I bow to be in the presence of royalty. 'I love your hair,' she says, and instinctively reaches out to touch it. 'It looks like pasta.'

'Pasta covered in tomato sauce, maybe?'

I love how cheeky and infectious her giggle is. I look up and clock Nick staring down at us. 'Do you like pizza?' she asks and takes me by the hand into the house.

I glance at Nick, who's smiling and shrugs his shoulders. 'Seeing as you're here... you're very welcome to have pizza with us if you want.'

Well, I am here and maybe this is the polite thing to do, especially when Nick has been so generous with his time in the last few weeks. Sofia clings on tightly to me and leads me down the hallway of the house, lined with family photos and all those little idiosyncrasies that make a house a home: jackets piled on bannisters, shoes thrown off by the stairs, pots of keys and scrapes and bumps that show you a family lives here. Sofia leads me through a door and it's a strange thing, I don't think I expected this at all. In this very large kitchen with a huge range cooker to the side and a Christmas tree (naturally) by the bay window, there seems to be a pizza-cooking workshop solely manned by children. I count five heads altogether and they all turn to look at me as we enter the room, Sofia's hand still firmly in mine.

'Hi!' I announce, looking at everyone in turn.

'Everyone, this is Kay. She's here to discuss a few things. Be nice, please,' Nick says in surly tones, but it's funny, the kids almost laugh at him for it, the teen girl at the counter mimicking him.

'Didn't you come to the farm once?' a teenage lad asks me, and I recognise him as the grumpy elf from the first time I visited. I put a hand up to wave.

'That's Nate. You've met Sofia and this is Zita, George and Evie.' I wave at Evie who looks up at me from a baby walker. Zita leans against the counter with a rolling pin; an older teen, she looks at Nate with her eyebrows raised, grinning. George, meanwhile, is about eight and has a face full of pizza. I'm not sure he's registered I'm in the room. Out of the corner of my eye, I see Nick warning Zita not to say a word to embarrass him, also trying to remove the superhero cape from his shoulders and struggling with the fastening.

'Hi Kay!' she says, grinning. 'Are you the book lady?'

'If that's the name that I've been given then yes, I am the book lady,' I say curiously, wondering how my name weaved its way into conversations in this kitchen. I take in the half-eaten/made pizzas on the counter and a light dusting of flour that seems to cover all the countertops and tables. It's a mess but one that shows fun has been had by all. I notice a pizza crust sticking out of Evie's clenched fist. 'I didn't mean to interrupt your dinner or whatever sort of pizza party this is.'

'You're not interrupting,' Zita says. 'Stay. Uncle Nick, get her a drink. You're a terrible host,' she jests. He slides her a look again and I grin to see him being told what to do by a teenage girl. 'I'll just have a water,' I say.

Zita watches him as he moves around the kitchen quietly. 'So what are you two discussing?'

'You don't have to answer her questions!' Nick shouts, getting a clean glass out of the dishwasher.

'It's fine. I'm here to discuss a book drive with your uncle. He's helping me.'

'Of course he is,' Zita jokes, and I hear Nick slam a cupboard door, glaring at her. I smirk to see his niece try and wind him up.

'So you are all... family?' I ask, trying to diffuse the tension.

Zita nods. 'Mine and Sof's dad is Noah. I think you met him the other day. But we're a small selection of the nephews and nieces in the family,' she explains.

'Selection?' I ask.

'Normally there are seven of us.'

For some reason, I let out a little chuckle when she says this. *Oh, she was being serious.* 'And you all live in this house?' I ask.

'Nah. It's just an Uncle Nick day. He picks up the little ones from childcare and school and then he lets us all hang here until our parents can come get us.'

I pause as she says this. *Don't think about that too much, Kay.* But it's almost like trying not to look into the sun. Nick has a day dedicated to him where he looks after all these kids like some sort of professional manny. I watch him go over to baby Evie, pull a face and kiss the top of her silky baby head. *I didn't see that, that had no effect on me whatsoever.*

Zita pulls out some dough and tops it with tomato sauce from a pan. 'Sofia, you want olives?'

'Yes please,' she says. I look down and see Sofia still gazing up at me. She pulls me over to a table to sit down. She watches me as I unravel my scarf from my neck and take off my coat. 'Do you like olives?' she asks me.

'I love olives.'

'Then I like you. You can share my pizza.' I like how her standards are so low. 'What have you asked Santa for, for Christmas?' she asks me.

'Strangely enough, olives. Hundreds of them.'

She giggles. 'Do you want a glitter tattoo? I have a whole box of Christmas ones. You can choose which one you want.'

'Then I don't see how I can say no. What do you have?'

A glass of water appears in front of me on this large wooden dining table. 'She says this as if she has a catalogue but really she only has candy canes,' Nick says, coming to sit down.

'Then you can match Uncle Nick!' she cheers. I notice the teens at the kitchen counter trying to hold in their giggles.

'Also, she says that like *she's* going to apply it, but really I am the tattoo artist here so I will have to do all the work,' Nick continues. He sticks his tongue out at her, but it does little to change this girl's affection for him. She comes and climbs on to his lap. I see why he's so good with kids now, the man has had practice. But it's seasoned practice – not something that has come out of obligation but love for all these little people in his family that he obviously holds dear. Sofia adjusts herself on his lap and rests her head in the warmth of his chest.

'You don't have to do this. In case you need to preserve your arms for anything else. A tattoo is a serious commitment,' he says dryly.

I shake my head. 'No, please do proceed. I have given this a lot of thought.' I put my arm down on the kitchen table.

'Turn it over so it's in the same place as Uncle Nick's,' Sofia directs me.

'Sof, big old bossy boots,' he says, but that makes her giggle all the more sweetly.

He runs three fingers along my forearm, almost stroking the skin and I try to distract myself by smiling at the child in his lap. He places a sticker on my arm, pressing it down and then using a damp sponge to wet the paper, holding it there to soak it through. Is his hand shaking? I hope not. No one likes a nervous tattoo artist.

'I'll time it,' Sofia says, looking at the stopwatch on a phone on the table.

'So is this your first tattoo, madam?' he asks, as we wait and I smile. He's trying to joke again. Maybe he took his time to thaw with me. He's at home here and I get to watch him in a habitat where he is so loved and feels comfortable; I am seeing him in another light. Damn that light. His hand still rests on mine as we both try to ignore the contact. Is this also intense for him? Why am I sweating around the collar of my t-shirt?

'I actually have a tattoo that I got done when I was travelling,' I say.

'I've never noticed it before?' he says.

I blush a little. 'It's because it's above my hip bone.' He widens his eyes. 'It's a dolphin.'

'I LOVE DOLPHINS!' Sofia squeals, and I'm grateful she broke up that slightly awkward moment.

'So I was looking at the schedule for the book drive. You're a bit mad, eh?' he says, changing the subject and reaching over to get one of my flyers that he's scribbled things on.

'I prefer the term "ambitious",' I say. 'If it's too big a favour to ask for transport then please say so.'

'I didn't say that. But were you really going to do this all on your own?' he asks me thoughtfully.

'Back when I had a working car maybe, but a grumpy man in a truck in the rain told me I might need to take on some help.'

I hear Zita laughing from her countertop. 'I like this one, Uncle Nick. He's very grumpy, all the time.'

'Zita...' Nick mutters moodily.

'It's a busy time on the farm. The twentieth, I can only make the morning... we'd need to do two deliveries on the twenty-second. But I can make myself available for everything. I've ensured the vehicles are available and rearranged a few things.'

'Really?' I say, mildly surprised.

He looks up at me, his green eyes earnest, searching. 'Yeah. I'd do it for—'

'The good of the book drive...' I say abruptly, interrupting him.

He chuckles under his breath. 'Of course.' He looks down at my arm.

'Well, what do you think, Sofia?' I ask her. 'Is it ready?'

She nods and Nick slowly peels back the paper to reveal a pretty red and pink candy cane with a green bow on my arm. 'Get yours out, Uncle Nick.'

I can hear Zita and Nate laughing from the other side of the kitchen but Nick puts his arm next to mine and we glance at each other for a moment, grinning. Look at us, matchy matchy.

'Is the lady happy with her tattoo today? If you are, make sure you leave us a good review on Yelp.'

'Most certainly. Thank you... and to you Sofia for the artistic direction.'

She smiles then turns and shouts across the kitchen. 'IS MY PIZZA READY?'

'Man, you are bossy. Come on then,' Zita says, and Sofia jumps off her uncle's lap.

'I'm sorry,' Nick says. 'It's bedlam here sometimes. You didn't have to come in and stay for pizza. Sorry about the twenty questions. I don't often have friends visiting.'

'You're telling me you have no friends?' I joke.

'None that are...' He puts a hand out, pointing to me.

'Book ladies,' I joke. And I snicker and blush and look at him curiously because I see those teens nudging each other in the chest so I suppose I have come up in conversation. They know about me. But what do they know? Is it because I'm a novelty in this house or because Nick has said something to them, about me specifically?

'You may need to leave before my mum and sister get here though. You think this lot are bad.'

'I heard that, Uncle Nick. Don't worry – I texted Aunty Nell already. She's on her way,' Zita shouts across the kitchen.

'They're an excitable bunch. Sorry. You are very welcome to take that pizza to go if you want. I won't be offended.'

Is he embarrassed by all of this? Does the cape, the fact he kisses babies and the sheer bedlam of the scene change my opinion of him? Surely that can only be for the better. 'Don't apologise for your family,' I say, watching baby Evie whizz around the kitchen. 'This is all very...' Don't say cute and wholesome. Don't say homely and warming. But there is something wonderful about a house full of people, full of life and love, and it hits me somewhere in my heart, because I don't have this. I'm an only child and I'll go back to a dark, cold maisonette after this that belonged to a family member that I'm slowly losing. So to be in the midst of all this love and noise and festivity in abundance is joyful, a huge hug for the soul. I look through to a large living and dining space. 'Do you seriously have a tree in every room?'

'Have we not met before?' he jokes.

I laugh, watching Nate nudge his niece in the ribs.

'I have pizza! Merry Christmas,' Sofia says. She returns carrying a plate very carefully towards the table. A plate with a pizza that has all the olives shaped in a heart. Nick turns around staring daggers at his niece whilst I take a piece.

'This is the best gift ever,' I say to little Sofia and she stares at me with tomato sauce all over her face, giggling.

TWENTY-FIVE

There is nothing London does better than theatre. In the West End, theatre is still an event, it feels grand, the ultimate escapism. This is most true at Christmas when you walk along the pavements, skipping across puddles that mirror the glow of the lights, with everyone wrapped up in wool coats, leaping up stone steps to buildings lined with pillars, foyers decked in dark wood, red velvet, glass and a soothing amber glow. There's a lady there with a giant fur muff. You don't see muffs anymore, I laugh to myself quietly, as I wait near the box office, watching the crowd.

A family walk past, the youngest daughter with brown uncontrollable curly hair, and I'm reminded of New Nick's little niece, Sofia. I only stayed for an hour at Nick's house that evening when I dropped in the books. I think Nick was desperate to get rid of me before the big guns came home to interrogate me. It was an hour of bedlam and very tasty pizza, and it grounded Nick. It showed me the messiness of his life, I could start to join the dots about where he belongs, who he loves in his life and how that love makes him the person that he is. It meant I came away from that house supremely confused about what I felt for him.

'I'm always late, I'm so sorry.'

I jolt back into the moment as I feel an arm go into my coat and around my waist and the familiar touch of Old Nick coming to hug me and give me a kiss on the cheek.

'You're not late. I was early. I wanted to just hang out here and soak up the atmosphere,' I say, looking up at the corniced ceiling, the people in velvet waistcoats in the concessions stands, trying to block any other men called Nick out of my mind.

'You look amazing as usual,' he remarks, looking me up and down and taking in my cocktail dress and long black wool coat. The tenderness of his touch and gaze makes me smile. I think that might be one of the things I like about our dates. Back at university, we had dates that involved Pizza Hut buffets and cheap cinema tickets, but now we're on these big romantic dates that are incredibly mature, that involve little black dresses, white linen tablecloths and wine lists. I'd never looked at a wine list before. I thought I was still at the age where I went for mid-list every time.

'So do you.' Old Nick in a suit will always be such a surprise to me, the way he carries it, and how it's miles away from the boy I once knew. 'We are super early though, yes?' I say, looking at my watch.

'Because we're having cocktails first,' he informs me.

This is what I mean by grown up. I don't remember a cocktails element to our dates unless they were cheap rum and Cokes in The White Hart. I let him take me by the hand as he walks me over to a lift. How does he know about all of these places? How does everything feel so effortless around him? There's the way he tells us we're having drinks, the command in his voice which is hugely arousing. He stands next to me in this lift with its brass fittings and checkerboard floor and reaches for my hand.

'I don't think we're in The White Hart anymore, Toto,' I mutter.

'That's a popular culture reference I actually got,' he snickers.

'Thank God. If you hadn't got that one, I'd have been forced to end this,' I say. He turns to me and sticks his tongue out. There's a ping as the lift reaches its destination and the doors open. I thought I was done with being shocked but it's pretty incredible to see this little whimsical bar stashed away on top of this theatre. It's flooded with fairy lights and greenery, like a conservatory where tables hide amongst the plants, where everyone sits in their little corners tucked away from the rest of the world. Outside, a gorgeous candlelit balcony overlooks Covent Garden – the place where we found each other again.

'I thought it best to go back to the scene of the crime,' he says.

'That would infer that something bad happened that day,' I say, as we wind around people to find a table.

'Define bad,' he says, putting a hand to my lower back. We find a corner table, a church candle to the centre, backlit by ivy and lights.

'Oh, I was very good, I was just trying to buy a teapot,' I jest.

There's a hugely flirtatious nature to our relationship since the igloo boat incident where everything got a bit steamy on the water. The texts, the emojis have gone a bit X-rated, not that I have minded one bit, but sometimes it feels nice to also slow things down, to have a conversation and get to know each other again properly. So this evening feels perfect, it's got a lovely old-fash-ioned romantic twist to it.

'Drinks for you, sir… madam?'

'Tom Collins for me and a Bramble for the lady.'

He ordered for me but I don't seem to mind. He knows what I want. I now just have high expectations for something garnished with fruit, aromatics and a paper straw. I look around adjusting myself in my chair, taking off my coat and noticing him watching my every move. I can't help but marvel at the attention. The lights are low, the music is jazzy and we're surrounded by similar couples, all infusing the collective dreamy atmosphere. I see a young couple on a table near us, barely touching, sitting awkwardly opposite each other. I ask Nick to follow my eyes.

'First date?' I mumble. 'He went big, possibly too big. She'd have been happy with the IMAX and a Five Guys.'

Nick looks over, smiling. 'Yeah, he over-egged it and went and booked the ballet trying to impress her. He had to borrow a suit off his dad,' he suggests. 'He knows nothing about ballet except he once wore a tutu at a stag do.'

'She did ballet classes until she was nine. She got wedgies from the leotards.'

His smile broadens into laughter. Our eyes glance to the next table over where a man has ordered champagne in a silver bucket. 'That's either an early Christmas gift or...'

'He's shagging his secretary and is trying to make it up to the wife.'

The synchronicity in how we finish each other's sentences is strangely arousing and makes me lean into the table. This is the sort of conversation that might keep me in this. An older couple sit at the bar and toast each other. 'They go to the ballet every year, a non-negotiable. A little Christmas tradition...' Nick goes strangely quiet at that point, looking at them dolefully. 'And their names are...'

'Tom Collins and a Bramble?' Not the names I'd have chosen for that couple but the waitress arrived just in time. I was also right about the drinks in this place. Mine is half-crushed ice and a mint plant sprouting out the top. She puts the glasses down and Nick raises his to clink against the side of mine. 'To us.'

It's a simple toast but one that makes me smile. Did the older couple at the bar prompt this sentiment? Either way, it feels apt to toast us, a version of us that could exist in the future. 'What do you think people say about us then?'

'Obviously, we are stunning and people are hugely jealous of the chemistry,' he jokes.

'Obviously. They adore your tailoring.'

'And I reckon people can see the history, the story. I like that we have a story.'

And I understand what he means completely. He reaches over to hold my hand and rubs a thumb over my knuckles affectionately.

'Nick?' I am snapped out of our moment by a blonde lady standing beside us, a glass of red wine in her hand. 'What are you...' She swings around to look at me and I see poker-straight blonde hair, blue eyes and a way her lips curl to a disapproving pout. She's in an olive backless dress which shows me she's not wearing a bra. I get no warmth from her; it's a cold front with super-frosty edges. I know her but I can't think how. Nick's demeanour changes to see her too and he moves his hand away from mine and sits up straighter in his seat. He's gone from casual and flirty to rigid, a snarky look to his eyes that I can't quite read.

'Oh, hi... yeah, we're here to watch the ballet.'

'The ballet? Seriously?' the lady says, one eyebrow raised.

So she knows him. Ouch. Is this an ex? To find out I'd have to ask or get out my phone to do some side-by-side comparisons with old Facebook photos but that might not go down well.

'Why not? This is Kay. Kay, this is Neve.'

I know that name, I really do know that name. This is an ex. This is an ex from New York because I've seen a photo of them on top of the Empire State Building. *You have really good hair.* Don't say that out loud. She looks at me but doesn't seem to want to engage in pleasantries. I will assume that Nick dumped her on account of her lack of manners then. She's judging, I can feel that gaze scanning my face, looking for zits, warts, an extra nostril, anything that can place me beneath her, and for that, I hate her immediately. *I hope that wine stains your teeth and you don't find out all evening so in all your photos, it looks like you've been sucking off a Smurf.*

'It's good to meet you,' I say, not really sure why I'm lying or feeling so angry. She nods back at me and her lack of etiquette immediately riles Nick. I'm secretly pleased he's so defensive of me in this moment.

'Well, enjoy. If I don't see you before, have a good Christmas,' Nick replies, not quite smiling. She doesn't reply. She just gives a slight shake of the head and walks away. I can't hide the look on my face as she does so. I see Nick turn to watch her go, then he turns back to me. 'Absolute bitch.' He takes a long sip of his drink and looks over his shoulder again.

'Am I allowed to ask?' I mutter.

'An ex.'

'I thought she might be. She's…'

'So far up her own sphincter, she can breathe out her own mouth?' he says.

'I was going to say a bit Grinchy, but that also works,' I say, trying to lighten the mood and then I see Nick's face relax, and he laughs loudly, enough for a few people to look up. Loud enough that someone at the end of the bar might be able to hear. I know his game. *Oh my, is she scrunchie lady?* Because that computes in a big way. There's a story there, right? That would have been a long relationship, something that travelled miles and obviously didn't work out, but this is not the right time to fish for details and kill the mood.

He sits, still slightly pensive. 'Do you believe in fate, Kay?' Nick asks me, stroking the side of his glass.

'I believe the universe has a plan,' I say. 'I think it's funny we met, broke up and reunited at Christmas. The timing is pretty impressive.'

'I've been starting to think that. Perhaps we were reunited for a reason.' He smiles broadly. 'Plus, Christmas seems to be the common theme here. That means we'd have to give our kids festive names.'

'You and the kids, stop it already. I'm not even ovulating,' I joke.

'Holly and Ivy.'

'Mariah and Rudolph.'

Again, he roars with laughter. 'That would be cruel.'

'But funny.'

'And this is what this is, right? Fun?' He looks down for a moment at my arm. 'Is that a… tattoo?'

I stare down at the candy cane tattoo on my arm that after a few showers still remains on my skin. We'll blame the six-year-old creative director for that one. 'It was a library thing, I joined in with the kids,' I explain, immediately feeling guilty for lying.

He chortles almost in disbelief. 'Fun.'

And there's that word again. This is fun. But sometimes we veer into this being more than that, and that's when I find I can't read him. *What happened with the frosty blonde, Nick? Why did it not work? Where is this going? Why do you keep the scrunchie?* And for a moment, I don't see present-day Nick in his suit, I see a boy I spent a year with in Bath, a boy I fell desperately in love with. A love that didn't exist in these fancy clothes and surroundings. Someone who used to wait outside my lecture theatre with a doughnut in a white paper bag. It was summer spent in the park, lying on the grass sharing headphones and getting slightly pink tans. Eight years ago, eight years apart. Could this be revived into a long-term thing?

'Fun, always.'

TWENTY-SIX

'Lola! Have you seen the Santa? It's not that caretaker man, it's some fit bloke! Come see!'

I should have thought this pitstop through. Griffin Road Comprehensive. Maybe I should have gone for a primary school, but, somewhere in my bleeding heart, I thought it might be nice to try and promote reading in teenagers. In my mind, I put a book in the hands of a fourteen-year-old kid and suddenly their world is transformed, they start to read again, they are transported out of London into an idyllic future where their imagination can expand, their literacy evolves and I become that story they tell in their speech when they've won the Oscar for Best Original Screenplay. *It was all down to that lady who dressed up as a Christmas tree and gave me a free book in my school library.*

Yeah, that isn't happening.

What is happening is that New Nick and I are hanging out in this lovely and well-equipped library space. There are four children in here, one who seems to be desperately finishing History homework, two on computers watching YouTube and one who is asleep on a bean bag. The librarian is trying so very hard, she's wearing a Christmas hat and has matching tinselled earrings. She's got a tree in the corner and filled the place with homemade paper chains. But this is hard work. It's the opposite of a captive audience. *Please, read a book. Try. They're free!* But no one is here, apart from some girls standing outside the window, their faces pressed up against the glass, waving and staring at the novelty that is Nick, someone to change up their lunch hours. Nick waves back politely. They giggle. 'Put away your phones!' I hear a teacher thunder down the corridor. I get it, girls. *This is premium Santa here, not a bargain basement granddad in a beard. But I'll only let you interact with him if you take a book.* I look over and watch as Nick texts someone on his phone and then switches to Wordle. I peer over curiously to see how long it'll take him to get it. The word today is ADEPT but I won't tell him that.

'I'm sorry. This book-drive stop was a bit of a waste of time,' I say, feeling a little guilty I brought him here.

'Or not. We had those Year Seven kids come in, they seemed excited. I reckon if we found them again, we could give them some extras,' he says, looking up.

'I like the optimism,' I add, smiling at him. 'At least you have amassed a fan club,' I joke, trying not to stare at the posse of girls outside.

'Yeah, I thought the old people were inappropriate.'

'DO YOU HAVE A GIRLFRIEND?' one of the girls says, knocking on the glass.

He looks up at them and then returns to his phone. He's not falling for their games but I'll admit I want to know the answer to that question. We met outside the school today, all dressed up and ready to take on this place. He was formal and polite as he always is, a school secretary gave him her telephone number and he paused in reception to see yet another fake tree reaching to the ceiling. I am quietly fascinated by how irritated he gets by fake trees. He intrigues me on so many levels but I remind myself that I'm seeing Old Nick. I went to the ballet with him. We had Mexican food after. And sex which is still fun and satisfying. All the fun.

'CAN WE HAVE YOUR SNAP?' they ask through the window.

'DO YOU WANT A BOOK?' he shouts back.

'A WHAT?' they shriek, as though he's offered them drugs.

He laughs. 'What's a snap? Is that a sex thing?' he asks me quietly.

'No, it's a Snapchat thing. Social media.'

'Don't have it,' he says, and they all moan with disappointment.

I didn't think he'd be the sort who would. I still don't know how to converse honestly with Nick. I want to tell him how much I adored meeting his family without overstepping, but I also have so many questions, so much interest in his past. But I can't. I can't give him the wrong impression, so I get up and start to stroll around the library. Schools are strange places in the run up to Christmas, out in the courtyard you can see children wrapped up in coats, random Christmas hats and the odd classroom that sparkles and glitters. It would seem these kids are far too cool to get into the season and I don't think we're going to change that any time soon.

'Oh, by the way, I got a lead on those letters, I think,' Nick says, and I turn back to face him.

'You did?'

'In the book was a ticket to a school play in a local primary school so I put a post up on a Facebook community page. Maybe I'll get a bite.'

Since he mentioned this to me, I must admit the way he seems intent on finding the owners of these letters is endearing and well, vaguely hot. It's giving literary hero on a grand quest to reconnect two lovers. This is the sort of drama and commitment that I live for in any main character. Naturally, I don't tell him that much.

'You are funny,' I say.

'Funny?' he replies. Well, not like that.

'I mean, it's quite a romantic thing you're doing there.'

'Well, if I get my teeth into something, I believe in doing things properly,' he says. I swallow hard as he says this, to think about his teeth, in something. I really do not like how this man is really perverting my thoughts on Santa. It's not right at all especially as I'm with another person now; it's inappropriate. *Stop it, Kay. You're also in a school.* 'And it just feels like a nice gesture to be able to get these letters back to the right people... before Christmas.'

'Like a gift?'

'Exactly.'

I run my fingers along the spines of some of the books and pick one out to read the blurb. I remember the time I spent in my school library, tucked away in a corner, deep in stories.

'So do you only write children's fiction then?' he asks, his attention away from his phone as his eyes follow me around the room.

'Oh yes, nothing that these kids would be interested in, I'm afraid.'

'And was it something you always wanted to do?' he asks.

'Ever since I was little, I was a writer. I used to fill diaries and write articles, stories. The curse of being an only child when you have to create your own entertainment,' I say. 'When I was about fifteen, I got glandular fever for three months and I remember being at home, sat at my nana's kitchen table and I wrote a whole series of short stories... a table I still write off to be honest.'

He smiles as I talk about it. 'What were the stories about?'

'A boy I fancied called Paddy Edwards, but that's not the point.' He laughs. 'He was very dreamy. He had frosted tips and a BMX.'

'I'm sure... You're strange.' I pause when he says that. I thought we had mildly warmed to each other. He realises his gaffe. 'What I mean is that you don't broadcast it, you don't announce it to a room. You should tell people you're an author. That's amazing.'

So, strange in *that* way. I smile back but say nothing. People usually assume my writing is a vanity project or a glorified hobby. I see it as doing something I've always dreamed of doing, even if people measure my success very differently.

'And you? You've told me you do a touch of carpentry but have you ever thought about turning it into something more?'

'Well, I design furniture,' he says quietly. 'It's what I did at university.'

'So basically, your life is about wood.' That was a joke, I am not flirting, that is stating the facts. He, however, remains unimpressed by my humour and shakes his head. 'Well, I'd love to see some of your pieces.'

'You already have. My office is full of them. The rocking chair in the corner of my room.'

My eyes are wide. 'You made that?'

'I did.'

'How?'

'With my hands and some tools,' he explains bluntly.

'And your wood,' I say.

'It's not my wood. It's general wood.' He looks at me, trying to gauge if I'm deliberately being an idiot, but in truth, I wouldn't know where to start in making a rocking chair.

'That you find in the forest?'

He narrows his eyes at me. 'Yeah. I have a family of beavers. They live with me, we go find a tree and they just fell it for me and we bring it back to my workshop.'

I try and hold in my glee that he made a joke. 'You see, now I think you're lying to me.'

'Don't be mean about my beavers.'

I try to hold in my giggle at the word beaver. 'What are their names?'

'Bradley, Belinda, Barney and B...'

'Betsy. And just like that, you've written my new book for me,' I say. Was that a laugh? Damn him. Where was this banter before? This warmth, this humour that's started to peek through. Because before he was a little moody, serious. I knew him as that rude man on the phone who still used the word 'wazzock'. But this, these stolen smiles and looks, are confusing because there's another Nick and these two don't know about each other and I don't want this to become a situation where I have to readjust my moral code. I'm saying nothing. It's safer that way. Actually, because there are two of them and they're both called Nick, they effectively cancel each other out. My dodgy reasoning is interrupted by the door opening.

'Hi! I was just popping my head in to say... hold up, why are you here?' At the door of the library stands a woman in a Christmas jumper and Converse, colourful lights flickering on her lanyard. 'You're the Christmas-tree man. I know you...'

'Beth,' he says. 'Lucy's sister. How's your tree?'

'Very good, thank you. You're...'

I wave across the room and Beth recognises me, heading over to my corner of the library, occasionally looking back to clock Nick. 'Yeah, I was told to come over and see why all the Year Nine girls were crowding the courtyard and had rolled up their skirts. Hey, Kay,' she says, coming over to hug me. Lucy is one of five sisters I've come to know over the years and her sister, Beth, is my main contact at this particular school. 'Why is he here?' she mouths.

We both watch Nick as a few girls enter the room to talk to him. He carries a pile of books just in case they may want to take one. 'Long-ish story. He volunteered to help deliver the books, outreach in the community and all that.'

'Lucy's boss?' she says quietly.

'Yeah... By the way, you girls never told me about him before.'

Beth peers over as he stands there turning his back to the girls so they can't take pictures of him. 'Oh, yeah – we call him The Timbersnake.'

'Because he's underhand and sneaky?'

'No, because Lucy saw him getting changed once and...'

'BETH!' I squeal. He looks over curiously at both of us.

'He's a nice fella. We all get fantastic Christmas trees because of him. In my opinion, he's almost *too* good looking though.'

'That's a thing?' I ask her.

'Look at him, I wouldn't know what to do with myself. It'd be like dating Ryan Gosling. I'd spend ninety per cent of my time staring at him, blushing, speechless.'

I giggle. 'Who are you texting?' I say, noticing the phone in her hand.

'The staff room. This last week before the Christmas break is the hardest one in the school year. We all need to find our joy somewhere,' she says. 'GIRLS, you are being too much, leave him alone. He's married.'

I see the alarm on Nick's face as she says this and I can't lie, something drops out of my stomach. He's what now? Married? But he doesn't wear a ring. It's not as if it came up or we discussed our situations in detail – at all, in fact. He's allowed to be married. We're not together. Why am I emotional? You idiot. I feel it hit my eyes and turn away. He was here because it was a community endeavour, nothing more.

'What? He's married!?' a girl shouts.

'Yeah, this is his wife so behave yourselves and roll down your skirt. I can see what you had for breakfast,' Beth replies.

Nick and I look at each other. I'm not his wife. *Oh.* She was saying that to calm down the girls so they wouldn't pursue him so aggressively. The girls look over at me and I'm unsure what to do. How does one act territorial? Or wifely?

'Yeah, I'm afraid I'm spoken for. I belong to her,' Nick says, shrugging.

I bite my lip as he says that, trying not to smirk. 'Yeah, I am his wife.'

'Lucky cow,' one girl says, looking me up and down as if I'm undeserving.

'I heard that,' I say. 'Not so lucky really. He snores. Loudly. Like a baby elephant.'

'This is true,' he says, looking over at me, grinning.

'His feet are also horrific. Like Monster Munch.' He gives me a look. I've taken this a little far, haven't I? I see Beth laughing under her breath as these very hard to please teenagers give me evils because I'd dare criticise their new crush.

'Girls, Mr and Mrs North have brought a lot of books with them today, maybe you should take them as gifts, broaden your horizons this Christmas? No?' Beth adds, trying to talk us up. Nick looks at me as we're referred to as Mr and Mrs. I must admit, with the North bit, it makes us sound especially seasonal.

'But it's like, reading, miss. It's like, work.'

'It doesn't have to be,' I say. 'I've wrapped up some of the *Heartstopper* novels.'

'Like that show on Netflix?'

I nod. 'Plus Mr North wrapped them. And if you don't take them, it'll make him sad.' The group of girls look to him as his bottom lip pops out. They take a book each.

'Well done, girls,' Beth says, walking them to the door.

As they depart, a hand falls onto my shoulder and squeezes it tightly. There's a word for how it feels. Natural. 'OK, wifey. My feet are like what now?' he says, slightly offended.

'They are awful. The way you leave your boots around and don't pick up your socks.'

'And what was that other thing you said?'

'That you snored.'

'So, essentially, I'm noisy in bed?' he smirks.

I can't exhale. 'Yes, you are very noisy. It's not good for my beauty sleep.'

'As if you need it.'

We smile at each other for a moment too long until he puts his arm around me, his fingers grazing the skin by my neck, and I feel that. I feel it in places I shouldn't, confused by the sudden need for physical contact until I see him waving to the girls by the door. I slide an arm around his waist and wave too. To keep up the illusion, obviously.

TWENTY-SEVEN

Isn't it strange how at Christmas we all become big fans of light? Anything that glows and sparkles, we ooh and ahh and watch it, entranced. Big flashing snowmen sitting on the gables of a house, strands of bulbs hanging off a lamppost, garlands festooned from doorways and windows. We like it when the season literally glows. The lights are some special form of festive magic; it's good for our souls, it helps us get our Christmas on. I look up now at the trees and I get it, those twinkling lights transport you back to being young and that sense of fascination you had with the world which seems to diminish.

'Mulled cider, madam?' A hand reaches out in front of me and I take the cup from Nick, the lights reflecting in the pupils of his eyes. 'I also got us some bratwurst from a man in lederhosen.'

'That's one steamy sausage,' I tell him, looking down as he attempts to juggle everything.

'That's what she said.'

I grin broadly. Old Nick. This season has felt as though we've gone through London's greatest Christmas hits on our dates – from watching *The Nutcracker* last week, to Harrods to ice skating. We find ourselves in Kew Gardens tonight, enjoying the illuminations and seeing the place lit up, from towering Christmas trees to archways and installations, sparkling in a kaleidoscope of colours.

Tonight, Nick's wrapped up in a beanie and puffer coat, and the cold has hit his rosy cheeks. He beckons me over to a bench and hands me a sausage swathed in mustard and sauerkraut. I can't lie. Hot wiener is an excellent idea, the temperatures have dropped considerably and I will take anything to feel a sense of warmth. I take a bite of mine and immediately wipe away at the remnants of mustard coming out the corners of my mouth to not have a repeat of the hog roast incident. But then I remember that was with the other Nick. Jesus Christ, I am mixing my meats here. *That wasn't with you.* I have no feelings for the other Nick at all. Honestly. I actually can't think about him because it almost gives me a headache. The last time we met at that school library, something had changed. There was open flirting. Possibly. It moved into innuendo and we don't normally do that. But then as soon as our time in that school library was over, we went out into the car park, back into his truck and it was as if it never happened. And so I pushed it all away. I can't even tell if it's a spark. It's almost like lighting the burner on a hob – it doesn't spark immediately but when it does, the flame goes out again. It's starting to become vaguely frustrating. It's almost made me grateful for Old Nick and the comfort I get from knowing we're into each other and can say that out loud. I glance over at him now, looking up at the lights in wonder.

'It's quite a thing, eh?' he says.

'It is. And if I forget to say anything later, I had a very cool time tonight,' I mutter.

'Why did you say that in an American accent?' he asks.

'I was trying to go all *Pretty Woman.*'

'Isn't Julia Roberts a hooker in that film?' he asks.

I stick my tongue out at him. Books and films, they're my currency. *Indulge me.* There's a way we sit next to each other which is comfortable, an ease I always have with him. It's strange how all this time later, that's not gone away. It's a jigsaw puzzle where the pieces will always fit.

'The electricity bill in this place must be off the chain,' he says, gazing up at the lights. It's a practical stance, he's perhaps less entranced by the magic of it all than myself.

'They must get through a lot of bulbs too.'

'Very true,' he says, sipping on his warm cider. 'How's that wiener working for you?'

'It's delicious.'

He smiles and I return that smile knowingly. We have been keeping up with the idea of fun, on our dates and in bed. It is different from our university days – sex back then was scrappy, we went into it with basic knowledge from few partners and were occasionally drunk or stoned. But now, we've learnt things, we are a little more confident in our own skins and skills set. It's certainly matured in a lot of ways, we're enjoying each other, regular orgasms can only be described as fun.

'It's very Instagrammable, isn't it?' he asks. 'People are just here for the social media filler, eh?'

We look at a family across the way in matching Christmas hats, all arranging themselves for a selfie. It's all a perfect picture ready to show the world how happy they are until their mum takes the picture and they all part, one of the children punching the other in the stomach before running off.

'Well, this is absolutely lovely, Nicky! Delightful! What a wonderful idea!'

I don't really register the voice at first as I'm still laughing at the two children who are beating each other up but Nick gets up from the bench and my head turns to see two people standing there, one of them in a giant fur hat as if she's going to visit the Kremlin. And then I realise who they are. Shite. They're Nick's parents. Marjorie and Lester. I stand up immediately, not knowing what to do with the half-eaten sausage in my hands, glad I did my best to eat demurely. I haven't seen these people in, well, nearly a decade. Such is a break-up, one minute you're part of a family and the next you don't see them, you don't get a chance to say goodbye. The last time I saw them was for a family birthday party at their house in

West Hampstead. I remember a really good carrot cake and one of my biggest regrets was never getting the recipe for that.

'And you... how have you not changed in all this time?' Lester asks, coming in for a hug.

I've been ambushed. I really have. I know I've met them before, Nick, but it's your parents and you could have warned me. You keep giving me mixed messages about what this is. You said this was fun; this is not fun, this is a relationship milestone where I'll have to be on my A-game and engage. I'm wearing one of my tatty old hats, jeans and trainers. This is not how to make an impression after all this time. I really need to find a way to get rid of this sausage too.

'It's so lovely to see you both,' I say, looking at Nick who clearly doesn't understand that this may be awkward for me.

'Kay, how wonderful. We were so happy to hear you were back in Nick's life,' Marjorie says, an eyebrow raised. Was that sarcasm? She's a bit posh and her brow carries all her judgement. 'Don't let us stop you. Finish your food, sweetheart.' I look over at Nick, who seems to have finished his bratwurst, and I do my best to gobble mine down as quickly as possible. They're not just ambushing me, they're watching me eat. 'Tasty? We were thinking of getting some, weren't we Lester?'

I nod, trying my best to get it down me, my throat tight with nerves. I put my thumb up in the air. As they look away, I stare at Nick. *What on earth is this? You told me sausage, lights and fun.*

'Mum, Dad... there's a cabin up there with mulled cider, go get some cups and we'll meet you there,' he says, clearing up our things. They stroll away as I swallow the last mouthful, still a little confused as to why they're here.

'I'm sorry,' Nick whispers. 'I should have...'

'Said something?' I'm trying to downplay any threat of a quarrel with a smile.

'It's not a big deal,' he says. 'You've met my parents before.'

'Yeah but... I would have worn my best trainers,' I whisper. 'It's kind of a big deal, no?'

'Or not. They always liked you,' he says casually.

'But I thought we were having... you know, fun,' I jest. You don't meet the parents if you're just having fun. I don't know by which parameters he measures his relationships but fun is sex, low-key dates and trading in memes. I'll be honest, were it not for the earrings, I was going to get him a joke Christmas gift – a wind-up Santa or a comedy pair of socks. Dates involving parents are always going to be a level up from fun.

'This is fun. Maybe just go with it. Chill. It'll all be good,' he says.

As we start walking towards the cider cabin he takes my hand, lights still reflecting off his face. I look into his eyes. I think the problem here is not being able to read him. There's an equivocal look there which I can't interpret. Does he want to be more serious? Should I be flattered that he can just introduce me back into his family with such ease?

As we approach Nick's parents, his mother comes up to him immediately, linking an arm through his and walking away with him. 'Darling, I have to tell you about John Partridge's daughter. She went to Thailand and got bitten by a monkey...'

This leaves me with Lester and we traipse along behind them. I never minded Lester but he always gave me labradoodle energy, a lot of bounce but a little clueless. I stare at the back of Nick's head confused that this is what our date has turned into.

'I am so glad that you kept your hair,' Lester says. 'I always thought you had terrific hair.'

'You too,' I say. Yeah, Kay, that wasn't the right reply there. This is because I've gone into this blind and completely unprepared, but also because he's certainly lost a bit more hair from when I knew him nearly a decade ago. He doesn't know if I'm joking. No Lester, that's me displaying my wondrous social skills. 'I mean, there's no way to get rid of this hair. It's literally all I have. It's how my nana used to find me in crowds.'

'What shade is it?' he asks.

'I've always gone with auburn.'

'Do you put anything in it to make it so... bushy?'

I bite my lip. Mainly because of his social awkwardness but because I'm a child who hears the word bush and takes it somewhere else.

'I use a good conditioner, Lester, and I take a B12 supplement.'

'Is that good for hair?'

'I think I saw it on the internet once and I went with it.'

'Maybe I should start taking it,' he says. I don't have the heart to tell him it won't make hair grow from scratch. I think he'd have to undergo a whole lot of crop regeneration for that. 'I take turmeric for my joints.'

I nod. 'Also excellent in curry.'

'Not the stuff in the spice rack, I take tablets,' he informs me.

'Oh yeah. I got what you meant. I love that for you. Which joints are causing you problems?'

'A few problems in my wrist,' he says, holding his right hand up. 'I think it's a repetitive strain thing.' Oh dear. Did you just make that hand gesture, Lester? Do I make a joke about this? *Because you wank too much or because you spend your life in fits of road rage calling other people wankers?* Don't say a word, Kay, just smile and nod. 'Bell-ringing.'

I down a bit of cider to mask the fact I want to burst into hysterics. 'You ring what now?'

'Marjorie and I are in a bell-ringing group.'

'Like Quasimodo? Sorry, he was the first bell-ringer that came to mind.'

I'm lucky he laughs. 'Oh no, they're much smaller bells.' He makes that hand gesture again. A family walks past and the dad gives him a strange look. That's one way to get kicked out of a Christmas lights event. 'I can play "We Wish You a Merry Christmas". Our group has a Facebook page if you want to see it. We're called "The Bells and Whistles".'

I marvel at how proud he is of that. 'That is quite the name. I will be sure to look it up.'

He looks at me as I sip at my cup again. 'I really can't believe it's you. After all this time. You'll think I'm daft but I always thought you were good for Nick. You were normal. Brought him down to earth a bit.'

I smile as he says it. 'Are you implying he's been dating a range of horrors since me then?'

'Oh, there have been a few proper Quasimodos,' he says, pulling a face. I'm glad the conversation has settled a bit, that we seem to have found a groove.

I can't help but dig though. 'I met Neve last week. She seemed—'

'Where?' His face is aghast at what I've just said, his interruption sudden, as if she's about to jump out of the darkness at us from a tree. Why has the colour suddenly drained from his face?

'The ballet. Nick and I went last week.'

'Oh.' I'm going to need more than that, Lester. Why is that significant? Why does he look disappointed? He's quiet for a moment trying to gather his thoughts, like he can't say too much. Why, Lester? Who is she? 'If I can be so bold, you're much better than her,' he says, his tone steely and resolute. 'In many ways, awful girl.' I didn't realise it was a competition but I'm both reassured and wildly curious. There's a story there and one I'm not sure whether to dig for because hey, Nick and I aren't serious. I mean, I'm strolling through a cascade of arches covered in shimmering lights talking to his dad about my bushy hair and his bells but hey, we're just having fun.

'Are you OK, Lester?' I ask, as his stance and gait feel a touch angrier than before.

He turns to look at me. 'How much do you know about Neve?'

'That she went out with Nick for a bit. That—'

'Lester, darling! Did you see the lake?' An arm loops into Lester's as Marjorie pulls him away. Lester, all I know is that she came across as an icy bitch and that I've possibly used one of her scrunchies. Is there something else I should know? He looks at me and curls his lips in before looking over to the lake. The lake is glowing. It's cute if a little cosmic. We all take it in as Nick returns to my side and finds my hand.

'Actually, Marjorie, Nick... I have an idea. Our Christmas Eve party at the house, Kay should be there.'

'I should?' I say, surprised by the invitation especially when I've just re-entered their lives. 'I mean, I wouldn't want to impose if it's a family thing.'

I look up at Nick and his whole nonchalant act again. 'Yeah, you should come along.'

Again, he seems to have missed the mark here. This is spending time with his family at Christmas. We have again overstepped the boundaries of casual and fun. I'll have to go out and buy gifts. His sister is a coeliac. However, as I try to gauge whether this is a forced invitation, I observe the interaction between Marjorie and Lester closely. She raises her thin spindly eyebrows at him, he nods lightly. It's that sort of non-conversational shorthand you have with someone you've been married to for a long time. What is going on here? Lester looks over at Nick, trying to catch his eye.

'Then it's done,' Lester says. 'Would you look at those fountains? How festive. I wonder how they get them to squirt to the music.'

And I stand there as they all gaze at a lake glowing in icy blues, whites and silvers, completely entranced. No one found that funny? Not even you, Nick? In fact, he almost looks sad. What has just happened here? But Lester is right, how are they squirting and keeping in time with the music? How is no one laughing at the word 'squirt?' That's amazing.

TWENTY-EIGHT

'Oi, oi! Christmas bitch incoming!' Lucy heads towards me in the car park of the North Christmas Farm, sashaying but also seemingly able to wave at toddlers driving away and look wholesome and festive at the same time. 'Have you heard my wanky shoes? They've got bells!'

I smile but think back to Old Nick's dad and his bell-ringing and the very odd evening I had two nights ago. I still don't know what to make of it but one moment I was biting into a hot sausage and the next I'm spending Christmas Eve with Nick's family. It all moved incredibly fast and I spent most of the time hypnotised by flashing lights but also completely dumbfounded by my lack of ability to read the situation. Do you like me, Marjorie and Lester? Was that a courtesy invite? Lester wasn't very keen on that Neve. From my interactions with her, I get that completely but there's more there. I can feel it.

Lucy is doing a jig and trying to play me a song via her shoes. Yeah, I won't get that without a tune and a starter note.

'You're jingly.'

'Always,' she says, coming over to hug me. 'Pray, do tell why you're here? Is it to see Nick?' she enquires, doing a little jig on the spot.

'Why are you still jigging?'

'Because I'm an elf. It's required by Christmas law.' She starts moving her arms around and a nearby family look on curiously. That's what being around all this pine will do to you.

'I'm actually here to pick up Nick,' I say.

She stops jigging to look at me intently. 'TO GO ON A DATE?'

The volume is a lot. I think they may have heard that in Lapland; it may have forever changed the course of the northern lights. 'No. He's been helping me do the book drive. We've been going from place to place delivering books. We're at a village Christmas fair tonight.'

'That's cosy.'

'It really isn't. It's mostly people lusting over him dressed as Santa.'

'Oh, we get that here too. He gets a lot of numbers...'

'He does?' I say that too quickly, almost panicked.

Lucy smirks at my reaction. 'So, I'll take it you're completely immune to his charms then?'

I realise that I can't say anything, mainly because it's Lucy and she's the most indiscreet person on the planet. 'He is a handsome man, for sure. But it's because I'm half-dating the other Nick. It would be morally ambiguous for me to show an interest.'

'Morally ambiguous are my middle names,' Lucy explains, smiling. 'What the hell does half-dating mean?'

'It means we are enjoying each other's company and not putting labels on anything.'

Lucy pulls a face. 'Did he decide that then?' I try and roll my memory back to that moment. I think it was mutually agreed. Bar the fact I have been reacquainted with his parents and will be spending Christmas Eve with them. 'I find men use those sorts of vague labels when they want to dip their wicks elsewhere. It means they can carry no responsibility or guilt later on.'

'It was mutually agreed but yeah, it's... complicated. I think we might be reigniting something there.'

'Tucking into seconds at the buffet?' she says, scowling.

'In so many words.'

'Well, I just hope that buffet is fresh as fuck, and that that boy knows your worth and how bloody spectacular you are,' she says. I lean over and give her a hug for the compliment. That's the thing about Lucy, the love she has for so many people always shines through. She looks me in the face, trying to read my expression.

'You look slightly worried though. Is it because you used to bump uglies so you don't know if it's a rehash or a rebrand?' Lucy says, pretty much summing up my feelings on the whole situation. I hate that she can read that just from my eyebrows and the wrinkles on my forehead.

'Perhaps.'

'And then there's also New Nick in the picture, dressed in red with the chiselled looks and the nonchalance, and he makes you a little twitchy in your lady bits so you don't know what's going on...' she says. Again, a little too astutely.

'Twitchy in my lady bits?' I say, giggling.

'Don't deny these things. Is he definitely not an option then?' she asks.

'I just think I can only really do one man at a time. Any more feels... tiring...'

Lucy winks. 'Then you've obviously not had enough fun in your life, young lady.' That could be interesting. Maybe we should be a throuple and it would remove any confusion, any need to choose. It would also be super handy to be able to say the name Nick aloud and it could refer to either of them. But I don't think I have the bottle or the nerve. 'You are spending a lot of time together.'

'I know.'

'Just saying.'

'Stop it.'

'I mean, you could do both. You know, like in those gelato places when they let you try flavours before you decide. Maybe take it to a testing phase?' she suggests.

'But when you don't choose the mint choc chip, its feelings don't get hurt,' I remind her.

'Who is the mint choc chip in this situation then?' she jokes.

'Mint choc chip?' a voice suddenly pipes up. I freeze but it's a female voice so I turn around curiously. Behind me is a lady with a fur cape draped over her shoulders, her hair pinned back in a bun, furry boots on her feet. She looks like a villager from *Frozen*, I feel like she's about to sell me ice.

'Natalia!' Lucy says, reaching over to hug her.

'Natalia, this is Kay, a friend of mine and Kay, this is Natalia North – Nick's mother,' she says half smirking.

I take a deep breath. What is it with the Nicks' parents sneaking up on me this week? I don't quite know what face to pull, what emotion to go with as I've had indecent thoughts about her son so seeing her kindly face in person feels slightly wrong. *You're tiny but you have the same green eyes as your boy.* She's wearing a long embroidered skirt as if she's going to lead a folk dance and bake me some pretzel. I never met her the day I stopped at his house. I saw photos, and she is how I imagined, this little matriarch that probably has all that family under her spell. I immediately want to hug her.

'You are the book lady,' she says, an Italian accent shining through.

'I guess I am. It's lovely to meet you,' I say, smiling. So she knows about me too. I wonder how much I have featured in the family gossip channels.

I see her scanning my face, and she grins broadly; there is no judgement there or at least none that I can see from her eyes, just joy that she's got to meet me. '*Bella...*' she mutters under her breath. She puts a hand to my face and then reaches into a pocket to get her phone. 'Why is my son keeping you waiting? Silly boy. I text him now.'

'Oh no, I'm early. It's been nice to catch up with Lucy, to be fair.' I look down to see her screensaver is a photo of her with all her kids, Nick may even be smiling, his arm tightly around his mother's shoulder.

'Thank you for getting my boy out there and doing this with him. I know his face doesn't always say it but he's a lovely boy really. He says he enjoys your company,' she informs me.

'He can be super grumpy, Natalia,' Lucy comments.

She tuts. 'Oh shush, he cannot change his face. He is a brooding, serious boy. That can be a good thing. You don't want a complete joker in your life, all of the time.'

'I do,' Lucy says, putting her hand in the air. Natalia narrows her eyes at her then looks back to me. There is something about her that is fizzing and excitable so I will assume Nick doesn't get his dour exterior from her.

'You like cannoli?' she asks me.

'I do.'

'Then I will make you a box. Nick says you have a long night ahead so you will need your energy,' she says. Naturally, this makes Lucy snort quietly with laughter, raising her eyebrows at me. I shake my head at her.

'You like mint choc chip, we do some fudge with that flavour and maybe we can see what paninis are left too. We'll put together a care package,' she explains. 'Lucy, do your job, sweetie. Wave to the people,' she says, blowing her a kiss as she links an arm through mine and drags me away. I look around, still no Nick in sight, but hell, I don't think I mind this. There is a lovely embracing energy there that reminds me of Nana, and which is sorely missing from my life sometimes. We walk along a wooden boulevard that winds around these log cabin buildings outside the farm and she looks at me, her eyes almost sparkling.

'You have lovely skin, sweetie. What do you use?'

I smile at her questions – all at once nosey, if a little maternal. 'Actually, for a moisturiser, the blue Nivea in the tin. It's what my nana uses and she passed down that skincare tip to me.'

Natalia throws her hands up in the air, almost as if she's praising someone. 'This is what I use too. It is the best, my daughter uses all these expensive things with gold and frog juice and honestly, it does nothing. You always lived in London?'

'Born and bred. You?' I ask.

'Oh, I was born in Milan but I met an Englishman and he stole my heart so I moved here in the nineties. I met a farmer, can you believe it? My mother always said, marry a doctor, a pilot, an accountant, but I married a man who sells trees.' She puts her hand out to indicate the farm, to the pine trees in rows, still waiting to be claimed.

'It's a unique business,' I say.

'It is, but you know why I fall in love? I think it takes a special man to nurture and care for something so it grows. It takes light and love.'

I like how we've just met and she tells this story with such fondness and affection. Is there a hidden meaning there too? Possibly. But you have to love a mother who bigs up her own son like this.

'So you've been together long?' I ask.

'My love, he passed six years ago. My Norman.'

'I am very sorry, I didn't know,' I say, a little worried I've upset her.

'It's good to talk about him. It keeps him alive for me,' she says, holding a hand to her heart to reassure me. She pushes at the door of the shop and leads me in, and I'm immediately hit by a gush of warm air, a spiced, sweet scent. I'd only been in Nick's office before so this place had passed me by, but I grin widely at how homely and gorgeously festive it is. It's draped in red and white Scandinavian-style decorations, panettones stacked in one corner, touches of festive everywhere from jars of jams to gingerbread, to those freshly baked mince pies Nick once told me about. I look around at the decorations, customers sifting around the tables with wicker baskets filled to the brim with parcels and boxes wrapped in ribbon and twine.

'You like my shop?' she asks.

'It's beautiful,' I say, still awestruck by the charm of it all.

'I told Norman, you go and plant your things and I will build this. Actually, we have fresh ravioli we made this morning, I will get two pots you can take away,' she says. 'You help yourself, anything in the shop, it's on me.' I'll assume she doesn't mean the fifty-pound bottles of alcohol I can see perched on a wooden shelf behind me but I smile at the generosity of her spirit, the way she greets all her customers and puts a hand to a member of staff's back to tell them she appreciates them. 'I also get you the good cannoli with the pistachio. I get you a box, you can share with your family.' The idea hits her eyes and lights them up. 'My Nick likes them too. My boy is fussy about what he likes.' Why does she smirk when she says that? 'Go out back and hurry up that son of mine. He should be in his office,' she says.

I nod as she scurries away. The office I remember. She points behind me to a door, swathes of holly on the frame, and I head on through. This time, I walk through the corridor slowly and carefully, mainly to dodge the parcels and boxes stacked up by the walls but also to see the photos of this farm lined along them, their family, photos of Nick when he was an older teen with a floppy fringe and an unfortunate love for jorts, but lovely pictures too of Norman with his family, his wife, a look of real pride in his beaming face and stance. I stand there for a moment to see how he envelops his wife in every photo, in an embrace that makes her eyes light up.

As I get to Nick's office, I notice the door slightly ajar and this is the thing, I shouldn't look. I should turn away. But he's the one who's left his door open and is standing there in his underwear. Don't look, Kay. Knock? Maybe close the door for him and wait patiently in the corridor, go look at those photos again. But instead, I watch through that crack of light in the door, almost frozen to the spot. Why is he in his pants? He raises an arm above his head, circling it to rub a shoulder and it's almost unbearable as it makes his bicep curl, it lets me see the curve of his shoulder, the shape of his abs. My lips go dry from my mouth just being open, staring. You absolute terrible individual. Look away. But then he turns and

I basically can see butt, perfectly rounded, the backs of his thighs, a back that I desperately want to trace my fingers down. I want to bite his buttocks. He pulls up a pair of red trousers over it. That's Santa's butt, Kay, what are you doing? I close my eyes and step backwards but as I do, I trip over what appears to be a sack in the hallway, stacked with parcels. Oh, shitbox. I see him turn to the doorframe as I scramble around on the floor, trying to put the parcels back and make it look as though I've not had peeks of him getting changed. I was just here, rearranging things. On the floor. He opens the door wider to see me there, crouching, looking up. Sweet Jesus. No. Santa. Urgh.

'Hey,' he says, rolling a white t-shirt over his torso. 'Why are you on the floor?'

'I'm clumsy,' I say, not really knowing how to look at him. 'I was early, your mum sent me through.'

'You met my mother. Oh God...' he says, his face filled with horror.

'She's lovely. She's making us food.'

'Of course she is,' he says, rolling his eyes.

I pout for a moment to hear him put his wonderful mum down. *You are lucky to have all that warmth and love in your life, it's quite a thing.* 'I'm sorry. If you're still getting ready, I can wait.' He shrugs his shoulders but urges me to come inside his office. I tentatively step in as he sits down at his chair and puts on his socks and boots. 'It's cold. You might need more than just a t-shirt.'

'It's fine. I will be going full Santa. I might stick warming pads in my pants too for good measure.'

I try not to laugh. Don't think about his pants. His hot pants. I need to keep a distance here. I need to not go near him.

He reaches over to a hook on the wall to retrieve his fur-trimmed red cape. I will admit, I like the authenticity of it, the fact it's thick and regal. But now I know what it's covering up. God, why is this so confusing? He's not an option. He's the other Nick. And I'm suddenly disappointed that I'm not being honest to either of them, that this pseudo-deception is not me at all. It doesn't feel kind. Maybe I just need to approach this with the clarity it deserves.

'Did it look like it was going to snow? The weather forecast said snow?' he asks me.

'It's frosty,' I say, looking out of a small window. But as I do, I notice a box below the sill. It's addressed to Nick but one of the flaps is up and I see a familiar picture, a book. I know that book. Because I wrote that book. That's one of my bears. I turn to see him go into a cupboard to fetch something and I slip my hand into the box. That's not just one book, that's a whole box of them and I see another three boxes below that. Why? Why has he bought all these copies? Why would he do that?

'Maybe I'll put on some thermals under this suit?' he says, opening a drawer.

I look down at the books and feel a tear rolling down my cheek. I wipe it away quickly and turn around. 'Yep, I reckon that's what Santa would do.'

'I may need to get changed again then,' he tells me.

'That's fine,' I say. *I don't want to lick you anymore. I want to hug you tightly.* I smile at him, probably holding the moment for a tad too long to be comfortable.

'You may have to get out of here then?' he says.

'Oh yeah,' I say. 'I'll go and check in on your mum and your cannoli?'

'My cannoli?'

My words are stuck in my mouth, they have no idea what they're saying or thinking. 'Cannoli,' I say, not before dashing out of the room, back out into the warm glow of the shop.

TWENTY-NINE

'And so this is free?' a woman asks me, sifting over the table at this village Christmas fair. She looks at me and Nick suspiciously, waiting for the catch. Does she have to give a donation? Throw a beanbag? Give us her email address and sign away her firstborn son? Thankfully, no. *Please have some books, re-gift them, embrace the power of reading. Please.* Because we wrapped a few hundred of these. I got paper cuts.

'When you say used, how do you know if they're sanitary?' she asks. 'Do you know where they've come from? Did you count the pages?'

'I counted the pages,' Nick says next to me. 'Every book was hand wiped too.'

'Because mites can live in books. I had a friend who caught nits from a book once.' Nick and I stand there quietly, not reacting. *That would mean your friend wears books on her head like hats.* Nick pushes a book in her direction. 'Well, given that it's free...' She takes one, putting it in her shopping bag. 'Thank you.'

'Merry Christmas,' Nick says, and we watch her walk away to smell a few candles in the next stall. Today is a little bit different. I was told by one of my library patrons about this Christmas fair in her little village – an event where the village comes together to create a nativity scene in the town square, school choirs come out to sing and they have market stalls all down the main street. She offered me a stall space to give away my books so I took her up on the offer. It's all wonderfully parochial from the lights to the hay bales and it's lovely to smell all the food and mulled wine, to see people bundled up and enjoying the season. I look at the dark inky sky and the stars sit there in formation, almost held up by the cold.

As Nick organises the books on our stall, I glance at him, still not knowing what I witnessed back at his farm. For the life of me, I don't know how to bring it up. I did some quick maths in the car and he's bought at least two hundred copies of my books. I checked that on my phone. I don't religiously check my sales and ratings anymore but I had seen that it had an immediate effect. Do I thank him? Do I tell him I know? Deep down, there's a reason he's done this, and it pains me that it's more than him wanting to do a nice thing. It's because there is more there than just friendship. On the way over, I was quiet, deep in thought, trying to unravel what it all meant. I say quiet, I was also stuffing three cannoli in my mouth. Nick's mum is a bloody baking genius. The pistachio in the ricotta filling is worthy of a thousand chef's kisses.

'Do we really count the pages so they're all accounted for?' Nick asks, his breath fogging the air.

'Of course, every last one,' I joke.

I wonder if he can tell that I'm trying to force this joke out of me. Because something has shifted. *Because you're not simply good looking, you've got a good heart and a kind mum who gave me a little cardboard box filled with ravioli with a wooden fork and a little separate container with cheese to sprinkle on top because she didn't know how much cheese I would want.* All the cheese, Natalia. All of it. I can't do this to him anymore. If he's done that big a gesture, I need to do the same and at least give him my honesty.

'Listen, after this... when we've given out the books, did you want to...'

'We should probably help them put the tables away?' he

suggests. 'I offered to help that old lady carry her jams too.' Of course he did. This would be far easier if he was awful and unhelpful.

'I meant, maybe we should get a drink?' I say.

His face softens. 'I'd like that.' I feel an immediate pang of guilt because what I need to say is that there's another Nick on the scene and I don't really know how to break that to him. 'What sort of drink though?' he asks. 'I think we use the term quite generically now but were you talking about a pint or a coffee from the petrol station?'

'I was thinking alcohol. There's a little pub over there,' I say, pointing across the square to a cosy little pub with a thatched roof and etched windows, smoke funnelling out of its chimney, Christmas lights glowing inside. Or maybe it would be easier to do this on a Shell forecourt.

He turns towards me, eyebrows slightly raised in surprise that I may be asking him on a date. Haven't we done this already though? We got a hog roast and shared a bench. We've sat in my library late into the night wrapping books. He rescued me out of a Christmas tree netting machine once. 'Then that sounds great. A drink sounds perfect.'

I can't look at him because I have no idea what that drink will entail but it immediately fills my heart with sadness that I will have to let him down, that I've not handled this situation very well at all.

'It's... actually, I—'

But before I can finish my sentence, a man arrives at the table, a little breathless and panicked. 'Mate, I couldn't ask you a favour?' he says, his hands gripping the end of the table. He points towards a woman stood by a lamppost, pushing a pram to and fro with what sounds like a very unhappy baby inside. To the side of the pram are two kids, mid-tantrum, one of them on the floor, his back arched as if he's possessed.

'Of course,' Nick replies.

'We just can't wait for Santa anymore. The queue is massive and my kids are tired and could you just...? Are you the sort of

Santa who'd be able to chat to my kids, hear their lists, you know? I'd pay. Can I buy something off your stall?'

I see the fatigue in the man's eyes and summon up a smile. 'The books are free, your kids are very welcome to take some.'

'But I can also help,' Nick says. 'I mean I don't look like traditional Santa with the beard or anything.'

'Seriously, I'll take anything at the moment. Tell them you've gone on a diet or something,' he says, taking out his wallet.

'Yeah, put that away. What are their names?' Nick asks, straightening out his fur robe and reaching down to a hessian sack, poring over the books on the table and selecting three. *Look at you. It's like we've told Batman there's a problem in Gotham and you've put on your outfit and are stepping up to the plate.* He's a hero, a saviour, this man's kids are going to sleep well tonight because of him.

'Louie, Anya and George in the pram,' the man says hurriedly.

'Last name?'

'Bailey.'

'You named your kid George Bailey?' Nick asks.

'Yeah, why?'

'Nothing. I'll need more, key facts on each of them.'

'Louie's into capybaras, Anya plays football, George is literally weeks old,' the dad reels off, and I hover by my stall, watching as Nick approaches them, just within earshot to hear what's happening. He stands over Louie and I see the little boy's face turn and look up at him.

'Ho, ho, ho.' Yeah, we still need to work on that. 'What's happening, Louie? Why are you on the floor?' he asks curiously. The little boy jumps to his feet, while his sister peers around from behind the pram, looking up. It must be like looking up at the moon. They're both silent. Not going to lie, Mum is looking over as well and then back at her husband as though this is a terrible plan. *This man is not some old grandpa and you might be shitting all over their Christmas dreams.*

'Who are you?' Anya asks.

'I'm Santa.'

'No you're not,' she replies quickly. I like this girl. Never stop questioning things, little one.

'Well, there's only one Santa but he has lots of people out there who represent him, who keep an eye out. Louie, Anya and George, yes?' Anya is silenced to hear her name. She comes out from behind the pram. 'The Bailey family. Hi, Mum.'

'Hi Santa,' she says, her voice a bit shaky.

'So you're not *the* Santa but you're also called Santa?' Anya continues.

'Yes.'

'Doesn't that get confusing?'

'Sometimes.'

I guess it's akin to when you're half-dating two people called Nick. I smile at these small people getting the better of him.

Nick bends down to their level. 'I'm just here to say hello. Are you being good tonight?' They both nod tentatively. 'I remember when I was little and got tired. Here...' He reaches into his pocket to find them each a chocolate coin, placing them in their tiny palms. 'And one for Mummy and Daddy too, because they do a very special job, wouldn't you agree?'

He's magic – all four of them listening, even the baby has quietened. Passers-by stop to look at this spell he's weaving.

'So you report back to Santa?' Louie asks.

'Yes, I have elf blood.'

'So you make toys as well?' Anya asks.

'I do. We are crafting you some very cool Nike Predators,' Nick says.

Anya inhales sharply. 'For me?'

Nick nods, smiling. 'And we're crafting some special musical instruments for Louie here too.'

Louie's dad's eyes widen in confusion. I cock my head to one side.

'Why?' asks Louie.

'Because you play the capybara?' Nick says.

I laugh and step away from my table to approach them. 'Santa, you are funny.' I turn to him for a moment. 'A capybara is like a giant bear-pig animal. Like a swimming wombat,' I whisper, and his eyes widen.

'I was just joking,' he says, turning back to Louie.

'You're sending me a capybara?' he says, his eyes lighting up.

'Is that possible?' he asks me out the side of his mouth.

'No, they live in zoos,' I say quickly, impressed by my own ventriloquism.

'We've sewn you one. A very special one,' Nick says, Louie's parents looking instantly relieved.

'Who are you?' Louie asks me.

'This is my wife,' he says, so casually. I could also be of elf blood, another of Santa's assistants, but instead it would seem I am Santa's wife. He's joking. It's all an illusion. This, what we have. I sigh deeply and smile at this boy and girl looking up at me.

'You don't look like a Mrs Claus,' Anya says.

Yeah, that's because I'm in fifty-percent Zara but let's roll with this, little one.

'I just make sure Santa is looked after. That he always has a supply of milk and cookies,' I say. 'And that he remembers to take out the bins.'

The children laugh. That was all me. 'I have a drawing for Santa,' Anya says. 'The real one, not you. In this drawing, he's fat and got a big beard. Could you give it to him?' she asks Nick, walking up to him.

Nick nods and she puts the drawing in his hands, scanning his face. 'If you know Santa then name all the reindeer,' she quizzes him.

'Rudolph, Comet, Blitzen, Vixen, Dancer, Prancer, Cupid, Dasher and...'

'Kebab,' I whisper.

'Donner,' he says confidently.

'I hope you have a nice Christmas fake Santa,' she says, reaching over to kiss him on the cheek. 'You smell nice.'

He smells of limes today, doesn't he? I sometimes know that smell when I'm near, when I hug him or get close to him. It smells like fresh laundry in a basket of citrus fruit. I watch as he fist-bumps Louie and then bends down to wave at the baby in the pram, before crouching down to let their mum take a photo.

'We also have some books for you...' he says, reaching into his hessian sack and handing them out. 'I wrapped those ones especially.'

I watch as they take the brown paper packages, their eyes lighting up because it's a gift. All of this is a gift. And just like that, the fatigue and tantrums of a few minutes ago have melted away. They're happy, they've rediscovered their Christmas spirit. I immediately think about how this man is perfect dad material. This is awful. I need to stop thinking that.

They run on and their dad turns and offers Nick a hug. 'Thank you, Santa.' He stays there for a moment too long, as if the inner child in him might need this moment and Nick allows for it, patting his back. He lets go and walks away and we turn to the table where a line seems to have formed. Nick and I look at each other. Time to give away some books, Santa.

'Could you go in my pocket and grab my keys?' Nick asks me as he carries a couple of boxes to the car.

It ended up being a longer evening than either of us anticipated. Nick was fake Santa for about thirty kids. He chatted to them, he learnt their names, he was frigging adorable. And I handed over books, watching, trying to convince myself that I felt nothing for this man at all. It was like having a herd of puppies at my feet. They're definitely not cute. Not one little bit. *Please don't make me put my hand in your pocket.* But he's waiting. I won't put the whole hand in. I'll put two fingers so the contact is minimal. I get them out and press on his key fob, opening his car boot for him.

'Are you OK? You look cold? I have a coat if you need it?' he asks. He puts the box in the back of the truck then steps closer to me, putting his hands to my shoulders and rubbing them up and down. My body tenses up. 'Sorry,' he says, stepping away almost immediately.

'It's fine. It's just this cheap cardigan underneath, that sort of friction might cause...'

'Combustion?' he smirks.

'Yes. I'd burst into flames right here and that would be...'

'Messy,' he says.

'I was going to say inconvenient.' My teeth are chattering slightly through my laughter. He's parked down a quiet street off the square, the lowlights of the streetlamps shining down on us but plunging the rest of the street into darkness. Down the road, the market winds down. It's been a lovely night to be among this small community, to meet families, curious old people, and to give them something free, without money, commitment or for anything in return. I enjoyed seeing the surprise in their faces, their gratitude, their joy. It's why I felt compelled to do all this. I gaze up into the clear sky, the stars twinkling down, and take in a deep breath of the cold night air.

'That was a good night, thank you for the capybara save,' Nick says, smiling and leaning against his car, looking at me.

'Haven't you heard the song?' I ask. Do I sing him the capybara song? Of course I do. I even make up moves because my charisma knows no bounds.

He looks at me curiously. 'Did you just make that up?'

'No! It's a thing on social media.'

'I don't do that.'

I look down, shaking my head, remembering. 'Well, now you know. Firstly beavers, now capybaras. We seem to run an excellent line in talking about small furry animals.'

He smiles. 'Did you hear that baby's name too? George Bailey.'

'*It's a Wonderful Life*. "You want me to lasso the moon, Mary?"' I say, doing my best Jimmy Stewart impression. He seems impressed that I'd get the reference, less so by the impression, standing there biting his lip as I laugh to myself. 'Don't pretend that you don't find me amazingly hilarious.'

He shakes his head at me, trying not to smile.

'The rest of that was excellent though. Well done, fake Santa.'

'Well done, fake wife.'

'Excuse me, please don't refer to me with a label. It's fake Mrs Santa,' I say, putting a finger in the air, trying to downplay the wife comment.

He takes a moment to catch his breath. 'You still up for that drink?'

'I am. It might warm me up.'

'You're still cold?'

I nod, breathing warm air into my hands. It's the sort of cold that makes you worry for the health of your toes, where you pray they will still be attached by the end of the day. A shot of something might help.

'Come here.' Without warning, Nick walks up to me and envelops me in his arms, holding me tightly, my head resting against his chest. This is far too close. I should push him away in the style of a Shaolin monk. But I lean into the embrace, and let him wrap me up, sighing quietly to myself.

'You should invest in a better coat, something down-filled,' he says. 'Your coat is a glorified picnic blanket.'

'It's wool,' I say, affronted.

'A wool picnic blanket then,' he says, rubbing his hands up and down my back. 'Is this too much? I just can't see you standing there cold. It's a survival technique, quickest way to get warm,' he says.

Yeah, I learned this in the Girl Guides too, except I was taught you had to get naked with someone in a sleeping bag for it to work. I can't think that way. Don't think about that at all. Accept the warmth of his furry Santa costume, that feeling of his arms tight around you, keeping you safe. I close my eyes for a moment, not wanting to ever escape from this cocoon. Because there is something so very right about our bodies close like this, our hips touching, the way I can nest my head in a space just below his chin and I can hear his heartbeat loud and clear. We seem to both realise we've probably held this for too long now. Maybe I'll pretend to have fallen asleep here to escape any awkwardness. But I glance up and see him smiling down at me, our faces dangerously close to each other, the closest they've ever been. And he puts his hand to my face, scooping it up but leaning down to kiss my lips gently. And I relent, kissing him back, at first with the softest of touches until his lips almost melt into mine, wanting to explore that kiss more deeply. I feel a rush surge through me, a moment of electricity, his hand moving to the back of my head, scooping up my hair.

'Nick,' I whisper under my breath. He doesn't say a word, I can hear his breath deepen, an intensity in the magnetism between us. I can't do this. What am I doing? 'I can't.'

He steps back on hearing those words, looking at me, snapped out of his daze. 'I'm sorry. I didn't—'

'I'm dating someone else.'

And I see his lips part gently, his body slump on hearing the words. His face is illuminated by the glow of the street lights and it's almost as though the lights have turned another colour, as if they've faded a little, as all the warmth that was there before goes and the cold returns to my bones, almost running through my bloodstream like ice.

THIRTY

'Look at what your mum and dad got me, another dressing gown. Leopard print, this time. This is the third one they've given me. What do they think I do? That I wear them all at once?' Nana says as she gets it out of her wardrobe.

'Leopard print is in you know, it's very trendy.'

'Well, that's good to know because it's a veritable fashion parade in this place with all the slipper shoes and tweed,' she laughs. I smile in return but it's strained and she looks at me curiously as if she can read that something is up. It's my weekly drop-in with Nana and I sit in my armchair in the corner of her room, curling my feet up into the chair and suddenly I'm twelve years old again and I'm round her house, eating all her biscuits and watching *Countdown*. It's that connection we always had when I was growing up that would make me gravitate to her every time. 'You know, last time you were here, everyone got very excited by the book stuff. Jeff upstairs loved that he got Bill Bryson, by the way.'

'I'm glad for Jeff,' I reply.

'You're a good girl for doing all of that. At Christmas when everyone is so busy. I was very proud,' she says.

'Thank you, Nana. It just felt like a nice thing to do.' I guess maybe I need to focus on the good because two days ago, I felt I didn't do something very good at all. I engaged in a kiss with a really lovely man when I shouldn't have. I let two Nicks overlap and something about my lack of control and honesty in that situation has made me feel goddamn terrible. It was never my intention for things to get so messy.

'So... I'm going to assume your sad face is something man-related. We never spoke about that tall glass of water you came here with last time,' she says, grinning, looking excited to finally be able to quiz me about him.

'That's one way to describe him I suppose,' I say with a smirk.

'I know my mind is going but you're telling me there are two fellas called Nick on the scene?' she asks, going to sit on the edge of her bed.

'Yeah. I messed up, Nana,' I say, my guilt consuming me so much I have to look out the window for a moment.

'Because you're seeing both?' she asks.

'Harrods Nick, the one who gave you the hamper, the one I dated a while ago, I think that's got a bit serious. I'm spending time with his family at Christmas. I kissed Santa Nick the other day after a book thing.'

'A peck on the cheek or with tongues and fettling?' she asks.

I burst into laughter and she looks mildly relieved to have broken my quiet. 'Nana...'

'He's a good-looking boy, you're young. If I had teeth I didn't have to glue in my mouth and my boobs from when I was in my twenties, I'd have a little go to find out,' she jokes.

'NANA!' I say. I smile but the guilt still sits in my veins like vinegar, stinging so very much. In hindsight, I should have said something earlier to avoid that situation. I shouldn't have kissed him back. And there are moments when I think back to that kiss, a heat rising up in me that turns into pain to picture his face when we parted, that disappointment. We didn't go for a drink after-wards. In fact, I was so mortified that I asked him to drop me at a train station so I could avoid any more awkwardness in the truck, so I could sit on a train platform, with tears in my eyes, looking vacantly into space, feeling so forlorn that a commuter stopped to ask me if I was OK. I just kissed Santa, I told him. He didn't stay any longer to find out more.

'How serious is it with Harrods Nick?' Nana asks.

'We've been on lovely, romantic dates. He bought me some earrings. Met up with his parents the other day. There are feelings there, we're sleeping together... and I guess...'

'I'm not hearing much certainty here, Kay,' Nana says.

'He's kind. He's generous. He's sorted in life, good job, a flat. He's handsome. It's different to last time. Last time, we were at university and we didn't know what we wanted out of life. We were so young. Now we're older and I'm thinking about the future.'

Nana looks at me, a little horrified. 'Who are you again?'

I pause for a moment, thinking this might be her dementia talking, that all my words have just disappeared into the ether. 'I'm Kay, your granddaughter.'

'Yeah, I know *that*. What I mean is that it doesn't sound like you, thinking about the future and serious things. The Kay I know is creative and kind and you've never been obsessed by money and what may or may not happen in the future.'

'But isn't it time to start, Nana? To start saving some money? Be sensible?'

'Why?' Deep down, I think I know it's because I need a better plan when it comes to looking after Nana in this place. I live in her flat, I don't earn a lot from the library work and sometimes even less from my book royalties but maybe it's time to be an adult, to think seriously about the shape of my future. Being with Old Nick would help mould that shape into place. 'Sweetie, when I eventually leave this planet, I won't be lying here thinking about that ISA I once put into place or how sensible I was to have paid off my mortgage. Oh yes, those saving bonds will do me good now.' I smile reluctantly to hear her mocking me. 'You'll think about words, people, deeds, memories of those who made your heart glow. Does he make your heart glow?'

'If my heart glowed, it'd be radioactive.'

'She's avoiding the question.'

'He makes me feel safe; he cares about me. He makes me think that maybe after all this time, life brought us back together for a reason.'

Nana looks up for a moment to take that in. 'But then life also brought you the tall glass of water, also called Nick, doesn't that mean something?'

'No.'

'It does. Life sometimes asks you to make choices too. I loved your grandad but there were other men I could have gone with. There was a postman called Alf who was sweet on me.'

'Why didn't you go with him?'

'Big chest like a pigeon,' she says, scrunching up her nose and laughing. 'You get thrown in the path of a lot of men in your life, lovely. And they are all sent to test you, you work out if they fit into the puzzle of your life.' I nod as I take in her pearls of wisdom. 'Your grandad made everything good, he was the first person I wanted to tell everything to, and he was one of these people in life that just raised you up. I always knew my happiness was the most important thing to him.'

'That's very romantic, Nana.'

'It is, for me. Don't get me wrong, there was plenty wrong with the bugger. He had wind strong enough to power a turbine, he hated Christmas – grumpy bastard at the best of times – but when it came to me...' She shrugs her shoulders, smiling broadly at bringing Grandad to mind.

I go over to the bed and put an arm round her and rest my head on her shoulder. Do any of those words help? I have no idea. I came here because I knew this was a safe place to be, to talk, to be under the wing of someone who well and truly loved me for me, so this was the place to get answers. I still feel none the wiser though. I feel confused. I know I hurt Santa Nick, that I led him on and I have no idea how to fix that. Maybe that's just the end of that? Maybe there's no redemption there.

'You still look very stressed, lovely,' Nana says. She takes a hand in mine and looks at my manicure, slightly chipped and grown out. 'Go out and treat yourself, get your nails done. Look after you.'

'I would. I've just got a lot of books to still give out. I've got writing deadlines. I've got to get gifts for Old Nick's family now I'm going round there. For Christmas Day as well, we're breaking you out of here, yeah? Shall I cook?' Nana pulls a face and I push her playfully. 'I'll get some bits from M&S and stuff them in the oven.'

'Then I am there. Can you get some nice cheese in?'

'Of course.'

She grabs both of my cheeks and holds my face up. I love how she takes in every inch of my face when she's looking at me, so she can put it into a part of her memory where it may stick. 'Katherine Redman, birthday the twenty-first of July, you find someone who sees all that light in you, you hear me? All of it.'

'I'll try,' I say, smiling sadly. I just have no idea who that person is. Because that person is usually you, Nana.

'You better. Now open your bag and show me what nice treats you have for me. You got them nice Lebkuchen from Aldi?'

'Of course I have. I'm not a bloody amateur.'

I leave Nana's before dinner that night and head over to the train station where they have a special bookshelf where people can leave books. I knew this was the case so had five wrapped in my bag especially. Maybe this is what I can do in the run up to Christmas, I can travel around London and find these book-shelves and stock them. I can hope those books go to good homes, that they entertain someone for a long train ride and then get passed on again. That's what should happen with books. I hope that's what happens with mine at least. Someone reads about my bears and then they pass that story on to someone else. The legacy is the joy, the words, it's how we should treat all stories. I look at the shelf, picking up a well-thumbed version of *Pride and*

Prejudice with passages highlighted, and I put it in my bag. To my left, I see a couple standing there, waiting for a train, holding hands.

'I really need a better coat,' she moans.

The familiarity of the conversation makes me eavesdrop.

'And finally, I have an idea of what to buy you for Christmas.'

'Christ, please don't buy me a coat.'

'Why?'

'Last time you bought me clothes, it was the wrong size and we fought and—'

'It was that dress,' he reminds her.

'It was red and far too large. I was a white bonnet away from looking like a handmaid.' He laughs so hard, he has to cough and control himself.

'Can I come with you to buy the coat at least? Then we can wrap it up and you can look surprised in front of the kids?' he asks.

'But then that will give the kids the impression that you have good taste.'

I smile at the banter, the sort of conversation and humour you pray exists in a relationship. An announcement echoes over the tannoy that the next train will be late and there's a collective sigh as those waiting stand there, looking to the sky exasperated, muttering profanities under their breath.

'Fancy a book while we wait?' the man suddenly says. I watch as the couple edge towards the bookshelf next to me and I step aside to see what they'll choose. 'Oh, there are ones wrapped up.' I get out my phone, pretending to scroll as the man reaches for one and hands it to his wife.

'So generous. I'm still getting the new coat, yes?'

'I guess.' She unwraps it and turns the cover to her husband. 'How did you know that I wanted a book of love poetry for Christmas? You soppy bastard.'

I look down and smile. I know that book. I know who wrapped that book and remember the moment in the low lights of the library when he read from that book to me. The man takes a strand of the woman's hair and tucks it behind her ear. 'You know me, all about the rhyming couplets and shit.'

She opens to a poem in the middle of the book, scanning the words. 'Ooh, I like this one. Husband...

Kindly return her tender gaze,
Press closely that little hand,
Whisper fond words and soothing praise –
They are ever at thy command;
It is all the harvest she asks to reap
In return for love as the ocean deep.'

And there's a moment between the two of them, a look. He takes her hand and she rests her head on his shoulder, him sweetly kissing the top of it. 'Is there any advice for you in there? *Maketh him cups of tea neverending, don't nag him to mow the grass, allow him the joys of golden ales, let him take you nightly up the—'*

'NICK!' she squeals, before they both collapse into fits of giggles.

And I turn away so they can't see that I'm laughing too. At them, at the fact my book prompted that moment, but also because of her husband's name. Nick. I look up to the sky and the stars. *I have no idea what you're trying to tell me or who I should end up with but you're not very funny, seriously.* My phone pings and I retrieve it from my pocket.

> Are you free? I need to see you about something?
> Nick

My heart beats out of my chest to see the message. But then I see the emoji that follows. Is that a squirrel? No, it's a beaver.

> I'm sorry about the beaver. There was no capybara emoji.

THIRTY-ONE

I wait inside the library, the doors locked to the outside world, looking for signs of life outside. An hour ago, Santa Nick told me to meet him here. I don't know how he feels about me, about us, if you can even call it that, but there was an emoji and emojis are all about playfulness and fun, so I'm going to take it as a sign that he doesn't completely hate me. I'm sitting behind the desk waiting when his figure appears at the door and I feel my pulse quicken to see him. He's not dressed as Santa which throws me a little but he's wearing the same coat he was wearing when we went for hog roast that time. I shouldn't be remembering little details like that. He waves at me through the door and I shuffle towards it to let him in.

'Hi,' I say, pushing the door into him, almost taking him out. My tone is also not natural. It's high and filled with too much fake jollity, trying to cover up the fact that we shared the sweetest moonlit kiss earlier in the week and then the most awkward moment pretty much straight after. He steps back and stares at me curiously, the same look he used to give me when we first met and he was trying to work out if I was a complete idiot.

'Evening. I'm sorry. I know it's late-ish but I just... I should have just called and done this on the phone.'

Oh no. Does he want a moment to find closure? A conversation. I guess that is owed. Maybe this is a chance to sit down and not skirt the issue anymore. *You're handsome, I'm confused. Thank you for helping me give out all these books. I'm sorry for kissing you when I shouldn't have. Please don't hate me.* This could be done in ten minutes and then I could go get noodles.

He comes in and inhales deeply. 'You can smell the trees when you come in now,' he says, admiring the tree in the foyer. 'The pine.'

I nod. Olga moans at us every day because of the extra hoovering but I won't tell him that. I let him follow me into the library as he looks around at the strings of lights illuminating the place. I feel his presence so closely that I can almost hear him breathing, the warmth of his body. I offer him Helen's seat behind the counter. 'Did you want a cup of tea or anything? I have some of Helen's Christmas cake here. She went a bit heavy on the marzipan but it's edible.'

'I'm good. How are you?' he says, turning to me.

'I'm OK. I've been with my nana. How are you?'

He sighs deeply. 'Can I ask you a question? Are you married? Kids?'

I shake my head. 'No. God, no. I... before I met you, I'd just reconnected with an old boyfriend, and there's...'

'Overlap,' he says. He takes a moment to let that sink in. 'Damn him for getting in there first, I guess.'

I stop because that infers he had been interested. 'I should have been more honest from the start. I like you, I appreciate everything you've done for me, the book drive.'

'I would have done that anyway. It's been nice to have been involved, to have got to know you. You're...' He pauses and looks around the library. *Please finish that sentence. I'm what?* 'You should open this place at night you know? Serve wine and people can connect over books.'

'That's not a terrible idea, you know,' I reply, trying to help him carry on the conversation.

We both sit there awkwardly in silence and I have the overwhelming urge to hug him, to hold him, in a way to let him know that I'm sorry, that deep down, I felt something too. For him. For the sake of transparency, I don't want him to feel as though I was dishonest about any of that either. There was something there.

He sits there trying to rearrange his thoughts, his words. I know he's not here to help me nurture library-based business ideas or check up on his Christmas trees. There was something to be said in person to each other. Maybe this is drawing a line formally, like proper adults. Maybe it all starts with an apology.

'You know I'm really glad you wanted to meet up,' I say, trying my best to catch his eye. 'I wanted to say—'

But he doesn't let me finish my sentence, I see panic in his eyes that I would even want to talk about us, or discuss anything emotionally charged. 'So yeah.' He reaches for his phone and it's strange to see him so hesitant and unsure of himself. 'Look, the reason I'm here is... remember those letters we found in one of those books. I told you I put some posts out on local community groups? Well, someone replied.'

Oh. I stop in my tracks to have been cut off. He scrolls through his phone and shows me a post from a few days ago. 'This person said they knew a Kelly whose husband's name began with N and they lived locally to here. Last name was Snowden. I was thinking that perhaps we could check your members and see if that computes?' he says.

I sigh warmly, knowing that in the background, this has still been a little project for Nick – the idea that while he may feel disappointment and sadness over us, he still held on to some belief in the story those letters told. I feel the emotion well up in me at the goodness of his intentions. 'What's her husband's name?'

'Nathan.'

I turn on the computer and log in, to look at our members and cross-reference the names. I find her: Kelly Snowden. She's a member, and so is her husband and all their kids. I smile to see her name and address there. 'She's here.'

Nick grins, looking satisfied that this story at least may have a happy ending. 'Is there an address? A phone number? Could we give them a call?' he asks, leaning over the desk.

I shield the computer from him. 'GDPR prevents me from disclosing that information but I can give them a call.'

I pick up the library phone while looking at Nick, the excitement in his face that we've managed to do something right here, that this will make him unfeasibly happy to get these letters back to their rightful owners. Maybe this is how I put this right. I put the phone on speaker and it rings three times before someone answers.

'Hello?'

'Hello, is this Mrs Snowden? This is Kay Redman from Hampton Grove Library.'

There's a pause as she tries to work out if this call is spam and why it's coming to her at 6.30pm. 'The library? We haven't been to the library in years,' she says bluntly. 'Is this a marketing call?'

I'm a little panicked by the curtness in her tone. 'Umm, no. We just... some books were donated to us recently and one contained letters that we thought might have belonged to you.'

Again, she pauses. 'What sort of letters?'

'Handwritten letters between you and possibly your husband.'

She laughs, almost a little too hard. 'Is this a joke? My husband left me two years ago for a tanning technician called Savannah.'

Nick pushes his chair back in horror at the way this phone call is turning out.

'I don't think I even got as much as a birthday card from the tosspot when we were married. Letters? Unless they were letters about child support? Christmas next week and I've received absolutely nothing from that twat.'

Nick and I stare at each other in horror. 'Mrs Snowden, I am so very sorry. It was just to check so we can reunite someone with their lost property. I didn't mean to offend.'

'Are we done?' she says.

'Yes, again, I'm sorry. You and your children are very welcome in the library this Christ—' But before I can finish my sentence, she hangs up, the monotony of the dial tone letting us know how much we flatlined there.

Nick looks at me blankly. 'Oh.'

'Sorry, that was—'

'She was so angry. Shame on that man for hurting her so much.' He looks down at the floor for a moment.

I feel bad to see Nick's disappointment that this didn't work out as it should have, that the story still doesn't have an ending. Or maybe because it means there's no reason to be here now.

'Well, maybe Facebook will come up trumps with other suggestions,' he says. 'Thank you for checking.'

'A pleasure.'

'One more book-drive stop in two days?' he says. 'I'd still like to help out if that's alright. It would feel strange not to.'

I smile at him. 'I would really appreciate that, sincerely. I can meet you there?'

'Sounds like a plan,' he says. He's a different Nick to the one I'm usually around. He almost looks a little defeated. 'Are you spending Christmas with your boyfriend?' he asks me. It seems almost painful for him to get that word out.

'No. I'm with Nana at home. I get her on day release. You?'

'We all get summoned to my mum's.'

'Bet she cooks up a storm.'

'You know it,' he says softly. He fiddles with his hands, still avoiding eye contact. 'Well, I'll be on my way, Kay.' There's a way that he says my name which still resonates deep in me, a light growl in his voice that trails off into a whisper. I watch him turn and a feeling surges up in me; somehow I already miss him and I want him to stay here, with me.

'NICK!' I say that too loudly, we're the only people here, but he smiles when I'm so clearly shocked at my own volume. 'I... I just wanted to say thank you for buying all those copies of my book.'

He pauses. 'Did my mum...?'

'No, I was in your office and I saw the boxes. I don't quite know what to say.'

'I have a lot of nieces and nephews and friends with kids,' he says, putting his hands in his pockets. It's the first time I've ever seen him blush. 'I heard you chatting to the manager of the care home about money and in the back of my mind, I just thought it was a nice way to support you, to help you out. I can sell them in the farm shop if you want.'

I pause for a moment to hear him say this, struck by how authentic and genuine he is with his care, his consideration.

'But really, why?' I ask, looking him in the eye.

He looks straight back at me, as if I'm all he can see. 'I've just never met anyone like you before, Kay.' His words make me stand still on the spot, piercing a part of my heart that was almost desperate to hear them. 'You radiate this energy, this kindness, I see it in your eyes. I don't really smile a lot. I bloody sell Christmas trees but I'm not sure I always like Christmas. But then there's you and you're just... you're like light. Your book drive, the way you invest all that energy into it, for nothing else than to make people smile, to give them a small gift, that's what drew me here, to you. I hope you don't mind me saying that. That I like that, I like you.'

'Nick...' I whisper, emotion soaring wildly through me.

'I like how mildly ridiculous you are. I like how your wild red hair looks like it belongs on a Disney character, I like that you laugh at your own jokes, I like how you eat and it ends up everywhere instead of inside your mouth. I like *you*. All of you. I need to say that out loud.'

'Please...'

He puts his hand up in the air. 'It's OK. I get it. I do. I'm not one to cross a line. Your boyfriend is a very lucky man,' he says, almost punctuating his sentence with that statement so I can't add any more. He turns to go and I want to throw myself in his path – but I know I can't. What about the other Nick? I can't think straight – everything feels a blur, a mix of flashbacks of being in my teens and thinking I was in love, images of kissing this Nick the other night and statements of love, commitment, labels, Nana telling me to look for the one person who'll raise me up. I just can't see who that is. I can't breathe. It's like being surrounded by this massive ball of big Nick energy and I feel defeated by it, unsure how to take it all on. 'I'll see you in two days, Kay.' And with that he heads towards the door and leaves the library, pulling the collar up on his jacket to shield himself from the cold before walking away into the bleak icy night.

THIRTY-TWO

'I don't get this film. I don't get why the kid doesn't just tell the police he's home alone. It makes no sense. They would get social workers in. They'd look after him instead of him having to fight off these thieves,' Nick says as he looks at his large flatscreen television, so huge I can pretty much count all of Macaulay Culkin's teeth when he screams. 'Pass the Sellotape, babe.'

I'm at Old Nick's flat, doing a bit of last-minute gift wrapping and trying my best to get into the season, to prove that being here is the right decision. This is Nick. Nick from back in the day, who you used to spend hours with, literally days at university where you'd go out on Friday and go back to his and sprawl over his bed, eating Domino's and tubes of Pringles. This is a safe love with history, potential. That said, did he used to sit here and judge films like this when we were together? This is Christmas canon. You don't get to sit here and pick holes in *Home Alone*. Because Harry would unlikely survive the flamethrower to the head if we're looking at what's wrong with this.

'How do you get your corners so straight?' he asks me, grappling with a small jewellery box.

'A lifetime of wrapping books. Here, let me sort that for you,' I say, reaching over. He seems reticent to hand the gift over, but I take the box and open it to see a pretty pendant in the middle.

'For my sister,' he says. 'That's her birthstone. Garnet.'

'The man has an excellent eye,' I say, though I am curious if birthstones are the only gift he knows to give.

'Well,' he says, gesturing in my direction. I blow him a kiss. I fold down the edges and then wrap the box in twine to make it look presentable. He watches me and then balances the box on his hand. 'You're amazing, thank you.'

He gets up to get another bag of gifts as I sit back, looking out at the river. Nick hadn't really bothered with making this place too Christmassy so I got him some decorations, lights and a small potted tree (not from the other Nick's farm obviously). Out across the way, the scene shows a scattering of coloured lights from other flats and houseboats in the twilight landscape to let us know Christmas is here, the river is still, the sky clouded over with snow expected in the next few days.

'More wine, madam?' he asks me.

'Always,' I tell him. He pours me a glass and clinks my glass. Tonight, it's another casual version of Nick. He's not in a suit but jeans and a t-shirt with bare feet, and this whole set-up feels like a grown-up version of us from eight years ago except we're not watching films on a laptop, sharing a large bottle of cider. I quite like how there's still a tube of Pringles on the coffee table though, along with some posh charcuterie and a large box of Celebrations. I'm also sitting here as myself, in leggings and a jumper, no make-up on and my hair bundled on top of my head. There are throws on the sofa, a fake fireplace fired up along the wall. He lines up a selection of toys along the sofa, ready to wrap them for his nephews.

'Hey, I'm sorry I never followed up on the book-drive thing, by the way. I did mention it at work and they said it was too small a venture to invest in, even for charity. I did try though,' Nick says, as he works out the best way to wrap the football in front of him. 'Did it go well?'

I shrug my shoulders, trying to push the other Nick out of my mind. The Nick who went the extra mile to help me wrap those books, deliver them and then ended up buying multiple copies of my own. It's not a comparisons game, it can't be. 'It was fine. Remember Lucy, my friend from school? She works at a Christmas-tree farm and they lent me someone to help.' Look at me, super vague but also imparting some truth there.

'Lucy works on a Christmas-tree farm? Is she the angel on top of the trees, shouting obscenities at everyone?' he says, chuckling at his own joke.

'She's doing meet and greet stuff in costume, it's a fun place,' I say.

'This is why Christmas is becoming more and more ridiculous. Next there'll be farms where you can name and kill your own turkeys but they'll turn it into an "experience".'

I try and summon up a laugh but inside I feel slightly protective about the North Christmas Tree Farm and their very special brand of family magic. I take a large sip of wine to try and remove them from my mind, to bring myself back into the room.

'So, I just need to ask about this whole Christmas Eve thing. If you think it's too much then I can stay away, I know your dad almost invited me out of obligation,' I say frankly.

Nick pulls a face telling me he thinks otherwise. 'Don't overthink it, hun. Just come along, grab some food. You'll know a lot of them. It's not a big thing.'

'It isn't?' I say, an eyebrow raised.

'You'll actually be doing me a favour. It'll save me from my family asking questions about my love life. Then I can point to you.'

'So really I'm just a cover to avoid awkward questions then?'

'The prettiest cover there ever was,' he says, a sparkle in his eye. I'm charmed, but also curious what this party has in store.

'Well, if you're free on Christmas Day itself, I'll be at my place with Nana if you wanted to pop in. I know you'll be busy but you're welcome to come for mince pies.'

He's distracted by the television at this point but turns to me, nodding. I don't quite know what that means but if this Nick is my choice then it makes sense to firm this up, to understand what all this fun might lead to. 'And I thought that maybe after Christmas, in the break, you and I could possibly go somewhere for the weekend? Surely the next stage of fun is a mini-break?' I ask him.

'Yeah? I may have to go to New York on the twenty-seventh though, for a few days. Work are doing a thing and New Year's Eve in New York is mega.'

Was that an invitation or an excuse? 'Oh, yeah...'

'We could do something when I get back. Maybe Paris?'

'Yeah. You can get good deals in January.'

'I could take you up the Eiffel Tower?' he mentions.

'Oi oi,' I say, and he laughs loudly. 'There's fun and there's fun.' He looks me in the eye, grinning, and I'm transported back to a bar in Bath just before Christmas where a boy tried to chat me up, giving me a look that told me he was serious, that he wanted to take this further. 'Can I ask you a question, Nick?'

'Uh-huh,' he says, gliding scissors through the wrapping paper. That piece is far too small for what he has planned but I won't say anything.

'What do you remember about us at university? I keep having flashbacks to it, moments, trying to piece it all together. It was so long ago that I can't remember all of it.'

'It was good, no?' I'm not sure how he's managed to qualify that year with a single word. 'We had fun back then too. You educated me on films. Before I met you, I'd never seen *The Shawshank Redemption*.'

'It was lucky I came along then,' I say.

He sits there, his scissors and hands hovering over the coffee table. 'I remember we had sex on a washing machine once? At that house party, the one where that bloke surfed down the stairs on a tray and then left a hole in the wall,' he says, chuckling to himself.

I try and laugh along but is it terrible that I can't remember that? Were we clothed? Was that washing machine on? 'I remember you had those jeans with the patchwork pocket. Do you still have those?' he asks.

'No,' I say curiously. He's going to have to give me more than a memory of a pair of patchwork jeans. 'I remember you were very gentlemanly, smart, it felt easy to be with you,' I say, trying to prompt him.

He looks at me. 'Yeah, it was easy. You were easy,' he smiles. 'You know what I mean. You're not like other girls.'

OK, this is warming up. I hate to do this but a few days ago, another Nick floored me with his compliments, he made me back into an armchair in an empty library and sob quietly with just a few sentences, so I need to do this to know I'm choosing the right Nick.

'Some girls are pure histrionics, nothing's ever good enough, there are terms and conditions, complications, nothing is ever black and white. So yeah, in that way, you're easy. I'm glad you get it.' He says this plainly, one eye on the film, the other battling with Sellotape, never quite looking me in the eye.

I sit there and take another sip of wine. I don't quite know what I'm feeling but I think it could be nothing, absolutely nothing. *What do I get? You? Us? Who are these other girls who I'm assuming you've dated in the interim?* I'm both wildly unamused but confused by all of what he has just said.

'Oh, remember that one time we went to the zoo in Bristol? We saw that monkey that was the spitting image of Will Ferrell. Remember how funny that was?'

My face is completely creased with confusion now. I have no idea what he's talking about. And for a moment, I do worry that I have romanticised this. I thought back to key moments, physical intimacy, conversations that would last for days. Does none of that stick in his mind? Why can't I remember this monkey? And suddenly, a flashback jumps into my mind. Not just one, a few. Moments where I waited for him outside lectures and he forgot about me and I shrugged it off. A time when he regularly drank all of my apple juice straight from the carton and said he'd buy me more. A time when he told me he had a cold sore forming so he wouldn't be able to go down on me or kiss me but if I wanted to go down on him then that would be fine. A Valentine's card that was a note written on the back of a coaster. And then a break-up. A conversation in a pub where he decided we would go off and do his own thing. I remember how blindsided I felt by all of that, but we broke up, and I nursed that heartache alone and without question because I was 'easy'.

'How upset were you when we broke up the first time round?' I ask him.

'Pretty hurt,' he says, bobbing his head around to gauge the feeling. 'I was young though and confused. In your late teens, everyone's a teeny tiny bit self-obsessed.'

'Some more than others,' I comment, smirking.

'I've changed though, no?'

I nod. I think he has. I hoped he had.

'I like that you haven't. I really like that.' But I have. Haven't I? We both have. And there's a reason I'm here. He's shown me kindness, generosity. He's still handsome and the sex is good. It's more than good. This could be good. 'You're great.'

I'm great. I think that is all I'm going to get here. I turn my head to one side, now starting to wonder if I've drunk too much red wine. I don't think you're wrapping that gift very well either. 'So tell me, what exactly does Kevin's dad do, because that house is massive? I'm counting six bedrooms at least.'

'I don't know,' I reply. 'I really don't know.'

THIRTY-THREE

'So what happened is that the ingrown toenail grew out to the other side of my toe so they basically had to lob the whole thing off because of the pus and the infection,' Mrs Michaels says as I sit by her bed. *I'm glad you've had help but seriously, I'm just here to give you a free book. Please take the book.*

'Well, I hope you feel better, madam.'

'That's very kind, love. Have a very Merry Christmas.'

It's the last day of my book drive today and we're in a local hospital. A mate of Lucy's has a husband who's a doctor, and he's allowed Nick and I to visit a few wards, give out books, and spread our very own version of festive book love amongst the patients. A hospital is a sobering place at Christmas, and it makes my heart ache to see people who will likely be here over the season, suffering and trying to get better, but also to see the selfless many who work here, who will spend time away from friends and family to help others. It makes my book drive seem a little ridiculous in comparison but it feels good to give all these people little pockets of joy where I can. And Nick is here. Santa Nick. It's our last stop today on this adventure and he's come through. He's here to finish the drive with me and to assist. He sits next to a lady on a bed by the window, chatting to her and nodding, holding her hand.

'Well, I really hope you get better. Try and have a lovely Christmas,' he says, signing off before posing for a requested selfie. I wait for him by the doorway, watching. His words still echo somewhere in my heart from last week. Who does that? Who just stands there and says words so profound, so moving to someone they hardly know? I hear them all the time, at night before I sleep, they play to me like a song over and over, like a lullaby to make my heart calm, peaceful.

'Hold up there, Kay,' he says as he wanders over to me. 'You're tangled...' He comes over and reaches up to my face. I would flinch but his hand moves to my hair where it would seem I've got myself caught up in one of the ward's foil decorations. That would be the other way the staff are trying to make these people feel better, they've lined every space and corner with decorations so bright and reflective that you have to close your eyes not to be blinded by all the light. 'You are free.'

I smile and look at him before averting my gaze. 'Thank you. Was she OK?'

'Gall bladder removal. Yours?'

'Ingrown toenail,' I say, pulling a face. 'Though I can't tell if they amputated the toe or just the nail.'

We look at each other and smile. I will miss this. I'll miss his company, but how do I communicate that? Can we still be friends? Is that a possibility in the future? But recently, I haven't really known what to do with the other Nick. The other night while we were wrapping gifts, I realised that I'm more confused than ever. We might be going to Paris. But he likes me because I'm easy to be with. None of it sang to me, not in the same way as when this Nick stood opposite me in the library telling me everything that was in his usually quiet soul.

'Hi, Kay and Nick, yeah? I'm Joe.' The man approaches us from a desk, dressed in scrubs, classically handsome as if he's on the set of a medical drama. Next to Nick, they make quite the duo. They could both be in some sort of handsome-man stage show and we could sell tickets for that. I shake his hand as he adjusts his stethoscope.

'That's a very good Santa outfit, mate. I used to have an elf one,' he says to Nick.

'Did you used to dress up for the kids too?' he asks.

'Oh no, it was a different sort of gig,' he says, blushing. 'So the Callaghans say you're giving out books, and Santa is doing a reading?' Joe enquires, and I nod. 'Then you're in the right place, come with me.' He escorts us down a corridor and I notice a pin of five gold rings attached to his lanyard.

'Like the song,' I say, pointing.

'Kind of, a gift from the wife. So are you two colleagues or...?'

Nick and I look at each other. 'Well, I'm from the library service and Nick is from...'

'The North Pole,' he says.

'Gotcha. How long have you been together?' he asks. Nick looks down at the floor at that point while I feel my cheeks start to burn.

'Oh, shit. Sorry. It's just...' He hesitates, but I nod so he'll fill me in about his little observation. 'You finished each other's sentence.'

Nick side-eyes me whilst I try and pretend I didn't hear any of that at all. 'We're friends.' He looks at both of us oddly and grins. 'Why are you smiling?' I ask.

'I just know this story, I've lived this story. Come on through.' Cryptic Joe flashes his lanyard at the door and we walk through to the brightly painted children's ward where the decorations are more cartoon reindeer and giant snowmen stuck to the walls. In the background, I can hear a child crying, the gentle beep of machines. I lied before, this shit is sobering. 'You're going to be in the lounge. Follow me.' I can see from the worried look on Nick's face too that this is a lot to take on, they're so little. We walk past cubicles where kids lie in their beds, wires sticking out of them, hear big hacking coughs and see stressed parents curled up next to them. 'Wait here and I'll let the Ward Sister know you're here.'

Joe leaves us in a corner of the corridor where Nick stands close to me, his eyes searching around the place. 'Can I give you some advice?' I say.

'Yeah?'

'The ho-ho-ho-ing. Yours is still very uneven.'

'Uneven?' he asks. 'Why are you telling me this now?'

'I don't know. It feels like the stakes are higher here,' I explain. 'Try it more from the diaphragm, from deep inside your gut.' I punch him slightly when I say this and he looks at me, smiling.

'You're trying to distract us because this is tough, yeah?' he says.

'There was me thinking we were just giving out books. Some of them are teeny tiny, Nick,' I say, concern etched in my face.

'I guess they're in the right place then if they're poorly.'

'But it's three days before Christmas.'

He takes my hand and squeezes it tightly. 'This is a friend grab by the way, to calm you.' I squeeze his hand back, not looking him in the face but feeling his fingers wrapped around mine.

Joe returns, smiling as he clocks our hands linked, winking at me. *I find you a little presumptuous, Joe.* 'It's through here, guys. Thanks again for being here.'

We walk through to another room, full of sofas and classroom tables, televisions and video game consoles. Again, the primary colours are strong but the Christmas decorations seem to have been crafted and drawn by the children. In one section of the room, a group of about seven children sit there waiting. They're all in a mix of hospital gowns and pyjamas. Some with IVs, one in a wheelchair wrapped in a dressing gown. I try to smile, I have to smile because *look at all of you.*

'Ho-ho-ho,' a voice bellows through the room, and I laugh because I think that punch to the stomach may have actually worked. I look up at Nick as he heads over to the children who all gaze at him with the same fascination and confusion as all the others. *We really need to get you some padding and a better beard.* Nick goes over to a seat laid out for him and one boy instantly takes a liking to him, hugging his knee, big hazel eyes looking up. Nick grins at him and puts a hand on his head. 'What's your name?'

'Alfie.'

I guess this isn't the same as the adult ward, it's not a time to ask these kids what they have and get them to relay all the details, because we're here to distract from that, to give them a little piece of hope, escapism.

'I've heard about you, Alfie,' Nick says.

'Really?' the little boy says.

'Bravest and kindest boy there is – that's what the elves tell me,' Nick says. I can't cry. That would be bloody awful. Another little girl goes up with a toy dog and rests it on his other knee. 'And who is this?'

'Cookie,' she says excitedly.

'I love me a cookie, especially with milk. Can I eat him?'

'Noooo.' She giggles as he pretends to chomp down on the toy. This is the Nick that's revealed himself to me in recent weeks. He's a quiet, sometimes serious soul but when faced with all these kids, with older people, he can turn it on like a tap. But it's not for attention, it's not charm or fake magic, it's something inside him that pours out. In that moment it's not about him, it's about making someone else feel better, special, seen. It's completely selfless and I want to tell him how I've noticed that, how it's all I can see.

'Well, this is my lovely friend, Kay, and we're here today to give you some rather special gifts.' He bends down into his sack and pulls out a selection of wrapped books, except they're not the ones I've wrapped. These are all the same size and shape. One of them rips the paper off and I recognise the font and illustrations almost immediately.

'Kay here is an author and she wrote this book about these bears and we thought we'd come and read to you and let you have some copies for Christmas.'

'Are you really the author?' an excited parent asks me. 'We have one of these at home, that's so exciting!'

I stand there, slightly embarrassed. This is not something I do, tell people about my books or what I do, and it wasn't the purpose of the drive at all to become some exercise in self-promotion, but the children shift their focus to me and Nick kindly nods in my direction.

'Can you sign my book?' one of the children asks me. A pen appears next to me from Nick. He knew exactly what he was doing, didn't he?

I take it from him. 'What's your name, honey?'

'Lucy.'

'I know a Lucy and she's one of my favourite people in the world.' I write an inscription and draw a smiley face next to my name. I've never really subscribed to the side of my job that's associated with fame or any sort of self-importance, but maybe at the same time I don't talk about it enough. I don't market myself very well. And even if I'm here doing just that to seven kids and their parents then maybe it's a start.

'Could I get a selfie?' asks another parent.

'I guess so and then we'll get Santa to read, yes?'

'Only if you help, Miss Kay,' Nick suggests. 'This is our last stop on our book adventures so I think we should read it together. You do the polar bear voice much better than me.' He pats a chair next to him and I go and join him reluctantly, nudging him slightly with my shoulder. 'So this is *A Beary Merry Christmas* and it was written by...' He waits and I sit there, shaking my head.

'Yeah, it was written by me,' I say grudgingly. The small collective clap their hands and I pretend to bow in my seat. 'Right, so... Once upon a time, before there was time and before humans actually lived, all the bears could talk, did you know that?'

'That's a Sharpie you know? It won't come off,' Nick says as we stand outside this hospital entrance, the cold air still circulating, the weather reports having threatened snow for days now but the South still not seeing anything except frozen pavements and windscreens in the morning. Nick looks at the back of my hand where one of the young people drew a massive star with a face.

'Maybe I'll leave it there, get someone to tattoo over it,' I say, holding it up.

'Cute.'

I don't know if he means me or the tattoo, so I quickly put my hand down. 'You didn't have to do that, you know, with the books. It was very kind though.'

'You don't really talk about your books much, your writing...' he says.

I shrug my shoulders. 'I guess it's because it makes me uncomfortable.'

'Don't be modest. It's a brilliant thing. You should feel proud of that.'

I don't know how to respond to that because I know what he's doing. I can almost hear my nana screaming at me from the corner of the room.

'How do I thank you, Nick, for all of it? I've had a lot of fun,' I say.

'Me too. Hey, maybe after Christmas, I can swing by the library, we can have a coffee. I don't want to overstep but we should keep in touch.'

'Because you know, it's still a collab, right?' I joke.

'Exactly.'

Maybe a hug is all that's needed in this moment. I know those words, those promises don't always come to fruition. They're said when you bid goodbye to someone to ease the finality of it, because this might be the last time we see each other. I really hope it isn't. It can't be. I reach for him and put my arms around him. He hugs me back and I reach up to kiss him on the cheek, to feel his skin next to my lips. I take a breath and close my eyes, stepping back from him.

'Actually, before we go. I did have a gift for you. It's a bit silly but I guess it is the season.' He watches me curiously as I pull an envelope out from my handbag. I watch him open it and his face slips into a smile.

'A capybara feeding experience.'

I shrug my shoulders. 'For your continued education.'

He laughs, this genuine sound that I try really hard to keep, to hold on to. 'Thank you, Kay Redman.'

'You are very welcome, Nick North. Have a bloody lovely Christmas.'

'You too.'

THIRTY-FOUR

'I think the man on the right is a tad sharp,' Helen whispers as we all wince slightly to try and work out where the bum notes from this choir are coming from. Is it the man in the penguin jumper or the woman who refuses to take off her gloves? My bets are on the man whose trousers look a tad too tight. That would affect your alto.

We invited the U3A choir in today as it's our last day open in the library and so we thought we'd go all out. We've put out arrangements of decent biscuits and we're all in Christmas jumpers; the last items for my book drive are stacked by the door, waiting to find new homes, and we've put the lights on a scatter setting, normally frowned upon by Olga who tells us it gives her migraines. The choir are singing about Santa Claus and how he's coming to town and, yes, when they do that I think of Nick. Santa Nick. I think of how he showed up here, how he came around this city with me and helped me give out all those books. And I think of his words, all the things he said. I look into space and smile, warmed by that memory. That's all it'll be because I drew a clear line in the snow there.

'Can I ask them to stop?' Olga mutters.

I elbow her in the ribs. 'Look how enthusiastic they are, they're all wearing antlers.'

'Which is ironic because they sound like dying deer,' Helen says out of the side of her mouth.

I stifle my laughter as the choir gear up for their final notes. God, my car used to make that sound when I went over 60mph. But they're here, they're making merry for our amusement and they're doing this for free. I clap enthusiastically and wolf whistle, encouraging all around us to do the same.

The lady in the front wearing a reindeer dress comes forward. 'Would you like us to do another?' she asks.

Helen steps in front of Olga before she has a chance to ruin this with her bluntness. 'We would ordinarily say yes but we're closing in about an hour. It was so lovely though, you are all so joyful.'

Bless Helen and her diplomacy. 'Please stay for biscuits though, and tea,' I say, so Olga won't complain that she had to get the urn out again for nothing. There are hums of approval from the crowd as we allow them to disperse. I always love a crowd at the library. It makes me feel as though people are investing in their community again, that the arts are important. There are cold, rainy days behind this desk when you get just one or two dropping in, to return books or find a place for their toddlers to be that isn't home. And that silence, though enforced because hey, we are a library, makes me sad, doubtful for this place's survival. Today, however, is different. That buzz, even if provided by a tone-deaf choir, is everything.

'Olga, I love your nails by the way,' I say as she stands next to me at the desk, eyeing up a man who's taken one too many biscuits. Olga has invested in nail art for the season, it's red and sparkly and I force her to let me examine the artistry.

'It is Christmas. I treated myself because we're going out for Christmas Day, to a nice hotel,' she says.

'Fancy schmancy,' I say.

'Who is this schmancy?' she asks.

I laugh. 'No one, it's a saying.'

'Your rich boyfriend is taking you out too, no?'

'On Christmas Day, no... But we talked about going to Paris in the New Year,' I say to the girls. 'And technically, not a boyfriend.'

'Oh-la-la,' Helen says. 'So a lover?' Her eyes light up at the thought.

'We're just... seeing how it goes,' I inform them. Both of them look at me with a mix of disappointment and confusion, so much so I feel the need to explain. 'Remember this love story started eight years ago. If I'm picking it up again then I want to be sure, certain.'

'You don't feel that already?' Helen asks, frowning.

And I pause. There is something there. But more importantly, this is someone who could fit into my life, my future, and Nick ticks many boxes in lots of ways. We were brought back together for a reason, bumping into him a month ago must mean something. 'I feel something.'

'And that is how all good love poetry starts. *I'll see how it goes... you make me feel... something*,' Helen jokes.

'For someone who writes books, your words about this man are very bland. Like potatoes,' Olga says. 'Boiled potatoes.'

'And you want a man who'll inspire your best words,' Helen says. She studies my face. She's been a quiet witness to the past few weeks, seeing how this story will pan out. I think she's hoping for a particular ending. Looking at her now, I'm not sure if this is the one she was rooting for though. 'And what of the other Nick?' I haven't told these girls about the other night, about the other Nick's declarations and kindness, because they're romantics and would have slapped the sensible right out of me. 'That's a man who could inspire poetry.'

'Most likely a dirty limerick in your case,' I jest.

She laughs heartily. 'Does he have any other costumes? We could put on events all through the year and get him to dress up for us. I'll find a kilt for Burns Night, a toga for Valentine's Day. I bet he has lovely legs.'

He does. Because I've seen them. I look down to hide my smile, trying to snap my attention away from him. That's done now, Kay. I need to move on from him to give the other Nick a chance. It's no longer a game of comparisons because that's not fair on either of them.

'Excuse me, I was wondering if you could help me?' a voice suddenly pipes in softly from across the desk. Amidst the crowd of library goers and choir members, an older woman stands there in a fluffy parka and hat, pulling her gloves off at the fingers, her eyes drawn to the ceiling, looking around this place.

'Of course,' I say, stepping forward, leaving Helen and Olga to tend to other duties and people.

'I'm sorry. I'm not a member here,' she says softly. 'Did you need to see a card?'

I shake my head, chuckling. 'We're not a country club. It's all good. Would you like to be a member? I can sign you up, it's all free,' I say, getting the form and a leaflet about the library service ready for her.

'Oh no. It's just... I was on Facebook and someone showed me a post about letters that had been found in some books. I think they might be mine.'

I stand there, looking into this woman's sweet face, the creases around her eyes and the softness of her curls. 'You're K?'

'Keira.'

'And the man who wrote them to you?'

'Nick.' Of course it was. It had to be. 'I was moving house and that book got put on the wrong pile. I'm so sorry. I don't even remember putting them in that book. He must have done that. And then...' I reach down to a drawer under the counter where I've kept the book, all the letters, and when I put it onto the desk the relief in her face is palpable. She puts her hands to her chest. 'Did you read them?'

'Some of them.'

'Then I am very embarrassed,' she says, blushing slightly.

'Don't be. We have a whole section dedicated to erotica – this was mild in comparison,' I joke. I can't seem to wipe the grin from my face that the mystery K is here and that we seem to have succeeded in this quest to find the authors of these letters. I say *we* though – there is another person who needs to see this, someone who made this happen, who was adamant from the start that this become a mission of sorts. He'd love this so very much.

Keira runs her fingers over the cover of the book, laughing, and then flicks through the pages to find the letters, carefully pressed and flattened out. She scans one of them and emotion overwhelms her, a single tear rolling down her face. I come around from my desk and instinctively go to put an arm around her.

'We have an office, a quieter space if you want to go there for a moment?' I say.

'Oh no. I'm... it's a happy tear. He always wrote a very good letter.'

And for a moment, I realise why she might be crying, why her Nick isn't here, claiming these letters with her. 'He wrote?'

'He passed away two years ago. Heart attack.' I tilt my head to one side, emotion rising up in my chest. 'Which was ironic as he had the biggest, kindest heart.'

'Were you... married?'

'Twenty-five years, three kids.'

'I'm very sorry.'

She smiles. 'Don't be. He was the most perfect man and I was lucky to have had that time with him. Some don't ever get that, at all. And now I have these which I thought I had lost forever. You know how many bins I went through trying to look for them? How many charity shops I rang? So, this is more than you'll ever know. The perfect Christmas gift to be reunited with these. I will forever be grateful...' She pauses, waiting for me to say my name.

'Kay.'

'See, it's a sign. Keira begins with K. Are you married, Kay? With anyone?'

I shake my head. I can't even begin tell her about signs, about my Nicks. 'It's complicated.'

She laughs. 'You youngsters all say that but in reality, love is the simplest feeling in the world.' I feel my eyes tear over to hear those words. 'I hope you have a really lovely Christmas, Kay. I don't know how to thank you.' She reaches over and gives me a very big hug before stepping back to look at me. Her eyes seem to have almost started glowing again to have these letters back in her possession, to be talking of her husband so fondly.

'You could join the library?' I joke.

'Deal. I'll bring my grandkids next time they're around. I saw a poster for a story-time session?'

'Every Tuesday and Thursday.'

She nods. 'Merry Christmas.'

'Merry Christmas.'

She exhales deeply but with a grin on her face, her eyes closing briefly, before walking away, that book clutched to her chest. I follow her figure to the door and then scramble around to find my phone. I have to tell him. He started this, he looked for her and she came. He did a good thing and made that woman's heart glow again with joy and remembrance of a great love. But that's Nick. She spoke of a man with a big and kind heart and that is him, as if the universe has connected him through that same energy. That wondrous Nick energy that's taken over my life. I laugh to myself, almost in realisation about what this all means, something in me almost fizzing with excitement. I hold my phone in my hands. I have to call him.

'Well, I didn't think it would look like this,' someone suddenly says from the crowd. Nick. Just not that Nick. The other Nick. Old Nick? *You're here?* He appears from around the choir, dressed in that same camel coat from that day we met in Harrods, smart jeans and boots, but with a Santa hat to his head. I pause because it's him. I wasn't thinking about him. I put my phone in my pocket. I force a smile, a surprised laugh, and point at him. 'You.'

'Me?' he says. 'You mentioned this yesterday and I got off work early. I thought I would come down and support you, say hello.' I look down and he has a paper bag full of cookies that he places on the counter. Nice cookies that look as though they've been hand-crafted and baked by artisan elves. I suddenly feel guilty that I didn't think him capable of such spontaneity. 'I didn't think it would look like this, your library. I thought it might be like some 1970s bunker. This is actually quite charming.' He looks through to the children's area, to large windows with seats where one child has curled themselves up reading a book, the choir milling around regaling each other with tales of seasonal mirth. He looks to the bookshelves stacked high, small pockets of space where people sit to read, to find safety and escape within our four walls. 'The trees are a lovely touch.'

I nod, my face stiffening with emotion. They are, aren't they? 'Tea?' I ask him.

'Why not?'

He takes off his scarf and heads over to my side of the counter, giving me a kiss on the cheek. I don't even have to see what Helen and Olga are doing, I think they all have an inkling as to the identity of this mystery man.

'NICK!' Helen says animatedly.

He turns to look at her and then back to me. 'I see word has got round. Nice to meet you, Helen and Olga.'

He has been listening. Olga looks at him with a more serious brow and I know exactly what she's doing, she's weighing up the choice she would have made. 'You are... Nick?'

'This is true,' he replies.

'You are handsome. You have hair.'

'Did she describe me as being without hair?' he chuckles.

'No. I see what she sees now. This is... appealing,' Olga says, and Helen scrunches her face up. Never mind the language barrier, it's the cultural one we need to look at, the one which says exactly what's on her mind in any language.

'I'm glad you think so,' he replies, grinning. Helen drags Olga away before she can say anything more and he starts to take off his coat, still looking around, bemused.

'I thought you still had gifts to buy?' I say.

'I do but maybe we can do that together, later? Grab an early dinner? Tomorrow is going to be pretty intense with all my family so I wanted to do something that was just us.'

'Just us?' I say, surprised to hear him crave something so small, intimate.

'Yeah. Also...' He reaches into his pocket and pulls out an envelope. 'It turns out that work do have funds for smaller fundraising projects and they said the library could have this. It's just a thousand quid but I thought it could buy you something for this place. I know your book-drive thing is over now.'

He puts the envelope in my hands and I look at it quietly. We could achieve so much with that small amount of money, not only for book drives, but towards fixing the roof, Helen could start laminating her signs, I could get a little sofa for the adults' reading area. I reach over to him and give him a hug. He is a good person. I knew there was something that brought us back together, I knew I wasn't imagining this man I fell for so many years ago. He hugs me back as I place a kiss on his cheek.

'Excuse me, can I ask if Santa's coming today?' a lady suddenly asks at the desk. I freeze and turn immediately.

'Umm, no. Lucy will be here at three for the final story time though.'

I see immediate disappointment in her face. 'Oh. I drove all the way from Raynes Park for him.'

'Raynes Park?' Nick says. 'Why?'

'A friend posted a picture of him on Facebook. She found out he's not married.'

'I'm sorry to disappoint.' I bite my lip because that is a low-cut top and a fair amount of mascara for a library story time.

'Is the tea free?' she asks.

'Yes and...' But she wanders off before I have the time to say she can have a biscuit too.

Nick looks at me, laughing as she does so. 'Either you've got a fit Santa in or she's looking for a sugar daddy this Christmas,' he says to me.

What do I say? Do I tell him about the other Nick? Do I

complicate this? But I see him leaning against the counter, starting to integrate into my life; he brought a cheque, he's here, now, after all this time. I need to give this time to breathe, to grow.

'I guess you don't know what people are into these days, eh?'

He laughs and puts an arm around me as we watch the choir start to form into a group again. Nick gives me a smile. I'd smile back but I know what this choir is about. He better brace himself.

THIRTY-FIVE

'Merry Christmas Eve!' Lester says as he stands in the doorway of Nick's childhood home, wearing a wonderfully festive dark-green Fair Isle jumper, a glass of something in his hand that very likely contains alcohol.

'You're drunk,' Nick says as he approaches him, giving him a hug.

'And you're not. How very disappointing, son. Kay, always a pleasure.'

'Lester...'

I look up at the big stone doorway in front of us, trying to remember the last time I was in this house. I am very West London, my family grew up around Shepherd's Bush and Hammersmith and my experience was little mews houses and winding streets. Nick's a North London boy and West Hampstead was his manor. I remember when I first told Nana that and she clutched at her fake pearls to tell me I was moving up in the world. *She's a posh bird now.* The thing is, she wasn't wrong. Their West Hampstead house has six bedrooms, the sort of terrace that looks unassuming from the outside but inside, it's a trove of large rooms, modern kitchens, loft conversions and, knowing London prices now carries a market value into the millions. They know how to do Christmas too. In the bay window sits a large tree, wide and tastefully decorated in gold, just gold. Garlands are festooned down the stairs and storm jars line the hallways carrying candles with holly and berries. I look through to see people carrying drinks, the tinkle of tasteful Christmas music in the background. I reach down for Nick's hand to find some reassurance and am grateful when he squeezes it back.

'You'll be fine,' he says, pulling my hand up to kiss it gently.

Last night, Nick's magic worked. It was almost what I needed, a gentle evening with him to reconnect and not be bedazzled by big dates and venues, to just chat, laugh and have faith that we were brought back together for a reason. And we did have sex back at his flat and it was perhaps less frenzied than before, it was tender and sweet and it led to us waking up together, getting ready to come here with all our gifts, almost like, dare I say it, a proper couple.

'Uncle Phil!' Nick says as we walk into the living room, removing our coats and scarves and embracing the warmth of the fire roaring in the hearth.

'Nicholas, you rascal! Come here!' I think I've met Uncle Phil. I think he's the investment banker who is very competitive when it comes to Monopoly. He's a large hirsute man, a fan of corduroy it would seem and he shifts his gaze to me.

'I believe you may know Kay?'

'Christ, I think I do.' He jolts his head to look at me and back to Nick. 'It must be years since we last saw you!' he roars.

'Nearly ten to be precise, how are you?' He comes in to hug me and I now remember him as the uncle whose hands dip a little too low when he hugs. We part but I can't quite read that look in his face. Disapproval, or maybe he's just shocked to see me after all this time? Either way, I put on my happy social face as I'm accosted by several other aunts, uncles, cousins, Lester's boss, Marjorie's best friend from university and a bloke called Calvin who I couldn't hear but I think he's either a neighbour or a Labour MP.

When I finally make it into the kitchen to see Marjorie, she's wearing a black velvet cocktail dress, low-dernier tights and a sensible heel, a red cocktail in her hand. I seem to live in jumpsuits at the moment and went a bit sparkly for the season. I don't think it's too much but I see her eyes scan me up and down. There's something about her smile which still doesn't sit right with me.

'I never understand how jumpsuits work,' she says. I'm not sure how you reply to that. Well, Marjorie, you step into them and zip them up. 'How are you, Kay? Welcome.'

I glance around the kitchen trying to remember this place. There used to be a big oak table in the middle with benches, possibly pushed back for the purposes of the party, but they still have an AGA and a big wall of family pictures, a rogues' gallery of all the Coles in one place.

'I'm glad to be here. You look lovely.'

'Thank you...' She looks past me to see Nick still grappling with bags of gifts. 'Oh, Nick, put those in the front room,' she says.

'The front room is packed, Mum. Is there room in here?' I look around, every single space seems to be taken with bottles of drink and glass crates.

'Maybe in your dad's office?' Marjorie says. 'But before you do, come and say hello to Sally. Do you remember she used to teach you the oboe?'

I smile. He played the oboe? This is news to me. I let him through before stepping in. 'Come, let me,' I say, putting my hands to his. 'Your dad's office is in the basement, yes?'

'You're an angel,' he says quietly.

'I know, Mr Oboe.'

I take the gift bags, shuffling through the corridor. It is strange how this place brings back a semblance of memory even though I must have been in here only a few times. I remember seeing his childhood bedroom and its dark-blue carpet, a garden space where his mother grew herbs and the way they had a lot of hand towels in their downstairs bathroom. I never got that.

But I remember his dad's office was through a small door to the basement, not somewhere I have entered before in this house but I head down the stairs with the gift bags, trying not to lose my footing. If anything, it's a good chance to just readjust myself after that bombardment of an entrance. Breathe, Kay. I spy a mirror and have a scan to see if anything is out of place, in case Uncle Phil was looking at an errant boob. Nothing. I put down the bags and have a peep inside. There's a hamper of sourdough crackers and cheese that seems to have unravelled in the bag so I take it out and tie the ribbon again, taking out the gifts that surround it.

But as I do, my attention is drawn to a small box. One I recognise because I wrapped it. It's the pendant that Nick got for his sister. I am very good at wrapping if I say so myself. I think it's my attention to the corners and the folding. I don't want this to get crushed though so I put it to one side, suddenly noticing the label.

N&N x

I take a moment to process what that means. Because his sister is called April. Is it a strange sibling joke? Possibly. I stare at it for a moment too long and then put it back in the large bag of gifts, heading back to the party. As soon as I re-emerge from that door, back into the hallway, I step right back into Christmas. I take a deep breath to compose myself.

'You're Kay! I remember you,' someone says to my right. I look at the person talking and I feign surprise to see Nick's cousin, Sean, standing there holding a drink. Everyone is holding drinks and I feel I need to get in on the act here. He reaches out for the obligatory double kiss to the cheek. I remember Sean as we went drinking together once. He was the sort of drunk who necked Sambuca shots and used to drool like an old dog. My memory really does work in strange ways.

'Sean.' Sean has already engaged in a lot of alcohol this evening it would seem, given the way that he seems to be leaning at strange angles against a wall that doesn't appear to be there. 'Wow, you look... great.'

'That's very kind. You look...'

'Exactly the same.' All this time has passed and he still hasn't updated his schoolboy haircut. Interesting. I'm going to predict that he works in the Middle East, isn't attached and drives a Tesla. 'How are you?'

'Well, you know...working out in Dubai now, having the time of my life...' Bingo. 'Good to be back in ol' Blighty for Chrimbo though.' I forgot he's also incredibly posh. And short. Or maybe I've grown. 'God, when Nicky told me you were back on the scene, I was gobsmacked. I never thought we'd see you again,' he says, in loud, brash tones.

'I am just as surprised,' I say. Seriously, where is the alcohol in this place?

'I mean, after everything that happened, I didn't think he'd move on that quickly.'

Hold that thought, Sean. I stand there, Nick in the corner of my eye as he's still chatting to Sally who taught him the oboe. 'Move on?'

'You know? From Neve?'

I reach round to the kitchen and grab a glass and half a bottle of champagne. It's time to drink. I top up Sean's glass.

'Rumour was her parents dropped thirty grand on that wedding.'

Wedding. The air sticks in my throat. Short sips, Kay. That will mean I don't miss any of the details. I still keep Nick in my line of sight.

'That's a lot of money,' I say.

'Yeah, especially when the bride doesn't turn up,' he whispers loudly. I take another sip of champagne. Maybe I should just drink straight from the bottle. 'He was broken, you know? I tried to get him out to Dubai for a change of scene but I think he stayed in London to pine. I still can't believe they work for the same company.' And an image suddenly jolts into my head of an icy blonde who looked me up and down at the entrance of the Natural History Museum. A girl who was rude to the staff and who didn't seem particularly happy to see me. I knew at the ballet that I'd seen her somewhere before. And she was so incredibly cold and dismissive there. The way Nick was so aggressively rude about her. 'But you know she's always had that effect on him, he followed her to New York all those years ago, like a bloody puppy.'

Oh dear. *Maybe now's the time to get real, to think about working on ourselves.* Those words echo in my head from the time we first broke up. None of that was true, was it? There was someone else. And if he went out to New York to be with her then that means for the last eight years, she's been a fixture in his life. I really am some special sort of idiot.

'I can't believe they'd been together for all that time,' I say. I can't believe I'm still able to stand here and hold this conversation so calmly.

'Right? So when I saw those pictures on social media of you and him together, I thought, OK, my boy is finally growing a pair and getting over that bitch.'

'Pictures?' I ask.

'Yah, there was one which was WOW, I can't believe he's saying that.' He gets out his phone to show me a Facebook photo from a few weeks back at the ballet. It's the first time I'm seeing it, maybe because I don't do social media too regularly but also because he's not tagged me. It's a photo of me outside the building, walking away. The caption below reads: *An old love in a new tradition x* It's not wholly inaccurate except we've not really used the word love around each other. 'He proposed to her at the ballet. In New York. It was on her birthday in January, a couple of years ago.'

All of the realisations start to settle like a thick dusting of snow, the music and chatter from the party fades into silence, and I let out a resigned and strangely calm exhalation. 'Which makes her birthstone garnet, yes?'

'I guess. I'm not really into that shit. I'm a Taurus if that matters?'

'N&N,' I mutter under my breath.

'I have no idea what you're talking about.'

'Thank you, Sean,' I say.

I glance over into the kitchen and see Nick standing there, still chatting. He catches my eye for a second and we exchange a look. *Yes, you are good looking, there is charm and attraction there, but now its effects are almost vanishing, a mist is clearing.*

You OK? he mouths.

The thing is I think I am. Despite the revelation that's been put at my door in the last five minutes, I feel weirdly calm and am strangely relieved. No wonder there was hesitation all along, because on paper this was lovely, but deep down I knew that it didn't work out the first time for good reason. Shame on me, I guess, for romanticising any of it, for shifting my focus to what worked as opposed to what didn't, for believing any of what that naïve young twentysomething of me felt for this man.

'And so I turned down Riyadh, I may do Bahrain next. Everyone is going to Singapore but who knows?'

I turn to Sean who's still talking. I don't think I asked, babe, but I smile politely.

'Exactly. Sean, could you be a doll and get me one of those mini quiche things? I need something to soak up the alcohol.'

'Right-o,' he says.

I wait until he disappears then head down to the basement office again. I don't know what to do. I can't stay. I don't doubt that Nick upstairs likes me. We've had sex, he's been generous and reasonable company, but I know now he doesn't love me. I think I may have been a rebound, someone to fill a gap and possibly make Neve jealous. The ballet, eh? At least that was fun though. I'd never been to the ballet. And it's then I suddenly think of the other Nick. And I realise I shouldn't refer to him now as the other Nick. Maybe he was always the only Nick.

I need to get out of here, don't I? I hear the doorbell upstairs and more guests being greeted. I don't think I would be too conspicuous slipping out now, but then I also don't want to cause a scene at somebody else's party. It should be a quiet departure, I should slink out of here. I look around. There's a window that leads out onto the street. Through there maybe? I look at the angles of it to see if I would fit. That could work.

I grab a chair from the desk and step onto it, holding the window open as I push my coat out first. This will be easy, just push myself up and slide through, like some Cirque du Soleil contortionist. Girl, you've fit through a Christmas tree netting machine before, you can do this. I suck in my stomach and hoist myself up, putting my head through the window, the cold air prickling my face. But something's wrong. Is it the angle? Is it my boobs? I try and push myself through. Please. No. I kick my legs like a small child. You're not underwater, you don't need propulsion, you need a crowbar. And just like that, a shrill alarm suddenly sounds in my ear, and I hear footsteps down the stairs to the basement.

Shit.

THIRTY-SIX

Eight years may have passed but it seems that they've still not updated the carpet in Nick's room. It's still a deep blue, a shade that resembles the colour of the deepest part of the sea. I look down at it and my bare feet. Yes, they had to remove my shoes as three grown men from the Christmas party hoisted me out of a downstairs window. I sit on the edge of Nick's bed, waiting because I also tore my jumpsuit so to really compound all my embarrassment, I will likely have to leave here wearing his mother's clothes. The door opens and Nick returns with a pile of clothes in his hands.

'So we have options,' he tells me. 'We have pyjamas, yoga pants, a tracksuit and a sweatshirt that I once bought her that has the Statue of Liberty on.'

Oh great, a souvenir from New York. I point to the sweatshirt quietly and he throws it in my direction. I put it over my shoulders and let the fleece lining hug my skin.

'I also brought us some supplies,' he says, pulling out some canapés and a half-full bottle of champagne from out of his underarm. He comes to sit down next to me and puts a hand on top of mine.

'Was it my Uncle Phil? I know he's handsy,' he says.

I'm still bathing in the shame of my failed escape but the shock of what I heard upstairs still overwhelms. 'It was actually your cousin, Sean.'

'Was he lechy?'

'Nick, he told me all about Neve. Maybe a bit too much about Neve,' I say pretty directly.

The mirth drops from Nick's face and he stares down into his inky-blue carpet, trying to find the words. 'Oh... Kay, look...'

'Why didn't you say anything?' I ask, less angry, more incredulous that he wouldn't share news that monumental with me. 'That's a horrible thing to happen to anyone, Nick. When was the wedding?'

'May,' he whispers. 'She didn't show up. She sent her dad with a note. I didn't even get an apology.'

'Nick...' I say quietly. 'I can see why you thought she was up her own sphincter then.' He doesn't laugh. 'That's incredibly awful of her and I'm sorry that happened to you.'

He still can't make eye contact with me and I can sense he feels guilty that he never told me about any of it, that in the last month or so, our relationship, which I thought felt safe and easy, lacked some truth.

'I have a question,' I say, trying to break the silence. 'Was it *her* scrunchie?'

He nods. I hope he didn't do strange things with the scrunchie as he was obsessing over her.

'I have thrown that away now though.'

'Good.'

'And at the Natural History Museum, when you disappeared, was it something to do with her?'

He side-eyes me. The thing about me, Nick Coles, is that I'm not just a pretty face with a ridiculous head of hair. I'm sometimes Jessica fucking Fletcher. 'Possibly,' he says sheepishly. 'She saw me there with you and she got angry. I'm not sure why when she was the one who didn't want me, but we had it out by the blue whale.'

'Sean filled me in about the ballet.'

He sits there in a place between shame and fear that I'm eventually going to kick off about all of this. 'I didn't know she was going to be there.' I pull a face. 'Well, I had an inkling.' He returns the same face to me, one of ick and sadness. 'I enjoyed the ballet though with you. And the bar with all the plants. It was a nice evening.'

I stare at a point on the wall. It was a lovely memory until about two minutes ago.

'We weren't stalking her at ice skating? Harrods?' I ask him tentatively, trying to work out if all of this was a huge charade to follow another woman around London.

He sits up immediately and looks at me. 'Christ, no. I'm sad but not that sad. Some of it was very genuine. I remembered you liked ice skating, Harrods felt like a big gesture for someone who I thought deserved it. I mean, we also had excellent sex and I wasn't pretending about any of that. I do like you, Kay. A lot.'

'I like you too. It's just not...'

'Yeah.'

We don't have to say the words because we know. This isn't it. As much as we try and force and fold it into an ideal of what we think a relationship should look like, there's no spark or at least we're trying far too hard to make one appear out of nowhere when that star burnt out a while ago.

'Wasn't it fun though?' I say, trying to make a joke out of all of this.

I see a glimmer of a smile. 'Very fun. I've said this before but maybe you came into my life at just the right time.'

'Really?' I say, surprised.

'To maybe remind me of what a good person should look like. How I could and should be with someone who's kind and hilarious and warm. You asked me what I remembered about you, Kay Redman, and what I did remember was that you were far too good for me.'

My face freezes with emotion and I put my hand on top of his, squeezing it tightly. 'I'll be honest, a lot of what I've heard in the past hour hasn't portrayed you in the greatest of lights but Nick Coles, you deserve someone good at least. Someone who dumps you at the altar after almost ten years of a relationship is not a good person.'

He pauses for a moment. 'We didn't get together before New York, you know? It was about five years ago.'

I look at him suspiciously. 'Hun, the maths is irrelevant.' I almost laugh. 'But I don't think I'm angry, I think it all makes a bit more sense now.' I think about how the sum of all those romantic dates wasn't love. 'You did lie about the pendant though,' I say.

'You guessed?' he asks, surprised at my own levels of intuition.

'I saw the gift card.' I reach into my pocket and retrieve the box. I'm not sure why but as I left I thought I might steal it, save this man from himself. Helen's birthday is in six weeks, she'd love it.

He looks down at the box. 'A mutual friend was here tonight, I was going to see if she would pass it on.'

'Nick...'

'Yes?'

'No.'

He looks at me, scowling at my abruptness. 'But what if there's a chance...?'

'No.'

'I love—'

I put a finger to his lips. 'I don't think that's what love should look like, Nick. And what about having some self-respect, acceptance? I don't know...'

A look of pain creeps across his face and I instantly feel bad. I guess in the greater scheme of things, it's been six months since it happened. Perhaps it is still too fresh to move on, to understand anything with much clarity when your heart has been broken in that way. 'Instead of acting lovelorn and desperate?'

'Your words, not mine. Using me to make her jealous,' I scoff. 'Do you think it worked?'

He shrugs his shoulders. 'She was pretty angry at the museum.'

'Then I'm glad your plan almost worked,' I say.

He sits there fiddling with his hands, unsure what to say. 'I have to say, it wasn't all a sham. It has been nice to see you again, to be in your company, to have you re-enter my orbit.'

'That would imply you're a planet.'

'And maybe you're a shooting star, a ray of light.'

I pause to hear the light comment. 'Does that make Neve an asteroid?' I ask. 'Causing catastrophic damage?' He sighs and nods at the comparison. 'Just remember, planets recover from those though. But it will take time. Is this why your parents were a bit weird with me then?'

Now this is intuition. 'Oh, we've had words, don't worry. Mum loved Neve like a daughter so it was always going to take a while for her to get over losing her. I think my dad quite liked you though. He remembers you as the one with the hair. I think he didn't want you to get caught up in the aftermath. I think he sensed I wasn't over Neve. Which is fair...'

'And why I always liked your dad.'

He laughs. We sit there for a moment to absorb the silence. Despite my eventful interruptions, the party continues to simmer, the faint jingle of Nat King Cole winds its way up the stairs. I reach over and take a canapé. Why is it that I only eat canapés at weddings and Christmas? I feel I need to turn little toasts with brie and cranberry and teeny tiny spring rolls into my everyday. I offer him a spring roll and he bites it out of my hands.

'Did we have sex in this room?' Nick asks.

'I think we did, you know.'

'Do you remember it?' I try and subdue my giggles because, frankly, no. 'Way to kick a man when he's down.'

'I remember you got out your scout badge collection for me,' I say.

He jumps up to his feet and goes to the top drawer of his dresser, getting out a shirt that's still impeccably pressed, both arms covered in fabric badges. 'Sexy.'

'Always.'

We smile at each other. 'I did get you a gift by the way,' he says.

'In case you thought I'd only got Neve something.' I hope he knows I will be going online to compare the prices of said gift. He reaches under his bed and I see a book wrapped up. Yeah, I know for a fact that pendant would have cost more. I slide my hand under the paper and unwrap it. *Poetry for Lovers*. I sigh to see the title, my fingers moving gently across the front cover. 'I saw it and thought of you. Because you know... books are your thing.'

'Thank you,' I say, unable to control my emotion, a tear rolling down my face. He tries to read the emotion, wondering if this is a complete misstep. 'Have you read any of them?'

'Is it bad if I say no?'

I shake my head, flicking through the pages to find a poem that a man read out to me once. 'I feel I need to be completely honest with you too. I've been spending time with another man since I've seen you. Not sleeping with him or anything, just someone else who I think I possibly have feelings for.' I exhale deeply as I say it, waiting for his reaction.

'I can't really comment, can I?' Nick says. 'What's he like?'

'He's OK.'

'You deserve more than OK, young lady.' That sounds genuine. I like how it harks back to what Davinia once told me, the day I met this Nick.

'I also got you something. It's a little stupid,' I say.

'I think we're way past stupid now, right?'

I go into my handbag and get out a small box by comparison. He opens it and he at least laughs. 'It's a Ferrari, you asked Santa for a Ferrari.'

'You are funny. Very funny.'

'Thank you. That much we can agree on at least.' We sit there for yet another silent moment. I reach over and take a swig from the bottle of champagne. 'I don't have to stay at this party, do I?'

'God, no. Can I ask one thing though?'

'Yeah.'

'Can we be friends? Unless you think that's a bloody cliché?' he says mockingly, and I cackle. I really laugh because maybe we've both remembered the same thing, the day we broke up. A day I thought I'd never recover from at the time. And yet here we are.

'Why not. Just not fun friends anymore... OK?'

'Deal,' he says. I go to shake his hand but he pulls me in for a hug. And now I know how I feel, without doubt: I feel pure relief, kindness and compassion for someone I once loved. *I feel a sense of care towards you because there was a point when what I felt for you was love.* Maybe that never dies. Maybe it can be transformed into something else which keeps him in my life. Maybe the coincidence of meeting wasn't because we belonged together. Maybe it was so I could help you heal. I grip my arms around him, around this person who just wanted to feel something else instead of intense heartbreak. I hope you'll be OK, Nick Coles. I really do.

'If you want to leave though...' he says, from over my shoulder.

'Use a door?' I suggest.

'Yeah,' he says. 'And Kay. Thank you. Seriously. For everything.'

'You're welcome, St Nick.'

THIRTY-SEVEN

'Well, that's the ugliest jumper I've ever seen,' Lucy says as she walks up to me in the Tube station, wrapping her arms around me. 'You look like a deranged tourist.'

'It's not mine. It's Nick's mum's. He bought it for her.'

'Does he not love his mum?' she asks. I let Lucy hold me for a moment too long in the harsh lights of the Tube station as I try and process everything I'm feeling right now.

'Oi, oi!' a man shouts at us from beyond the barriers. We look over and he hangs a sprig of mistletoe over his crotch.

Lucy turns around. 'Oh, go swivel, you sausage.'

I laugh under her as she pushes my body away. 'What on earth are you wearing? Aren't you cold?' I ask her, looking at her winter coat tied tightly around her waist but realising her suspenders might be showing. Her heels are patent black leather with shiny silver spikes. She could slash people's tyres with those.

'I run everywhere so I'm never cold. And it's Christmas Eve. I've got a shift in a bar, double pay to be a different sort of elf, you know? But...' she says, looking at her watch, 'I can give you two hours. Where we going?'

She puts an arm through mine. 'Back to mine? I don't think I can do the frenetic Christmas Eve mess of a pub.'

Lucy nods. 'Fear not, I came prepared with tequila in my bag. I also brought a lemon,' she says, digging around in her belongings to find it. 'Let's pretend I wrapped it and it can be my Christmas gift to you,' she says, grinning. We start walking and she huddles in close to me. Outside, the high street is a mix of two extremes. The lights attached to each lamppost flicker sporadically in fluorescent shapes and colours; there are people still out, still partying but most shops have closed their doors for the festive period, you can sense there's a city waiting to go into hibernation, waiting for the big day to come tomorrow. We turn the corner, past a pub, bold and brightly still pumping out Christmas anthems. 'So...'

'Is this where you say I told you so...' I ask her, giving her a mean dose of side-eye.

'Told you so.'

'You are mean, it's Christmas.'

'Not yet. It's the Eve. I do have half a mind to go round and tell him he's a twat though. He essentially used you. That's not cool,' she says. 'Can I go on his social media and cause beef? I can find that Neve too?'

'Or not?'

'Boo,' she says, smiling.

'He's asked to be friends,' I say.

'They all say that. So you didn't get angry, not one little bit? I think I would have broken things. I would have made that party an event. I would have thrown a brie.'

'Because that's you,' I joke. 'I just felt a bit stupid that I believed there was something there. I did like him but I think I was forcing it a little.'

'Like a fart?'

'Not the romantic vibe I was going for, but yes. I think I was thinking too much about what's good for me, what the future had in store. The man was excellent on paper, good prospects.'

'...When really the man had some leaky foundations,' she says. She's not wrong. I enjoyed the time we had together but the whole Neve situation is messy. I'm just glad we didn't drag things out.

That I found out now rather than months down the line when feelings could have been more entangled, more hurt. We walk past another wine bar, watching as people have last-minute dinners and gatherings, fogged-up windows reveal glowing lights and seas of decorations. 'So are we saying that with that Nick gone, done with, kaput – we can possibly move on to New Nick? My boss, Nick. Are we going to give that a go?'

'He's not a fairground ride?' I say.

'Au contraire.'

'We did kiss, you know?' I say sheepishly.

'WHAT?' I'm lucky she doesn't push me into moving traffic with how affronted she is that she's only hearing this now.

'It was brief and a non-event really and—'

'The first thing you should have done as soon as you parted lips was texted me,' she says. 'So we jump on that now, yes?' Who bloody knows? I kissed Nick. We made up. We left things civil. He said things to me that have made my heart so wound up with emotion that I felt my ribs could shatter. But what do I do? Do I just rock up at his place? *Hey, I'm done with the boyfriend? Fancy a go? Merry Christmas, by the way.* It doesn't feel right to rush into that, to be so careless with his feelings when he's been so honest and genuine with me. Maybe it would be better to wait. Maybe I can have a moment to simply enjoy the season, he can have the Christmas with his family he deserves, and I will find him afterwards, and see if that chance is still there for us to be something. 'I'm too confused, Luce. I've literally been overwhelmed by Nicks. I just need some breathing space.'

Lucy looks at me oddly then howls. 'I thought you literally said you'd been overwhelmed by dicks. And I thought what a unique conundrum?'

I fog the air with my laughter. 'I'm just going to enjoy my Christmas.'

'With me?'

'And my nana.'

She looks at me and beams. 'Then you do you. Nick can wait.'

We cross the high street to a side street and proceed to walk towards the mews and my maisonette. However, as we do, we see a large van parked up by my door and a man waiting outside, knocking on the door. Lucy looks at me as our pace slows but my heart picks up a beat. I can't make out who it is. Could it be him? But as the man turns to face us, the light picks out the face of a complete stranger.

'Hi,' I mutter into the darkness.

'Kay Redman?' the man asks. I try and work out if I've missed paying a bill and the man is here to take away my television. *If your name is Nick as well then I'm running away from here.* Lucy stands there adopting a pose that says she could take him on. I'm slightly glad for the back-up.

'I have a delivery for you.'

'For me? I didn't order anything,' I say.

'Well, let's assume it's from Santa then,' he chuckles. Lucy and I look at each other as he goes into his van and begins to drag out a piece of furniture, wrapped in wood and bubble wrap. He places it by the front door as Lucy looks it up and down. 'Can you sign here?' he asks. I'm too dumbfounded to take anything in so Lucy takes the pen and puts her initials down on the monitor. It beeps. 'Are you two OK?' We both nod, silently. 'Well, Merry Christmas then.'

'Yeah, Merry... Christmas...' I say.

He laughs under his breath and gets into his truck as Lucy and I examine the parcel from afar. She looks at me unable to hold in her grin.

'Stop it,' I say. It's because she knows what this is, she knows who it's from. I bet the cow even gave him my address. 'Take that end. We better get it in.'

She heads to one end of the package and grips her fingers over it while I do the same, both of us angling it as best we can through the hallway and into the space of my front room. 'Told you the man was all about wood,' Lucy says. I put a finger to my lips. I dig my fingertips into the plastic and tear it away, unwrapping until the gift reveals itself. It's a table... a desk? I run my hand over it until I get to one corner and see my initials carved into the surface. Don't cry. Too late. I don't know why but I kneel down and rest a cheek on the wood. 'There's a card.'

'I can't read it,' I say, sobbing onto the desk.

'Would you like me to...'

'Yes,' I whisper.

Lucy opens the card and bends over laughing. '*For your next book about beavers...*'

I manage to smile through my tears.

'I thought you hadn't slept with him?'

'I haven't.'

'*A special desk for a special author. Keep telling people (and yourself) that. Merry Christmas, Nick...xxx*' Lucy says, reading the rest of the card. She fans the card with her hands and stands there with her hip out. 'My boy's done good.' I just hope this thing is varnished because I seem to be soaking it with my tears. 'Who knew my grumpy boss had this in him. I mean, even I'm a cynical bitch but this... this is pretty slick Nick.'

'He made this?'

'Well, yeah.'

'For me?'

'Those are your initials?' she says, slightly bemused. 'Are you crying because you didn't get him anything?'

Tears continue to stream down my face. 'I got him a capybara-feeding experience.'

Lucy doesn't quite know how to reply to that. 'He's at the farm, you know? Until ten-ish?' I look up at her as she approaches me, wiping my damp face with her hands. 'Kay, maybe this doesn't have to be very confusing at all.'

'It doesn't?' I say.

'Nah, I'm getting you an Uber, bitch. Go find your boy. And that's my bloody Christmas gift to you.'

· · ·

I'm sitting in the back of this Uber, on my notes in my phone, trying to write down something. It's because when I finally get to that farm and see Nick, I know I won't be able to say anything. I need words. Good words. I should have brought Lucy but she needed to get to work and we both knew this was a solo trip, something I needed to do alone. Words, words, words. I need to know exactly what to say to him to show him how much that desk is everything, how since he's come into my life, the world has started to glow in every bloody different colour imaginable.

'Lady, are we sure this place is here?' the Uber driver asks. I nod enthusiastically. 'Who gets a Christmas tree on Christmas Eve?'

'People who've realised they've missed out.'

'Disorganised people,' he says in a thick accent. 'My sat nav is saying it's just woods here. If you are luring me here to mug me and take my organs then please know I have a family. I have kids.'

'I want nothing to do with your organs. Trust me. Have a little faith.' He looks at my face in the rearview mirror again and smiles. 'Take the next left.'

I'm not sure what I expect when we turn into the drive, but the farm isn't lit up the way it was when I've been here previously. 'See? Closed,' he says. 'I think big Tesco is still open. We can find you a tree there. It might have to be a fake one though?'

However, in the distance I can see a light on in the buildings, the gates are open and there's a familiar truck in the car park. I feel a shiver of excitement run through me to be here, near him. I know that truck. 'It's cool. I'm going to stop here. What's your name again?'

'Nikos.'

'Of course it is,' I say, laughing. He pulls a face. I wasn't laughing at your name. Shit, I'd better leave a tip. I close the door, waving him off before standing there looking up at the sign on the farm, slowly wandering into the building where I can see lights. 'Hello?' I shout into the darkness. There's no answer. This is when I realise it's not Nick's truck. It belongs to a cleaner or a brother.

Maybe there's really no one here at all and I'm stuck hoping Nikos might return to give me a lift back into town.

I wander over to the building with the light on but the door is locked. I knock on it and try to look through the window. Do they have security? Maybe dogs. God, this would not be a good way to go out. 'NICK!' I shout.

Right, this is awkward because I don't think he's actually here. I hear a noise. It's the dogs, they've come for me. Or we're also in the woods. Maybe it's an urban wolf. I should have just called him, instead of coming down here to ambush him. But then I see another truck parked up by the gates. I walk over to peek inside the cabin but it's empty, though the keys are in the ignition. Someone has to be here. In the back of the truck are thirty to forty Christmas trees all lying there, stacked, ready to leave. They're not netted up. I run my hand over one of the branches, the needles still intact and waxy in my hands. Wait, why are the branches moving? I pause for a moment, waiting for whatever is going to come out and eat me, until I see a pair of yellow eyes watching me, mewing lightly.

'Hi,' I say. A black cat comes over and puts her head under my hand so I can stroke her. I sit up on the back of the truck and she climbs into my lap and I read the name tag on her red collar: Bonnie. I think I've heard about her. 'Hey, Bonnie. I know your daddy.' That sounded less wrong in my head. She suddenly jumps off my lap and burrows further into the trees. 'Bonnie? Bonnie? You can't go in there.' These trees may be headed for a wood chipper, a bonfire, a bin. I turn from being perched on the end of the van and begin crawling in amongst the trees. 'Bonnie? Please?' I lift up branches, peering between them and wriggling under to try and see where she's hiding. 'It's cold, honey. Let's get you in the warm. I'm nice, I really am. Bonnie?'

I'm not really sure what happens next. But I hear the tailgate of the truck bang up into place and a noise that sounds like it's being locked. Nick? I crawl to the end of the van and out from under the branches as quickly as I can, but I can only see his back as he heads to the cabin and climbs in. Are those ear defenders? Earphones?

'NICK!' I shout. Whoa. What is going on here? And then the engine starts and we're off. Bonnie suddenly jumps out of the branches and leaps into my lap. Ring him. Call him. I have my phone in my hand but the truck suddenly jolts over a bump and I drop it. Shit. Bonnie, help me look for my phone. The cat looks at me as if I'm mad. 'You're not much help are you?' She meows in reply, looking up at me with her big eyes as her fur starts to get dusted with snow.

THIRTY-EIGHT

I think back to the number of times I've watched an action film and someone jumps from a moving truck or car or train and I've thought, *you know, it doesn't look that hard*. Jump and roll, right? Well, it's not until you're in a moving truck trying to keep hold of a terrified cat that you realise how hard it really is.

I look out the sides of the truck, and the traffic and the road are moving incredibly fast, and it's not an entirely smooth journey. We're getting tossed around like we're at sea here. I mean, what if he's taking us to the dump? Or it's a long overnight drive to somewhere far away? I mean, he will stop eventually and maybe then I'll have to think what to do. In the meantime, I am also on all fours in this thing clutching a cat and attempting to look for my phone. I knock at the back of the cabin again. How the hell do I explain this? Really? Maybe Nick was right. I am slightly ridiculous. This is all slightly ridiculous.

On the other hand, as this truck is open topped, it's a lovely way to see London by night. Is that Hammersmith? I guess this could be worse? The snow, which has been looming for weeks, falls in light, magical drifts. I could be wearing a really awful coat. I pull my hat over my hair again. I sit back against the branches, letting Bonnie settle on my chest, and look up at the lights, the sky. I guess there could be worse ways to spend Christmas Eve. Hold up, that's the Natural History Museum on the left. Yeah, I was there just a few weeks ago. That must mean Harrods is approaching. I lie back again. But as I look out, I realise I'm being watched by a whole row of people on a double-decker bus, who all turn their heads to look at me. I know how this looks. I'm either being kidnapped or a tramp. It's kind of neither. A woman puts her thumb up at me. I do the same to signal that I'm alright. Someone takes a photo. Do I smile?

The truck starts up again and takes a sharp left. I have no idea where we are now but we must nearly be there, right? I look out of the side, hugging Bonnie the cat, and feel a sense of relief when the truck eventually rolls to a stop and the ignition halts. I watch as Nick's door opens and he steps out. I see glimpses of his face, a green beanie on his head, wearing a thick checked jacket and jeans. I smile for a moment. I don't think there is a way to explain what's happened here, not at all. I see another man come towards him and greet him. Nick finally takes off his earphones and I realise now is not the time to call out to him.

'Nick North?' the man asks.

'Yep, that's me. Mr Douglas?'

'Yes, I'm Tom – thank you. It means a lot that you're doing this on Christmas Eve.'

'No problem, they're not wrapped but they're all in good condition. Shame to let them go to waste.'

'Do you do this every year?' he asks.

'Yeah, we put all the old trees on Facebook Marketplace and see who wants them. Saves us putting them in the chipper.' And as soon as he says that, I shut my eyes tightly to think of a moment about five years ago when my nana answered an ad on Facebook and a handsome yet faceless man delivered her a ten-foot tree that I had to saw in the street so she could get it in her house. I spoke to that grumpy man. Maybe if we're talking about the universe and signs, maybe I should have listened to Nana all along. Even back then, she stood on those cobbles and tried to set us up. She said we'd make a good couple. She knew. I'm so distracted by these thoughts that I don't hear the tailgate of the truck opening. And now Nick is standing there with a very distressed-looking man called Tom who thinks that I possibly come with the trees. I don't.

He looks at Nick who does a double take to see me standing there. 'Kay? What the hell? What are you doing? Is that my cat?'

The cat and I will be forever bonded by this trauma. She sits in my arms in the same way a feline would nestle in the arms of a Bond villain.

'Funny story...' I start to say, and then I try to descend off the end of that truck as majestically as possible whilst Nick offers me a hand. As soon as my feet hit the pavement, the cat jumps down and sits there as if ready to watch the impending drama. Oh, it's coming. I push Nick on the chest with both hands. Given how tall he is, I am impressed that I have that much strength to make him topple a little. 'Who drives with headphones on like that? I've been knocking at that cabin for most of the trip!' Tom stands there, looking at both of us, and I turn to him. 'Please, take your trees. If you see a phone in there, can you give it to me?'

I turn to Nick and he seems to be laughing. 'Why were you in the back of the truck?'

'I went to the farm to look for you and then your cat went in the back of your truck and I was trying to beckon her out,' I explain. 'Why didn't you check before you closed the gate?'

'Because...'

'Health and safety,' I say, flaring my nostrils. 'I want to fill in an incident form.' He's doing his best to contain a rather large smile but he's also scanning me from my shoulders to my forehead. 'I've got half those trees in my hair again, haven't I?'

He nods, reaching over to pick out pine needles. 'And a bit of snow?'

I look up at where we are, and it seems to be the back of a hotel right in central London, the Thames to our right, lit up as far as the eye can see. A line of people have appeared to remove the trees from the truck. 'Someone's getting married here tomorrow, they wanted some more trees to add to the magic,' Nick explains. He watches as Bonnie jumps into the truck and curls into a ball on the driver's seat. 'You came to the farm?'

'Because some idiot made me a desk,' I say, still angry, still feeling huge swathes of emotion that make me literally fizz.

He pulls me away from that hotel loading bay onto stone steps, lit up by a single lamppost. Snow lands on his shoulders and gets caught in his eyelashes. 'You could have texted "thank you".'

'You made me a desk.'

'It's just a desk. It was actually quite easy.'

'I usually get my desks flatpack from IKEA,' I say. I can tell that makes him wince a little. 'No one has ever done anything like that for me before.'

'Made you something?'

'Just... raised me up.' As soon as the words leave my mouth, I think of Nana and see her smiling. I think about what she said. How love is supposed to elevate, to leave you almost floating. 'I wrote this all down on my phone before I dropped it. You just... you're pretty special, aren't you?' He looks at me, his breath quickening. That probably wasn't as eloquent and meaningful as I'd wanted but I can feel a single tear running down my cold cheek. 'Oh. And do you know who came into the library before we closed? A wonderful woman called Keira. The mystery K.'

'The letters? You managed to return them? Find the owners?' he asks, his face softening to hear the news. I nod. 'They were from her husband. He passed away so she was worried she'd lost them forever.'

He looks at me with pained eyes. 'But you know when that woman came in and talked about her husband and how a simple gesture like yours made her happy again, it made me see you with such clarity. You have such goodness. How you love people, how you exist so quietly. You give others your time, your attention, you're wonderfully gentle and sweet but not for you, never for you.' I say all of it frenetically, not catching a breath. 'That wasn't what was on my phone at all.'

'What was on there?' he mutters.

'It was a full outline for that book about the beavers.'

He laughs so loud the people at the truck turn to watch. See, I am hilarious.

'Did you like the desk?'

'The desk is beautiful, sincerely the most beautiful thing I think I might ever own.'

'I had a great muse.'

'Are you saying I look wooden?'

'Exactly that,' he replies, beaming. He stops to look at me, wondering what all of this might mean and I melt to look into his eyes, to try and show him how much I care.

'I don't have a boyfriend anymore. I also came down to tell you that.'

His mouth opens slightly, his face still with the revelation. 'Oh.'

'I wanted to give you that information in person.'

'Noted. What happened?'

'Nothing. And that's probably where it all went wrong.' He cocks his head to one side as if trying to understand what I've just said. 'He was a relationship that didn't quite work out first time. I thought the universe was trying to tell me to give it another go, but really maybe the universe was throwing you in my direction again.' All these Nicks, like cosmic bumper cars, all running into my life at different times.

'After I delivered that tree to your nana,' he realises. 'After I shouted abuse at you down the phone?'

'Yeah, maybe the universe was trying to show me you're not all bad,' I say, giggling slightly to remember how ridiculous that Christmas tree really was.

'So it was the universe that made you get in that Christmas-tree machine, was it?' he asks me.

'Shush now,' I say, trying desperately to keep some romantic cool about me, trying to hide all the joy in every ounce of my being that he's here, that what I feel is so very bright, so very clear.

He still doesn't look away from me, his face filled with hope, anticipation. 'What do I do now? Can I ask you out?'

'You can.'

'Can I also do something else?' I nod.

And he sighs almost with a low growl, reaching around to grab my cheek and pulls me in for a kiss. His skin is icy cold against mine, his lips soft, parting gently. I stand on my tiptoes to meet him, to let him pull my body into his. As we part, he rests his forehead against mine. That felt right, so very perfect that I can't speak.

'I'm really sorry about your boyfriend,' he says.

'No, you're not,' I smile.

'What was his name?' he asks me.

'Funny you should ask...'

'Hold up, there were *two* Nicks? You conveniently left that bit out of your story! Were you sleeping with both of them at the same time? This is the sort of detail I wanted to hear,' my agent Davinia says, her hat the size of a small satellite dish. I reckon we could pick up Sky sports and movies with that thing.

'Yeah,' I say. 'I'm not marrying the one from university. God, please don't bring that up if you talk to him. This is another one,' I say, laughing.

Davinia looks into space trying to work it all out. When the New Year happened, all she knew was that there was a Nick in my life, a very special Nick who made me desks and who inspired me to believe in my writing. The bear books I wrote after that were some of my best work, she said, and those books helped me secure my merch deal which means you can now buy all my bear characters as cuddly toys. The panda is my favourite but don't mention it to the other bears.

'I guess the only thing you need to know is that I'm marrying one of them today. The right one,' I tell her cheekily.

She looks me up and down and exhales a wonderfully long, satisfied sigh before coming in for another hug. 'You are a marvel. It's my honour to be here. I will see you on the dancefloor later,' she promises, winking. 'Love you,' she says before scurrying out of the room.

I don't usually tell that story anymore. The one about the short festive time in my life where I dated all the Nicks. Mainly out of love and sincerity to the Nick that did win my heart. But I often think back to that heady month when the universe threw both of those men in my direction and how that story didn't really end, it just gave me a new chapter, a story that continues to thrive and blossom more than I had ever hoped. How every day, I do feel raised up in the best possible way.

'You should have told her the bit where you got stuck in the Christmas-tree machine,' a voice behind me says. I turn to see Lucy holding a glorious bouquet of amaryllis and roses. 'Because really, if it wasn't for me then none of this would have happened. I am the cosmic glue that held this all together and told you that going back to old Nick was a terribly bad idea.' I glance over at Lucy, always stunning in any situation but today she's wearing a fur wrap and black tea dress, her hair pulled back, ready to take on this day with me. I don't think I'd want any other bridesmaid by my side. She pulls out a little flask of brandy which proves me right.

'I'd like to say this is for Dutch courage but it's mostly to keep you warm. You're absolute nutters to get married in the winter, you really are.'

'But it links in to how we met, right?' I say.

'Possibly. But I've had to rub Deep Heat into my toes so I don't get frostbite. That's not sexy.'

'It is to me.'

Lucy cackles wildly. 'You gorgeous thing. Look, I have to get buttonholes to the men and corral the little flower girls. Little Sofia is a dynamo, no? But stay here, I'll leave you my flask, yes?'

I nod as she trots away on her heels and I head over to sit in the rocking chair in the corner of this room, next to a log fire blazing in a burner. Quite interestingly, this is the room in which I met Nick. We chose this venue because obviously there was no other place to exchange vows than on this farm, down an aisle lined with

Christmas trees. The party will happen in a hotel down the road but for now, we have nearly every fairy light in South London hanging off every branch, chair and trellis to make this ceremony glow.

I take a deep breath. It's been one of those mornings dashing around with hair and make-up and people, like Davinia, have been popping back here to say hello and give me their best wishes. Helen made me a sandwich, Olga is in fur-lined boots. My parents have flown in. It's overwhelming in the best possible way. My phone pings and a message pops up.

> I believe it's today. Have a magnificent day, Kay Redman. From the Other Nick xx

I smile, because that's how that Nick signs off these days when he gets in touch, and, despite any reservations I may have had eight years ago when we first split up, lo and behold, it would seem that Old Nick and I can remain friends.

After our dalliance, he did his best to get over Neve and went to live in Singapore. I don't think there's anyone else in his life but there seems to be evidence in his pictures of him enjoying life and taking advantage of the excellent and cheap tailoring they have over there. And it makes me happy that we were able to move on, that he seems reasonably content with his life, that whatever we had between us helped that process. I send him a heart back and close my eyes for a second to steady myself.

A sudden knock on the door interrupts the peace and I stand up, turning to face it. 'Come in.'

'I can't,' says Nick's voice, and I smile at his superstitions on today of all days. The Nick North I know is scared of nothing.

I go over to the door and stand next to it. 'What's up?'

'I needed a breather. My mother is trying to feed me. She tucked a napkin in my shirt. There's a woman out here dousing me in hairspray. It's a bit of a circus out there. I hope you know the family you're marrying into. There are cousins out here that I've never seen in my life.'

I smile through the door. That family I'm marrying into is everything. I put a hand to the door.

'Shouldn't you be out there welcoming them all?' I ask him.

'Yeah, but I needed a moment of calm. You're my calm.'

He still has a way with words that makes me melt. I rest my head next to the door and open it a little, putting my hand out. 'Close your eyes. Take my hand.'

I hold my hand out and feel him search for it, holding it, rubbing his fingers along the outline of my engagement ring and then I feel him pull it up to his lips to kiss it. That tenderness he's always shown me, that way he extracts the love from every touch is always soothing, it always feels like our own personal magic.

I take my hand back, feeling him still there. I always seem to sense him when he's close. 'I will give you the trees,' he whispers through the door, laughing.

And I laugh back because that was a line from one of those love poems he read out to me. Of course you'd give me the trees, it's technically your business.

'And I will give you the journey,' I say back.

'Love you, Mrs Claus.'

'Love you,' I whisper, and hear his footsteps pad away from me. My heart feels full, ready, and I run a hand across the wood of the door. 'I can't wait to marry you.'

'And there's the whole world thinking that I'm the crazy one and you're talking to a door,' a voice sounds behind me. I turn to see Nana, a festive vision in bright red, a cross between a First Lady and someone who's about to take a turn on the dancefloor in Blackpool. I love the extravagance, the joy in her wrinkled little face as she sees me in my wedding dress, a huge white taffeta creation that I love because it does allow me to wear thermal underwear underneath. She comes over and runs her fingers over the skirt then reaches up to put a hand to my face. I've never seen her beam like this before.

'Katherine Redman, twenty-first of July,' she says.

'That'll be me.'

'It'd be weird if it wasn't.'

'That's some meringue you've got on.'

I spin to let her see how much it billows out and she claps her hands, smiling.

'I am possibly the happiest I've ever been, my dearest girl,' she says, choking back the tears.

'Well, it was on your bucket list. You wanted to see me married, eh?'

She takes pause to remember saying that, tears forming in her eyes as we let the emotion of the moment sit there between us. For as long as you're around, I'll try and remember everything on your behalf. 'I hope you're not going to tell me this is my Christmas gift though – I'll still need a proper present, something I can unwrap, nothing in an envelope.' I cackle and take her hands in mine. 'It's quite a thing out there you know? Christmas trees lined up for days, it's very magical. I think I saw doves.'

'It felt like the right place to get married.'

'Surrounded by your fella's good wood?'

I shake my head, grinning at her. 'The fella has a name, you know.'

'Nicholas North, sixteenth of March.' She taps her head. 'I've got it locked in. Got to remember the name of the boy who's looking after my granddaughter. And he better. Or I'll be having words.' I tilt my head to the side to know his name is in her heart too. She weaves an arm through mine. 'Right, let's get you out there and give you away. What do you say?'

'I do.'

'Yeah, you say that to him, not me.'

And I laugh, picking up the skirts of my dress and opening the door, stepping out into the glow of fairy lights and the hum of Christmas music in the air, a perfect winter's sky shining blue beyond all those perfect trees.

A LETTER FROM THE AUTHOR

Hello, there! You're bloody marvellous! Thank you from the bottom of my heart for reading *Big Nick Energy*. If we've met before then hello again but if you're new – welcome, take a seat... it's a pleasure to meet you. I'm Kristen 😄

I hope you've loved reading about Kay and both of her Nicks. If you like your romance with big heart, lots of ridiculous laughs and a healthy dose of innuendo then do look for my other titles, and keep up to date with all my latest releases and bonus content by signing up at the following link. Your email address will never be shared and you can unsubscribe at any time.

www.stormpublishing.co/kristen-bailey

And if you enjoyed *Big Nick Energy* then I would be overjoyed if you could leave me a review on either Amazon or Goodreads to let people know. It's a brilliant way to reach out to new readers. And don't stop there, tell everyone you know on social media, gift the book to your mates, drop WhatsApp voice notes to everyone you know.

So let's start with some festive greetings. Merry Christmas, reader. I hope it's snowing where you are and Santa has got you everything you wanted and more. May you have the loveliest time with the people you love, that's all that matters. That and a great big fucking trifle.

This is my third Christmas book and man, they do get more and more fun to write. And maybe this one has some personal meaning too because if you've linked up the names then you'll know that I'm married to a Nick. My Nick doesn't sell Christmas trees nor is he a finance wanker in the City but I think the spirit of him sings very loudly in this book. He does refer to my jumpsuits as onesies, he will openly admit that I am completely ridiculous, and he gets angry with me when I don't tell people I write books.

However, he also thinks Christmas is a completely awful, materialistic affair. It makes him unbearably Grinchy. So what fun it is to write this festive book in his honour, to be able to tell people that despite that grumpy Scrooge you think you see, there is also a man who loves his family fiercely, who believes in his wife more than she believes in herself, and who once wrote me a note saying, and I quote: '*every day with me was like Christmas Day.*' You romantic old bastard, you. So here, have a book dedicated to all that big Nick energy that has remained at the core of my being for the past twenty years.

However, I hope *Big Nick Energy* speaks loudly in a lot of other ways too. Despite the very Christmassy settings and themes, it was nice to explore the idea of what ifs, those relationships past that are sometimes sent to haunt us (you know the ones I'm talking about!), the idea of second chances but also the idea of what love should look like. I'm forty-five and I'm still working that out all the time but dear reader, I hope that you do have the sort of love that raises you up every day. Please listen to Nana because beyond all the meet-cutes, sparks and small moments that align, love should also look like someone carving you a desk with their own hands, it should be someone who tells you exactly what they like about you but more importantly, it should be an all-year-round kinda thing. A Nick is for life, not just for Christmas. But it should also be about family, loving yourself and what you do and a love that you project out into the world. God knows, we could all do with a bit more of that these days.

I also hope you loved seeing all of my Bailey Universe characters again. What an absolute joy to revisit sexy-elf Joe back in that hospital. I'm glad he went back into medicine. But I also loved meeting my Three Kings and their Maggie in the museum, finally invited to the big office Christmas party. And Lucy, you big ol' Christmas lush, you. Thank you for your candour and big laughs. I always love intertwining those characters so you can see where they all are now. If you want to read their origin stories, just go and find them in my back catalogue. I'd love for you to meet them all.

I will leave it here. I'd be thrilled to hear from any of my readers, whether it be with reviews, questions or just to say hello. I'm more on Instagram these days as TikTok scares me, so do pop over. I also have a Facebook author page and website, too, for updates, ramblings and so you can learn more about me. Like, share and follow away – it'd be much appreciated.

With much love and festive gratitude,

Kristen xx

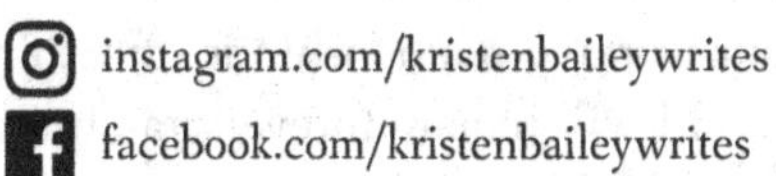

instagram.com/kristenbaileywrites
facebook.com/kristenbaileywrites

ACKNOWLEDGMENTS

Firstly, a huge thank you to all at Storm for all they do in transforming my manuscripts into fully fledged books. Seriously, my synopses always change halfway through, I constantly switch perspectives and overuse the word 'just' but somehow you weave your magic to help those stories emerge. My biggest champion at Storm remains Vicky Blunden who tells me to run with all my ideas, has unwavering belief in me and when I first gave her this title and idea, she held on to it so tightly. No notes, you are writing this book 😄 Our working relationship is something I continue to hold very dear and I will remain forever grateful to you for everything. To everyone else behind the scenes, my eternal thanks especially to Alex Begley, Emma Rogers for the gorgeous cover, and Harrie Dobby for her brilliant narration.

I've mentioned Nick far too much already but again, I thank you for being so miserable about Christmas that I thought it would be personally hilarious to write a book about you, with your name on the cover and everything. You're a love, an unlikely muse, a best friend. Thank you for all the children, all the letters, and that time you made me go in the loft when I was eight months pregnant to retrieve all the Christmas gifts because 'I don't really do that sort of thing.' I nearly divorced you that Christmas. I'm glad I didn't. There are so many other anecdotes but I will save them for future acknowledgements of other Christmas books that I will continue to dedicate to you to wind you up.

Jake, Tess, Oscar and Maya. Thank you for propping me up especially over these past two years. Still the greatest privilege to be your mum and see how you bless my world with your smarts, kindness and spirit. I'm going to write this down here hoping you may read it some day but my favourite moments with you are when we are all in the kitchen and you're all crammed around someone's phone, all laughing at some meme I don't understand, doing weird dances, eating all my food, teaching me what a full heart really looks like. A special thank you to Tess for coming up with the New Nick storyline about the Christmas-tree machine whilst we were zipping down the M3 on the way back from a hockey match.

I had a Nana and I still remember how bloody warm, vibrant and glorious she was. I hold on to that a lot at the moment. I think it's a lovely thing to think how that touched me and so many in my family. Along with my dear dad, my grandmother's memory was affected by age and dementia and so I write of Nana's experiences with pangs of sadness. Maybe the lesson in writing about all of it is that whilst it's so incredibly painful to see ones you love fade and become shadows of themselves, it is important to hold on to the love you feel for them, to remember their influence and everything that made them so important to you. I adore how their light still lives on, how I feel it everyday. What an incredible gift. My Nana was called Lydia and my dad was called Barry, and just to tell you their names and how brilliant they are feels special.

I wouldn't write without a readership and the people who still continue to support my writing leaves me absolutely floored. I have some of the loveliest readers in the land – faithful sorts who read all my books, tell me I'm funny and write me such wonderful reviews, posts and messages. It is completely overwhelming to know that people get joy out of what you write, that they seek it out, and get comfort and entertainment from it. It is probably why I keep doing what I do. So a big thank you to the readers, the lovers, the bloggers, the Instagrammers, the people who approach me at book festivals and tell me they like my books. I don't think you understand that when you do that, I am sobbing inside, I really am. It's incredibly lovely.

I borrowed some poetry for parts of this novel so I acknowledge the work of a great Syrian poet Nizar Qabbani and his poem *Love*

Compared and Rosanna Eleanor Leprohon and her poem *Husband and Wife* – during my research, I found both poems incredibly special and have held on to each. Their work is in the public domain and I urge you to search out these poems in their entirety.

The library in this book is a real place – Hampton Library – and somewhere I spent many an afternoon as a little girl running up a lot of overdue fines. It really is a magical building but then so are all libraries so a thank you to those who continue to fund them, champion them and support these little corners of the world that are an escape and sanctuary for so many.

I can't lie, it's now been eighteen months since I lost my dad, and a year since Nick moved away for work and whilst writing has been a joy and distraction, life remains busy and eventful and my emotions ebb and flow. I've done a lot of what I do alone – moments of stress, sadness and solitude sent to test and fortify, that have forced me to prioritise myself and what's really important. But still, I write. I spend a ridiculous amount of time coming up with seasonal surnames (e.g Redman; Coles) and getting side-tracked by research to do with hog roast food truck names, Harrods, capybaras and Demis Roussos. So Kristen, give yourself some fucking flowers.

Do I dare mention the exes that inspired Old Nick's story? Why not? You won't read this. CM, BR, JR. I don't hate any of you. In fact, I hold you all in the greatest esteem. But there's a reason we happened and a reason why we didn't. To the one who still messages me occasionally to reminisce, stop now. It's kind but it's only romantic because it didn't happen. I hope that makes sense.

And a thank you to the following people who just continue to be there with their smiles and friendship, people who champion me, who remain a constant in the life of me and my family in so many different ways: Sara Hafeez, Neil Charles, Rachel Ellis, Graham Price, Dan Turkington, Leanne Paul, Bronagh McDermott, Andrew Barber and Hayley Fisher.

www.ingramcontent.com/pod-product-compliance
Lightning Source LLC
Chambersburg PA
CBHW010431170726
48283CB00011B/3164